CLARITY

R. JAMES STEVENS

I hope you enjoy reading 'Clarity' as much as I enjoyed creating it!

Peace.

R.

EPSILON (BOOK 1)

CLARITY

R. JAMES STEVENS

Clarity is a work of fiction. Names, characters, places and incidents either are the product of the author's imagination or are used fictitiously. Any resemblance to actual persons, living or dead, events, or locales is entirely coincidental.

ISBN: 0989682609
ISBN-13: 978-0-9896826-0-2

To my awesome, beautiful, *witty* wife.
Without your never-ending love and support, this book would
not have been possible. Thank you for believing in me.

ACKNOWLEDGMENTS

Thanks first and foremost to my wife for believing in my ability to tell this story and for always being there when I needed you; you are the true meaning of the term "better half".

My son-in-law, K, who helped me brainstorm the basic idea of this story back in the day (when we designed it for a comic book!). My sister, who gave me the encouragement to write it the way I wanted to tell it – and for her tireless efforts helping me edit (and re-edit).

And the rest of my family, the best a guy could ask for!

1:
BROKEN, BEAT & SCARRED

Present day (2084)...

Brigadier Stroud stumbled into the dark alleyway, a light, misting rain making his already disheveled, shoulder-length hair that much more tangled and unkempt. Several dumpsters, some empty, others overflowing with putrid trash that had been sitting for months or years, lined the narrow passage on each side. A small, dim bulb swayed in the slight breeze at the top of one wall, its dull light slowly crawling back and forth across the deserted path.

As he staggered forward, he tripped over the base of a smaller receptacle next to a rust-eaten dumpster and fell to the ground, barely catching his near-two-meter frame with his hands as he hit the cold, wet, gravelly surface.

"Where the Hell is he," Brig grunted in his West Texas accent, his face contorted with pain. He gathered himself enough to sit back on his haunches against one of the walls of the alleyway and placed his head in his hands.

"Can't think straight, been too long since the last hit..." he groaned, trying to wipe away the cobwebs from his mind.

He leaned his head back against the wall and tightly clenched his firm, square jaw, slowly sinking to a sitting position on the wet ground.

Brig closed his eyes.

"Ah, what's the use? S'not gonna help anyway, damn it." Brig tried to shut out the world, to drown out the stabbing pain in his skull even for one second, but his head pulsed in rhythm with his racing heart.

"You can do it, just a little longer. Been in much worse shape than this. Funny though...just don't remember when."

A sharp spear of pain stabbed at his brain. It had become unbearable.

"Oh God...gotta make it stop..."

He grasped around for something, anything that might help get rid of his misery. Something jabbed at his ribcage from inside his coat pocket as he shifted his weight backward. He had a weapon.

Reaching in with one hand, Brig slowly pulled out the small handgun and stared at it resolutely.

No! That can't be the answer, he argued in his mind, laying his head against the brick facing of the wall.

But it would stop it, a voice in his head whispered. *All of the suffering, all of the pain – all gone in one stroke.*

Brig forced his eyes shut and tried to reason with the demons.

Do it! the voice hissed.

His will to fight gone, Brig slowly lifted the gun to his temple and closed his eyes in a trance. The cold steel of the barrel massaged its target; his finger instinctively located the trigger.

A loud thump in an adjacent alley shook him back to coherence. Hopeful that his contact had finally arrived to save him from his suffering, he pulled himself to his feet and wobbled forward.

Brig peered around the corner and into the other alley; his steely, blue eyes squinted nearly shut. A medium-build, bald man with menacing tattoos that spanned his neck and arms, stood over a smaller man lying prone in front of him. The man on the ground looked up with terror in his eyes at the other, as the raindrops pelted his face. The standing man pointed his weapon, a TR-31 Ripper, the only choice for those wanting to make a silent kill, at the other as he barked at him with a thick, Cockney inflection.

"You don't pay up, you don't live, it's that simple, meat!" he growled, spitting down onto the other's face.

Still dazed, Brig curiously leaned in toward the confrontation. However, he misjudged as he reached for the jagged brick edge of the building next to him. His feet lost traction on the wet, oily surface of the alley beneath him and he tumbled forward into a pile of garbage.

The attacker swirled around on one heel in Brig's direction. "Well, well, what do we have here? One of your buddies come to save you, huh?"

"Not who I thought you were, pal. Don't mind me," Brig murmured, gathering himself and turning to make his way out of the alley – staggering still.

His hasty exit was short-lived.

The distinct, and familiar, sound of a slug coming from the Ripper in the stranger's hand filled Brig's ears like a starter pistol in a sewer pipe. Brig instinctively dove to his left, narrowly avoiding the certain killing blow that would have resulted from a hit of the deadly armament.

Before Brig could pull himself to his feet, his attacker was next to him, sending him sprawling to the ground with a heavy blow to the back of his neck. Brig grimaced in pain as he got back up to his knees.

"Don't take much to warnings, do ya, bloke?" the attacker snarled. Grabbing Brig's hair, he quickly pounded his head into his knee. As Brig jerked up from the impact, the attacker gave him a quick boot to his abdomen, sending Brig hurtling backward with an echoing crash into the side of a large dumpster. Brig weakly pushed himself to his knees, spitting blood, flesh and a little vomit, as he desperately gasped for air, having had it knocked out of him on the last blow.

With two more kicks to the side by the attacker, Brig fell to the ground face-first. As he lay on the broken asphalt of the alley, he could feel blood oozing from a cut that had opened on his forehead. Ripples from his hot breath wrinkled the warm, sticky fluid that pooled in a puddle of water into which he had fallen.

Brig feebly lifted his head a few centimeters to locate his attacker, his hair dragging through the bloody muck as he turned his face. Suddenly, as he looked along the ground at his attacker's feet, a warm sensation came over him and a red glint filled his eyes.

"Mistake," grumbled Brig, leaping to his feet, knocking the Ripper from the attacker's hand with a swift kick while spinning and grabbing the man's neck with one hand. A quick twist, a sickening crack, and the attacker fell to the ground...lifeless.

The misting rain had subsided, replaced by an ever-growing fog that had silently oozed into the alleyway. Brig, snarling like a rabid beast, quickly turned his head from side to side. He lurched into a defensive stance as he peered into the foggy mist, and even though there was no one there, *he* saw groups of shadows approaching him from all sides. He took a step back and grasped for his assault weapon – to no avail, he had none on him.

An intense, searing burn surged through his brain. Losing his balance, he fell backward into a pile of scrap metal with a loud clang that echoed off the brick walls. He gripped his head tightly in his hands, trying desperately to squeeze out the agony.

"No! Stop! You'll never take me!" The wraith-like figures converged on him from within the fog, each of them brandishing fierce-looking assault weapons. Suddenly, he felt the fiery metal of their ordinance tear through his side. Brig twisted as he winced in agony. He jumped to his feet once again and began swinging wildly in a desperate attempt to connect with the specters.

"Retreat now, or I'll kill you all!" Brig shouted maniacally. Spittle flung from his mouth as he looked from one phantom attacker to the next.

Brig stretched his hand back towards his neck and grasped at a spot that stung like the payload of an enraged hornet. He fingered, and then released as quickly, a small, metal tube protruding from the skin, before he collapsed onto the slick asphalt of the alley.

Brig opened his eyes and glanced around the room. Through the thick haze that clouded his mind, he immediately determined that he was no longer in the alley, but rather in a large room of a dank, deserted warehouse. The rhythmic patter of drainage from the roof above echoed loudly in his ears.

He shook his head rapidly from side to side to gain perspective through the fuzz on his brain. He could not distinguish if anyone was there, and he quickly found that metal shackles bound his hands and limited his movement almost entirely. His ankles, fastened in a similar style, held tight against the legs of the chair on which he was sitting. He could taste the salt of the caked blood around his lips, and his sides burned with fire from the beating he had taken in the alley.

"Well, well, look who's awake," a voice from behind him jibed with a thick Australian accent.

"Where the Hell am I, Australia?" muttered Brig, knowing that was not the case.

"Australia? Hell mate, there hasn't been an Australia for years. That beating you took mess with your brain?" the captor chuckled snidely. "But you're awake now, so let's get down to business. You're in a heap of trouble."

"I don't even know who the Hell you are. What do you want from me?" Brig slurred, his lips cut and swollen.

"What do I want from you? Ha ha, that's rich, mate. What do I want from you..." the Australian continued to chuckle mockingly. "It's not what I want from you, it's what we're gonna take from you."

The Australian's voice grew angry as he grabbed Brig by the back of the neck. "Who do you think you are that you can take out a couple of our collectors and no one's gonna be the wiser? I got news for you, friend, you're not walking out of here alive."

"So just kill me already, unless I got something you're looking for." Brig stared at the captor out of the corner of one eye, trying to gauge what he was *really* after.

"Oh no, mate. You've got nothing I want. Besides, if it were my job to kill you, you'd have died in that alley after you took out my partner there," the Australian chimed with a sly grin on his face.

"That's why you attacked me from behind there in the alley, huh? You slimy chook, get outta my face if you're not gonna be a man," Brig snarled, wrestling futilely against the shackles on his wrists.

"Now, now, that's no kind of language to use with someone who's got the upper hand, now is it, mate? From where I'm standin' you're tied up in a chair with your hands clamped behind your back. All kinda bad stuff can happen here if I want it to."

The captor stood, released Brig's neck from his grasp, and flipped his own shoulder-length hair back from his face while lighting a cigarette.

"Besides, you're time's coming, friend. The Regional will be here in a minute, and he's gonna have a little fun with ya before he turns your lights out for good. Don't you worry. But you'll be wishing I were still here after he gets through with you."

The Aussie stared down at him with a condescending smirk, forcefully exhaling a white puff of smoke into Brig's face. "Ya see, I'd just put a bullet in you – knock that smile right offa your face. But the Regional, nah, he's gonna take his time with you. Real methodical type. He'll take you apart one piece at a time, but the beauty is that you'll be alive to experience it. Fun times, mate."

"Super," Brig grumbled, looking away. "Don't suppose I can bum a cigarette from you, huh...*mate?*" he quizzed sarcastically, examining the room around him for potential escape routes.

"Of course. I'm nothing if not cordial. Here ya go. Don't think you're gonna have enough time to reap the health benefits anyway." The captor laughed again as he pulled out another cigarette. Lighting it from his own, he then leaned towards Brig, offering it to him.

As the Aussie neared, Brig whipped his head forward and spat into his face. "Kill me you son of a bitch!"

The Aussie recoiled and quickly wiped the saliva from his face with his forearm. "Mate, honestly, I'm trying to be a good host here. Make your last moments on Earth a comfortable one," he retorted with obvious sarcasm. "But you're makin it awfully hard to do when you keep acting like an animal. But here, just to show there's no hard feelins..."

Again, the captor leaned in towards Brig with the lit cigarette, but this time he viciously drilled the lit end into Brig's forehead. Brig jerked backward in pain as the cigarette burrowed into his skin, leaving a small, black burn mark just above his eyebrow ridge. "That's for the chook comment, you Yankee prick. I've got a half a pack of ciggies left here that could just find their way onto that pretty little face of yours, mate. So just you settle down."

A loud click from the far end of the warehouse drew the captor's attention away from Brig. The Aussie stood up and turned in the direction of a set of doors across the room, as they swung open. "Ah, that would be your new best pal arriving right now. Nice knowing you."

Brig turned his head in curiosity. A medium-height man, wearing an armored mask and walking with a noticeable limp, slowly strolled across the dusty floor. "How long's he been here?" the man asked, the voice changer in his mask tuning the sound of his words into a squeaky hiss.

"Been since last night, mate. Didn't think you'd ever show up," said the Australian, backing away from Brig, picking the cigarette from his mouth and billowing another cloud of smoke from his nostrils. "This son of a bitch took out two of our collectors. Woulda done me in, too, if he didn't have some kinda weird episode or something – gave me just enough of an opening to drop him with a tranq dart."

"Anyone else know he's here?" queried the man, staring intently at Brig.

"Nah. I followed protocol, just like I'm supposed to. You and me are it, bossman," insisted the Aussie. "Mind if I stick around and watch how the Regionals get it done? Never seen you guys operate in person, mate. That would be a treat for me," he said cheerily, snuffing out his cigarette on a nearby table.

"Good man, but I don't think so," the other remarked. However, before the Australian could open his mouth in protest, the masked man raised his handgun at the Aussie's chest and fired two quick slugs, thrusting the Aussie backward and onto the floor, dead.

"...the *Hell*?" grumbled Brig in a slight whisper, peering up at the masked man through the hair draped over his face and eyes.

"A little too chummy for my liking. How about you, friend?" the masked man inquired. He tilted his armor-covered head sideways and peered at Brig through the small eye slits. "Seems you got yourself in a bit of a bind here."

"You could say that...but then I doubt you're here to talk *either*," resigned Brig, shaking his head slowly. He knew his fate was near.

"Sadly, no. You broke a cardinal rule of this organization, one that you're going to have to pay for," the masked man said, his tone suddenly more serious. The man put his weapon up to Brig's forehead. The barrel, still warm from the previous two blasts, made Brig flinch from its metallic heat. "Give me a reason not to put a bullet through that thick skull of yours right now," the man taunted through his unseen, gritted teeth.

"Does it matter? If I broke one of your precious rules so badly, then just *do* it already. Don't let me waste *your* time," Brig growled, sneering up at the masked man.

"Ah yes, *always* the hothead. When will you ever learn, *Brigadier Stroud*, the world's a little smaller place than what you want to believe it is. Actions have reactions...and consequences," The man turned his back on Brig while removing the armor from his head.

"Do I know you?" Brig twisted his neck further to try to catch a clear glimpse of this new stranger.

"Sorry, should have said...*Rage*...right?" The stranger turned to face Brig, his tanned, stubbled face suddenly visible in the lower light of the warehouse.

"Crypto? What the Hell?" cried Brig with a look of sheer bewilderment.

"Yep, here I am to save your sorry ass...*again*." Crypto began to unclamp Brig's hands from the restraints. "Did you make the pickup? Did you get the vials and syringes?"

"No, stumbled on two bagmen having it out before the contact ever showed up."

"Well, that explains this guy saying what he did. Did you take out both of them?" Crypto shook his head while he removed the last restraint from Brig's wrists.

"I took the one because he tried to kill me with a Ripper. The other was on the ground when I got there, so I don't know what happened to him," explained Brig, removing the chains holding his legs to the chair. "And in answer to your earlier question – because I've saved *your* sorry ass more times than I can count. *Fraternitas Aeternus*, remember?"

"Brothers forever, yeah, I know. But Brig, sooner or later your luck is gonna' run out," Crypto said, still shaking his head while helping Brig up from his chair.

"You call this luck? Luck is when that bullet with my name on it finally finds me."

"I guess for someone like you, that might be true, *Rage.*"

"I told you I don't *like* that name," growled Brig.

Crypto rolled his eyes and turned away from Brig, as he started towards the door. "Yeah, well, we all have our demons. At least *yours* has a name. Now let's get the Hell out of here before these cockroaches start putting things together and figure out what happened."

Crypto grabbed Brig's arm and draped it around his own neck for support.

"You know, you're kind of a sadistic bastard, Cryp," taunted Brig, glancing over at his friend, who stared forward, expressionless.

"Yeah, I get that a lot."

2:
Hero of the Day

Present day (2084)...

Clive 'Crypto' Underwood sat at his workbench, his shoulders slouched, tinkering meticulously on a small circuit board laid out in front of him. The bright, LED light attached to his bench silhouetted his short, dirty blonde hair; its subtle curls matted against the side of his sweaty scalp from the lack of air conditioning in the small room.

It had been almost twenty-four hours since he had rescued his friend, Brig, from the clutches of his captors, and the two had not spoken about the incident since.

Brig lay on a cot behind and several meters away with his face against the wall, as he tried to rest from his ordeal the previous night. However, unbeknownst to Clive, Brig was wide-awake and staring at the bare wall next to his cot, his mind vividly replaying his and Clive's first dealings.

Guess this isn't the first time you've been there for me, bro, Brig thought.

Nine years prior (2075)...

Brig and Clive huddled closely to each other, their extreme cold-weather gear bundled about their bodies. Their hoods mostly obscured the flesh of their faces, aside from the remaining bare skin around their mouths. As they spoke, thick clouds of cold breath flooded the air in front of them.

"Man, I thought solo survival training was rough. At least it was warm outside – this is *ridiculous*," Brig said, dipping his mouth into his scarf, a thick puff of breath spewing from the cloth as he spoke.

"Thank your maker that you've got me here, Brig. There's no way you'd have come up with this shelter on your own," Clive chuckled aloud, scanning around the makeshift tent he had crafted out of wild animal skins earlier that day.

"But I would have eaten well in any case," Brig mumbled,

poking a stick through the flames of the fire that blazed in front of them, sending small tufts of smoke up through the rough opening at the top of the tent.

Clive opened the slit he had cut at the front of the structure. He quickly peeked outside to gauge the fierceness of the blizzard that had forced them to take shelter.

"Doesn't look like this one's gonna let up anytime soon, man," Clive observed.

"We've got extraction in two days, hopefully it'll let up a bit by morning so we can go out and make sure we're not buried here." Brig watched his partner close the flap and head back to the corner against the large, flat rock next to him.

"So, Brigadier Stroud," Clive said in a deep tone, mocking as if he were an authority figure giving an interview, "what brought you to the Epsilon Warriors?"

Brig chuckled. "The same thing that brings most of us, I guess. Adventure, wanting to serve our nation, become a man. That sorta stuff," he quipped, staring forward in thought.

"Ooo-*rah* all the way, huh?"

"Yeah, sorta. But you know having been in military boarding schools since I was fourteen, I guess it was my destiny to end up somewhere like *this* anyway." Brig stared blankly ahead of him as the memories, still fresh in his mind, played like a silent movie in his head.

"Ah, your Pop trying to toughen you up or what?" asked Clive.

"Never really put much thought into it. I suppose it *might* be that, but he had always had grand ideas of running for political office. I always figured it was easier for him to get me out of the way. After all, hard to win an election when your teenage son gets busted for messing around with the local police chief's daughter," Brig replied. "*True* story, by the way." Brig turned to look at Clive with a smirk that curled up one corner of his mouth.

"Hell, he made Regional Governor just a couple of years into my stay at school," Brig continued, "so I guess he was onto something. But lately, I think it's more of me wantin' to prove somethin' to him. To show him that I can make somethin' out of myself, just like *he* did. That I'm not just some young troublemaker. Politics aren't my thing, though, so I just followed what I knew – and *here* I am."

"A bad boy with something to prove, I like it brother!" Clive gave an approving nod and raised his heavily gloved hand to pat Brig on the shoulder.

"So what's *your* story, Underwood?" Brig asked, glancing over at Clive.

Clive nodded subtly, as he bent over their chow pack to fetch a K-Ration, his bare hands quivering from the chilled air.

"My story's not all that great, bro." Clive popped open the small container and handed it to his partner. "Lived a pretty normal life. Got into athletics at an early age. Did all kinds of track and field, played football, basketball in high school. After graduation I was gonna go and try to qualify for the decathlon in the Hemi-Games..."

"Hemi-Games?" Brig looked up from his freeze-dried fruit bar. "What's *that*?"

"You know, like the *Legacy* Games. The Olympics is what it used to be called, you've heard of *them* right?" Clive opened his food container, as well. "Well, for the most part the government prohibits us from travelling to countries outside the United Republic of the Americas, and athletics just don't cut it for an excuse anymore. So they came up with the Hemi-Games, which lets anyone from within the URA or its immediate neighbors to the north and south compete."

Clive paused as he took a bite of a granola chunk. "If we win the gold in an event," he said with his mouth full, "that qualifies us for a chance to go to the Legacy Games, even without a promise of anything, especially with the current political climate."

"So you're a jock then?" Brig jabbed.

"Not in a typical sense, no," Clive answered, politely shaking his head. "I actually liked school – I was good in math and science. Hell, I was pretty decent in my other subjects, too. But something that really drew my interest early on was when I was studying the ancient Greeks," he continued as his round, slate black eyes widened; he was now engrossed in his own story. He gritted his teeth slightly, the muscles in his squared jaw subtly pushing the sides of his hood outward. "They were one of the first ancient civilizations to utilize ciphers to encode messages."

"Ciphers, you mean like cryptography?" Brig asked with a puzzled look on his face, what little could be seen of it. "What's a kid doing getting into *that* kinda stuff?"

"I don't know, man, it just *spoke* to me. And with my background in math and science, I just took to it naturally," Clive muttered as he finished his food, crumpled the container and threw it into a receptacle on the other side of the makeshift tent.

"So how'd you end up in the EWs then? With those kind of smarts you'd think you coulda' gone to any college you wanted," Brig asked with an air of amazement.

"Well, that's where the story goes to Hell, man. See, I had planned on doing the whole Hemi-Games thing while going to a first rate university. But then, my folks split up a few years before graduation. My Dad didn't leave me and my Mom much to live on, so I had to start working earlier than I wanted. That took away time from me being able to study or even train. So my grades fell a bit - and I couldn't compete with low grades." Clive also dug through the flaming pile of wood in front of him with a smaller stick. "So after graduation, stuck at a dead-end, low-paying nothing job, no chance at the Hemi-Games, no chance at college – what choice did I have?"

"So you joined the EWs..." Brig added.

Clive nodded his head subtly as he stared forward at the flames, the disappointment of what could have been glowing inside the reflection of the flames in the pupils of his eyes.

"And the rest is history," Clive concluded. "It's not college, it's not the Games, but they allow me to do what I love – cryptography – as a specialty. Plus, they pay for just about everything else, so I can't really complain too much. Well, except for being in a makeshift tent in the middle of the Alaskan wilderness in the dead of a winter blizzard."

Clive looked at Brig to judge his reaction.

"I'll bet you weren't too happy about them creating these new two-man survival training missions then, huh?" Brig patted Clive on the back with a gloved hand.

"Nah man, but if it means that I get to do more of what I like on actual missions instead of just going in with guns blazing, I'm all for it I guess," Clive answered self-assuredly.

Present day (2084)...

Brig quietly sat up on the cot in the corner of the small room. He could see the figure of Clive, his back turned towards Brig and hunkered over a workbench, various electronics strewn all about him on each side. Faint tinkering sounds filled the side of the room where his workbench stood, a sign that Clive was hard at work... as usual.

Detecting that Brig was awake and stirring, Clive turned to face his comrade. "You need some rest, Brig. You've been through *Hell* the past couple of days..."

"...Past couple of *days*? That's an understatement..." Brig remarked, looking up at Clive from a sitting position on the cot.

"Regardless, man, you need to recover and the only way you're going to do that is by lying back down and getting some sleep. I gave you some serum, so you should be able to relax for a while without having to worry about...well, *you* know." Clive silently stared at his friend for a moment. "Besides, I have something to take care of and I think it's best if you just hang tight right here til I get back – alright?" Clive turned his back on Brig and focused on his workbench once again.

"Sure man, whatever you say," Brig mumbled. "I got nowhere to go anyhow."

Clive gathered a couple of small components, stowed them in a small, black container, and then arose from his stool. As he walked to the door, he turned his head at Brig and motioned with his finger. "Remember what I said, *stay* here," he commanded, his eyebrows furrowed intensely.

Brig chuckled, nodded his head and lay back down on the cot. "Yes sir, Cryp."

As the door slid closed behind Clive, Brig glared back up at the ceiling, his mind still replaying the events that helped shape his and Clive's friendship. "Guess I owe you *that* much."

Nine years prior (2075)...

The following morning, the blizzard had broken and both men had ventured outside, hiking in the direction of a nearby clearing next to a frozen lake just beyond a heavy grouping of trees where they had made camp the night before.

"Twenty-four hours to go, man. Can't wait to get back to base and get as far away from this cold weather as possible," Brig hollered over the howling wind to his comrade, who was walking several meters ahead of him.

"You said it, man," answered Clive. "But we still have some stuff we need to take care of before the extraction tomorrow. Here, take these comm-markers," he said, as he turned and tossed a wrapped bundle to Brig. "You need to head over to the edge of the lake, then up to the hill just on the north end and place them so that we can complete our morning task." Clive pointed to a spot just on the other side of the lake.

"Oh, I get to hike up the hill? How's *that* work, bro?" Brig held out his hands to his side in protest.

"Age has its privileges, and being younger I think you can handle it!" Clive thrust the bundle of markers into Brig's arms. "Now get going, we need to have those markers in place before noon so that we get credit for our task for the day." Clive turned from Brig and started back for the tree line.

"You're the boss," Brig barked in jest. "Try not to over-exert yourself setting your markers *right here* along the tree line, old man. I know *that* job's gonna be tough."

He turned from his partner and began his trek to the hill, holding the bundle of markers tightly under one arm, his feet crunching crisply in the fresh snow as he briskly strode away. Reaching the base of the rocky-sided hill, he dropped the markers with a dull thud.

"Just great," Brig mumbled to himself. "Just what I wanted to do today – go rock-climbing with forty pounds of winter gear on."

Brig thought for a moment as he stared up at the hill. He had an idea.

"Easily fixed," he quipped confidently.

He unbuttoned and then shed his heavy, fur-lined military commando jacket and placed it neatly on the ground, restringing the small pack over his lightly clothed shoulder. Picking up the bundle of markers, he strapped them to his pack and jogged towards the rock face to begin his climb.

"Let's light this candle," he said, stretching his arms out in preparation.

Although the cold bit into the bare skin of his hands and arms, he realized he was correct in his decision to shed the weighty clothing, as he found himself quite easily scaling the jags jutting out from the rock face of the hill. In just moments, he was at the pinnacle, heavy puffs of foggy breath chugging from his open mouth as he pulled himself upright to a standing position.

Brig turned and looked down at the edge of the tree line 50 meters away.

"*This* is what youth does for you, man," Brig shouted. "*You'd* still be huffing and puffing your way at the bottom of this baby!"

Over near the tree line, Clive glanced up to see his partner at the top of the rocky summit and waved his hand in dismissal of Brig's taunts.

Having planted the communication marker at the top of the crag, Brig had already begun his descent. "Now, the easy part," he chuckled, quickly scaling down the slick rocks.

As he reached the base, Brig decided to forego putting his heavy coat back on, deciding instead to do a quick dash over to the lake's edge to plant the corresponding, and final, marker.

A sharp crack filled the air. Brig abruptly lost his footing and plunged into the lake through a gaping hole that had suddenly opened beneath him. He flailed his arms wildly, grasping at the sides of the hole in a futile attempt to keep his head above the water line, but found that the ice kept shattering and expanding the chasm as he made contact with the jagged edges.

The super-chilled water burned his face and stung his hands as he splashed about, still trying to gain a hold on the rapidly expanding edges of the hole around him. In a last ditch effort, Brig managed to get his head above water long enough to scream out "Warrior down!" and then slipped back down into the depths of the black, icy water.

Clive, near the tree line having just placed his final marker, turned sharply towards the sound of the cry. He caught a glimpse of water splashing out from a breach in the ice at the edge of the target hill. Dropping the marker that was still in his hand, he made a mad dash towards the frozen lake to save his friend.

Clive came to a halt at the edge of the fissure. The water had become calm with no sign of his fellow EW beneath the murky depths. A deep thump shook the ice a few meters away. He recoiled, seeing the shaded outline of Brig just beneath the shimmering surface.

Clive instinctively scanned the area at the base of the hill and spotted a smaller boulder with most of its apparent mass above ground. With no time to waste, he managed to free the boulder from the earth, lifted it over his head and slammed it down onto the thick ice of the lakebed.

The loud crash of the rock crushing the icy lake surface echoed off the side of the ridge. Large jets of chilled lake water spewed out in all directions, as a three-meter hole opened up where he was standing just moments before. Clive spotted Brig's motionless body near one of the edges of the jagged ice and quickly grabbed the back of his collar.

"Not on *my* watch, soldier," Clive growled. He panted wildly as he pulled Brig from the freezing lake, despite being a good fifteen centimeters and having a more slender, tone build than his partner. However, before Clive could administer any life-saving procedures,

Brig gurgled, coughed, and then began spewing water from his lungs out of the corner of his mouth.

"Alright, there you go, Brig. Come back to me now – take a breath," Clive said, helping his friend to a sitting position.

"D-d-d-damn that's some c-c-cold water out there," Brig stuttered, spit and icy clouds of breath sputtering from his mouth. His hands shook violently from the frigid water, as he reached out to Clive for assistance in getting to his feet.

"Good then, at least we know your *brain's* still workin'. We gotta get you back to the shelter before you go into hypothermic shock." Clive yanked on Brig's hand.

"Ow, shit, I can't feel my left leg man!" Brig yelped, falling back to the snow-covered ground, grasping at his calf.

"And *that's* why we need to get you back, now come'on hold onto my shoulder we gotta get goin'!" insisted Clive, pulling Brig back up on his one good leg.

In moments, both men were back within their hand-made shelter. Clive diligently examined Brig's lower left leg for frostbite while Brig bundled the rest of his body in a heavy blanket. "I'm starting to get some tingling back in it now, *that's* good right?" he asked, stretching his leg out near the fire.

"Once again, you're lucky I was there, Brig. I don't see any frostbite damage. So I don't think you're going to *lose* that leg or anything."

Present day (2084)...

Brig sat upright on his cot again, his arms resting on his knees and his hands clasped loosely together.

"Lucky me," he muttered, staring thoughtfully at Clive's empty stool.

3:
Communication Breakdown

Eight years prior (2076)...

Brig and Clive strode abreast along the corridor. The overhead lights of the hallway reflected off the portions of their scalps exposed by their short crew cuts. Their crisp military fatigues rustled with each brisk step.

Clive, realizing they were late for the mission briefing, increased his pace.

"What do you think this briefing's about, Clive?" Brig asked his partner, as they rounded a corner.

"Hard to say, but you can bet your ass they're not sending us on *another* sensitive mission so soon. Not after the stunt *you* pulled last time," quipped Clive, a half-smile adorning his face. "My guess is they'll have us babysitting some politico as they walk their dog or something – or at least *you* will be."

"We'll see about *that*..." A wry smile grew on Brig's face.

"Aw, Hell. What are you gonna go and do *now*, Brig?" Clive replied hesitantly, rolling his eyes without looking at his partner.

"Do? You mean *done*, pal," said Brig, the wry smile now turning to a knowing smirk.

The two men entered the mission-briefing center, where several other Epsilon Warriors had already found seats. A tall man with peppered, black hair, stood at the front of the small room, his back to the group while he studied a holographic map display. His combat fatigues fit snugly over his muscular frame, with the sleeves barely rolled up over his massive, bulging biceps.

"Underwood, Stroud – glad to see you ladies could make it. Now have a seat!" he barked, turning to face the small assembly of soldiers. "I hate to take away from your morning constitutionals, but we've got some important business to take care of, so..."

"Sorry we're late, Commander Falco. Underwood's training for the squadron triathlon..." Brig replied.

"...I don't give a *damn* what you're doing, Stroud! Now *can* it so we can get this over with!" Falco growled through his bared teeth. "Now men, we've been given a very sensitive assignment that needs to be handled immediately..."

"Yesss!" whispered Brig, pumping his fist lightly to himself while leaning towards Clive. Clive did not react, but instead continued to focus his attention on Falco.

"...it's a two-man mission that's going to require both Warriors to be very alert – but also very stealthy. We're not expecting any resistance – or at least not any that should pose a credible threat. Probably a lightly armed security guard or two, but nonetheless you have to be as covert as you can. *Zero* body count."

With a quick swipe of two fingers at the base of the display, the Commander called up a strategic, holographic map behind him.

"We'll make the insertion at oh-two-hundred hours just beyond this ridge right here." Falco pointed at a location on the map marked with a small, pulsating red flag. "You'll follow along this tree-line until you come upon a cluster of buildings..."

"I can't stand all this tip-toeing around garbage, man. That's *not* what we do," Brig mumbled at Clive, incensed that stealth was the order of the day.

"...Once inside and past any security that might be present, you will locate and access the special security terminal shown here, and retrieve the data onto your data pad. It's expected that the terminal will be protected by some sort of security, which is why we need two of you for this job. Your crypto specialist will handle this portion while the other will provide lookout and cover, if needed. As soon as you make the retrieval, you are to exit the premises immediately. You are *not* to engage non-military personnel if you don't have to."

Falco faced the group again, scanning them with an unwavering glare. "You are to be back at the extraction point at oh-five-hundred, no later...or you'll lose your ride."

"Oh great. Couldn't he just get his secretary to do this job? What do they need the EW squadron for on this one?" Brig shook his head at Clive.

"Sir, you mentioned non-military personnel. Are there military personnel *at* this location that we should be wary of?" Clive asked, continuing to ignore Brig's display of frustration.

"There are none in this immediate vicinity, which is why we are expecting very little resistance," Falco responded gruffly.

"What kind of data are we retrieving, Commander?" Brig asked.

"That's not your concern, Stroud. But let's just say that a

successful retrieval is essential to ending the conflict we're dealing with in Spain."

The Commander focused on the rest of the group.

"Now, I've got Stroud as the leader of this covert op. I had intended Thompson to be his crypto spec, but someone got his daddy to pull some strings for him," Falco continued, with a gratuitous look towards Brig. "So...congratulations, Underwood – *you're* running crypto for Stroud on this one."

Several of the other EWs began to chuckle and whisper to each other, as Clive glared at Brig.

"Did I tell ya?" Brig remarked to him with a wink.

"This is a covert op," the Commander continued, "you must take great care not to be detected, and most of all, not to be *captured*. As always, if you are discovered or captured during this mission, the URA will disavow any knowledge of your activities and you will essentially be on your own."

Falco leaned in on the rail that separated the front of the room from the seating area, and craned his neck towards Brig.

"Don't screw this one up, Stroud! You get in, get the package, and get out. Any extra-curriculars *this* time and you both can kiss your time in the EWs good-bye. Do I make myself *clear?*" Falco hollered, his face turning several shades of crimson.

"Yessir," both Clive and Brig said simultaneously, their eyes widened in reaction to Falco's rant.

"Dismissed!" the Commander yelped, and the small grouping of EWs hastily began to exit the room.

Clive strode ahead of Brig as they entered the corridor. The scowl on Clive's face did not mask his obvious anger.

"I can't believe you *did* this, Brig! You trying to get me booted out of the EWs or what?" Clive snarled without looking at Brig.

"No way, man. This is a walk in the park, you'll see. We'll be back here and getting kudos before you know it. Hell, you never know, we might even get *promos* out of this one," Brig offered optimistically, trying to keep up with Clive.

"I don't care about that right now, man. I'm tryin' to keep my nose clean, and man I just get the feelin' this *ain't* the way to do it! Besides, I'm in the middle of training for the 'tri'. I got a chance to win it this year, Brig."

Clive stopped and turned abruptly to face his partner.

"And where do *you* get off pulling strings to get me put on this duty?" he said, jabbing his finger angrily at Brig.

21

"Hey, I thought you'd be *happy* to do it," Brig retorted, looking somewhat surprised.

"You just don't get it, do you? Every time you do something like that, pull strings with your father, all the other EWs are *laughing* at you, man!" Clive began walking again, but then stopped and threw his arms up in the air. "And now you got them laughing at *me*! I've busted my ass to get where I'm at, and I don't like it! You think just because your daddy's a Regional Governor you can use that to your advantage. *Some* of us have to *work* to get where we're at, man!"

"Give it a rest already, man. I'm tired of hearing how I'm the teacher's pet around here. Besides, this isn't about my father. Sure, he may have some pull with our outfit, but he doesn't make my decisions for me – especially not with my *life*. I wanted the best crypto guy on this mission, and that's you. Maybe I should just go and get Jonas Slade to do it?" Brig pursed his lips and furrowed his brow in disgust.

Clive rolled his eyes and crossed his arms over his chest in protest.

"Yeah," Brig continued in defense. "That's what I thought." He brushed Clive's shoulder with his own as he forcefully moved past him, but then turned abruptly to face him.

Brig softly tapped Clive's forehead in jest.

"And if you think this is about anything other than you being the best crypto guy in this squadron, you're delusional."

Present day (2084)...

As Clive walked alone on the deserted sidewalk along what was once a bustling city park, a slight whisper grabbed his attention from just beyond the hedges that grew wildly along the edge.

A dark figure stepped partially out from behind a thick, unlit lamppost. The person remained within the shadow of the trees branching out over the roadway, which conveniently hid most of the stranger's features.

"Over here," the voice prompted, piercing the silence of the night.

"You here for the drop?" Clive asked quietly, moving slowly towards the figure.

"That's right," the figure responded. "You've got the package?"

"Right here," Clive answered assuredly, patting the shoulder pouch hanging down to his side under his arm.

Clive pulled a small, black box from the sack and presented it to his customer, who was still standing within the shadow of one of the nearby trees.

"Pretty heavy duty stuff here, although that encryption scheme was old, even when it was new. But I'm sure you knew that already," Clive offered.

The shadowy figure took the box from Clive.

"Did you look at the data on these cards?" the shadowed stranger asked curiously, while opening the box and thumbing through the enclosed white, plastic, cipher cards. The small interface connectors on each glinted in the moonlight as the stranger moved them from side to side.

"Not my business. My job is to decrypt customer data and hand it over," Clive said dryly. He closed the pouch and placed it back over his shoulder while glancing around, ensuring that unwanted eyes were not in the vicinity.

"Good," the stranger said in a reassured tone. "Syndicate credits will do?"

Clive turned his attention back to the stranger. "The *only* kind that matter anymore, aren't they?"

The stranger nodded subtly, dropped a small, jingling bag into Clive's hands, whispered, "I'll be in touch," and then quickly disappeared into the shadows.

"I'm *sure* you will," Clive muttered softly, turning to head back to his workshop.

Eight years prior (2076)...

The intercom buzzed over the whirring of the heli-jet's multiple engines as it dove deep around an oncoming ridge, briskly came to a stop and hovered near an opening in a small forest some twenty meters below.

"Captains Stroud and Underwood, we're over the target now, sirs. Prepare for insertion," the pilot instructed over the speaker.

Clive sat and gazed pensively out the side of the cabin window at the blackness below. He gripped the stabilizer bar above him, as he swayed back and forth with the subtle motion of the idling vehicle.

"Wonder what we're gonna' find down there?" Clive asked Brig, sitting opposite of him.

Brig, preoccupied with fastening his supply pack to his shoulder and mentally reviewing his preparation checklist, answered without looking up at him. "Cake walk, bro, cake walk," he said flatly.

"Wish I had *your* confidence," Clive murmured as he, too, picked up his pack and threw it over his shoulder.

"Besides," Brig said, smiling and patting the rifle that he had strapped to his other shoulder, "they don't stand a chance with *us*."

A subdued, red light began to pulsate at the top of the cabin, accompanied by the muted chime of a claxon from the speaker next to it.

"Let's rock n' roll," Brig urged, giving Clive a quick nod.

The door clunked as it began to swing upward into a gull-wing shape and out of sight above the cabin. Brig, showing no apprehension, grasped the outside of the fuselage in one hand and a rappelling rope in the other. He dexterously kicked off against the side rail with a spin, and quickly disappeared downward out of sight into the murk.

Clive took a breath and stood silently, still staring at the abyss below him through the open door, and then followed his teammate.

Brig leaned against a tree just beyond the opening of the compound gate and motioned to Clive with two fingers. Clive, behind another tree across the path from Brig, peered around the side of it and visually confirmed what Brig had seen. Two security guards, each brandishing small rifles, stood watch over the entrance. Brig motioned once again, and the two men stealthily disappeared within the tree line nearest the compound.

Moments later, they had emerged at a point fifteen meters from the compound gate, just beyond earshot of the two guards. A metal chain-link fence, three meters tall, stood in front of them. It stretched back towards the main gate in one direction and disappeared at a solid block wall that began twenty meters to their right, surrounded by thick brush that partially hid a security light at the corner.

As Brig approached the fence, Clive grasped his upper arm and pulled him back.

"Electric?" Clive whispered.

Brig scanned the fence to the limit of his sight in both directions.

"Nah, don't see any terminals anywhere – just a plain chain

link," Brig replied, shaking his head. He quickly hopped onto the fence and scaled upward.

"Great security," Clive mumbled, "makes you wonder if the data in here is what we *think* it is." Looking hesitantly towards the guarded gate, Clive silently leapt onto the fence and began to climb.

After having weaved in and out of several smaller facilities within the complex, Brig and Clive stopped at the rear of a taller building at the center of the compound.

"This's the one. Terminal's on the second floor," Brig whispered.

Clive nodded silently.

A tiny, red dot from Brig's wrist-mounted laser finder danced along the top edge of the building.

"Fire it there," Brig said softly, pointing upwards at its target.

Clive pulled a small, black tube from his pack and aimed it towards the building's top floor. With a subtle squeeze of the back end, a small, metal grappling hook zipped silently upward, and expanded as it latched with a light 'clink' onto the top edge of the wall. Clive yanked firmly on the lower end of the rope and then nodded to Brig.

Brig grasped it and hastily made his way up the side of the building, effortlessly removed the glass from a window on the second floor, and disappeared inside.

Glowing red with the light of the laser finder, Brig held his arm through the window and gave a 'thumbs-up'.

Both men exited the stairwell to the second floor and approached the target room. Suddenly, a security guard, making his rounds, entered the intersection of their current hallway and another.

The EWs quickly flattened themselves against the wall, just enough of them in the shadow of darkness that the security guard did not spot them.

The guard continued his patrol into an adjacent hallway.

Brig motioned to Clive to follow him into the terminal room. Clive shadowed the mission leader and quietly closed the door behind him.

"Piece of cake, like I told you." Brig pointed to the terminal on a desk against a far wall.

"I'm just glad these people don't believe in security, or this could have gone *much* differently." Clive pulled his data pad from his shoulder pack. "Give me a few minutes after I hook up to get past any security measures. Although seeing as how we just waltzed right in here, I doubt there will be many at all."

Brig positioned himself next to the door, keeping a keen ear for anyone that might be approaching from either end of the hallway just outside. After a few minutes, he turned to Clive, gave him a shoulder shrug with arms outstretched and silently mouthed, "Well?"

Clive, flustered, looked at Brig, pointed at his pad and made a slashing gesture against his own throat.

"Crap," Brig muttered, reaching into his own shoulder pack and pulling out another data pad. He lightly tapped against the device, carefully tossed it to his partner and whispered, "It's not secure..."

"We're taking a real chance here, Brig," Clive replied in an elevated whisper.

"We got one shot at this, *make it happen,*" Brig encouraged sternly, turning his attention back to the door.

Clive subtly shook his head, faced the terminal, and completed the hook-up of the unsecured pad.

Once again, Brig glanced at Clive for another silent status update. Without looking up from his effort, Clive responded with a quick 'thumbs-up'.

Clive silently tapped his gloved hand on the edge of the desk as he waited for the data download to complete, and then quickly stowed it away in his pack. Clive's part of the mission completed, Brig quickly motioned to him and silently exited into the hallway.

Moments later, and without incident, both men trotted quietly along the backside of the building as they moved towards their infiltration spot.

As they neared the compound's perimeter fence, the sound of several voices from beyond a nearby wall halted Brig in his tracks. He stood at the base of the rock wall listening attentively to determine the source and potential danger, motioning to Clive to hold his position.

One of the voices piqued Brig's interest; it was that of a teenager. He signaled to Clive once again, but that *this* time that they were going to go investigate.

Ignoring the incredulous look on Clive's face, Brig began to scale the nearby wall. Clive, knowing he had no alternative but to follow his partner, began to climb as well.

On the other side of the wall, just beyond a small grouping of trees 25 meters from where they were perched, they saw the source of the noise.

Three guards, armed with standard assault weapons, led a long line of teenage boys, shackled together at their hands, waists and legs, from one building of an adjacent compound into another.

Brig and Clive leapt stealthily, and simultaneously, from the top of the wall onto the ground beneath just behind a thick patch of brush, landing silently with cat-like precision on the soft earth.

Brig extracted his night-vision binoculars from his pack and focused on one of the teens nearest one of the guards. From what he could determine, *they* were the ones doing the talking.

He gathered focus just in time to catch the teen spit into the nearby guard's face, prompting the guard to rear back with his rifle and clobber the teen directly in the side of his cheekbone with the butt.

Brig tensed. The anger flamed within him as he watched the teen crumple to the ground in pain.

The guard, upon silencing the insolent teen with his violent response, turned to the others and shouted an obvious taunt. Although incomprehensible to Brig, as it was in Portuguese, it let them know *he* was in charge of the situation.

"What do you suppose *that's* about?" Clive whispered to Brig.

"That's what we're about to find out," Brig replied, not taking his eyes off the confrontation unfolding in front of them.

"I know you're kidding...*right?*" Clive glared at Brig without blinking. "We can't do this, man, extraction's in an hour!"

"Don't start with me, Clive, we're *doin'* this. Besides, you *know* this is the *right* thing to do," Brig replied, eyes still fixated on the guards.

"We have our orders, Brig! Get in, get the data, get out – *no extra-curriculars* – *remember* that?" Clive insisted while grabbing the front of Brig's shirt collar, and swiftly, but quietly, shoving him against the wall behind them. "I'm not going to let you do this, you *hear* me?"

Brig took his focus from the guards and glared intently at Clive.

"Not going to *let* me? You're forgetting – *I'm* in charge of this mission. Man, there are kids over there getting led in *shackles* to who knows where, getting beat by guards with *guns*. You wanna' just turn your back on that and let it happen? That's fine, go ahead. But *I'm* goin' in to do something about it, so either we come up with a plan together or you can just head back over the wall to the extraction point and I'll see you in an hour." Brig forcefully pulled Clive's hand off his jacket and shoved him to the side, then headed back towards the brush.

"Man, if you don't get us both killed you're gonna' get us run out of the EWs," Clive conceded while slowly shaking his head, taking up a position next to Brig. "This *better* work."

"Nice to see you come to your senses, bro," Brig remarked with a sly wink of his right eye. "Here's what we have. Three guards. From left to right, I'll take numbers one and two, you take number three. When they hit the ground, we converge and get those kids out of there. Understood?"

Clive reluctantly nodded while pulling the strap of his rifle over his head, readying it for the task.

Their sniper rifles emitted three quick, silent bursts, and the guards quickly flopped to the ground, all victims of perfect headshots.

The EWs swiftly emerged from the brush and sprinted towards the group of teens, who strained against their shackles in horrified confusion, as their former captors lay motionless on the ground at their feet.

"Grasnado agora!" Brig shouted in imperfect Portuguese, motioning to the group of teens to come to him.

Suddenly, terror flooded the face of one of the boys closest to Brig.

"NO! Don't come any closer!" the boy screamed in broken English.

Two small beeps emitted from the boy's waist shackle, followed by a loud 'kachoom!' and a quick flare that lit the area briefly in orange.

The explosion tore apart the boy and several others closest to him before their eyes, and the shockwave of the blast sent both men reeling backward onto the ground.

The harsh grit of dirt coated their tongues, and the pungent odor of ignited sulfur seared their nostrils, as Brig and Clive strained to see through the cloud kicked up by the bomb blast. Neither could make out anything more than two meters in front of them.

The remainder of the line of teenagers flew haphazardly to the ground, some still in their shackles linked to one another. Several others, blown clear of the group, lay motionless in various spots. The boys that remained alive and conscious shrieked in terror at what had just transpired, as they looked at the remains of members of their group lying in crumpled piles about them.

Brig and Clive pushed themselves from the ground. Suddenly, a set of double-doors on one of the nearby buildings burst open and several heavily armed soldiers wearing riot gear stormed out, heavy assault weaponry at the ready.

Realizing that they were hopelessly outnumbered and not wanting to endanger the teenagers further, Brig and Clive sprinted back to the brush from where they had emerged just minutes earlier.

Mere meters away from escape, Clive heard an all-too-familiar 'whoosh' from behind them.

"Shit!" Clive screamed, as he and Brig, both recognizing the sound of a rocket-propelled grenade launch, dove in opposite directions to avoid the deadly projectile.

The shell was fortuitously off-target and exploded harmlessly against a nearby rock formation.

Both men managed to scamper to the safety of a nearby wall, but quickly found themselves pinned down by heavy gunfire raining on them from the edge of the compound.

"Got some cover right over there!" Brig barked to Clive, pointing to the edge of the forest bordering the wall next to them.

"Too much fire!" Clive shouted over the zing of bullets around him. "Have to draw them off or we're toast!"

Thinking tactically, Brig pulled a small object from his pack and held it up for Clive to see.

"Flashbang!" Brig yelled, tossing three in succession over his head at different angles towards the camp.

Several loud explosions, accompanied by brilliant flashes of light, filled the area. Aside from the initial, frantic shouts from the enemy soldiers, the camp fell silent.

"Move! Move!" shouted Brig, leaping from his crouching position.

The two EWs sprinted frantically towards the tree line, their only chance for escape to run while still under the cover of darkness. Additionally, the effects of the stun grenades Brig had lobbed would be wearing off very quickly, and bringing with it resumption of the enemy attack.

Brig's leg muscles burned as he neared the edge of the tree line, and from behind, he could hear the footsteps of his partner following closely.

Suddenly, a deafening blast, and ensuing shock wave, knocked him forward into a heap.

"You ok, man?" he shouted at Clive, getting to his knees without looking back.

The blast created a deafening buzz in Brig's head. He shook his head and rubbed his shoulder, turning to peer back at his partner.

Where his fellow Epsilon *should* have been standing, was Clive's motionless body, lying two meters away from Brig.

As Brig knelt to revive his partner, an enemy soldier emerged from the brush ten meters away. Brig instinctively drew the high-powered sidearm from the top of his pack and fired a quick shot at the soldier, hitting him squarely in the chest plate.

The soldier recoiled backwards at the force of the impact, but then stood upright, hoisted a massive assault rifle to his shoulder and aimed at Brig, while shouting in a language Brig knew was not Portuguese. Before the soldier could squeeze the trigger, however, Brig sent another slug into him, shattering the soldier's facemask and obliterating a good portion of the attacker's head.

A second soldier emerged from the brush just as the first fell to the ground in a heap. Brig dispatched him with a shot to the throat before he could act. The soldier dropped to his knees and then fell to the ground. His weapon thudded into the dirt next to him as he frantically grabbed his slick, bloody throat in a desperate, but futile, attempt to breathe.

Brig knew that these two were just the beginning, and that more soldiers would come in numbers too great for him to fend off with just a handgun and a sniper rifle. He also knew aiding his partner while engaged in a heavy gunfight would prove difficult. Brig hoisted Clive with a hearty grunt, placed him over his shoulder and dashed into the brush.

The gunfire tapered off as he put distance between himself and his pursuers. Brig found himself in a small, quiet clearing just on the opposite side of the ridge, where extraction was to take place. Brig propped Clive into a sitting position against a flat rock, and began to reach into his shoulder pack for smelling salts.

The snapping of a branch from the brush made Brig draw his sidearm again as he whirled around.

Staring back at him with the barrel-end of Brig's gun against his mouth was a young boy, terror filling his eyes. Brig recognized him as one of the boys that were shackled together back in the compound. Brig lowered his weapon, but continued to stare in hesitant suspicion.

3: COMMUNICATION BREAKDOWN

"You must leave now. Dawn coming soon, you soon be greatly outnumbered," the boy urged in broken English.

"What was that all about back there? Who were those men and why did they have you all chained up?" Brig questioned the boy, although realizing the futility of his statements.

"No time," the boy said, tilting his head to the side quizzically. "You go...these...Conquistadora Fantasma," he continued after a short pause, pointing back in the direction of the compound. "Your friend need medical help, you go now!"

The darkness surrounding the chaos that both he and Clive had just endured clouded Brig's awareness to the reality of the situation. It had not occurred to him that Clive might have sustained a serious injury from the blast, and although he still could not see anything, he realized that the boy must have noticed something that Brig had not. After glancing back at Clive, Brig turned his attention to the boy.

The boy was gone, having already fled back into the brush.

Brig was winded from carrying Clive during the sprint from the compound. He knew he would have to try to revive his fellow EW so that they could both make it back on foot to the extraction point. Brig quickly waved the small pack of smelling salts under his partner's nose.

Shocked back awake, Clive began to speak.

"What the Hell...just happened," Clive muttered, shaking his head to gather his wits.

"Think that RPG blast must've knocked you out and off your feet, but I got you out of there," Brig responded, sitting back on his haunches and taking several quick, deep breaths. He gazed in relief at his now-conscious partner.

"Aw, man. My ears are ringing, can't hear what you're saying, Brig," Clive leaned upright away from the rock. "My leg's caught under something, man. Can you help me out?"

Brig, perplexed, peeked at Clive's legs. His eyes widened in silent alarm.

One of Clive's legs was missing from the knee down.

He must have stepped on a mine, damn! Brig thought, hastily pulling off his jacket to use as a tourniquet.

"You're gonna be alright, man, it's all gonna be fine," he reassured Clive. He quickly wrapped the remainder of Clive's leg to ease what he could only assume was now massive blood loss.

"What's going on, man, *what's going on?*" cried Clive, trying to get a glimpse of his leg where Brig had just bandaged it.

"Sit tight, it's gonna be ok!" Brig commanded. He tapped at the built-in sat-com device on his shoulder plate. "Condor, this is Eagle One, do you read," he barked.

"Eagle One, this is Condor – you are *not* to break radio silence, do you...." the voice on the other end of the radio tersely responded.

"Negative, Condor, we have an emergency situation. We've got a unit down. We're under heavy assault from enemy combatants and we need assistance with the extraction, do you copy," interrupted Brig in a heightened tone.

"That's a *negative*, Eagle One. You know the parameters of this mission. Proceed to extraction point as outlined."

"Patch me through to HQ. I need some authority to modify the parameters – *NOW!*" Brig bellowed.

Clive pressed his back against the rock and groaned in terrified agitation as he listened to the conversation.

The transmission went silent.

Brig looked at Clive. "I need you to be calm, man. You got an injury on your leg, but it's gonna be ok, we're gonna get you out of here, don't worry."

"No way, man," Clive cried, grasping at where his lower leg should have been, but only pulling back greasy, blood-covered hands. "No way no way...shit man I can't feel my leg. I can't feel my God-damned leg! Where's my leg?"

Brig grasped Clive tightly around the shoulders. "Come on, man, hang in there bro. It's gonna be ok, we're gonna make it out of here, I *promise* you!"

"They're not comin' for us, Brig. You heard 'em - they're gonna leave us here to die!" Clive continued to shout, wrestling against Brig's grasp. "It's over man *it's over*! I'm gonna bleed out!"

Still clutching Clive tight with one arm, Brig extracted a syringe from his pack and quickly injected its contents, a sedative, into Clive's shoulder.

Within seconds, Clive's struggling ceased and he sat back against the rock, the thick sweat on his forehead gleaming in the moonlight.

As Brig removed the needle, the sat-com crackled to life.

"Eagle One, this is Phoenix Alpha. Stroud, this is Falco – what the *Hell's* going on over there?" the voice on the other end shouted angrily.

"Commander, Underwood has a critical injury and can't make it back to the extraction without some assistance - I just can't get him over this ridge without an extra body," Brig pleaded.

"God damn it, Stroud, I outlined the parameters of this mission, *no exceptions*! You find a way back to that heli-jet in time for extraction or you find your own way home!" Falco roared.

"We're only sixty meters from the extraction point!" Brig insisted. "This is an EW, damn it, I'm not leaving one of ours behind, and I know you don't want to do that either. So get me the *God damned* help or they'll slaughter us here!"

A few seconds of silence passed before Falco once again spoke. "You've got one unit inbound to assist in extraction. Don't make me regret this, Stroud! *Your* ass is on the line here!"

Brig tapped at the sat-com to silence it. He glanced at Clive, who was more at ease with a dazed expression, leaning against the rock.

"You alright...Crypto?" Brig asked softly.

"Crypto?" Clive muttered, wrinkling his brow and blinking his eyelids slowly at Brig.

"Figure everyone needs a good nickname, so there ya go man. Crypto – it fits," Brig quipped with a nervous chuckle, trying desperately to keep Clive from panicking over his situation.

"Whatever, man...by the way," Clive stammered, hardly able to keep his eyes open from the sedative, "that half-assed...Portuguese bullshit you spouted back there? You told those kids to 'quack like a duck'. Or some crazy shit like that. You always did suck in foreign language training," he joked with a dazed half-smile, closing his eyes.

Brig sat back in a seat nearest the open door of the heli-jet. He propped one foot on a landing strut as he gazed out into the heavy brush and beyond the nearby ridge where the compound lay.

Clive, strapped onto a stretcher in the cargo area just behind Brig, lay motionless, as the sedative had taken full effect.

"Sorry man," Brig thought.

The craft completed its ascent, made a half-circle, and then dashed over the ridge away from the area on its way back to base.

Present day (2084)...

Brig stood next to Clive's workbench, thoroughly scanning the work surface.

Knowing him, he thought, *he's got this place booby-trapped against anyone with a curiosity.*

After several minutes of fruitless searching, he sat back down on his cot in frustration. "Typical Underwood, always was a neat freak..."

His thought trailed off however, as a momentary, metallic glint from the floor just underneath the edge of Clive's desk caught his eye. He got to his feet and squinted at the floor beneath the bench. Underneath, lying in partial shadow, was a small, silicone computer chip.

"Well *that's* not going to talk to me," he frowned, muttering aloud and reaching under the desk to retrieve it. "Even if it did, I ain't the crypto wiz here anyway."

He started to place the chip back on the workbench, figuring that it was a dead end for him. As he moved his hand, however, the small work light reflected onto the gray surface of the chip, and exposed the letters 'URASA' in print on its top.

"URA...*Security Alliance?*" he pondered. He stared intently at the chip. "Crypto my man, what have *you* been up to?"

4:
Unforgiven

Eight years prior (2076)...

It's been three weeks since I've seen Cryp, Brig thought, hastily striding down the main corridor of the base infirmary, his destination the patient recovery bay just ahead. *Three weeks since his life changed forever. Funny how things can change in an instant,* he pondered.

As he rounded the final corner that led into the hallway outside the main patient bay, he spotted a doctor reviewing a holo-chart emitting from a data pad in his hand. Just beyond one of the propped open doors, Brig could see Clive lying on a cot three rows down from the entryway.

"Excuse me, doctor?" Brig asked the white-coated man, quickly peering through the door at Clive. "Are you Captain Underwood's doctor?"

Still looking down at the colorful, 3D chart, the doctor responded coolly, "Uh, yes I am. And *you* are?"

"Captain Brigadier Stroud, 81st EW Squadron Special Ops. Captain Underwood...Clive..." Brig hesitated in reflection, imbibing the heavy aroma of sterility and rubbing alcohol that hung in the cool air. "He's my partner...he's my friend. How is he doing?"

The doctor shut off the display, stuffed the pad under his arm, and then brought his eyes up to meet Brig, who stood almost a third of a meter taller.

"Captain Stroud, you're here to see Captain Underwood? I don't seem to recall your name on the visitor list – let me check my pad just to make sure." The doctor quickly took the pad out from under his arm and typed a few commands, wrinkled his brow as he tabbed through a couple of screens, and then shoved it back under his arm.

"Not on the list, but that wouldn't be the first time the admin staff overlooked a name or two," the doctor said with a smile, looking up at the organizational insignias that adorned Brig's shirt.

"I can see you're with the same outfit as Captain Underwood, so you're free to see him if you wish."

As the doctor turned away, Brig placed a hand lightly on one of his shoulders.

"Doc, I'd like to speak to you *first*...if *that's okay*," Brig implored, lowering his voice considerably to just above an audible mumble. "How's he doing? You know, with the injury and all."

"Well, Captain Stroud," the doctor began, "Captain Underwood is *physically* in the best shape that we could hope for. He's a strong, healthy individual and, the injury notwithstanding, he *should* make a complete recovery," he concluded with a raised eyebrow.

"That's *great* news, doc." Brig patted the doctor's arm.

"However, the physical injury isn't usually the *hardest* part of recovery in these instances, Captain," the doctor cautioned, looking past Brig into the recovery bay at a still-sleeping Clive lying on the cot. "The psychological trauma that comes along with an injury such as losing a limb is something with which many patients have difficulty. I'm afraid Captain Underwood has a big hill to climb to completely recover from his condition."

The doctor raised two fingers together and pointed towards Brig's forehead, looking over the eyeglasses perched at the end of his nose.

"And it all has to start up *here* for him," the doctor added.

Brig's brow rumpled in thought. "But you can give him a new leg, *can't you*? Wouldn't that help?"

"We've developed amazing prosthetic technology, yes, that's for sure," the doctor lauded, crossing his arms on his chest and smiling broadly. "Ones that are completely melded with the host's nerve endings at the site of the amputation to give them the feel of a real leg. But in Captain Underwood's case he has sustained some major nerve damage in that area and wouldn't be eligible to have one of the higher tech prosthetics. At least...*not yet*."

"So there's hope?"

"Most definitely," the doctor replied. "Fortunately, we also have developed some amazing pharmaceuticals that actually aid in the re-growth of nerve tissue. It will take some time, say...eighteen to twenty-four months. But with the proper physical *and* psychological treatment, intense physical rehabilitation and the aid of some of our miracle drugs, I see no reason why Captain Underwood can't enjoy a normal life with very little discomfort from his injuries."

Brig nodded his head, smiling lightly at the doctor's hopeful news. "Thanks, doc, I'm glad I got to talk to you."

Brig began to enter the recovery bay.

The doctor spoke once more.

"Captain, remember what I said though. This all begins with *his* ability and *willingness* to cope with the hand that he's been dealt. I've seen *many* a patient fold," the doctor concluded with an understanding nod, before he strode away.

Brig watched the doctor disappear into another room. Exhaling deeply, Brig poked his head into the recovery bay.

"There's my man," Brig bantered, approaching Clive's cot. "Cryp, how you feeling, brother?"

Clive peered at Brig without turning his head, and then rolled over. "Who let *you* in here," he grumbled.

Brig had figured that Clive would be a bit down after going through his ordeal, so he overlooked the agitation in Clive's voice. "It's great to see you, man. You look like you're feeling *much* better!"

Clive hesitated, blinked his eyes shut briefly, and replied, "Well forgive me if I don't get up to greet you, but I seem to be missing a leg. But you *knew* that."

"Well...yeah," Brig countered. "But hey, I just spoke to your doc over there and he says that with your physical conditioning you should be back on your feet in no time."

Clive continued his silent stare at the other end of the recovery bay.

"And Clive, you know..." Brig added with slight hesitation, "...no matter what you need, I'm here for you. *Always.* You need someone to rough it with you through rehab, a cheering partner, whatever you need – I'm your brother for life. And that's not just because we're EWs, *remember that.*"

Clive fluffed the pillow under his head. "I'm tired and I need some rest if that's ok with you."

"Sure man," Brig conceded.

As he began to exit the room, Brig stopped and faced his friend.

"For what it's worth, Cryp, I'm truly sorry about what happened back there in Portugal. I never meant for it to go down like that but I still feel like we made the *right* decision. I just hope that one day you can *understand* that."

Brig pursed his lips tightly and stared down at the floor, his hands at his hips. "*Really* good to see you again, man."

R. JAMES STEVENS

Several weeks later...

"I told you that you didn't have to be here for this, man," exclaimed Clive, forcefully pushing the wheels of his temporary wheelchair near the curb outside of the infirmary and to the awaiting transport. "I can do this on my own."

Brig chuckled. "Don't even think about it Cryp, I'm here for you whether you *want* me to be or not."

Clive approached the curb and locked the wheels on his chair. Brig held out a pair of crutches in both hands. Clive jerked them from him.

"You've done *enough* already, don't you think?" Clive groused.

"What, bro? I'm just here to help my EW brother leave the hospital and get on with the first day of the rest of his life is all," Brig cried, holding both hands in the air in protest.

"And I *told* you," Clive bristled, leaning on his crutches and angrily pointing a finger at Brig, "*you've* done enough already! You're the reason I'm even at this place!"

"Now, Cryp, c'mon. We've talked about this already. You know I was just tryin' to do the right thing back there."

"The right thing?" Clive shouted. "The *right thing* was to follow orders and not go off and do your own little mission on the side...*again.* How'd *that* turn out?" Clive clumsily spun away from Brig and leaned on one crutch that rested on the steps of the transport.

Brig stared at Clive blankly. He did not want to argue with Clive. This was his friend and he knew that he was hurting. Brig blinked his eyes nervously and looked around, trying to mask his discomfort with the situation.

"I'll tell you how it worked out – you nearly got me killed!" Clive continued, rotating on his one good heel to face Brig. "And ruined my life in the process! And for what? What did we get out of your latest act of insubordination?"

Resigned to ending the confrontation, Brig began to walk away, waving his hand back at Clive as if to say, "That's enough."

Clive, however, continued the barrage.

"There are other people in the world besides you, Brig, and sometimes you just have to suck it up and do what you're told or those other people can get hurt. *Regardless* whether *you* think it's right or not! And being a 'Daddy's Boy' doesn't exactly make people like you much, either."

38

Brig stopped and gritted his teeth. "I told you not to *call* me that," he growled, still facing away from Clive.

"Oh yeah, *there* it is," Clive spouted. "If you'd spend more time paying attention to the mission briefings and doing what you're TOLD instead of worrying about what people think of you maybe...just *maybe*, things might turn out a little different!"

Brig rotated his head to the side. "You're angry, you're frustrated – I *get* that. Maybe we need to let this one fade a bit. I'll talk to you soon," he said calmly. He walked a few more meters before stopping one last time. "I already said it, but," he dolefully added, abruptly facing Clive, "I *am* sorry about what happened. We did get some valid intel that the URA is going to act on out of that mission – but I didn't mean to put you in a dangerous situation, and I hope that one day you can forgive me for that."

"That'll be a cold day in Hell," Clive mumbled under his breath, having already taken two steps into the transport.

Two months later...

"...And I'd like to take a few more moments of your time before you're dismissed to recognize a couple of individuals," the Commander insisted, leaning back from the podium, proudly scanning the gathered audience of EWs.

"Not me, not me, not me..." Clive chanted to himself quietly with his eyes squinted shut.

"For nearly fifty years," the Commander continued in a more grandiose tone, "the Epsilon Warrior squadron has been a vital asset to this United Republic of the Americas. From intel gathering to 'first-look' scenarios to 'flash resolution'. Without this critical component, the URA would be limited in its use of conventional forces and would lack stealth operations and the overall element of surprise that has aided this great group of nations since its inception."

"The core of this squadron is each troop, each soldier, each commando, all working together in harmony. Not only to complete any mission given to them, no matter how overwhelming the odds, but to complete it with a sense of unity. These men take an oath, one that binds each of them together as a family. They even have a creed – 'Fraternitas Aeternus'. 'Brothers Forever'. And it's not just a creed, it's an oath of loyalty that each one of them takes to heart, and takes very seriously. EWs over the years have been known to go through extraordinary circumstances to save the lives of their partners, often sacrificing their own."

Clive's gut sunk. He knew what was coming next, and it was unavoidable.

"I'd like to recognize a pair of EWs that embody the ideals, the loyalty and the creed that *are* the EW squadron." The Commander focused his attention on Brig, sitting next to Clive, as he spoke. "The EW commando that I'm speaking of risked his own life in the face of overwhelming odds against a fierce enemy that greatly outnumbered him and his partner to save the life of that partner when he had been taken down by an enemy mine. Without hesitation, he went against enemy fire and carried his partner to safety where he could receive life-saving medical attention."

The commander raised his right hand and pointed in the direction of Brig and Clive. "Captain Brigadier Stroud and Captain Clive Underwood – would you please come up to the podium to be honored by your peers."

Knowing that he could not refuse recognition, Clive pulled himself up onto his crutches and hobbled to the front of the auditorium alongside Brig.

"Captains Stroud and Underwood were part of a covert operation several months ago that netted some very valuable intel that could aid in the safety of our troops engaging in counter-warfare. Some in our very own squadron," the Commander lauded.

He greeted Brig and Clive with a strong handshake, and then faced the audience with his left arm outstretched as he spoke, "Men, these two soldiers exemplify what it is to be an EW." He leaned over and whispered to the two partners, "Fellas, give 'em a strong EW handshake, would ya?".

Clive gnashed his teeth at the thought, but did not want to create an embarrassing spectacle. He held out his hand for Brig to shake. Brig beamed a broad smile as he grabbed Clive's hand strongly, and pulled him in for an emotional hug.

The audience erupted in raucous applause with *nearly* every Epsilon present jumping from their seat to give a standing ovation to the pair.

After taking in the moment, Brig whispered to Clive as they released from their embrace, still grasping his hand firmly. "Man, I'm glad to see you're starting to let things go – that's great to see."

Clive's face became void of expression as he glared at Brig.

"You're incredible man. *Just incredible*," Clive droned, shaking his head.

Present day (2084)…

"Hey! Not so *hard*," Danil Chekushkin exclaimed with a thick Russian accent, as one of the Webb twins, Pollux, slammed him face-first against the wall of the hotel hallway.

"What are you doin' here, Danil?" Pollux grunted into Danil's ear, stretching Danil's arm farther up his back.

"I…I… I am here to see Bruno," Danil cried, his round face distorted with pain.

"Bruno?" Pollux snorted. "Hey Cas – ol' Boris here is on a first name basis with the boss!"

Castor, the other Webb twin, standing with his arms crossed and watching the proceedings from just outside of the hotel room door, nodded his balding head in derision while brandishing a wry smirk. "Is 'zat so…"

"…I mean Mr. Muldoon," Danil corrected. "I am here to see Mr. Muldoon."

His grip unrelenting, Pollux snarled into Danil's ear. "Now what's the boss want with a two-bit Ruskie snitch like you?"

"He…he…" stuttered Danil, "he asked me for some…information. And I am here…to…to give it to him."

Pollux glanced at Castor with a slight motion of his head, at which his brother reached for the doorknob.

"For your sake, you better be tellin' me the truth. I haven't broken anybody's legs in a few weeks now," Pollux grunted.

Castor opened the door and began to enter.

A forceful voice greeted them from within. "Pollux, please show our guest in – I've been expecting him."

"Sure thing, boss," Pollux responded from the hallway. He released Danil, and then grasped the upper portion of Danil's other arm, wrapping one hand entirely around it as he led him into the room.

"Pollux, could you give us a bit of privacy," Muldoon commanded in an Irish inflection, standing on the balcony of the hotel room looking outward. "And thank you for being so…protective."

"You got it, boss," Pollux replied.

As he released Danil and turned to walk out of the room, he stopped next to him, pointed into his face and growled. "You better behave, Igor."

Danil glared at Pollux with a punishing scowl, watching the big man swing the door back open.

41

"Mr. Chekushkin, you have news for me..." Muldoon continued, pensively surveying the openness outside.

"Yes sir, Mr. Muldoon," Danil replied quietly.

"And that is?" Muldoon prompted, raising his right hand up in expectation.

Danil stepped forward, stopping a few meters behind Muldoon. "We put a tail on the woman that broke into your warehouse."

"And what have you found out about this 'mystery woman'?" Muldoon solicited, clasping his hands together in front of him while looking out at the azure, desert, evening sky.

Danil hesitated in silence and ran his hand across his short, flat black hair.

"We....do not know much of anything about her right now, Mr. Muldoon, but..." Danil offered softly.

Muldoon turned his head to the side and barked, "You've come here with nothing? What have you been doing for the past week, Danil?"

"We did not want her to know we were following," Danil explained. "But she is very...how do you say...*crafty*. It is like sometimes she knows that we are there, never giving away anything of what she is doing. You might find it interesting though..."

"Interesting? Oh please do tell," Muldoon mocked, bowing his head to peer down at the empty swimming pool below.

"She met with your friend... the Underwood gentleman," said Danil, hoping to gratify his boss with *some* good news.

Muldoon remained silent for what seemed like an eternity as he scanned the horizon, with its mountains providing a crisp silhouette against the starry sky. He abruptly turned to face Danil, his long, dark, slicked hair flinging from behind his ears. "Underwood. Are you certain?"

"Yes sir," Danil quickly retorted. "And they made some sort of exchange, but we do not know what was exchanged."

Muldoon stroked his thin, black goatee. "Castor," he snapped, striding across the room past Danil.

The door opened and the hulking mass stuck his head in through the crack. "Yeah, boss?"

Danil looked on in curiosity at Muldoon, as the pair privately conversed.

As their discussion ended, Muldoon approached Danil once again. Castor exited the room and silently closed the door behind him.

"You've done well, my friend," Muldoon praised. "But I need you to gather some more information for me on our 'mystery woman'. Find out everything you can about her, but as before do not let her find out that you are tailing her – is that understood?" he said, placing a hand on Danil's shoulder and glaring into his eyes.

"Yes sir, Mr. Muldoon."

"And I expect you back here in forty-eight hours with some solid data," Muldoon instructed, staring savagely at Danil, as if telepathically implanting the vision of a potential punishment in his mind.

"Of course, sir," Danil said unevenly.

Muldoon paced out onto the balcony, leaned onto the railing with his elbows and pensively folded his hands underneath his chin.

He glared out into the desert beyond the hotel grounds. The half-mounted sign that used to read 'Welcome to Fabulous Las Vegas', now with the word 'Fabulous' partially smashed out, and the word 'Las' overwritten in spray-paint with 'New', flickered unevenly in the darkness beyond.

"Well, little girl," he muttered aloud, "no one breaks into one of my warehouses and gets away with it. And if you *did* steal something, you and the fine Mr. Underwood will pay dearly."

R. JAMES STEVENS

5:
Heaven and Hell

Present Day (2084)...

Clive reached into his pocket and felt around for the keys to his workshop, the metal on each radiating cold from the chilled, night air.

As he smoothly inserted the first key into a deadbolt on the rear door, a gruff, deep voice from behind made him freeze.

"'Bout time you showed up, Underwood," Pollux Webb growled, his massive form appearing from within the shadows just beyond the barely-lit doorway.

"Ah, one half of the Twin Terrors," Clive quipped, looking down at the lock. He hesitated turning the key to unlatch the deadbolt. Maybe Pollux would go away without wanting to come in. After all, it was late; what business could he possibly want at this hour?

"That's 'Twin Towers'. Get it right, egghead," Pollux quickly responded, looking thoroughly incensed.

Nodding in amusement, Clive turned the latch on three separate locks with different keys for each, and then looked at his visitor. "Don't suppose you're just in the neighborhood and wanted to say 'hi', are you?" he asked facetiously with a raised eyebrow.

"Nah, we got some business to take care of," Pollux grunted, pushing his gargantuan frame up against Clive's back, towering over him as he waited for Clive to open the door.

8 years prior (2076)...

"...77, 78, 79, aaand, 80. That's it for that set, Clive," the physical trainer marveled. "And that makes twenty-two-hundred crunches for the day – you're setting an incredible pace!"

Clive sat up, sweat glistening on his forehead and chest. "Have to be...in the best shape...that I can," he managed to respond in-between hard exhales of breath, wiping the heavy beads of sweat from his head onto a towel.

"Well, I'm proud of you," the trainer gushed. "Why don't you take a break before we start in on the balance training," he asked, getting up from the floor and holding out a hand to Clive.

"No!" exclaimed Clive, waving away the assist, as usual, and instead using the side of the weight bench to pull himself up to his one good leg. "I need to keep pushing, no breaks."

"I'm already impressed, Clive, you don't need to..."

"I told you I want to do this, I'm ready for it and I have to do it *now!*" Clive snarled, gathering his balance and standing on his prosthetic leg.

The trainer subtly shook his head, partially out of impressed disbelief, partly out of frustration, and then put his hand out to 'spot' Clive during the exercise.

Clive had been training maniacally for almost six months and showed no signs of letting up, or wanting sympathy.

"So you're looking forward to having a new prosthetic soon, huh?" the trainer asked.

"Yeah," Clive muttered through gritted teeth, showing his obvious pain while putting his weight on the bad leg in-between grunts. "Doc says I've still got another twelve-to-...fourteen months of healing to do nerve-wise to get to the point where they can...fit the new leg though."

"Well if your PT sessions are any indication, you'll be ready for it!" the trainer remarked amazedly at Clive's strength.

The trainer's data pad softly chimed from within its pouch sitting on a nearby stool. "Clive, I have to take this. But I'll be right here if you need anything – *just take it easy...*"

"I'll be fine," Clive droned, glaring forward, his face intense with concentration. "Just take your call."

The trainer nodded politely, walked a few meters away and then began to fidget with the device.

With the trainer focused on his call, Clive hobbled his way along the back wall slowly while holding onto the handrail in an effort to reestablish his balance with both legs.

"Once I get done with this rehab," Clive thought, "things are going to be *different*. I'll be stronger than *ever before*, and more *importantly...*"

His thoughts trailed off as the intense pain in his leg forced him to stop and grasp the handrail tightly with both hands. "...more importantly, I've gotta find a way to keep my distance from Stroud. Things have *gotta* be different this time..."

"Captain Underwood, sir," a voice from the doorway barked, "there's a Colonel Jacobs here to see you, sir."

"Jacobs? Wonder what *he* wants?" Clive muttered, releasing the handrail with one hand and standing up straight.

"Captain Underwood. Clive, my boy," the Colonel prattled warmly, approaching Clive with an outstretched hand.

Clive instinctively stiffened and delivered a crisp salute. "Colonel Jacobs, *sir!*"

Jacobs gently pulled Clive's hand from its saluting position and gave him a firm, friendly handshake. "Relax, son. We're in a medical facility, there's no need for so much formality. Besides, you're not even in uniform," the Colonel chuckled mockingly.

"Oh. Sorry sir, if you can give me two minutes I'll..." Clive faltered, his face turning crimson with embarrassment.

"Clive, Clive..." the Colonel continued to laugh, shaking his head. "Have a seat son. I know what kind of soldier you are. And besides, you look like you need to take a breather."

"Th-thank you sir," Clive responded, hobbling pitifully to a nearby chair opposite of Jacobs and plunking down onto it. "What can I do for you, sir?"

Jacobs hesitated as he looked at Clive with admiration. "Your doctors tell me that you've been working *really* hard to recover from your injury."

"Yes, sir! Non-stop, every day that I can, sir," Clive offered eagerly. "I think I'm in the best shape of my life *right now*, sir."

"That's just great, Clive. We're all *really* proud of how you've approached a *very difficult* time in your life, son," Jacobs said with amazement, nodding his head in approval.

"Thank you, sir. And in about twelve months, God willing, I'll have a new high tech prosthetic leg and I'll be mission ready once again."

Jacob's smile slowly faded. "*Mission ready?* Clive... you *do* know that you're being discharged...*right?*"

Clive's face contorted in confusion at the Colonel's response. "*Discharged?* Sir...um, no. I'm...in rehab right now. And once I get the operation for my leg I'll be...right back with my squadron, better than ever!"

Jacobs slowly shook his head while pursing his lips. The pity in his eyes told Clive what he needed to know, but did not want to hear.

"Son, I'm sorry if anyone here has misled you on this. But you know as well as I do that with your injury it's *impossible* for you to return to active duty. There's just too much liability there, Clive. It's not fair for you to ask your squadron to look after you, and it's not fair to you to have that expectation of them," Jacobs calmly responded.

Clive stared blankly at the Colonel for a moment, and then dejectedly looked down at the floor beneath his feet. "Then what are my options? *Sir?*"

"Well, Clive," the Colonel started, and then paused. "There's really only one way to go here. You'll finish up what rehab you can in the next thirty days here at this facility. Then...you'll be discharged and your rehab will be transferred to a non-military facility off base. But don't worry, son. Your rehab and whatever procedures your doctors deem necessary are on us – the URA's got the tab on this one, we're *not* going to let you down," Jacobs reassured Clive warmly, standing up from his chair.

Clive, speechless, continued to glare at the floor in front of him. Finally, with a heavy sigh he responded, "Yes, sir."

Noting the obvious dejection in Clive's voice, the Colonel placed his hand on Clive's shoulder and leaned over to make eye contact.

"Clive my boy, let me give you a little bit of advice. Man to man," he advised. "You should be proud of your service in the EWs. I know that we are all very proud to have served with you. But take my word from experience – don't let your time in this service *define* you. Take from it the parts that have made you strong and successful and move on with the next chapter of your life. Your service was a moment in time - *don't let that moment alter your course.* You'll *never* find true happiness if you do."

Clive gazed blankly at his trainer, now off his call but purposely avoiding intruding on the Colonel's conversation. Clive grudgingly nodded his head.

As he walked away, the Colonel added, "Carry on, soldier. We'll be in touch," and left the room.

Present day (2084)...

Clive strained a hard breath as Pollux's massive fists gripped tighter on his jacket collar. The gargantuan held him forcefully against the wall, his legs dangling 30 centimeters from the floor.

"Come on, Pollux, you don't want to do this," Clive calmly reasoned.

"This is *exactly* what I wanna do, egghead," Pollux growled, clenching his jaw fiercely. "Now start talkin' or I'm gonna paint the wall with ya!"

"What do you want me to say, Pollux, that you're a fine, upstanding gentleman..." Clive quipped, trying desperately to lighten the giant's mood.

"Very funny," Pollux retorted, turning and flinging Clive across the workshop like an old pair of socks, where he landed with a loud crash into a pile of boxes and a couple of aged, wooden chairs. "You *know* what I'm talkin' about – the girl! Tell me about the girl!" Pollux shouted, as advanced on Clive.

"Well if it's a date you're looking for I know some lovely young ladies..." Clive began to jest, getting up to his one good knee and choking out a bit of dust.

The frightening shade Pollux's red face told Clive all he needed to know... he was not in a joking mood.

"What *about* her?" Clive resigned, pulled himself upright and gingerly rubbed the small of his back.

Pollux curiously glanced around the workshop. "How do *you* know her?"

"I *don't.*"

"You're lyin', Underwood," Pollux grumbled, rotating his head slightly to one side so that he could see Clive in his peripheral. "We saw you and her makin' some kind of exchange a couple'a days ago, so there's *somethin'* you ain't tellin' me."

"What I'm telling you is that I'm Muldoon's top operative on this continent, so I have no interest in making *outside* deals," Clive responded emphatically. "Besides, Pollux," he jabbed with a smirk, "you know I wouldn't lie to *you.*"

Pollux hesitated for a moment, fruitlessly scanning the workshop for visual evidence.

"Heh. Lyin' to me ain't the problem here, chief. The boss thinks you're up to somethin' – and ya know what? I think he's *right,* I think you're on the take," Pollux offered, turning to face Clive. "Ya see...that girl there? She broke into one of the boss's warehouses a few weeks back." Pollux hissed, rubbing his chin in feigned cogitation. "Don't know what she took for sure, but my guess is it's important. 'Specially if she shows up on *your* doorstep lookin' to make some sorta' exchange. I may not be as smart as my brother, but it don't take no genius to figure this one out." He tapped his finger to the side of his head. "So what's it gonna' be. You gonna tell me who the girl is and what you're doin' with her, or do I gotta' tell the boss that he's right and…well…*you know the rest.*"

Clive's smirk washed away as he considered Pollux's ultimatum. "She's no one, believe me. Just a user lookin' for a score," he droned, turning his attention away from Pollux to glare at his workbench. "And I gave her a contact…that's *all.*"

"If you're bein' straight with me, Underwood, then I'll tell the boss he's got nothin' to worry about, and you and me don't have to do this dance no more," Pollux muttered, looking over towards the workbench at which Clive had just glanced.

"But if you're not," he continued, grabbing the side of the bench and tipping it up, toppling everything on it to the ground with a deafening crash. "I'm sure you know why Mr. Muldoon's nickname is 'Brutal'…*don'tcha?*"

"Because *'brilliant'* was a stretch?" Clive calmly uttered with a slight, silent grimace at the sight of his delicate equipment in a heap on the floor.

"A wise guy," Pollux chuckled, turning to Clive. "See, *I* can appreciate that. The boss? *Not so much.*" As Pollux strode to the door, he grabbed Clive by the collar once more and yanked him forward. "Watch your step, Egghead. Just remember…I'm right behind ya'."

"*Always* a pleasure, Pollux," Clive quipped, gathering his balance as the giant released him from his grasp. "Stop by anytime. And say 'hi' to your brother for me."

As the door slid shut forcefully behind Pollux, Clive faced the mess of components and equipment. "Damn it," he moaned.

Outside, from just beyond a fence line bordering a property across the street from Clive's workshop, a shadowy figure watched Pollux Webb emerge from the building and mount his retro-bike.

As the roar of the bike's motor cascaded through the empty neighborhood and quickly faded away, Brig stepped from the shadows and focused intently on Clive's workshop.

"Keeping some *odd* company these days, friend."

6:
Down in a Hole

Eight years prior (2076)...

Clive winced as he painfully forced himself up the training step and then back down again, a stern expression on his face.

Gotta' get what I can from here, no tellin' what that other facility is like off-base, he thought.

"Hey Underwood, lookin' *good* man..." a voice from beside him chimed, his South American accent rolling smoothly from his tongue.

"That's *Captain* Underwood, *Lieutenant,*" Clive answered authoritatively without breaking stride, rolling his eyes sideways quickly and then forward again.

"Oh...uh...yeah. I mean...yes sir, *Captain* Underwood. Sorry, I guess when I'm in here rehabbing I feel like we're all just mano-y-mano, no ranks, ya' know?" The man patted Clive on the shoulder.

"Easy for *you* to say." Clive gnashed his teeth and looked more intense than ever. "I've worked very hard to get where I'm at, so if it's all the same – it's *Captain* Underwood."

A broad grin transformed the man's face as he gave Clive 'two thumbs up'. "Hey haha, it's all good, Captain." The man looked past Clive and up at the television monitor mounted on the wall above them both. "Mind if I turn this up, sir? One of my buddies says there's some announcement coming up about one of his friends – that ok with you?"

"Sure, *whatever,*" Clive retorted, having lost interest.

"...and the Senator's assistant tells us that the cuts will take effect immediately. Here's Blaine Thomas with the details... Blaine..." said the news anchor, himself a military man in standard dress sitting behind a desk in front of a large URA flag. The other rehab patient turned up the volume.

"Ah, just news right now, man," the man said, exasperated. "But I think it's coming up." The man took an interest in Clive's serious demeanor. "You're working hard there, Captain. But you're in great shape, what you in here for, man?"

Looking annoyed, Clive answered, "Leg injury."

"Leg injury? Really?" the man said in an incredulous tone. "You're punishing those stairs, man. I think you're ready to rock and roll!"

In the background, the news correspondent continued to deliver his story. "...and Senator Hawthorne, you're one of the hardliners in the new representative regime that's just taken office. Do you think it's too soon to be making military cuts like *this*..."

"Hrmph. Tell that to the brass, I'm *more* than ready..." Clive grumbled under his breath, ignoring the television entirely.

The news broadcast continued with the Senator speaking. "...I'm just saying, Blaine, that if outfits like *these* want to stay under the radar and aren't willing to operate with *complete* fiscal transparency then the people of the URA should be under *no* obligation to continue..."

"Can you turn that down, Lieutenant...?" Clive commanded, continuing his work on the training stairs.

"...*Trujillo*, you can call me Trujillo...sir," the man responded in a friendly tone. "And sure, I'll turn it down. Sorry, sir." He muted the television monitor and peered at Clive. "You getting back to action soon, sir? You're an EW...*right*?" he said, eyeing the EW insignia tattooed on Clive's bicep.

"Yeah. Well...was. I'm being discharged at the end of this month. They say my injury makes me a liability, *total bull*..." Clive trailed off through gritted teeth.

"Aw, no way, man! That's rough, dude," Trujillo said sympathetically. "But you got it made on the outside, bro, the ladies love the soldiers – 'specially the macho ones that took one for the team, am I right?" He playfully bumped his elbow into Clive's side.

Before Clive could respond, Trujillo aimed the remote at the monitor. "This is it, man, here's what I wanted ta' see."

"...And now for promotion news," the anchor continued. "Brigadier Stroud, a member of the famed, elite Epsilon Warrior squadron based near White Sands, is set to be promoted to Major tomorrow for his heroics during a classified mission two months ago. Stroud also received the URA Silver Star last month for that same mission in which he rescued a fellow EW in the face of *insurmountable* enemy combatants..."

Clive rolled his eyes at the announcement, not caring for the reminder of his *own* predicament.

Trujillo, on the other hand, showed great interest in the story.

"Man, that's a hero right there for you, dude. *That's* what it's all about, ya' know?"

Clive grumbled audibly through the sneer on his face.

"When they came to my village in Colombia looking for recruits for the EWs, that's all I could hope to be, man," Trujillo recited in amazement while watching the monitor, which showed a file picture of Brig in full dress uniform. "That's what all EWs should be, ya' know? *True heroes.* Always looking out for your *brother*, am I right?"

Present day (2084)...

Brig rapped on the wooden door of Clive's workshop and peered around the neighborhood. After another knock, he shoved his cold hands inside the pockets of his worn-out overcoat to wait for a response, the crisp night air evident in the breath flowing from his mouth every few seconds.

"No answer...hmph. That's strange, 'specially since I saw that big lummox coming out of here a minute ago," he muttered. Brig reached for the door, glanced around the area once more, quietly slid it open and took a step inside. "Cryp? You here, man?"

He slid the door shut and glanced around the room from just inside the doorway. Clive was not there. "Empty, what the Hell?" he puzzled.

The lighting in the room was as he had seen it about a week prior – dim, except for a spot on one wall, where brightly focused LED lighting shone onto Clive's workspace. Squinting to distinguish things in the rest of the room, Brig spied the dishevelment of objects and equipment towards the rear where Clive's cot lay overturned. Partially crushed boxes and a broken wooden chair lay scattered in front of the cot. "That doesn't look good."

"Sorry if my housekeeping skills aren't up to *your* standards..." a voice from behind him mocked.

"Jesus, you scared the *crap* outta' me," Brig said. He could see a partially open doorway behind Clive leading down into the floor, and another bright LED light streaming from its opening, preventing him from determining what was inside. "Did I *interrupt* something?" he said, curiously glancing at the doorway.

"No. Just grabbing a snack from the pantry down below," Clive answered tersely. He turned away from Brig and focused on the pile of equipment, some apparently broken, in front of his workbench.

Staring after him intently, Brig continued. "Your *friend* didn't want to stick around and break bread with ya?"

Looking up briefly in silent contemplation, and then refocusing his efforts by picking up a small gizmo and placing it back on the workbench, Clive responded, "Friend? I don't *see* anyone here, do *you?*"

Brig shook his head, chortled aloud and pointed his thumb over his shoulder at the door. "Really? The guy that *just* left here? You know, big ogre-lookin' dude, could barely fit through the doorway?"

Clive gazed at the door. "Oh...*him*. Old acquaintance. Dropped by for a visit," he said in a dull tone and looked away.

"You two catch up on your wrestling or somethin'?" Brig peered over at the pile of boxes and wooden pieces that used to be a couple of chairs, and scratched his head with one hand.

Clive continued to pick up small pieces of equipment and metal boxes, containing what presumably were electronic components, from the floor without responding.

Brig knew from his experience with Clive that this was how his friend handled ending an uncomfortable conversation. He also knew that if he kept pressing, Clive would eventually say what was on his mind.

"...'cause I can only guess from the looks of it that a lot of stuff was thrown around in here..." Brig continued, still glancing around the room.

"Has it been two weeks already, *Rage?*" Clive jabbed, obviously trying to change the conversation.

Brig snorted, trying to ignore the obvious insult even though it stabbed at him every time he heard it. "Nah. I'm good for *now*, but thanks for asking."

From inside the room below the floor, the computer display facing away from the pair of men glowed into the darkness. The title, 'URA DMST CLASSIFIED – TOP SECRET' emblazoned the top of the screen. Underneath, a heading read 'Project: Advanced Weaponry Engineering (A.W.E.)'.

Eight years prior (late 2076, three months later)...

As Clive finished the final repetitions of his military presses, the buzzer from the front door of his apartment sounded. Without losing focus on his exercise, he shouted, "Its open!"

"Man, you are *always* workin' out, Cryp!" a fully uniformed Brig said, stepping into the apartment.

"What's up, Brig," Clive grunted. He glanced at Brig for a second, lowered the bar and began to change the weights for the next set of exercises.

"Not much, bro. Just stopping by on my way to the base to see how my *favorite* partner's doing," Brig responded.

"Hmph," Clive grumbled. "I see you couldn't resist doing it when you were in uniform." Clive clicked the slide lock on the weight bar and began to rub his hands together in preparation for his exercise, all while avoiding eye contact with Brig.

"What's *that* supposed to mean?" Brig quipped with a puzzled, but serious look.

"Oh, I don't know," Clive groaned, lifting a set of weights up behind his head. "What do you think it means...*Major* Stroud?"

Brig shook his head in frustration. "So now you're mad at me for getting promoted. Is *that* it?"

"No!" Clive growled, dropping the barbell suddenly with a loud clang and a thump that shook the floor. "That's *not* it, don't you get that?" he bellowed, hobbling on a crutch towards Brig with an angry finger pointed at him. "It's that *you* get a medal. *You* get a promotion. *You* get the world. And what do *I* got? I got *nothing*, man! And you come over here sportin' your fancy new insignias trying to rub it in. And you wonder why *I'm* upset. Shit, wake up man."

"I'm not trying to rub in *anything*, Cryp!" Brig defended, raising both hands in protest. "I came by here because I *care* about you and I want to keep in touch with you... to make sure you have what you need to make a full recovery."

"Oh, *guilt*. I see."

"No, it's not guilt. We went into that mission as *brothers*, and we came out of that mission as brothers. *Nothin's* gonna' ever change that!"

"That mission was a complete disaster, and you know it," Clive screamed. "From the moment we walked into that briefing room, after you had pulled your little strings and got your way, *as usual*." Clive turned away from Brig, focusing once again on the barbells on the floor. "And *my* life will *never* be the same."

"Man, I understand how you're feeling right now. You're bitter about everything, and I get that. But you'll see, the time will come...*soon*...when you'll be able to let this anger go." Brig paused for a moment, waiting for a reaction from Clive – but did not get one. "You can't let this *define* you, man," he said sympathetically.

"What the Hell does that *mean*?" Clive exploded in response, whipping his hands into the air in disgust. "I keep getting told that, and damn it man... I don't know what the Hell it's supposed to mean! So, let me tell *you* something," he said, forcefully pointing his finger into Brig's chest, "it's not about *letting* anything define me. It *has* defined me. And unlike you *I* didn't have a choice." As he backed off, his tone changed from anger to resentment. "And just when I think it couldn't get any worse, I get more great news from the brass..."

"You're getting discharged...yeah, I heard," Brig added compassionately.

"Yeah. You heard. And yet here you are, sticking your finger in a fresh wound like you don't *know* any better."

"That's not it, man. Look...it's not the end of the world, things are gonna' get better. With your resume you'll be able to write your own ticket out in the civilian world."

"You don't get it. It's the end of *my* world. The world *I* had planned. *My* future. The EWs were my ticket, and now that's gone." Clive paused, his voice cracking as he glared at a large grouping of trophies atop a small hutch along a wall of the apartment. "And I can't even fall back on my athletic career now. It's hopeless. And *that*," he concluded, once again gesturing at Brig, "is why I don't think I can *ever* forgive you."

Brig paused to absorb Clive's feelings. "Well. I *am* sorry that things turned out this way. But understand that I *will* be there for you, no matter what the circumstances. We may follow the creed, but it's more important that the creed follow us. Just remember that."

Clive hobbled to the door and opened it, and then faced Brig. "I made a commitment to honor my EW creed, and for that reason alone you'll always be my '*brother for life*'. But don't mistake that for *friendship*. As far as I'm concerned, I don't want to have anything to do with you *ever* again."

Present day (2084)...

"So...yeah, the mess here. What gives?" Brig persisted.

After having finished cleaning up the pile of junk nearest his workbench, Clive sat and began to tinker with a broken circuit

5

board. "It's nothing, just a little frustration is all. Trying to get something to work and couldn't – blowing off a little steam."

With Clive's back to him once again, Brig craned his neck and leaned backward to get a closer look into the half-open doorway in the floor. From his vantage point, he could barely make out the glow of the computer display in the room.

Frowning, he focused his attention back on Clive. "So, Cryp," he began quizzically, "last time I was here and you were out I found this *chip* on the floor."

"Yeah...*so?*" Clive immediately droned, not taking his attention from the object in his hand.

"Sooo...it had the marking of the URA Security Alliance on it."

Clive sat in silence for a moment. "So what's your point?"

"It just seems more than just a little odd. And quite frankly a little *suspicious.*"

As if stumbling from Brig's comment, Clive let the circuit board flip from his hand and onto the floor. "Damn!" he grunted to himself. Picking up the board once again, he glanced at Brig without making eye contact. "It's just nostalgia. I've got a lot of stuff from....*before*...that I keep around, just because it reminds me of *better* days. You're making too much of it," he said dismissively.

Brig took a few steps and stood behind Clive, placing a hand on one of Clive's shoulders. "Cryp...*Clive.* Listen to me, man. All of this looks like you're into *something* a little too deep. And I'm *worried* about you..."

"Worry about *yourself*, Brig!" Clive barked, forcefully pushing the chair away from the workbench and getting to his feet, shoving Brig's hand from his shoulder in the process. "I'm just fine. I've got my own place here, I do my own thing and I'm just fine. What about *you*? What...you're out living on the street somewhere, showing up here every couple of weeks for a fix. Don't worry about me – *save yourself!* I've got everything under control!"

Brig stepped backwards, his face revealing his shock and unease, as he watched his friend limp to the door.

Clive reached for the handle without making eye contact.

Brig recoiled. "Clive, I didn't *mean* anything by it, man. I just..."

"Save it," Clive responded tersely. "I'm tired of the twenty questions and I've got work to do," he said as he slid open the door, stood to one side and gave Brig a stern look. "See you in a *week*, man."

7:
Critical Acclaim

Present day (2084)...

The hooded figure sat at the end of the dimly lit bar, condensation beading on the half-empty cocktail glass in front of her. Beside the glass lay a small, black box with an open lid. She quietly thumbed through a set of odd-looking, white cards in her hands, staring at them intently.

What secrets are you holding? she thought, as if expecting the cards to answer. *And why did he want me to steal you?*

"Hey lady..." grunted a voice from farther down the bar. The bartender, wearing an unfriendly sneer to go along with his eye patch, motioned his thumb towards the door as he spoke. "Think you might wanna' get outta here...it's gettin' dark, and this ain't no place for a woman to be without protection."

The woman, slender and just above average height, silently nodded from underneath her hood and sipped the last bit of drink from her glass. She dropped a few Syndicate credits on the bar in front of her and swiftly strode to the door.

She reached for the handle, turning her head to scan the bar behind her. Several tufts of auburn hair poked out from underneath her hood, as the small amount of light in the room highlighted her fair skin and glinted in her green eyes.

"Thanks for the tip," she said, turning and gliding out the door.

As the door clicked shut, a shadowy figure quickly rose from a corner seat and slithered out the door behind her.

Outside in the cool, Flagstaff night, a dim, makeshift streetlamp hanging above the establishment's entrance illuminated the figure standing beneath it.

Peering down both ends of the alleyway to spot his prey, Danil Chekushkin closed his jacket and started in her direction, ensuring that he stayed within the shadowy part of the building to avoid detection.

"Ok, little girl..." he muttered to himself, "let us see where you are going to lead Danil tonight."

Wanted to be out of here by nightfall, the woman thought. *Stupid, Steele, just stupid.*

As she made her way past an abandoned grocery store, she caught a hint of movement in the reflection of the broken store window in her peripheral vision. She decided to subtly increase her pace and cross the street, unsure that anyone was there, and equally so that they were following her if that were the case.

She reached the other side of the narrow road and quickly glanced over her shoulder.

"No one there. Just my imagination. Still...can't be *too* sure." At the next corner, she hastily ducked into a nearby alleyway and disappeared from view.

Danil crept to the corner where he had seen the girl vanish, and pressed himself against the edge of the burned-out building. He guardedly peered around the edge of the charred remains and once again spotted the woman darting out of the opposite end of the passage. He scurried into the alleyway and sprinted to the other end.

"You are not *that* clever, girlie," he reassured himself with an inaudible chuckle.

As quickly as he could finish his thought, a broken shovel handle swung wildly from around the corner.

Danil anticipated the attack, however, and quickly parried, grabbed the makeshift weapon from Steele and yanked it from her grasp. The force threw Steele off-balance and she tumbled backward to the ground.

"I...I don't have any money...if that's what you're after..." she said meekly. She panted heavily, her breath forming dense clouds in front of her face.

"You *know* what I am looking for, do not make me get physical..."

Steele felt around her with one hand, desperately trying to find something with which to defend herself. She found nothing.

"What do you want..." she exclaimed, back-pedaling while still lying on the ground.

Danil grasped at Steele's arm.

An abrupt kick met his groin, rapidly followed by another to his mid-section, and finally one to the side of his head. He reeled backward awkwardly and fell to the ground with a dull thud.

Her attacker was down, and she had but one quick moment to flee.

Steele quickly sprang to her feet and turned to run, but was halted instantly by Danil grabbing her by the lower leg. She dexterously performed a spin, in place, and hammered Danil in the side of his face with a devastating kick. Danil again crashed to the ground, as Steele sprinted from the scene into the darkness.

Danil sat up and wiped the blood that oozed from his mouth and nose, catching a final glimpse of his prey running from him.

"You little bitch. Muldoon may not have much to worry about after I get through with you," he muttered in Russian.

Twelve years prior (2072)...

"...and in conclusion, to the class of seventy-two," Steele proclaimed, her voice reverberating through the PA system. She peered out across the sea of graduates seated throughout the arena.

"If this *Brit* can leave you 'Yanks' with one *possible* vision of the future..."

The crowd chuckled in polite amusement.

She continued, "...advancements and the partnership through the disciplines of Plasma and Particle Physics will someday, soon, yield us the results we have been looking for..."

"What does *she* know," a man in the audience whispered to another, as Steele continued her speech. "She's just *eighteen*."

The other nodded his head in agreement. "And did you read her dissertation? No *factual* basis whatsoever. Goes against *everything* we've been taught from day one. Complete garbage."

"Her father's a government big-wig, too – any *wonder* why she's the *Valedictorian*?" the first man answered snidely.

Unable to hold his tongue, a third man chimed into the conversation. "You guys know she *does* have doctorates in both fields. I would imagine she might know a *bit* more than you think," he chastised, glaring back and forth at the pair of doubters.

After the ceremony...

"Steele, my little flower!" Bronson Fox gushed. "Magnificent address!" he said, leaning in to give his daughter a peck on the cheek. "I'm so proud of you, my dear."

'Proud' did not begin to describe Bronson's feelings about his daughter. After all, at the tender age of eighteen she had already earned two doctorates in two very difficult fields of study, and had made several *very* tangible contributions in each. He, along with various other industry notables, had been watching her progress acutely. To say that she was a *'special'* individual would have been an extreme understatement.

"Oh Daddy, thank you," she modestly responded. "But I felt that the lot of them didn't take me seriously," she said, pulling the graduation cap from her head, tucking it under her arm and mussing with her long, flowing, brunette hair.

"Nonsense, Steele," Bronson replied gruffly. "The people that matter were listening, and that's what's important. And *speaking* of," he said, holding out his hand in the direction of a man next to him, "I'd like to introduce you to William Hanley, director of the URA Security Alliance."

"Mr. Hanley, it's a pleasure to meet you," Steele remarked, quickly returning the cap to her head while stiffly holding out her other hand.

"The pleasure's all *mine*, Miss Fox," Hanley said, shaking her hand rapidly. "We've heard *great* things about you, and I have to say - I'm *quite* impressed with your accomplishments at the University."

Steele blushed, as she was not one to expound on her own accolades or accomplishments. "Well, thank you, Mr. Hanley. Although I must say, accomplishments that anyone else could have achieved with a bit of hard work – *and* skipping the parties," she said shyly.

Both Bronson and Hanley chuckled loudly as they shared a grin between them.

"Ah... modesty. Impressive young lady, Bronson." Hanley patted Bronson on the back and walked away.

"*Honestly*, Daddy," Steele chided her father in a hushed tone, as Hanley strode out of earshot, "why do you insist on making me converse with those stuffy *government* types? Downright *dreadful*."

"Those stuffy government types," Bronson replied smugly, "are going to be *your* bread and butter, my dear."

"I told you I don't wish to work for the government. My interest is in the *civilian* application of my theories."

"Steele," Bronson pressed, "the key to your future *is* through the government. There you have access to so many resources not available to the civilian sector. Make it there, and you can write your own future *anywhere*."

Present day (2084)...

Steele lightly knocked on the door of the estate and peered around at the empty rural street that led up to the house.

Rather deserted, as usual, she thought. *Never can be too sure after that little run-in though.*

The heavy, linen drapery on the front window, completely masking the view of anything inside, moved aside slightly.

A male voice, frail but stern, sounded from inside the door. "Who's there..."

"It's *me*, Daddy," Steele responded just above an audible whisper, enough for her father to hear her. "I'm *alone*."

Steele glanced once again around at the unlit road, as her father clicked through several heavy locks on the other side of the door. She turned her focus back to the house. The door slowly opened inward to reveal near darkness inside.

"Come in, dear. *Quickly*," Bronson Fox commanded, his own voice also in a heightened whisper. He backed away from the door as Steele stepped into the house. The moonlight faintly glinted against the metal on her father's wheelchair as he rolled into the sitting room just beyond.

"Daddy, you really do need to turn on some lights in here," she chided, closing the door gently behind her. "You'll hurt yourself."

"And *you* shouldn't be out this late, you know how dangerous it is after dark in these parts." He wheeled his chair around to face her.

"*These* parts?" she mused, "...you live in the absolute wilderness. I don't think you have to worry about a thing. Except maybe a bear or two."

"If only that were true," Bronson added, nodding in bemusement. "No, my dear. The less visible I make myself...*and you*...the better. Now, to what do I owe the pleasure of this visit? And can I get you a cup of tea?"

She removed her coat and placed it over the back of a nearby couch, and then knelt next to her father's wheelchair.

"I've fetched what you've asked for, Daddy. You know...the *cards*. I've got them," she said eagerly.

"Oh, brilliant, Steele!" her father prattled, his eyes widening. "I knew I could count on you. Now, that tea..." he tapered off, rolling out of the sitting room and into the adjacent kitchen.

"Father," she quizzed pensively, "I don't quite understand the significance of these cards. Or *why* you so needed them."

"Hmm? What's that darling?" Bronson responded absent-mindedly from the kitchen.

"The cards, Daddy. I recognize them as being from the Department, but I don't recognize them as anything that *I* worked on," Steele continued, sitting on the couch.

"You know the nature of classified data, my dear," Bronson reassured Steele, rolling back into the sitting room carrying a tray, on which he precariously balanced two steaming teacups.

"Some of us know some things, others know other things," he continued, looking sheepishly into his daughter's eyes, "but no one knows *everything*. Here you go sweetheart." He placed the tray on a nearby table and handed her a cup of tea.

Eleven years prior (2073)...

Two colleagues walked abreast down the plush, quiet corridor en route to the conference room.

"So do you know what this meeting's about, Tim?" the first asked his partner.

"There wasn't a memo about it," Tim, responded. "But if I had to guess I think Director Fox is gonna' go on the warpath again about missed deadlines. That *never* gets old, does it?" he said, rolling his eyes upward.

The other man chortled as they approached the conference room, entering one after the other and taking seats along the oblong table in the center of the room. Several others filed into the room, filling the remainder of the empty chairs.

The room remained eerily silent. Each of the men fiddled with their data pads, desperately recalling information to present their director if he so demanded. However, none of them had noticed the demure brunette sitting to one side of the room.

She sat in a chair, offset from the others. She eyed each one in turn and glanced down, gently tapping at her own data pad after each fruitful glare.

"Good morning, gentlemen," a stern voice projected from the doorway. Bronson Fox briskly entered the room and took the seat at the far end of the table.

Bronson, tall and lean with silvery-tipped dark hair and carrying an air of 'all business' about him, glared sternly at the men seated around him.

"And, of course...*lady*," Bronson said with a smile, briefly standing and bowing towards his daughter.

Suddenly aware of her presence, the men seated at the table spun their necks in the direction of Fox's bow to catch a glimpse of the woman they had all failed to notice.

"Who's *she*?" one man whispered. "New intern?" observed another.

"If I could keep your attention, please," Fox reprimanded the panel, "...we have *important* business to discuss. Now...it's no secret that we've been falling behind in productivity, and subsequently missing our deadlines. *Again*."

"Told ya'," Tim jabbed at his friend in a hushed tone. The other smirked and rolled his eyes again.

"And to that end," Fox continued, "I've decided that an *addition* to the department is warranted. No doubt, you've noticed the young lady sitting at the side of the room. Gentlemen, I'd like to introduce you to the *new* Senior Architect for the Department of Military Science and Technology, Miss Steele Fox."

Hushed murmurs filled the room.

Some of the men turned to look at Steele, while others, with concerned expressions on their faces, talked to each other as if they were telling secrets in middle school.

"Did he just say *Senior* Architect?" Tim asked his partner incredulously in a loud whisper. "That was supposed to be *my* position!"

Others also grumbled to each other, many with the topics of "Fox huh? Shoulda' figured – he went and hired his own daughter" or "Where's he get off hiring a *college* girl for a position like that?"

"Gentlemen, please," Bronson urged, stretching both arms and placing his hands on the table in front of him. "Miss Fox is a recent graduate of the Oxford Science Institute...*URA* chapter, of course...with doctorates in both Plasma and Particle Physics. I believe she will be a *great* asset to our department as we strive to design and apply the next level of military technology."

"But sir," Tim pleaded, leaning forward to glare at Bronson at the head of the table. "With all due respect, we have so many *other* qualified candidates, right here in- house. Was anyone else even *considered* for the position?"

"Tim Fredericks," Steele interceded. "*You* were the architect of the 'Shield On Demand' mobile battlefield armor projector, were you not?"

"Yeah...I was," Tim responded proudly, looking around the room with an arrogant smirk.

"It's an honor to meet you, Mr. Fredericks. And I must say, *excellent* work..." Steele commended with a grin.

"Thank you, Miss Fox. You see, Director Fox," he said, focusing his attention back to the head of the table. "...a *perfect* example of the qualifications that I have to..."

"That's *Dr.* Fox. And *unfortunately*," Steele continued, "the SOD54, when exposed to dusty terrain... how can I put it. Well...*fails miserably.* Leaving soldiers precariously exposed to even the most *archaic* of weaponry."

"She gotcha' *there*, Freddie," one of the men mumbled to Tim, jabbing him with an elbow.

"Mr. Long, I presume?" Steele asked, turning her attention to the man next to Fredericks, whose grin had suddenly transformed into a conceited scowl.

"Yeah...that's me," Long, the man that jibed at his counterpart, responded arrogantly.

"*You* were the designer of the SuperPOD Transport, yes?" she asked, unfazed.

Before he could answer, though, she persisted with her review.

"Very well thought-out. However, if plied with even the *slightest* amount of negative electro-magnetic charge, this vehicle's protection mechanisms seize. Causing it to be nothing more than..." She hesitated for effect. "...An *expensive* death trap."

Except for the weighty breathing that exuded from the two engineers as they struggled for intelligent retorts that never came, the room fell into steep silence.

At the head of the table, Bronson sat back in his chair, a wicked smile growing on his face.

"I've got my notes on the *rest* of the team, if you would like me to go on..." Steele prodded, scanning the rest of the men seated at the table.

Present day (2084)...

"Did you *bring* the cards with you, my dear?" Bronson asked Steele, the anticipation obvious in his eyes. He took a sip of his tea.

"No. I put them in a safe place." *Her* tea had remained untouched on the tray, a small wisp of steam rising from the cup. Obtaining the cards was a strange request from her father, and she was too preoccupied with their importance and his reasoning for wanting them to partake in their nightly ritual.

"Good. *Destroy them.*"

Steele looked at her father blankly. "Did you just say '*destroy them*'? Father, I thought the cards were important?"

"Oh, they *are*, Steele. Which is precisely why they need to be destroyed...*immediately.*" Bronson took another sip and set the cup on the table next to him. "This kind of data cannot be allowed to surface. Not now, *not ever*," he cautioned, giving his daughter a stern look.

"You're not making any sense." She paused, as she stared at her father with a raised eyebrow. "Daddy...have you been *drinking* again?" she added with an air of mocking derision.

"Oh, my dear, you worry too much," Bronson chuckled, waving the palm of his hand at Steele.

"What's on the cards, father?" Steele prodded, firmer this time.

"It's not important for you to know, Steele. Suffice it to say, its data that could lead to the Syndicate gaining more power. More than they have now. *Much* more." A mildly glazed expression fell over Bronson's face as his mind began to wander off in thought. "Can I count on you to do what I ask?" he quizzed Steele, once again focused on her.

Steele hesitated before responding, pondering the alternatives to her father's directive.

"Yes, Daddy. I will destroy them tonight," she said dolefully, standing up to retrieve her coat.

"*That's* my girl," he cooed, holding out his arms to receive a hug. "Be careful getting back to your place. And don't let *anyone* know what you are doing."

"Yes, Daddy." Steele finished putting on her coat, pulled the hood over the top of her head and stepped out of the house onto the porch, closing the door tightly behind her.

After re-latching each of the locks, Bronson pulled aside the window drapery and stared out after his daughter. "I'm sorry I have to *lie* to you now, sweetheart. But soon the *truth* will set us free..."

R. JAMES STEVENS

8:
Before I Forget

Present day (2084)...

The glow of the monitor projected onto the wall of the room, as the user clickety-clacked several commands into the keyboard.

After a few whirs of the laser drive, the screen flickered several times. The display switched to the URA Security Alliance logo, a crimson and blue eagle holding four arrows in its beak with three large stars about its head, all surrounded by twelve smaller stars in a circular pattern.

The user wiped off the dust obscuring part of the display. The speakers crackled to life and a computerized, female voice emanated from them.

"Please speak your security code, and then the security phrase listed on your terminal to complete voiceprint identification," it asked politely.

"Victor...one...two...alpha...four...seven. Security Alliance protocol twelve..." the user responded. As the user completed the phrase, the display went blank and the drive began to chatter. Several seconds of no activity ensued. The user banged the top of the computer case, causing a loud 'clunk' from the internals.

The drive whirred once more and the voice answered, "Voiceprint identification failed."

The user gently blew the dust off a small rectangular pad, pressed the small button at the bottom of it, and placed a thumb snugly against the recessed center portion.

"Biometric identification confirmed. Greetings, *Ms. Fox*," the computer responded hospitably.

"Bollocks," she cursed aloud. "That voiceprint ID has *never* worked for me. Surprising enough that this old dinosaur even works at *all*."

"Ms. Fox, the Hyper Nebula cloud was not detected, would you like to troubleshoot your connection?" the computer voice prompted.

"Maybe because it doesn't *exist* anymore..." she mumbled to herself. "No, I wish to use local resources only," she replied, speaking up once again.

"Very well," the voice responded. "How may I assist you?"

"Cipher dump and analysis," Steele commanded with deliberate annunciation.

"Ms. Fox, please place the first card of the cipher set into the reader so that I may verify its contents," the computer instructed.

Steele reached into the pocket of her coat, hanging on a hook nearby, extracted the set of five cipher cards and inserted the first of them into the reader slot.

After several moments, the voice once again replied, "I'm sorry, Ms. Fox, but I was not able to locate the record identifier on this card. Are you sure this is the first in the set?"

"Not sure of *anything*, really," she quipped, yanking the first card out of the slot and replacing it with another. "Re-analyze."

Again, after a brief pause, the computer repeated the error. Again, Steele replaced the card in the slot with the next in the set, until she had attempted all five.

"Is it possible that there was data present but was *deleted?*" Steele asked the computer.

"I'm afraid the design of this type of cipher card prohibits the determination of..." the computer began.

"...I know, I know. I *designed* it, I should have *known* the answer to that already," she interrupted, biting her lip in pensive thought.

It's got my personal URA SA security marker on the outside of it, she thought, examining the first card, wrinkling her brow. *But yet there's no data on it... at least not anymore.*

"I don't know what's more curious," she said aloud, "the fact that my father desperately needed me to intercept what appears to be *nothing* before the Syndicate realized they had *something*, which they *didn't*. Or that I don't even vaguely *remember* this cipher set. *Very* curious..."

She leaned forward and flicked at the computer's power switch, then placed the set of cipher cards back into her jacket pocket and arose from the chair.

"But I do believe *Mr. Cryptographer* might have some explaining to do." She shut off the small lamp at the desk and strode the short hallway to her bedroom.

Later that evening...

Steele crept slowly down the corridor. The dull, monochromatic coloring of everything around her, much like what she remembered from the century-old classic movies that she and her father had enjoyed watching when she was a child, made her wrinkle her brow. The strange sight reminded her of a smudged print from a copy machine. The walls, however, were a brilliant crimson.

People passed by her, people that she did not recognize, each with a look of shock on their face, as they stopped and stared at her. Steele found it uncomfortable to return the strange glares and continued walking. She grasped at her neck and rubbed a spot at the base of her skull that pulsated like a cattle branding.

Walking farther, she stepped into a grand lobby. A large mural of an eagle adorned the main wall. She immediately recognized the eagle from the URA SA logo, of which she was very familiar.

She squinted at it, noticing the oddity of a blindfold over its eyes. Where there had typically been fifteen stars, three large and twelve small, there stood only one just above the eagle's head. Below the logo, on a gold ribbon that stretched from left-to-right, were the words, "Pro Nos Es Totus Caecus".

Steele stood and stared at the logo in both fascination and puzzlement, furrowing her brow and tilting her head in confusion.

The sudden feel of someone grasping her upper arm shattered her gaze.

"Ma'am, you shouldn't be *here*." Turning abruptly, she came face-to-face with a brawny, familiar-looking security guard holding her arm tightly and pointing back at the corridor from where she had just emerged.

"But, I...I...*work* here," Steele stuttered in confusion, forcefully trying to free herself from the man's grasp, in the process sending a vase crashing to the floor from a nearby table.

The vase's single carnation landed face up within the broken glass, its gray coloring turning a bright crimson to match the walls.

She scanned the lobby, looking for a familiar face that could vouch for her identity. Suddenly, she heard another, recognizable female voice from behind.

"You shouldn't *be* here," the voice said in a heightened whisper.

Steele spun around once again. Where the security guard had been standing just seconds before, stood a woman the same height

71

as her, with similarly colored hair in a tight bun at the back of her head, still grasping Steele's arm.

Steele gazed at the woman curiously. Her facial features blurred to an extent that she could not distinguish whom she was seeing, as if there were a small cloud surrounding the woman's head.

A male voice drew Steele's attention from behind the strange woman.

A tall man stood a meter behind the woman, and oddly, had the same blurred facial features. As she listened to the man speaking to the woman, she realized that she could not understand them. The more she listened, the more she realized it was not another language, but either gibberish or double-speak.

"What are you *saying*?" Steele asked the man.

He did not answer. He continued speaking to the woman in front of her, every few seconds pausing to peek over the woman's shoulder to look at Steele.

"What is he *saying*?" Steele pleaded to the woman, tugging desperately at her arm.

The woman also ignored Steele and began to speak to the man, also conversing in the same, strange jargon.

Steele glared, perplexed, back and forth at the pair as they chatted. She had never been so confused in her life, but something seemed familiar about what she was witnessing.

The man began to raise his voice and pointed at another corridor as he spoke. The man's inflection rose, even though she could not comprehend his meaning. As she tilted her head like a dog in an attempt to understand its master, she managed to catch one word at the end of his sentence: '*Diversion*'.

"*Diversion*?" Steele cried loudly.

Steele's eyes fluttered open and began to scan the ceiling above her bed. She sat up on her elbows and looked around her bedroom, as if expecting to find someone there, but found she was still alone.

"Bloody Hell. What was *that* all about?" she exclaimed aloud to herself, laying back in her bed and pulling the blanket up to her shoulders. "No more late night tea for me..." she mumbled sleepily and drifted off once more.

Twelve years prior (2072)...

The alert on the flat-panel display chirped, as Bronson Fox focused on manipulating the data hovering above the holographic projection device mounted on the desk in front of him.

"Fox," he said mindlessly without turning to look at the device.

"Bronson. Hanley here," chimed the voice from the panel, which had switched to displaying the director of the URA SA's live picture in the center of the screen, his rotund face filling a good portion of the feed.

"Ah, William," Fox replied warmly, spinning around in his chair to greet his boss. "Glad you could set aside the time to speak to me today. Have you had a chance to review the mass ejection forecasts that I forwarded to you?"

"Yes, I have," Hanley replied guardedly, removing his glasses. "And I'm concerned that it's leaving us blind. And we can't afford that in our line of work. We can't get any further out than fourteen months?"

Fox shook his head while pressing his lips together tightly. "I'm afraid not, William. The current projection algorithm just won't take us beyond that limit. But I'm hoping to *rectify* that shortly with a bit of added...*talent.*"

"Funny you should mention that, Bronson. I just got your memo," he continued with a stern look. "I have to say I'm a bit surprised at your recommendations here."

"Really, William, why should *you* be surprised?" Bronson cooed furtively. "This is everything we've discussed... *is it not?*"

"Fox, let's not beat around the bush here. We discussed giving her a position – but senior architect? *Really?* Is that wise?"

"I couldn't imagine a *better* person for the job, honestly," Fox said, placing his chin in his hand, his index finger raised along his cheek.

Hanley chuckled. "You don't say. You don't feel her qualifications are a bit...*light?*"

"She's the best and brightest in her field, past or present," Fox boasted. "In just a few short years, before even turning eighteen I might add, she's managed to *drastically* change the theory of Plasma and Particle sciences...*forever.*"

"Says the proud papa," Hanley continued to chuckle. "Can she handle the *pressure* though?"

"She's got her old man's fortitude, of *that* I'm certain. This group needs someone of her ilk leading the way, not following in others' footsteps."

Hanley paused in obvious thought. "Security of this nation is my number one concern, Fox. I hope that *this* doesn't distract your group's attention from that fact."

"Worry not, William. We *both* know what's at stake here, and she's just the type of revolutionary, outside-the-box thinker that's going to guide us through this," Fox said, raising an eyebrow at Hanley to cement his point.

Present day (2084)...

Bronson opened the cabinet at the end of the hallway just outside of his bedroom, the creaking of the doors echoing crisply throughout the quiet estate. He fumbled around underneath a few blankets and sheets, pulled out a small telephonic-looking device and placed it on his lap.

As he rolled his wheelchair back to the sitting room, he opened the front flap on the device and flicked on the power switch. The display came to life in a bright flash of LED blues and greens, and the speaker crackled with static.

Closing the flap and focusing on the keypad just below the display, he picked up his reading glasses from the desk next to him. Perching them just below the bridge of his nose, he peered down at a small piece of paper lying on the desk, and typed in a series of numbers on the device.

"And...SAT," he muttered aloud, pressing a larger, green button at the bottom of the keypad.

A long, deep, droning tone emitted from the small speaker beside the display, followed by a few short, high-pitched beeps and then a pulsating buzz.

"Is this line secure?" a graveled, electronically altered voice responded through the speaker.

"Y-yes," Bronson stammered, leaning over closer to the device "This is Bronson Fox..."

"Although we are on a secure channel, I expect to maintain anonymity at *all times*," the voice commanded after a few seconds.

"Y-yes, sir."

"What do you need?" the person asked, small speckles of static filling the silence in between sentences, as if speaking from a great distance.

Bronson glanced hesitantly towards the draped window, and then at the lock-secured door. "I've acquired the data you requested," he said, lowering his voice an octave.

There was no response. After a long moment, the voice spoke again. "That *is* good news. I assume it was without incident?"

"No problems encountered," Bronson answered quickly.

More seconds passed in silence. Then the voice chimed once again. "*Good.* You've done well. I'll be in touch."

"*Wait!*" Bronson barked desperately before the connection broke. "I've done what you've asked. I believe it's *your* turn to live up to the terms of the...*arrangement*," he said condescendingly into the device.

The voice on the other end of the connection remained silent for several seconds again, and then responded in a harsher tone. "Arrangement? I don't believe that you've yet completed *your* part of the bargain, now *have* you?"

Bronson was perplexed. Had he not followed instructions to the letter?

"But...I retrieved what you requested," Bronson cried, astounded. "What *more* am I to do?"

Once again, silence preceded the answer. "I have other... *items*...that I will require you to procure, and more work to be completed," the voice said matter-of-factly.

Bronson bowed his head and rested it in the palm of his hands. "You do realize," he asked the voice, "that I am wheelchair-bound and cannot perform very many physical tasks?"

"The able mind," the voice responded after another silence dotted with brief spikes of static, "...is stronger than the able body. You're living proof of *that*," it said suggestively.

"I would say more luck and timing than skill!" Bronson said, now highly agitated, glaring once again at the device. "We were *lucky* to have gotten the data for you without being caught!"

"*We?*" the voice questioned after a moment. "Am I to understand that *you* did not perform this task *alone?*"

Bronson was speechless. He had said too much. He knew he had to mitigate further damage. He sat back in his chair and stared blankly down at the brightly lit display.

"Need I remind you of the importance of secrecy of any mission on which I send you?" the voice chided without waiting for a response. "And *who* assisted you?"

"I hired...a *mercenary*," Bronson answered hesitantly. "More likely...a *professional thief.* But not to worry," he reassured. "This individual has no vested interest in what was *procured.* Or the *Syndicate* for that matter."

"You had better hope not," the voice responded gruffly, "for *your* sake."

The device emitted an audible click and several high-pitched squeals before falling silent. Bronson sat in uneasy reflection, rubbing his forehead.

9:
Scream With Me

Seven years prior (early 2077)...

Clive slurped the last of the whiskey, glancing over at the bartender as he tapped the edge of his glass.

"Keep 'em comin'," he said, blinking away the effect of what he had already imbibed. The blaring of local news headlines filled the background from a television mounted above the bar.

"Hey soldier, can I buy you a drink," a voice said from behind him. Brigadier settled down on the stool next to Clive, playfully grabbing and shaking him by the back of the neck with one hand.

"You're not my type. But what the Hell," Clive replied with a blank expression.

"I'll have what he's havin'," Brig said to the bartender while gesturing at Clive's glass. "Back at the ol' watering hole," Brig quipped, peering around the crowded room. "We had some *good* times in here, huh?"

Clive nodded silently and raised his glass to his mouth to take another swig of the freshly poured whiskey. "And what're you here for – you get promoted *again*?" he asked sarcastically.

"Nah, man," Brig replied, taking a gulp of his own cocktail. "And look, no insignias today," Brig offered while leaning back and holding both hands out at his sides. "I realized that was pretty lame of me to do – and I'm sorry man."

"Eh... it is what it is, Brig." Clive emptied the drink into his mouth, and then tapped on the edge of the glass once again as the bartender passed. "I heard your father won the election – congrats, *I guess.*"

"Thanks, man. Kinda odd though, being called the '*President's son*' and all," Brig countered, taking a moment to look at his reflection in the mirror behind the bar. "But I guess he's worked hard for it, so I'm happy for him." Brig took another mouthful of his drink.

The news anchor on the television continued to report a story. "...officials confirm the deaths of two more military members this week, both apparent *suicides*. This brings the total number of deaths by suicide in this unit to seven in just the last nine months. No comment was given by officials other than to say that they are continuing to investigate..."

"Don't s'pose you can get him to push his weight around and get me back in the EWs, huh?" Clive jibed with a hint of sincerity, but knowing it was a moot point.

"Favors, he can do. But man, policies...that's another story. I wish I could help there," Brig replied, shaking his head.

Clive leaned onto the bar with both elbows and looked down at his drink. "Probably a good thing I didn't vote for 'im then," he slurred.

Brig snorted and patted Clive on the back. "Classic, bro, classic. It's all good." Brig spun his glass around a few times between his fingers and then stared at Clive. "Speaking of favors though. How 'bout I pull some strings and get you in over at SecForce?"

"The biggest government security firm around - you kiddin' me?" Clive answered, looking at Brig with his eyebrows raised.

"Not a bit, Cryp. You just say the word."

"Hey soldier, whatcha' drinkin'?" a woman said flirtatiously, approaching Clive and softly placing her hand on the top of his back.

Without taking his focus from Brig, Clive replied, "Whatever you're buyin'. And Brig – I told you before, I don't *need* your help." Clive turned to the woman, clumsily pulled himself up from the bar and leaned over to her. "You wanna get outta here and go somewhere more...quiet?"

"Sure baby."

"See, Brig," Clive said sloppily, poking a finger into Brig's chest, "I'm jus' fine. *Save yourself.*"

Brig shook his head as he watched his friend stumble out of the bar, Clive's arm held tightly around the woman for support.

The auto door slid open gracefully as Clive removed his hand from the bio-signature pad mounted on the wall next to it.

"Nice place, soldier-boy," the woman cooed, standing behind him and draping her arms over and around his shoulders.

Clive smiled and pushed the door release pad on the interior wall, as she slinked past him into the apartment. He balanced himself on the doorframe and then the wall just inside. The door quietly slid shut.

The woman, already reaching for a bottle of tequila from the shelf in the pantry next to Clive's kitchen, gave him a coy look. "Need any *more* encouragement?" she said, waving the tip of the open bottle in his direction.

"I think I have all the incentive I need," Clive answered devilishly.

As the two locked together in a passionate embrace and kiss, the auto-monitor on the wall emitted several, small chimes.

Pulling himself away from the woman, Clive glared at the wall-mounted display. "Mind if I jus' check that out for a sec?"

"Sure thing sweetheart, I'll just go make myself comfortable in your room," the woman replied, stepping into the hallway towards the bedroom. "Don't keep me waiting *too* long..."

"Mail..." Clive commanded to the display.

He smiled and began to unbutton his shirt.

Clive stared at the email already open on the screen. His smile faded slightly as he skimmed over it once more. Another chime sounded as one new item popped up on the screen.

"Open new..." Clive said, finishing unfastening the final button on his shirt.

The display instantaneously switched to a picture of an electronic form, with a bold letterhead that read "URA Office of the Veterans' Health Advocate".

"Dear Mr. Underwood," Clive began to read aloud. "*Mr. Underwood*," he muttered, "I'll never get used to hearing that..." As he continued to read the letter his smile died, replaced with a cold, blank stare.

The next morning...

The steam from the shower billowed throughout the bathroom, as Clive wiped clean a small area on the mirror. He gazed blankly at his reflection for a moment, and then, leaning forward to support his weight, looked down and shook his head subtly in dejection. Putting his head down into his arms on the vanity, tears began to stream from his face as he gazed at the empty spot that used to be his leg.

Hope he enjoyed himself last night, Brig thought amusedly, as he stepped up to the entrance of Clive's apartment, dark sunglasses concealing his eyes from the bright, Southwest sun.

After a few loud knocks on the door, Brig leaned over to one side of the doorway and tried to peer into a window.

"Probably still asleep," he muttered aloud, pressing a hand against the wall and curling the other around his eyes to block out the sun.

To his surprise, the auto door slid open. Noticing that his other hand was unwittingly resting on the bio-identification plate, he mused, "At least I'm still on the guest list – I guess *that's* a good sign."

Brig apprehensively poked his head into the doorway. "Cryp? You here? Clive?" There was no response.

He stepped fully into the apartment and the auto door smoothly slid shut behind him. Brig removed his shades and placed them inside the front of his shirt, as he slowly walked through the living room into the kitchen area. Several empty liquor bottles littered the countertop, some standing, some on their sides.

"Hey man, you awake?" he shouted, standing just outside of the hall that led to Clive's bedroom.

Brig turned his ear and listened for signs of any activity.

"You sure tied one on last night, dude," he said, walking slowly towards the bedroom, noticing the sunlight flowing out of the open doorway just beyond.

Out of courtesy, he stopped just outside of the bedroom, but shielded his eyes just in case his friend might be otherwise indisposed.

"Rise and shine, buddy!" he barked, taking a quick peek with one eye into the small room.

Tangled sheets and pillows sat atop the mattress, but Clive was nowhere to be found.

"Up and about already," Brig said aloud. "The man can hold his booze!"

As he strode the hallway and into the living room, he noticed that the auto-monitor on the wall was still active and chiming for attention. On the screen were several emails, all open for reading. Brig scanned through the body of the top email curiously.

"Aww, *shit*."

"The honorable Senator Romulus Hawthorne," Clive read aloud from the placard just outside of the entrance to the grand hall. "Let's see how *honorable* he really is..." he muttered. Repositioning his tie and straightening his sport coat, he limped into the entrance, using his small walking cane to aide his progress.

Inside the great hall, what seemed to be hundreds of people scurried between corridors and across the room like ants, several stopping at a large desk in the middle to speak to the clerk manning it. Some appeared to be deep in conversation with each other as they walked. Others, their eyes glued to the data pads in their hands, worked furiously with their screens, oblivious to their surroundings.

Hanging precariously from the ceiling of the lobby, over the clerk's desk, was a large, bronze sculpture of the URA eagle. A ribbon-shaped placard reading, "Unus Populus, Iunctus Nos Sto" stretched beneath it. Fifteen stars in two separate rows, three larger stars on one and twelve smaller stars on the other, adorned the sea of navy blue above its head.

"Sir...sir? Can I *help* you?" a woman clerk from a desk to the side of the hall asked, leaning over to catch Clive's attention.

"Uh, yeah. I'm here to speak to Senator Hawthorne?" he answered, still glancing around at the people bustling back and forth.

"And *you* are?" she said impatiently.

"Last name's Underwood – Clive Underwood," Clive offered, hobbling over to the receptionist's desk.

The receptionist rapidly tapped at her transparent, desk-mounted display. "And what time was your appointment, Mr. Underwood?"

"Uh...I didn't *have* one, but I *really* need to speak to him."

Making graceful swipes across the display, moving in and out of different screens, the woman replied to Clive without breaking focus. "Lots of people *need* to speak to the Senator, sir. He is a very busy man, Mr. Underwood – *that's* why we have appointments. Is there anything else I can do for you today?"

Before Clive managed to respond, the woman's display emitted several chimes.

"Sheila, I'm going to take a break for thirty minutes," a gruff voice said from through the small speakers embedded within the display.

"Yes, your honor," Sheila responded quickly.

"*Please*, miss," Clive pleaded, leaning on her desk, prompting a stare of incredulity from her. "Sorry," he said, releasing his grip on the desk and standing back upright. "My name is Captain Clive Underwood, 81st EW Squadron Special Ops. And if there's *any* possible way I could just get a few minutes of the Senator's time, you'd be helping me out *more* than you could imagine."

For the first time since beginning the conversation, Sheila broke her concentration from the display in front of her, rotated her chair slightly to face Clive and sighed as she wrinkled her lips.

"I'm probably gonna catch Hell for this, but you *seem* pretty sincere." Pondering some more, she added, "The Senator doesn't like to pass up opportunities to speak to the troops, though. Give me a moment, Captain Underwood."

Sheila quickly rose from her chair, darted down a short hallway just behind her desk and disappeared from view through a large, oak door.

Clive took a breath, adjusted his tie again and exhaled heavily, as he turned and stared at the eagle sculpture at the center of the hall. "You *owe* me," he mumbled aloud.

After a few moments, Sheila caught his attention once more. "Captain, the Senator has a small amount of free time on his schedule right now. But you have to make it fast – right down that hallway," she said, pointing to the room with the oaken door.

"Thank you. You're a lifesaver," Clive gushed, limping past the desk and into the hallway.

Giving a polite knock on the large, partially ajar door, Clive stuck his head through the opening. "Senator Hawthorne?"

"Yes, yes! Come in, Captain!" the Senator boomed, springing from a chair behind his desk.

"Thank you sir," Clive said, making his way into the large office.

Clive glanced around at the room. Full bookshelves lined each wall, perfectly framing a giant picture window just beyond the Senator's desk. Positioned along the length of the windowsill were seemingly endless pictures of the Senator with various heads of state and other assorted dignitaries. The centerpiece of the sill was the familiar URA eagle, also a bronze bust, with wings spread and beak agape in a silent scream.

Before Clive could sit, the Senator rushed to hold the chair for him.

Hawthorne found an empty spot at the front edge of his desk and perched, one leg raised partially from the floor while the other firmly held his considerable weight. He placed his hands in his lap and looked fondly at Clive.

"What can I do for you today, son?"

"Well, sir," Clive began hesitantly. "I wanted to speak to you about some legislation that was just recently passed."

"Oh?" Hawthorne replied in surprise. "Well...heh. I'm always happy to discuss law with my constituents. Especially the *uniformed* ones," he said, leaning forward to pat Clive's good knee. "I'm afraid you're going to have to make it brief though, I'm on a bit of a tight schedule today."

"Yes sir. It's about the termination of health benefits for discharged veterans," Clive responded tersely. "Specifically, for the *Special Ops* units."

Hawthorne stared at Clive in silence for a moment. His wide smile faded into a simmering glare.

"Captain," he said, as he glanced belatedly over at Clive's walking cane, "I'm afraid there's not much I can do to help you with this...*issue*."

"But *sir...*"

Hawthorne quickly stood from the desk, waved away Clive's comments with one hand and leaned over to his own transparent, desk-mounted display.

"You see, son, once it becomes a law, my part of the job is completed. This is something that you should be bringing up with your Health Advocate." Hawthorne peered through the blank portions of the display at Clive, as he tapped a few quick commands into it. "You have spoken to your VHA, *haven't* you?"

"Yeah, I've spoken to them," Clive said, the irritation growing in his voice. "And they basically told me I was shit out of luck."

"It says here that you were recently *discharged*, is that true?" Hawthorne questioned, standing up fully behind his desk.

"Yes, sir," Clive responded bluntly.

"Yet you come in here under *false* pretenses, all in an effort to protest a law that was *fully* supported by this government *and* its people?" Hawthorne growled.

"Have *you* ever served, Mr. Hawthorne?"

"That's *Senator* Hawthorne, or 'Your Honor', MISTER

Underwood," Hawthorne replied angrily. "And your question is *irrelevant. My* job is to pass laws that enable this great republic to remain in the budgetary black. *That,* Mr. Underwood, is how it works."

Pushing himself to his feet, Clive angrily pointed at his prosthesis. "I lost my *leg* serving this great republic, Senator! Don't tell me what's relevant or not. And now my benefits are *terminated!* Not only that I *owe* the URA for my treatment retroactive to the end of last year!"

Rounding the corner of his desk, Hawthorne continued his tirade while stabbing his finger wildly in the air.

"This is *exactly* the lack of convention that I've come to expect from units such as yours. Units that feel they can operate outside of the laws that govern this republic. Special Operations units have been a *bane* to the budgetary process – *never* wanting to fall within the constraints that are required to keep this republic afloat. *Never* divulging the *true* nature of their '*missions*' or the costs involved. Well, I tell you, Mr. Underwood," Hawthorne concluded, pacing the floor behind Clive. "I had *no* intention of slowing the passage of this measure – and I will *not* see this republic plunge into debt because of *careless* behavior such as this."

Clive's face flushed red with anger. "What can *I* do to get this changed?" he asked through gritted teeth.

"Oh, *now* you're willing to talk about procedure, are you?" Hawthorne gasped in jest. "Feel free to file a petition with your VHA. But I should warn you – it takes more than just one man's protests to change a law that a *lot* of people worked hard to pass. Now if you don't mind, I am late for my next appointment. *Good day,* Mr. Underwood," he concluded, grasping the door and pointing determinately in the direction of the hallway.

Feeling his head swell with rage, Clive grabbed his walking cane and hobbled to the door. On the way out, he sneered in the direction of Hawthorne. "Thanks for *nothing.*"

The door slammed behind Clive. He wound his arm sideways and delivered a hearty blow to the wall next to him, cracking the plaster underneath and making an indentation just a bit larger than his fist. "Damn it!" he screamed, as he began to make his way back to the great hall.

The pain in his head began to pulsate, as a small glint of red appeared in his eyes. Using the wall to guide and balance himself, he reached the end of the hallway just behind the receptionist's desk.

Clive's skin suddenly went cold and beads of sweat began to form on his forehead. His surroundings warped oddly outwards and rotated, as the sounds of the great hall muted themselves. Covering his eyes with one hand, Clive protected himself from the sunlight flooding in from the skylights above. He stumbled as he exited the corridor, but managed to catch hold of the corner of the receptionist's desk, propping himself back up.

"Captain Underwood, are you ok?" the receptionist asked. She leapt to her feet in an effort to assist. "You look absolutely pale – can I get you a glass of water?"

"N-no. I just need to get some...cold water on my face. Where's the... restroom?"

Sheila leaned over into Clive's line of sight and pointed past him. "The next hallway to the right, second door on the left. Are you *sure* you're going to be ok? We have an in-house physician I can..."

Before she could finish her sentence, Clive had already begun to quickly head into the hallway. Using the walls for stability, he turned his head to Sheila and used one hand to wave away her offer of assistance.

Crashing through the door to the stall, Clive stumbled inward and fell to the floor next to the toilet. Sweat streamed heavily from his brow and into his eyes. Clive groped blindly, searching for something with which to pull him up to a more comfortable position.

He felt inside his jacket pocket and extracted a syringe filled with an oddly colored, blue liquid inside. He tried to roll up the left sleeve of his jacket, but his muscular forearms prevented it from going much past his wrist. Instead, he desperately tore at the shoulder of the jacket and pulled his left arm free, and then immediately jabbed the needle into the soft skin at the bend of his elbow.

As the liquid began its course through his blood stream, Clive's eyes flickered rapidly, as if he were in an intense dream state, but awake.

After a few moments, his eyes closed and he lost consciousness.

Present day (2084)...

Mercury McGraw clenched his fist and cracked his knuckles, as he peered into the dark corridor just beyond the entrance to the deserted warehouse. The bright moonlight shining in from the windows at the top of the wall behind him glinted off the clean-shaven portions of his head. The stiff tuft of blonde, spiked hair at the top of his scalp nearly glowed in the dim room.

He turned quickly and sneered, as the rusty door to the front of the warehouse clamored open.

His contact had arrived.

The contact maintained anonymity by staying in the shadow of the wall of the front of the warehouse, beckoning McGraw forward with a quick hand motion.

"Got a job for ya," said the contact in a graveled voice.

"Hmph," McGraw grunted, "didn't figure ya' wanted to have tea or nothin'."

The contact extracted a small envelope from inside his jacket and handed it to McGraw. "Need this guy...*eliminated.*"

McGraw nodded his head in amusement. His glare at the shadowy outline of the contact penetrated the darkness while he opened the envelope.

"Elimination. *That's* my specialty." McGraw pulled a photograph from the inside of the envelope. "Who's the mark?"

"No details," the contact said gruffly, "just take care of him."

"The guy do ya' wrong?" McGraw asked sarcastically.

"Let's just say...he's gettin' a little too close to one of our operatives. Askin' too many questions. Gettin' in the way."

McGraw squinted at the photo in the dull light. "The Syndicate doesn't do their own work anymore? Gone soft?" he snorted.

"It's more complicated than that. We don't want any internal trails on this one, for reasons you don't need to know," the contact remarked tersely. "Just do the job."

10:
Good Day to Die

Nineteen years prior (2065)...

The group of cadets quietly stood at ease in the calisthenics yard of the Amarillo Military Academy, waiting for the drill instructor to return from an impromptu meeting with the Dean of Discipline.

"You're that new kid, aren't you?" said the taller, stockier boy named Jesse.

"Hmm? Oh...yeah," the fourteen-year-old Brigadier replied in his subtle, West Texas drawl. He quickly glanced at the other boy and then re-focused his gaze on a spot of grass in front of him.

"Hey guys," Jesse shouted to the boys standing just to the left of him, "this is the *new kid* I told you about!"

As the three other boys gathered, all a bit taller than he was, Brig peeked at the remainder of the teens outside of the circle. While some were still in position, others had begun to take an interest.

"Yeah, that's Stroud..." one of the taller boys, standing next to Brig, said with a sneer.

"*Stroud?*" Jesse remarked with a surprised tone. "You related to that Stroud guy running for Governor?"

"He's my Dad," Brig mumbled.

The circle of boys began to grow.

"Ha ha! Hey guys, this kid's got a *big shot* for a father!" one of the other boys shouted to the group, as he pointed at Brig.

"Big shot, huh?" another boy, Mercury, cried.

Mercury was tall like the others, but leaner and much more muscular in tone, his head shaved on the sides with a bright blonde line of hair that stretched from front to back.

"My Dad says that Stroud guy's a *jerk!*" Mercury sniped. He stepped into the middle of the circle and stopped just in front of Brig.

"He's *not* a jerk," Brig defended. He pushed futilely with both hands at Mercury's chest. "*You're* a jerk!"

Mercury, who was a full fifteen centimeters taller than Brig, immediately shoved back, sending Brig tumbling backwards onto the ground. The crowd of boys pointed and laughed at Brig, who pushed himself back up into a sitting position. He bit his lip in a semi-pout, as he glared at the group surrounding them, and then at Mercury.

Brig let out a primal scream as he leapt to his feet and drove his body into Mercury's midsection, shoulder-first. Mercury grasped his powerful arms around Brig's neck and torso, as the two boys dropped onto the freshly cut grass and began rolling around, each attempting to gain a superior position over the other. Several boys screamed, "Get 'im Merc!" while most of the others chanted, "Fight! Fight!"

Brig managed to free himself and started to stand upright. However, before he could mount a defense, he found himself on the receiving end of two quick, heavy-handed punches – one to his right eye and the other to the side of his mouth.

He laid out both hands behind him as he landed on the ground from the second punch. A bright stream of blood trickled from his mouth. Levering himself on one knee while wiping the blood from his face with his t-shirt, Brig focused intensely at Mercury.

The taller boy, now up on his feet, stalked menacingly towards Brig.

A whistle screeched shrilly from just beyond the large group gathered around the fight. Mercury leaned over and grabbed the back of Brig's neck with one of his large hands.

"You're gonna' have a hard time here, Stroud, if you don't show a little more *respect*. Your Daddy's not gonna' be around to *save* you."

A few hours later...

"Cadet Stroud," the Commandant barked, as he entered Brig's dorm room. "You've been here exactly *three* days and *already* you're in a fight. That's *not* the kind of behavior we expect out of our students here!"

"Yes, sir..." Brig replied. He sat at the edge of his bed and gawked at the floor while he held a cold, wet towel against his eye. "I mean...*no*, sir."

The Commandant paced in front of Brig. "We're all a team here, Stroud, so we expect you all to put aside your differences and work towards the common goal!"

"But sir, I *didn't*..."

"I don't care, Stroud! *You* are your own man here – *you* have control over what *you* do!" screamed the Commandant, stopping next to Brig and pointing angrily at him. "I want this to be the *last* incident that I hear about."

Brig knew it was no use arguing. His father wanted him here, and it was up to Brig to make the best of it. "Yes, sir," he said to the Commandant, watching him exit the room.

The next day...

Brig had just finished putting a shine on his field boots. He stood back and admired his locker, satisfied that he had reduced the clutter to pass inspection a little easier next time.

A voice from the doorway gathered his attention.

"Brigadier, my boy!" the voice boomed.

Brig did not have to turn around to know who was there. It was his father.

Dressed in a dark blue, silk suit, and holding a pair of sunglasses that he just removed in one hand, Devlin Stroud stood at the doorway with both arms outstretched.

Devlin was a tall man, a tad under two meters, with facial features chiseled from marble. His jacket gracefully outlined his slender build and small amount of muscular tone about his shoulders. Behind him, two burly security guards stood watch at the door.

"*Dad!*" Brig exclaimed, slamming shut one of the drawers inside his locker and dashing to embrace the elder Stroud.

Devlin released from the hug and stepped to the center of the room, as he soaked in the surroundings.

"It looks like you're settling in nicely, Brig. You getting along with the other boys?" he asked, peering out of the small window situated equidistant on the wall between the two beds.

"Yes, sir," Brig mumbled, as he headed back over to close his locker.

"You don't sound too *sure*," Devlin replied, throwing a half-glance over his shoulder.

"Well, sir...I..." stammered Brig, glaring down at the floor in front of his locker and grasping nervously at his upper arm with one hand.

Devlin faced Brig and, as he approached him, leaned in and gruffly tilted the boy's face in his direction with one hand. Devlin's expression quickly turned to a scowl. "*Brigadier!* What is this all about?"

Brig pulled his face away from his father's grasp. "It's nothing, Dad, just got into a little fight with one of the other..."

"A *fight?*" Devlin bellowed, moving backward a step and throwing both hands into the air. "Did I send you here so you can cause trouble and pick fights?" Before Brig could respond, Devlin spun furiously on one heel. "I thought we got *past* this, Brigadier."

Devlin placed his hands on his hips, leaned forward and growled, "I thought that attending this school would make you into a *man.*"

"It wasn't my fault..." Brig whimpered, once again focusing his gaze to a point on the floor away from his father's glare.

"It never is..." Devlin grunted, turning just as he reached the door. "This is just like before, son. I'm *very* disappointed in you. I thought things had changed for the better." As he forced the sunglasses onto his face, Devlin angrily pointed at Brig and growled through gritted teeth, "Grow up!"

"So does this mean I get to come home, Dad?" Brig asked meekly, peering at his father out of the corner of his eye.

"*Brigadier,*" his father continued to scold, stopping to glare at his son, "we're not going to have *that* conversation again."

Devlin nodded to one of the security guards. The guard returned the nod and exited into the hallway in front of his boss.

As Devlin and his guards made their way down the corridor and out of the dorm, Brig dove onto his bed. He forced his eyes shut and faced the wall, as he wiped away the tears.

Present day (2084)...

The night was clear, chilly and serene. A chorus of crickets harmonized in the bushes nearby, as a lone coyote bayed somewhere off in the distance. Glowing embers crackled within the remnants of a campfire a meter from the shell of a downed heli-jet.

Inside the weather-worn fuselage, Brig lay on his side on a pile of old clothing and seat stuffing fashioned into a bed. He had been asleep for several hours, but it had not been a very sound slumber.

Although the air inside was relatively crisp, small beads of sweat lined Brig's forehead as he once again tossed over to his other side.

It had been several days since he had paid a visit to his friend, Clive. Something did not seem right with his EW brother, and it bothered him. Clive was hiding *something,* and Brig's instinct told him that Clive was in trouble.

Suddenly, a faint noise from the darkness outside blared in his ears like a wailing siren. A metallic 'clink', barely audible to most, alerted him to sudden danger.

Brig's eyes popped open and a voice inside his head ordered, *Move now!*

His heart slowed to a deliberate cadence as he rolled from his bed onto the metal floor, listening to the other voice that told him to be as stealthy as possible.

The frame creaked lightly, as Brig slowly slid along the floor, until he dropped out of the door onto the soft dirt outside. He quickly stood and darted to a nearby tree for cover.

He surveyed the area just beyond the edge of the forest where he had set up camp. The forest thinned and led out to a small clearing filled with mostly sagebrush and several large, half-buried slabs of rock jutting from the ground. The moonlight glanced off their tops, creating large, monolithic silhouettes that dotted the landscape.

One hundred meters beyond the clearing was the edge of town and a handful of tightly clustered, small houses on the left. Packed together on either side of the main road were rows of darkened commercial buildings. While they were mostly old storefronts and storage warehouses, several unlit, taller buildings rose above the small city skyline.

Brig squinted as he scanned the area around the rocks, which posed a perfect hiding spot for someone, but could not distinguish anyone that might be lying in wait.

Behind him, the forest was impenetrably dark, except for the few spots where the silvery moonlight filtered down through small gaps in the thick canopy of treetops. He peered into the darkness, hoping that he was close enough to the tree that the moonlit clearing would not make him into a perfect, backlit target.

The silence of the wooded area was suddenly shattered as the heli-jet violently exploded into small fragments of flaming metal and other material. A small plume of fiery, black smoke rose quickly from the spot where it lay just seconds before.

"Oh *shit...*" Brig grunted.

He quickly sprung from his crouch and began to sprint towards the clearing, knowing that the shot came from within the forest behind him. Trees splintered around him as the assailant continued to fire. Brig allowed his military training to take over, instinctively darting back and forth between the trees as he ran. Those same trees continued to burst into kindling as the attacker traced his steps.

The firing stopped as he reached the clearing, allowing him to catch his breath. Brig pressed himself against the back of a smaller set of rocks and exhaled quietly. He knew that his pursuer was either reloading or recharging his weapon. That meant that he had precious few seconds to make a break for town before the onslaught picked up once again.

Brig glanced back. He could see the smoldering ruins of his campsite.

Damn it, he thought.

His only refuge – *gone*, and now *someone* was trying to kill him, someone with a dead aim and *serious* hardware.

He emerged from his resting spot and began to dash towards the next group of boulders. The sound of running and the telltale rattling of a weapon on a strap around the person's shoulder urged Brig forward. He did not dare look back, as that would only give his pursuer a chance to close the gap on him. Instead, he continued to progressively race towards the city, zigzagging between rocks.

A hail of bullets rained around him as he reached the final slab just 30 meters from the main road.

"Great, he's got more than *one* weapon..." Brig cursed, recalling that it was something much bigger than a bullet that had disintegrated the heli-jet just a few moments before.

Scanning the desolate street, Brig spotted several charred pickup trucks and cars in front of a burned out hardware store. If he could make it to them, the lack of street lighting and relative cover that they offered would be adequate for him to stop and regroup. At the very least, he would be able to scan the area and choose a more suitable hiding place in one of the buildings without presenting such an easy target.

He rounded the end vehicle and slid to a sitting position behind it. The truck next to him suddenly lifted several meters from the ground, burst into multiple sections of twisted, molten metal and then rained down around him. Brig leveraged the ensuing billow of fiery smoke to make his escape to a nearby warehouse, dashing through the unhinged, front doors of the facility.

Moments later, a lone figure stood in the lot outside of the warehouse, his weapon propped over his shoulder with one hand on his hip, as he stared at the half-open door. Behind him, the fragmented remains of the pickup truck still lay smoldering in the street.

"Gotcha now..." Mercury McGraw purred with a satisfied sneer.

Seven years prior (early 2077)...

Brigadier, camouflaged and perched high in the tree on the edge of the enemy encampment, peered through his electro-binoculars at the two armed guards patrolling the main gate.

"Not goin' in the front door, that's for sure..." he mumbled aloud, lowering the binoculars and staring intently at the compound below.

A narrow stream wandered in and out of a small wooded area along the eastern edge of the camp, reaching the back edge of the encampment where it disappeared behind a grouping of several large rocks.

"*There* we go," he whispered.

Shimmying down the side of the tree and landing with cat-like dexterity at its base, Brig spoke with a low tone into the communications device strapped to the back of his wrist.

"Bravo, this is Condor. I've reached the camp and I've located an entry to get to the objective," he said purposefully.

"Roger, Condor. Proceed with stealth," the voice on the other end of the radio chirped in response.

Brig weaved through the small trees that lined the stream next to the camp, pausing at each to ensure that the guards within had not taken notice of him.

As was the standard with any of these types of training missions, live ammunition was not used. Despite the lack of physical danger posed by weaponry, it was still a blemish on anyone's record to fail to achieve the objective due to carelessness.

Although very few considered his previous real world mission a failure, as it did produce highly valued intel, training missions were different. It was success or failure – there was no room for interpretation, and Brig knew it.

Clearing the last tree and approaching the rocks, Brig quickly glanced over his shoulder at the camp. The final sprint to that area was fifteen meters and he could not afford to blow it now. As he rounded the edge of the first rock, his face met the force of a blow that knocked Brig's feet from under him and laid him flat on his back into the dirt.

Brig sat and shook his head as he rubbed at the side of his face. A warm, salty flow of blood oozed from his nose into his throat. He looked up. Mercury McGraw stood over him, rubbing the elbow that just cold-cocked him, a devilish grin on his face.

"Not as stealthy as you *think*, Stroud," McGraw snarled sarcastically. "I heard you comin' a mile away. This objective's *mine*."

McGraw quickly leapt to the chain link fence at the back of the camp, turning to flex one of his arms into a 'V' shape, his chiseled bicep straining against the torn sleeve of his shirt.

"But then, they don't call me '*Victory*' for nothin'," McGraw chortled, swiftly scaling the fence and flipping himself over to the other side.

Present day (2084)...

McGraw made his way into the entrance and stood in the lobby, slowly peering around for signs of his prey. The warehouse was deathly quiet, the only lighting provided by the moonlight flooding in from the windows at the top of the building.

Not in the main storage area... he thought, noticing that the heavy doors leading to it were still in place with no signs of recent movement.

A steel staircase led up to an office running the length of the complex on the second floor with large, plate glass windows on the side.

"Come out, come out, *wherever* you are..." he hissed lightly, glaring up at the windows while moving over to the stairs.

Up on the second floor, within the office, Brig crouched behind several large filing cabinets. The moonlight cast a ghostly glow across part of the floor, enough to make out only the silhouette of solid objects. Another set of large windows adorned the opposite side of the office and offered a view of the entire warehouse floor below.

He held his breath and listened. It was very faint, but he could hear his attacker ascending the staircase. He would be in the room in mere seconds.

This is it... Brig thought.

Seven years prior (early 2077)...

Brig sat on the bench, his elbows propped on his knees, and stared down at the small puddle of blood that had slowly formed on the cold tile beneath him.

What a bastard... he thought, reaching for a towel to sop up the blood still dripping from his nose. Just less than an hour ago, he was well on his way to successfully completing his solo jungle training. That was, until Mercury McGraw showed up and ruined his chance.

What was he playing at? Brig quizzed himself silently, as he painfully applied pressure to his face to stop the bleeding.

He could hear several voices approaching the locker room. Brig pulled the towel from his face and peered over at the entrance.

Mercury McGraw entered the room along with two other EWs in tow, both engaged in sycophantic conversation, patting McGraw on his back. Brig shook his head and sighed lightly, returning the towel to his face.

"Well, look who it is. Brigadier Stroud...A-K-A *Looo-sa!*" McGraw jeered, as he approached Brig.

Brig remained silent, still holding the towel to his face and staring down at the floor. *He's trying to egg you on, just ignore him...* he assured himself.

McGraw stepped closer to the bench, leaned over to Brig and growled, "You're a disgrace, Stroud. *I'd* be ashamed to call myself an EW if I were you."

Still not saying a word, Brig removed the towel from his face and placed it on the floor next to his feet, then arose from the bench and opened his locker door.

"You hear what I *said*, man?" McGraw continued to taunt. "Breaking the rules, as usual, and you don't *care* about the consequences," he emphasized, slamming Brig's locker door shut and nearly catching one of Brig's hands in the process.

The line was crossed and Brig could not hold his tongue any longer. He whipped around and jabbed a finger into McGraw's chest. "That's funny coming from *you*, jackass...*you're* the one that broke the rules today!"

"What?" McGraw griped in mock innocence. "I just picked up where you failed. *I'm* not the one that broke radio silence..."

"Aw, bullshit McGraw!" Brig bellowed. "You were running backup – you had *no* business bein' at the camp. You *knew* I was gonna be there!"

"Hey, when a teammate drops the ball *someone* has to pick it up. Blame *yourself*, loser," McGraw said, swiping Brig's finger from his chest.

Brig snatched McGraw's hand quickly and without hesitating, delivered a titanic blow to the side of the taller man's chin, sending the surprised Epsilon tumbling backward into a set of lockers with a mammoth crash. "Pick *that* up, asshole."

"Careful, Stroud," McGraw said with a snort, as he levered himself, one hand on his knee, the other rubbing his jaw. "Your *daddy's* not here to make sure we all play nice, now *is* he?"

As he finished his taunt, McGraw launched forward and into Brig's midsection, this time sending Brig into another set of lockers, the metallic clamor echoing loudly throughout the locker room and beyond.

The men tumbled to the floor, burying their balled fists into each other's midsections. One of the other two EWs that had escorted McGraw into the locker room began to move forward to intervene. However, the second Epsilon held out his arm to stop him, allowing the altercation to continue.

After a few more moments of intense fisticuffs, Commander Falco rushed into the room, tossed his outer shirt aside and jumped into the middle of the fray.

"That's *enough*, you two idiots!" Falco exclaimed, grabbing Brig and McGraw by the backs of their necks and lifting them up to a standing position. "Into my office! *NOW!*" he bellowed, releasing them and stalking off to the latrine.

Both men stood at attention up against the tiled wall, as Falco took turns bawling at them just centimeters from each other's faces. "Just tell me what the *HELL* you think you were doing out there, McGraw!"

"Just teachin' Stroud here a little bit about followin' the rules…" McGraw said cockily without making eye contact with Falco. "…*Sir.*"

"And what the Hell kind of God damn rule is it that has you attacking your teammate?" Falco growled loudly, hovering even closer to McGraw's face.

McGraw hesitated before responding. "Sir, you'd be better off asking Stroud what kind of rules *he* broke during the mission today. I was just ensuring our *team* was victorious."

Falco allowed his lips to cover the gnashed teeth that were previously showing. He exhaled an exasperated breath as he backed away from McGraw and stepped in front of Brig.

"I'm waiting, Stroud!" Falco shouted after a moment.

"*I* didn't do anything wrong, sir," Brig answered confidently, maintaining his gaze at the opposite wall of the latrine. "It's *this* jackass over here that insists on pulling crap like he did today that makes us *all* look bad."

"Well...isn't that just fan-damn-tastic..." Falco muttered loudly, turning his back on both men and beginning to pace. "Do I have to remind you two numbskulls that you *are* teammates? You go out of your way to make sure your *team* succeeds – whether you personally look like a hero or not doesn't mean jack shit!"

Then, once again facing both men and pointing angrily at both in turn, he yelled, "That means following the rules! That means no dirty crap to try to make the other look bad! And that also means both of you – NO FIGHTING!"

Falco turned his back to Brig and McGraw once more.

"At least not where I can see it. You wanna take this outside away from here, be my guest, but when you're here you two are gonna' be like two peas in a pod – you *get* it?" Falco said, spinning to face them.

"Yes sir..." both Brig and McGraw uttered simultaneously, although with little enthusiasm.

"So congratulations, men," Falco continued, now with a smirk. "You've both earned a three-day pass...to the desert just outside of the missile range. There's three kilometers of fencing that needs replaced, and you two strapping young studs are gonna' be the ones to do it." Falco chuckled, as he began to stride out of the latrine room.

He stopped for a moment to glare back at both of them. "And boys, bring your sunscreen, it gets *hot* out there."

Present day (2084)...

Brig waited for his mystery attacker to finish climbing the stairs, crouching next to the cabinet adjacent to the door and readying himself to make his move.

Only got one shot at this, gotta' make it count, Brig cautioned himself.

McGraw tapped the door open with his boot. He knew what was waiting for him inside, but he also knew his prey was trapped and unarmed, making him unpredictable.

In a *previous* life, McGraw was an EW. No civilian could match the raw fighting power, cunning and skill of an Epsilon – *especially* in close quarters. This was the final showdown and he was a professional killer. McGraw *knew* he had the upper hand.

Showtime, McGraw thought with a devilish smile.

The door swung open slowly, its hinges creaking loudly from years of inactivity. As the door tapped against the wall, a small, broken piece of glass, evidence of a looter from years past, fell from its frame to the floor and broke into smaller shards. The stinging rank of dust and mildew wafted outward from the room and flamed at McGraw's nostrils. He ignored it. He had tracked his prey, and he was too focused now to let anything stand in his way.

McGraw stood in the doorway and peered inside, his finger resting just off the trigger of his tri-barrel S-37, its Rhodium-tipped armament eager to find and destroy its target. He quieted his breathing and listened with tuned ears. His prey was here.

As McGraw stepped into the darkened office, Brig wasted no time, reaching from his hiding spot behind the cabinet and grabbing McGraw's ankle. With one swift motion, he flipped McGraw into the air and onto his back, sending his weapon sailing from his hands and skidding across the dusty floor of the office, out of sight under the darkness of a desk.

Brig leapt to his feet and pounced into the air at McGraw, but McGraw, already anticipating his move, countered with a solid kick to Brig's chest. Brig stumbled backward and caught himself on one of the cabinets, giving McGraw enough time to spring to his feet and advance for the next attack.

McGraw continued his assault, and despite the darkness, delivered a deft roundhouse kick to Brig's face, sending him careening into another file cabinet and knocking both it and Brig to the floor. As Brig choked off the flow of fresh, warm blood in his mouth, McGraw grasped him by the shoulder, pulled him from the floor and railed Brig with two solid knee butts to his face.

His attacker reared back with one hand to deliver a mighty blow to Brig's head. However, Brig planted a heel, spun quickly and delivered two stunning, mid-air kicks to McGraw's midsection. McGraw staggered backward and gasped for breath.

Not wanting to lose his opening, Brig quickly jumped forward and began pummeling McGraw in the gut with a rapid succession of uppercuts. Brig followed with several blows to McGraw's head – the last of which painted a spattering of blood on the window behind them that glowed oddly in the moonlight trickling in from the main warehouse.

With savage precision, McGraw interrupted Brig's attack with two quick head butts, hurtling Brig to the floor with a dull thud onto his behind. Brig shook his head to gather his wits as the room wobbled around him.

Closing one eye, he peered at his attacker. The blurry figure of the man's moonlit silhouette filled the large office window in front of which he stood. Brig ignored the throbbing in his skull. He surged to his feet, bull-rushed McGraw, and wrapped his arms around the muscular torso of his aggressor, lifting him from the floor.

The momentum of Brig's desperate attack carried McGraw forcefully backward, Brig in tow, bursting through the large pane of glass and onto the metal walkway just beyond with an echoing clatter. The combatants exploded through the aging, pipe railing and tumbled into a small pile of wooden pallets eight meters below with a thunderous clamor.

Dust scattered and filled the air like a dense, midnight fog. Brig rolled over onto the cold, concrete floor of the warehouse. Sweat poured heavily from his brow as he weakly shoved himself up onto his knees, holding his hands out for support. He turned his head, peered out through his sweat-soaked, scraggly hair, and saw the motionless form of his attacker in the pile of rubble into which they had fallen.

Brig, dazed and exhausted of all energy, began to make a break for the exit and disappear into the night. He placed a hand out in front of him onto the floor for stability and tried to push himself up to a standing position, but the motion of the room around him and his utter exhaustion caused him to fall again. Behind him, he could hear his foe stirring.

Gathering his remaining strength, Brig forced himself upright and staggered towards the exit of the warehouse ten meters away. He could feel the welcome wisp of the cold, night air seeping in from the doors just ahead. Safety was almost within his reach.

Just a few steps from the door, his right shoulder erupted in a searing heat, forcing him back to the floor, flailing in pain.

The sound of McGraw's boots, slowly clunking across the floor as he approached Brig, filled the void of silence in the great room. McGraw reached down and with a slow, deliberate motion pulled the enormous blade, buried up to its handle, from Brig's shoulder. Brig howled in agony and grasped his arm, flipping over onto his back in the process.

Brig glared up at the hulking figure, who held the blade that felled him off to his side.

Brig was beaten and he knew it. While not as merciful as he had hoped, the *end* had arrived.

McGraw took a step forward, brutally pounded his knee into Brig's chest and stepped onto the side of Brig's head with his other foot, exposing his bare neck. Brig sputtered more blood onto the floor and gasped for breath, as McGraw raised his blade high above his head, drawing a blackened outline in the moonlight above.

As he glared down and aimed for the killing shot, McGraw suddenly halted his final attack. Within a ray of moonlight that shone on Brig's neck, partially covered by his shirt collar, was the very distinct Epsilon Warrior insignia – a Greek 'Epsilon' character set between two brandished swords.

Quickly re-sheathing his knife, McGraw leaned forward and grabbed Brig's hair, forcing his face into the sliver of moonlight. McGraw squinted and puzzled at the sight. Brig's unkempt appearance, grizzled beard and long, scraggly hair, made it difficult for McGraw to discern his prey's identity.

"You're an *EW*? Who the Hell *are* you?" McGraw growled, grabbing Brig's face between his fingers and forcing it fully into the moonlight.

Brig coughed as he slapped away McGraw's hand from his face. "You're the one...tryin' ta kill me...the Hell you *think* I am?"

"*...Stroud?*" McGraw answered incredulously after a silent moment.

"*McGraw?*" Brig barked, craning his neck to get a closer look at his attacker in the darkness. "What the Hell..."

McGraw quickly sprung to his feet, grabbed Brig's hand and pulled him to a sitting position beside him. "Let me look at that wound," he muttered, spinning Brig around and exposing the area where his knife had penetrated just moments earlier.

"You gonna' answer me..." Brig groaned, turning to glare at McGraw through the corner of his eye. "Why are you tryin' to *kill* me?"

"Wouldn't be the *first* time someone wanted to do that, Stroud. 'Specially me." McGraw reached into a small pouch located on the back of his belt, and extracted a metallic-looking packet. He tore it open with his teeth and emptied the powdery contents into the gash on Brig's back, making Brig flinch as it worked its way into his open flesh.

"That'll stop the bleeding. Go get some medical help and get that sewed up." McGraw tossed the empty packet aside, stood and peered up at the office on the second floor.

"Who hired you..." Brig yelled. The room began to spin even more as his head throbbed wildly with pain, and dizziness crept in from the loss of blood.

McGraw turned to Brig, the typical 'McGraw smirk' lighting up his face.

"Now...*you* know how it is. Mercs don't give up their employers – kinda bad for business," McGraw chortled. "But I'll tell ya' that you *did* piss off the wrong...*organization*."

"Syndicate?" Brig questioned, shakily getting up on one knee.

"All I know is that someone *up there* is lookin' out for you," McGraw offered, peering up at the moonlit windows above. "If I hadn't seen that 'tat, you were finished."

McGraw quickly strode to a metal staircase that he spotted at the other end of the warehouse. As he reached the bottom, he stopped.

"Watch your back, Stroud. The next guy they send might not have the high moral standards that I do," he chuckled, mounting the staircase three steps at a time until he was at the top. He flung open the door to the office and disappeared into the darkness.

Brig sat for a few moments, trying to hold back the pain from his shoulder while he gathered his dwindling strength. He weakly pushed himself upright and, after steadying himself from the spinning room, staggered to the exit door.

He reached for the handle and pushed his weight against the door, as the pain thundered against the inside of his skull. Brig closed his eyes and leaned his head against the metal surface, relishing the peace of the moment.

The door unexpectedly gave way and fell off its hinges, forcing Brig to lurch forward off balance. He stumbled onto the sidewalk just beyond the doorway and out into the small street that ran between the warehouse and a smaller building next door.

"Well, well...look who it is..." a tinny voice with a Brooklyn accent mocked. "Don't look like you're in too good'a shape to fight back *this* time..."

11:
The Infection

Present day (2084)...

Brig lifted his head from the cold pavement. Although a cloudy sludge coated his mind, he could see the figure of a man, smaller in stature, standing half a meter away. The man, his legs partially spread in a defiant stance, had his arms folded across his chest as he stared at Brig. Propped over one shoulder was a weapon.

"Yeah, that's *right* you son of a bitch," the man snarled, bending over to let Brig get a closer look at his face. "You remember me from the alley a couplea' weeks ago, dontcha?"

The man grabbed a handful of Brig's hair, stretching his neck backwards. He gritted his teeth centimeters from Brig's face, inflicting small droplets of spit onto it.

"You tore up one of our guys pretty bad, snapped his neck like a twig. Saw the whole thing." He released Brig's hair, causing his head to thump to the ground. "Didn't want some maniac taking me out so I just laid there and played dead. But I saw what ya did. And ya thought ya *got away* with it, huh? We all might not see eye to eye, but we look after our own. And no one takes out one of *ours* without gettin' somethin' *back*."

The man circled Brig as he spoke, glaring down at him in disgust. "You hear me, punk?" he screamed, letting loose a vicious kick into Brig's side.

Brig grabbed his midsection and recoiled in pain. His body ached to its core from the brutal beating by McGraw, and his head burned with an intense fire as he stared out at the world spiraling around him.

The man delivered two ferocious kicks to Brig's side, causing Brig to curl up into a fetal position.

"What's the matter, why ain'tcha fightin' back, you piece of *shit*..." the man snarled, wiping the drool from the side of his mouth with the sleeve of his jacket.

A small chunk of blood spewed from Brig's mouth, as he coughed and let out a yelp of pain. The bagman pulled his weapon, a Ripper, from his shoulder and placed the edge of the cold, titanium barrel fifteen centimeters from Brig's head.

"Ya know what a Ripper can do at point blank, dontcha? It makes its way nice and clean into your skull. Then it spins and scrambles your brains like a bowl of eggs. You'll only be alive for just a second...but long enough to feel it..." the man said with a cool, sarcastic tone.

"That'll be enough – drop your weapon and step away from him," a voice with an Indian accent commanded from behind the bagman.

Behind the bagman, three meters away, stood a man holding an old-style pistol aimed at his back. Just beyond the other man stood a woman, partially hidden from view behind a burned-out street lamp.

The bagman grinned and let out a sardonic chuckle as he glanced over his shoulder. "Now why don't you just move along, buddy. You got no business here," he said calmly. He turned his attention to Brig, who was lying motionless on the ground but still groaning like a wounded animal.

"I said drop the weapon...and step away."

The bagman cockily rotated to face the other man, holding both hands in the air just above his shoulders. He deliberately flashed the Ripper for the other to see. "You're steppin' in a whole big mess of it here, pal. You know who you're dealin' with?"

The other man stepped sideways as the bagman took two steps away from Brig. He glanced down at Brig and spied the dark trail of blood coming from Brig's shoulder.

"I know exactly who you are. You're Syndicate. And you're not welcome around here," the man said in an unwavering tone.

"That so?" the bagman chortled. "And who says? You?"

"That's right," the other man replied confidently. "I'm the local Constable... the *law* if you want to see it that way."

The bagman cackled heartily, lowered his hands and sarcastically placed them on his knees. "The *law*? That's a good one, buddy. And what're you gonna' do if I don't play nice?"

The Constable pursed his lips and straightened his aim at the bagman. "The Syndicate's days of ruling these streets in fear are *soon* coming to an *end*, so why don't you just drop the weapon and walk away so that we can get this guy some medical attention."

Taking a step towards the Constable, the bagman pointed his free hand in his direction, as the smirk on his face faded into a sneer.

"This ain't your business, hero. Now turn around and go back in your house before more of us come and burn it to the ground to teach you a lesson." The bagman pointed his weapon in the direction of the woman standing behind the Constable. "Besides, you wouldn't want us to hurt your girl over there...now would ya?" he hissed.

The Constable twitched his eyes to the side, remembering that his wife was still in harm's way. "Your threats don't mean anything to me. We're pushing scum like you out of our town when we get the chance. Now do what I *told* you."

"I ain't got time for no hero," the bagman grumbled. Once again facing Brig, he lifted his weapon to the side of his head. "Say goodnight..."

However, before the bagman could squeeze the trigger of his Ripper, the Constable fired three quick shots into his back. The Ripper dropped from the bagman's hands with a clank onto the ground as he fell to his knees and then forward onto his face.

The Constable cautiously approached the bagman's lifeless body, still sharply aiming his gun at the prone man's head as he jabbed him with his foot. He placed his fingers on the bagman's neck.

"This one's dead," he called to his wife, who was still hiding behind the lamppost. "Quick! Give me a hand with the other!"

Brig lay on his side, moaning, as the Constable carefully peeled away the ripped portion of Brig's shirt and exposed the stab wound on his shoulder.

"We're going to have to sew this up. Rah, go back to the house and get the med kit. I think I have a needle and thread in there that should do the job," he barked, examining Brig for other signs of injury.

"Peter, we shouldn't have gotten into the middle of this," his wife said, her light Hindi accent casting a veil of innocence over her.

"We had to do *something*," Peter replied assertively. "This man was surely going to be killed, and we can't allow that to *keep* happening. The Syndicate *must* be stopped!"

"But why us, Peter?" she cried, placing her hand on Peter's shoulder. "It's bad enough with everything that is going on in the world. I just want to live my life...our life, and picking fights with these types of men is just inviting trouble."

"I'm not picking fights, Rah. I'm saving this man's life," Peter said, exasperated. He sat in a crouch, staring at Brig for a silent moment, and then turned on his knee to face her.

"This is how society is rebuilt. Someone has to stand up for what is right. The law *has* to be enforced or *all* is lost." Peter faced Brig once again. "I know it's only one man, but we have to do all that we can to right this ship."

"Peter, *please...*"

"Namrah! Do what I told you. Go to the house and get the med kit, this man's life depends on it. Now...*go!*" he bellowed. "And please, bring some extra towels as well..."

Shaking her head and throwing her hands up in indignation, Namrah turned and quickly made her way back to a house 50 meters from the road, nestled at the edge of a deep set of trees, and disappeared inside.

Peter leaned close to Brig's face and spoke. "It's going to be ok, I've got a med kit and I think I can help you with that stab wound. Do you have any other injuries that you know of?"

Brig did not respond. He continued holding his side tightly with his left arm while exuding a low, throaty moan.

"It's ok, friend," Peter reassured, patting Brig lightly on the leg. Rotating around while still crouched, Peter yelled towards the house. "Rah! Hurry!"

Nine years prior (2075)...

Brig sat upright on the exam table, looking around at the various charts on the wall while clutching the small bandage at the bend of his right elbow.

He was no stranger to physical exams. Being an Epsilon, he probably had more done to him in the past five years than most had in a lifetime, so this was no different for him.

A small thought did linger in the back of his mind though. He had just come back from Arctic training with Clive several days prior, and there *was* the incident with the frozen lake. Were they testing him to make sure he had no lingering effects from the near-freezing temperatures he endured while submerged in the lake, or was this just the run-of-the-mill physical to ensure that one of the URA's finest was still at his physical peak?

The lab door swung open slowly and the technician, a shorter, stockier man in his early twenties, entered backwards while propping open the door with his weight, holding a small, silver case.

11: THE INFECTION

"Alright, Captain Stroud, everything looks to be in order..." he said cheerfully, reaching the center of the room and placing the case onto the table with a small thump.

"The doc gonna be in soon?" Brig quizzed, glancing around the room while pulling the bandage from his arm.

The technician peered up at Brig and smiled. "Doc? Uh, heh. No, no doctors needed today, sir. Besides," he said, as he looked down at the case, opened fully to reveal several large syringes, "we're not a medical facility, per se. We're more of a *research lab* than anything else."

Brig glared at the technician in puzzlement. "Research? Why do they have me taking a physical at a *research* lab?"

The tech raised his head and gently pushed his glasses back onto his nose. "Physical? No sir, we're not administering a physical today, sir. We just ran your blood sample through the scanner is all," he reassured Brig, tapping his own arm at its bend.

Brig's forehead wrinkled intently as he pondered the tech's answer. "Then why the blood test?"

"Oh, you know, sir. Gotta run a check for specific antibodies, mutagens, pathogens. Those sorts of things," the tech said casually, nodding his head in rhythm to his own comments. "Can't have any unknowns floating around when administering *these* types of modifiers."

"Modi...wait, is this some sort of *experiment*?" Brig questioned, watching the tech remove a multi-stage syringe from the case, its two-tone green and red liquids swirling in the bright LED backlighting emanating from the wall.

"*Result* of experimenting. Lots of it, and a ton of research, too sir," the tech corrected, still focused on the syringe, as he mounted a needle on its end.

"Alright. So...what does this stuff *do*?" Brig asked concernedly.

"Well," the tech began, scratching the back of his head with his free hand, "I don't know all of the details for the entire program, but... this one here," he emphasized, tapping on the side of the tube in his hand, "gives you *clarity* in certain...battle situations."

"*Clarity*. You mean like...*focus*?" Brig replied, staring at the syringe. *How could an injection give someone clarity?* he thought.

"In a manner of speaking...yes," the tech replied. "Think of it this way. When you're in a particular...scenario, you can read situations better, see them in a way you've never seen before. The ultimate battle edge. *Clarity*."

Brig stopped and bowed his head in thought. "And I signed up for this experiment...*when?*"

The tech choked back a partial laugh as he pulled up Brig's sleeve and swabbed his upper arm with alcohol. "When you signed on the dotted line to become an EW..."

Brig knew the tech was right, and if this meant that he would be an even more efficient soldier, who was he to argue with the brass?

"Well I guess I've been through worse – one shot isn't gonna' kill me, *right?*" Brig jabbed.

As the tech held the needle to Brig's upper arm and fired the first payload into him, he snorted again. "One today. But you'll be coming back every week for twelve weeks to finish the program."

"Are all the EWs getting these shots?" Brig said, looking down and bracing for the second payload.

"Don't flex..." the technician instructed, as if it were just part of the conversation. "*All* of your squadron will get them in time," he responded, as the second payload jetted into Brig's arm. "We're doing them in batches of twelve, and you're the *first* group to go..."

"Lucky me," Brig said sarcastically.

The tech pulled away the needle and wiped Brig's arm. Brig flexed his arm a few times, massaged it vigorously and then stood up from the exam table.

"You'll thank me later..." the tech bragged, placing the empty syringe back into its case. "See you next week, Captain."

Present day (2084)...

The masked man sat like a silent shadow at the edge of the thin cluster of woods, his back to the small collection of trees that provided him cover. He focused his gaze at the house 100 meters down a slight embankment nestled in between several others on a rural cul-de-sac.

Most of the houses had no windows, broken windows or boards where windows once were. The lawns were in such a state of neglect that it was obvious that most of them were vacant, long since abandoned by their owners during a time of crisis.

One home stood out, however. It was set back a small distance from the others at the head of the street and had rod iron fencing that encircled the entire estate. A large, tarnished brass 'F' embellished the entrance gates, which sat in the middle and connected both ends of the fencing. One of the doorways was propped open just enough to allow a smaller-sized adult admittance. This was not a welcome feature for the estate, but one born of necessity since the electronic locking mechanism ceased to work years ago.

The feature that set this house apart from the others, however, was that it appeared occupied. A small amount of light crept its way out from around the edges of the inside window coverings. Every hour or so, another light would go on, albeit very briefly, in another part of the house – but only on the first floor.

From his vantage point, the man had a perfect, panoramic view of the property, one that could afford him the opportunity to see anyone entering or exiting the front or side doors. Additionally, he could detect anyone approaching or leaving the premises via any portion of the fence or driveway that stretched from the front gate, and ended in a large garage at the back portion of the home.

A light on the back corner of the house popped on. The man leaned forward and pressed his eye against the scope of his tripod-mounted rifle.

"Can't see a damn thing through those shades," he muttered. He leaned back once again against a larger tree in front of which he had encamped himself, and then took a large bite from an apple.

After another fruitless hour of watching, the man rose to his feet and stretched his arms over his head, interlocking his hands and exuding a silent yawn, all while keeping one eye on the estate below.

Suddenly, a faint sound like the snapping of a small twig echoing from within the trees behind him snatched his attention. He quickly flattened himself against the tree and peeked out around one side towards the darkness of the woods.

Despite the glow of the moon that trickled from between the gaps of the trees and created a soft glow, he could not discern any movement within, or any interruption of the group of shadows cast out onto the floor of the woods.

"Imagination..." he whispered, squinting into the pitch, as his eyes fluttered side-to-side.

He turned around. The house had become completely dark.

Good, bedtime. I could use a little shut eye... he thought.

Then, something caught his eye; a silvery glimmer peeking out from underneath the overhang of the front porch of the large house.

He leapt to his observation spot, quickly got to one knee and peered into the scope, his finger gently locating the trigger of the rifle.

He was ready. The moment had arrived for his target to come out into the open. However, to his surprise, it was not his *target* that he saw.

12:
Primal Scream

The night was cool. A blunt chill rode the air and the full moon beamed a blue haze across the plain. In the distance, a coyote howled a welcome to its lunar friend, as a placid breeze rustled through the tall wisps of grass out in the clearing.

In the center of that clearing, a lion lay on his side, wounded and oozing blood from his mouth and back. His breath was shallow and labored, and his chest rose very slowly every few seconds, as the great beast stared forward with his eyes nearly closed. A meter away laid another animal, of what type the lion could not discern, but it appeared freshly dead despite the fact that the plains' scavengers had already gotten to the carcass.

Next to the lion stood a tiger, his head cocked downward at the lion as he cautiously sniffed the fallen animal. Not sensing a threat, the tiger turned his head and grumbled in the direction of a small grouping of trees just beyond the clearing.

Answering the call almost immediately, a tigress, somewhat smaller in stature than her mate, trotted from the tree cover and made her way towards the other two animals.

The tigress approached the pair and saw the prone lion, slowed her gait and came to a halt a few steps behind the tiger. She stretched her neck outward to the lion and took a few investigative sniffs, emanating a throaty growl as if to voice her concern to the tiger.

The tiger responded with his own closed-mouth groan, rotating his head towards the lion and jabbing him several times in the side with one of his enormous paws.

The lion did not react. He continued to lie still, only emitting a low, pitiful rumble after a few additional jabs from the tiger.

The lion knew his fate. He *knew* he was dying. He lacked the energy to simply pick himself up and find an isolated spot to pass, and certainly did not have enough to pick a fight with two hungry tigers, even if it was merely a defensive move.

He was still the king of the jungle, and he had hoped that the tiger and his tigress would leave him be out of respect. He had also hoped that the dead beast lying next to him would have provided an adequate feast for the pair. However, given the opportunity for fresh meat, the savage animals had no choice. They had now shown too much interest in him. It was becoming apparent that they had succumbed to bloodlust and were waiting around for his demise, or were planning to make the kill themselves.

However, it did not matter. The lion had nothing left in him for this fight.

The tiger swiped a few more times at the lion's side, growling heartily after each contact. Behind him, his mate began to purr with the relish of the possibility of eating well tonight. As the lion let out another guttural groan, the tiger ran his massive tongue over the lion's back wound. The lion flinched, blinked his eyes several times and then shut them tightly.

The end was near. The tiger had tasted his blood and was preparing himself for the kill.

As the tiger laid his weighty paw on his prey's back, a small blaze suddenly ignited in the back of the lion's brain. The lion could feel the heat growing moment by moment, until it felt like a torch sitting on the back of his skull. His eyes flickered open with a glint of red, and he stared forward, taking in his surroundings.

He could see the breeze wandering through the grass around him as if it were a slow-moving butterfly. In the distance, he could hear the wind whispering through the trees as if it were a wandering brook. In his mind, he could feel the stiff hair on the neck of the coyote that stood on the hillside a hundred meters or so away, its back arched and its snout shot out towards the sky in a celebratory howl.

Closer to him, he could smell the fear of his predators as they continued to lick their chops in anticipation.

Suddenly the lion leapt to his feet and turned swiftly to face his foes with a hearty snarl, his eyes opened alarmingly wide. The abrupt movement of the lion took the tiger and tigress by surprise, so much that they tumbled backward and onto the ground. The lion set himself into an aggressive stance, his front quarters slightly lower than his rear, and coiled his tail upward into an arch, as he bared his teeth at the pair.

The tiger let out a couple of subdued barks, as he got back to his feet and squared off into his own stance against the lion.

The lion could sense the apprehension of the tiger, as well as the confusion of the tigress now getting back to her feet behind him. It was what the lion was *counting* on, and what he *hoped* to use to gain the upper hand in this fight. Out of the corner of his eye, he could detect a minute twitch in one of the tiger's front paws.

He knew the tiger was getting ready to make a move.

Without hesitation, the lion reared and made two wild swings of his mammoth paw at the tiger. The tiger, taken by surprise again, flinched backward and thrust his own front paws out towards the lion in defense, just barely redirecting the other's massive claws from their intended target.

Seeing a chance to take the offensive, the tiger flung himself across the back of the lion, grabbing his neck with both of his paws, as the two tumbled to the ground. Both beasts roared ferociously as they spun around on the ground, their blood-hot drool spurting from their mouths. Several times the tiger attempted to swipe at the lion's face with an outstretched paw, but each time the lion snapped with his enormous teeth.

Dust spewed into the air as the two tumbled about, forming a strange, pale mist in the moonlight. The sharp odor of animal sweat hung heavily around them. The tigress stood just out of the fray, taking a step towards the two when she thought she saw an opening, but then stepping back abruptly as the ferocity mounted.

The tiger managed to find himself on top of the lion. As he reared back to take a brutal swipe at the lion's head, the lion pushed with all four paws and forcefully tossed the tiger into the weeds three meters away. Clearly dazed, the tiger rolled over onto his paws and tried to stand, but fell dizzily back to the ground.

Roaring her disapproval, the tigress began to advance on the lion, which had just gotten back to his feet.

Spinning the front of his torso at the tigress, the color in his eyes having grown to a crimson glow, the lion opened his gigantic maw to twice the size of the tigress's head. He emitted a titanic roar that thundered off the nearby hillsides.

The tigress recoiled, her ears curled backward in sudden fear. She began to retreat slowly, walking backwards while facing the lion.

The lion once again turned his attention to the tiger, who had now re-established his aggressive stance and appeared ready to make a move on the lion.

It was clear to the lion what the tiger's next move would be. He could see it in the tiger's eyes, he could hear the tiger's pulse increasing in anticipation, and he could sense the sudden tensing of the tiger's hind leg muscles.

As the tiger pounced forward, the lion swiped an enormous, taloned paw with pinpoint precision across the side of the tiger's head like a mallet. The lion's brutal attack ripped open the beast's skull, causing the tiger to recoil off-balance and land awkwardly headfirst against a large rock nearby. The tiger's neck snapped with a nauseating crunch as it fell lifeless to the ground, and a small ooze of blood and brain matter streamed from the open wound on the side of its head.

As the tiger twitched out its remaining life, the lion quickly whirled around to face his remaining foe.

The tigress, alarmed at the dispatch of her mate in such a heinous manner, exuded a whimpering growl as she continued to retreat in reverse. The lion slowly twitched his tail back and forth and glared intently at the tigress, a low rumble emitting from his throat.

More are coming...more are coming... the lion thought. He knew he had to finish her off or she would return with reinforcements.

In a rapid blur of motion, the lion reared onto his back legs and swiped twice at the tigress with a monstrous front paw. The final blow ripped a deep gash across the tigress's neck.

The tigress stumbled backward for a moment, dazed and in shock, as a flow of warm, dark, crimson fluid spewed from her neck onto the ground at her feet. Desperately gasping for precious breath with a sickening gurgle, she pitched forward and collapsed next to her mate, as the thick puddle of blood beneath her quickly stained the other's fur.

The lion, victorious, and once again king of its domain, staggered away to tend to his wounds.

Eleven years prior (2073)...

Steele stared in an intense gaze at the holographic computer image hovering above her desk as she furiously swiped at it. Each finger dove into the three-dimensional model and moved around various formulas and equations. With her other hand she blindly fluxed some of the modified formulas into a set of graphs. Then, shaking her head as she glared at them, scrambled them and started once again.

"Damn..." she cursed to herself.

"Steele, my dear," Bronson cooed from the doorway, leaning in and gently knocking on the door. "Busy?"

"Yes, Daddy," Steele responded curtly without stopping or looking away from her work. "What is it that you need?"

"I can't just drop by to visit my favorite engineer?" Bronson jabbed, pulling a chair from the side of the room up to the front of Steele's desk opposite her, and gracefully sitting down.

"You *never* just drop by, now do you, father?" Steele said sarcastically with a raised eyebrow, looking through her transparent work surface momentarily at Bronson.

Bronson smirked. "You know me too well, dear," he chuckled, as he sat back in his chair. "I wanted to commend you on the latest revision of the projection algorithms. Simply outstanding work."

"Well...thank you," Steele said, curling one side of her mouth upward in thought. "But it's a work in progress, and there's so much more work to be done."

"Ah, that's my modest little flower," Bronson remarked, shaking his head in amazement. "You've already tripled the length of projections out to forty-two months in just your first six months on the job..."

"...Which means I'm a bit behind, so...is this *going* somewhere?" Steele interrupted, swiping a few more numbers around within the holograph.

"I'm not ashamed of the desire to stop and marvel at your accomplishments, my dear," Bronson quipped unabashedly, resting his chin on one palm. "You shouldn't be, either."

"It's amazing you got fourteen months out of these algorithms. They are a bit...lacking," Steele said flatly.

"Well, now Steele," Bronson replied, a more stern tone to his voice, "that is the work of your counterparts. A *little* respect is due. Some of the brightest minds in the field worked on those algorithms."

Steele stopped for a moment and pursed her lips.

"I'm not saying they are lacking intelligence, Daddy. Only that when you get attuned to one way of doing things, you tend to not see it from other perspectives." She paused again. "Sometimes you need to extract yourself and come at it from a different angle...turn it upside down, as it were."

Bronson raised his eyebrows in concession and nodded his head. "Indeed. Can't argue with results..."

"Besides," Steele continued, "I've merely tweaked the existing algorithms. I've already begun work on creating a whole new set – one that will extend the projections out beyond five years. And if we can get the *others* to *properly* modify the simulation program to accommodate the new formulas, we could potentially project well beyond the next century."

"Astonishing...truly astonishing. Bravo, my dear," Bronson applauded.

He stood and made his way around the desk. Leaning forward, he typed a few commands onto the flat, hard surface in front of Steele.

"By the way, if you could take a look at *this* material..." he said, as several folders of images and virtual textbooks appeared at the center of the display.

"And *there* it is..." Steele laughed, sitting back in her chair. "I knew all of this gushing had a purpose."

"Well, dear...I *am* the Director, after all," he quipped in a deadpan tone. "I need for you to look through this material. Study it. There are also some seminars that I would like you to attend on the subject material as well."

Steele leaned forward and expanded one of the textbooks. "This isn't quite in my area of expertise, father," she said reservedly. "Not even my *field*, for that matter."

"But if anyone can make sense of it...even excel at it...that would be *my* girl." Her father stood fully, patted her lightly on the back and began to stride towards the door.

"Is this for the Department?" she quizzed, continuing to browse through the material within the display.

Bronson stopped at the doorway, placed a hand on the doorframe and peered back at Steele.

"Of course, darling. And by the by...no pressure. No one's expecting you to be an expert in this field overnight. But I know *you* won't let me down..." he said as he winked and turned the corner.

Several minutes later...

Bronson exited the turbo lift that had swiftly propelled him 30 floors above his daughter's office to the complex reserved for executive personnel, which in this case was mainly him.

Reaching the end of the massive corridor, he strode swiftly into his office and dropped into the chair behind the desk in seemingly one move. He quickly tapped a few numbers onto his own surface screen with one hand while opening a small drawer beneath his desk.

"Hanley," a voice droned from the speaker, as the image of the Director of the URA SA, portly and somewhat balding, appeared on the screen.

"Good day, William," Bronson said, pulling his hands from the drawer and sitting upright in front of the display. "I'm transmitting the latest mass ejection forecasts right now," he said, his fingers dancing across the surface next to Hanley's image.

"Something *new* that I haven't seen, Fox?" Hanley asked without making eye contact.

"I think you'll be pleasantly surprised, William," Bronson replied furtively, expanding the rotating graphs on his own screen.

Hanley remained silent for a few moments as he examined the data. His eyebrows rose suddenly. "Forty-two months? Am I reading that right?"

Bronson chuckled lightly. "That you are, my dear chap...that you are."

"*Incredible*, Fox. You've bought us a lot of extra time here," Hanley commended, pulling the glasses from atop his nose and rubbing his eyes.

"*She*...has bought us a lot of extra time, William. Let's not forget that," Bronson emphasized, leaning forward at the screen.

"Of course," Hanley replied. "Have these numbers been confirmed using other methods?"

"We ran projections against the past fifty years of live data with the modified algorithm and she's correct almost to the hour for the entire time period."

"Incredible!" Hanley exclaimed, placing the glasses back on the bridge of his nose. "Good work, Fox. Well then, that gives us a more solid timeline to proceed on *Project 42*."

"Indeed it does, William," Bronson replied warmly. "Things are looking up."

"Will Steele be working on that project as well?"

"She will remain...*in the loop*. But I have her working on a couple of other important...*projects* for the department."

"Very good, Bronson. I won't keep you, I know you've got some important deadlines to meet now that we have a clearer timeline," Hanley said, as his image disappeared from the screen.

Bronson once again reached into the desk drawer and pulled out a small, clear cocktail glass, placing it on the desk. With his other hand, he extracted a small, silver flask, smoothly removed the top and filled the glass with a clear liquid.

He sat back in his chair as he sipped the drink and stared pensively at the screen.

13:
Cathedral

Present day (2084)...

The moon continued to shine brightly across the cul-de-sac, its spectral, blue hue shimmering off the asphalt of the road, which had crumbled somewhat with age and lack of use. Long tufts of grass and weeds protruded from the edges of the street. Bushes, at one time manicured regularly, grew wildly from several of the lawns and hung over into the roadway. The empty houses on the street, having fallen into disrepair, gave the impression of a ghost town and not a rural, residential neighborhood.

A dark figure stood just outside of the central estate's entrance gates, taking great care to stay within the shadow cast by the moon onto the rock columns attached to them. With one hand, he traced the outline of the bronze 'F' adorned at the center of the twin, rod iron openings. Beyond the gates, he spied the lightless house. He reached over and gently pushed aside a set of hedges that had grown haphazardly up the side of the pillars. Underneath, he spied a tarnished, brass address plate and quickly recited the number to memory.

He slowly released the hedge limb. A silvery glint coming from the porch of the house twenty meters up from the gate caught his eye. While remaining hidden by the overgrown hedges, he pushed his way closer to the entry and squinted. He opened his eyes wider at the sight of an elderly man sitting in a wheelchair, staring farther down the street. The figure quietly looked behind him. He did not see anyone.

The faint sound of footsteps coming from farther down the road broke the quiet of the sleepy neighborhood. With a quick, silent motion, he dove behind another overgrown bush and waited in anticipation.

After a few moments, the man peeked out from the bushes. Coming towards him from the end of the street was the shadowy outline of a woman.

There she is... he thought.

Steele approached the gates, turned to look over her shoulder and quickly scanned the other properties in the small neighborhood. Feeling relatively certain she was alone and unnoticed, she made a quick turn to the partially open gate and disappeared quickly into it.

The man slowly emerged from the bush and peered around the corner of one of the stone edifices. He purposefully watched the woman trotting up the walk towards the front of the house.

She stopped as she approached the front porch and began talking to the man in the wheelchair. The stranger stood still for a moment, watching the pair converse. The woman then swiftly climbed the stairs of the porch, and both she and the man disappeared into the front door of the house.

The dark figure reached into his jacket, withdrew a handgun and held it down at his side, as he stepped towards the open gate. Reaching in once more, he extracted a small, black silencer adapter. He threaded it onto the end of his weapon, casually glancing around and then peering determinately at the house.

As he put a foot into the opening, a sudden, forceful pull from behind threw him to the asphalt onto his back with a sharp clump. His gun slipped from his grasp and skittered across the pavement, out of his reach.

He instinctively reached with both hands in an attempt to grab his attacker. However, before he could seize the unknown assailant, the other man forced a forearm onto his throat, rearing back with the other fist to make a critical blow.

Looking up, he recognized his attacker.

"*Underwood*...what the Hell are you doing?" he managed with a strained voice.

Clive stopped and instantly released the man, pulling his forearm away from the man's throat and standing upright.

"Danil...I could ask *you* the same thing," Clive replied gruffly, puffing hard for breath and pulling Danil up from the ground with one hand.

Danil brushed himself off and then looked around for his gun. "I am taking care of some business," he said tersely.

"I see that. But what *kind* of business?" Clive asked, staring intently at the shadowy outline of the diminutive Russian.

"*Syndicate* business," Danil barked in a heightened whisper, "and that is all you need to know."

Clive glanced at the house and then back at Danil, and then

over at the gun lying several meters away. "This doesn't look like *Syndicate* business. This looks...*personal.*"

Danil caught the object of Clive's gaze, his gun, and strode over to pick it up. He unlatched the clip, checked the chamber and then pushed the clip back into the bottom of the gun with a solid, metallic clunk. He placed the gun behind his back as he strolled toward Clive, quickly stowing it in-between his shirt and pants at the beltline.

"It does not matter what this looks like," he said sternly in his thick, Russian accent. "I am taking care of a problem. One of *Muldoon's* problems."

Clive grabbed at Danil's jacket as the Russian walked towards the entrance, and pulled him in close. "*Muldoon* doesn't want it taken care of this way. He doesn't *want* the girl hurt," he growled softly into Danil's face.

Danil stared unconvincingly at Clive. "What do *you* know about this girl? Mr. Muldoon did not tell me anybody else was part of this job."

"I know *enough* that *you* aren't supposed to be taking out personal vendettas on her," Clive grumbled, releasing Danil's jacket. He reached around Danil's back and yanked at the gun. "And...I know that *this* wasn't what he asked you to do," he emphasized, holding the gun in front of Danil's face.

Danil calmly plucked the gun from Clive's hand, pulled the clip, ejected a single round from the chamber into his hand and placed them inside his jacket pocket.

He stared over at the house and rubbed at the stubble on his chin. "You are not supposed to be here, Underwood," Danil murmured. "I know *that* much. So I wonder if *you* are up to something as well."

"I'm here at Muldoon's request," Clive said bluntly, tightening his jacket around his neck.

"I do not believe you," Danil replied hesitantly, squinting and tilting his head at Clive. "But then...that is my nature." He faced the house and stared silently for a few minutes. "How do I know that *you* will not just go after the girl instead?" he asked without looking back at Clive.

"Muldoon doesn't have trust issues with *me*," Clive countered slyly. "If you want, we can go and ask him."

Danil continued his pensive gaze at the house a moment longer, and then turned to Clive.

"If you are playing me," Danil grumbled, pointing his finger angrily into Clive's chest, "I will not only take care of the little bitch, but I will kill you, too."

Turning his back on the house, and Clive, Danil quickly departed into the night.

Clive glanced curiously at the front window of the house, its small bit of light trickling out from around the shade, shoved his hands into his pockets and walked away.

One of the two large, ornate, oak doors creaked open slowly. The blue shaft of moonlight flowed forward onto the floor from the outside, carrying with it the dark outline of a man's shadow.

Brig stumbled into the dimly lit room and fell with a groan against the wall next to a table holding several small, lit candles. Despite the cool air outside and the visible breath coming from his mouth, sweat dripped steadily from the stringy hair that hung down in front of his face, pooling onto the floor beneath his feet.

The door shut with a thump behind him, magnifying the close silence inside the building. He could hear the faint flicker of the candle flames next to him as well as across the other side of the room. A larger table of candles sat opposite from where he leaned, a small handful of them lit, their flames dancing solemnly in the darkness. A basin, with a small bust of a woman attached to it, adorned the wall next to the doors.

Brig rubbed his eyes and pushed himself upright. He could see faint light trailing in from the room just to the left of where he stood, and began to make his way towards it, still holding onto the wall for balance.

He turned the corner and propped himself up against the doorframe. He had entered a church.

The sanctuary, also lit only by flame, was brighter than the vestibule that he had just come through. The main aisle led up the center of two sections of dark, oaken pews, twenty rows in all. Ornate lanterns hung from the walls on the outside sections of the pews every fourth row, the flickering of their flames casting moving shadows on the wall behind them.

13: CATHEDRAL

Brig slowly staggered up the center aisle, holding on to the end of each pew as he passed. The walls, divided into sections of stained glass with colorful pictures on each, composed a grand mural.

The moonlight filtering in from behind the glass, coupled with the gently slithering light from the lanterns, created an eerie, three-dimensional effect that made the murals seem to come to life, silently writhing back and forth. Brig's throbbing headache did nothing to make the odd sight any easier to witness.

Depicted in each section of the stained glass murals were large groups of people, most on their knees or having fallen completely, and trampled by others. Some of the people appeared to be blind, either grasping out desperately with both eyes closed or wearing some sort of small, cloth blindfold across their eyes.

Portions of the other scenes illustrated the masses with their arms and hands madly outstretched forward, some holding small babies or children aloft above the crowd around them, almost seeming to be offering them up to the heavens. The commonality, however, was that all were portrayed with their mouths open, as if lamenting their plight and clamoring to be heard.

Both murals led forward to the front of the sanctuary and, where the stained glass ended, they continued, becoming paintings on the solid wall nearest the head of the room.

On the center wall behind the altar stood an enormous, full-length section of stained glass that visually divided the area into two sections. The image on the glass was that of the Christ in robes, his hands held out and downwards, with palms facing out towards the throngs around him to each side. His head tilted slightly upwards with sympathetic eyes peered at the heavens, as a single tear rolled down the bare portion of his face.

Brig stood for a moment and absorbed his surroundings. The place was empty. He did not dwell on it for long, but he knew that the presence of the ignited lanterns on the walls and the candles in the vestibule meant that *someone* had to have been here very recently, a caretaker or clergyman perhaps. It did not matter, though, he needed to rest, and he could not have found the solemnity of this church at a better time.

He stumbled into one of the rows of pews midway up the aisle and fell to a sitting position. Brig brushed the hair from in front of his eyes and looked around the sanctuary once again. Then, leaning forward onto the pew in front of him with his elbows, crossed his arms, placed his head on top of them and lost consciousness.

Brig bolted upright, his hair flipping forward around his face, as his arms flailed in reaction.

"Sanctuary...sanctuary..." he called almost incoherently, looking around with a dazed expression.

"Yes, my son," a soothing voice responded with a modest, comforting chuckle.

A tall, slender man 30 years his senior, stood next to Brig with one hand on his shoulder. He was dressed in blue jeans and a light jacket, which opened part way at the top. Within the opening of the top of the jacket, Brig could see a white strip wrapped underneath the man's shirt collar.

"Oh...sorry, *Father*..." Brig sighed, pulling a clump of hair backward over his ears.

"It's ok, son. You're right, there *is* sanctuary here. You're safe," the priest said reassuringly, staring at the deep scratch marks on the side of Brig's face that led down his neck to his shoulder.

"I...I didn't mean to fall asleep. I just needed a moment to rest," Brig said apologetically. "I'll go," he mumbled, as he began to get to his feet.

"*Please*," the priest responded, gently forcing Brig back to a sitting position with the hand still on Brig's shoulder. "You need your rest, and as you can see," he said, holding out his other hand towards the emptiness of the chapel, "you're not bothering anyone else here."

Brig sat back and closed his eyes. "I guess business has been better, huh Father?"

"Yes," the priest replied with a sigh. "That's true. But we'll always keep our doors open even if many have gone away." He leaned over and looked at Brig's face. "Are you sure you're ok, son?"

"The world isn't such a nice place, Father," Brig remarked gruffly, grasping and gently massaging the area around his right shoulder.

The priest nodded his head in agreement. "That's seems to be a common feeling anymore, I'm afraid." He sat down next to Brig and peered at the empty pews. "At a time when it's needed most, the world seems to have lost its faith." He faced Brig again. "What's your name, son?"

Brig leaned against the pew in front of him. "Brigadier," he responded softly.

"Ah, a '*leader of men*'," the priest said thoughtfully. "Yet even the *leaders* sometimes need guidance," he said, gazing forward at the altar.

Brig did not say anything, choosing instead to stare down at the floor, closing his eyes every few seconds to shake off the buzzing in his brain.

The priest, smiling broadly at Brig, rested on his elbows alongside of him. "You know, a lot of my congregation…" he began, and then stopped to chuckle, as he glanced around briefly once again, "…well, a lot of what *used* to be this congregation… would come here looking for *The* answer. The Light…the Almighty Hand to help pull them from the depths surrounding them. When they would find that I couldn't provide that for them, at least not in the way they anticipated, they would move on." He paused in thought. "Many times to head down the wrong path."

The priest beamed warmly at Brig, placing a strong hand on his other shoulder. "When far too often the Light…the guidance that they so desired…was *within* them."

Pushing himself upright, the priest stepped out from the row, and into the center aisle, and then faced Brig.

"I've got some bandages and medicine that might just help take the sting out of those cuts. I'll be right back," the priest said. He strode quietly to a door located in an alcove just off to the side of the front of the sanctuary.

Alone once more, Brig peered up and gazed intently at the mural in front of him.

After a few moments, the priest re-emerged from the door holding a small, wooden box in his hands. He extracted a spool of white, gauze bandages from the half-open box with one hand while precariously balancing it with the other.

"It hadn't struck me right away, but Brigadier is a *very* uncommon name," he said, putting the spool under his arm and continuing to dig around in the box, walking back to the center aisle. "I believe the President's son's name is…was…Brigadier, wasn't it?"

Brig had gone.

The priest stared down the center aisle and out at the vestibule. One of the large doors had just swung shut, closing out the small stream of moonlight that had seeped in from outside.

The priest placed the gauze back into the wooden box and closed it with a soft clunk. "Lord, help *him* find the inner strength he needs," he said softly, gazing on at the empty sanctuary.

14:
No Quarter

Present day (2084)...

Bruno Muldoon gazed out at the empty road that led past the hotel that housed his headquarters. From his perch on the 22nd floor, he could survey the massive, panoramic view of what was once a busy thoroughfare packed with cars, both retro and the newer magnetic types (of which the old Las Vegas was one of the pioneering cities to have).

He had chosen this spot not only for its view, since it offered great visibility of any intruders that might be approaching, but also because it was one of the few larger buildings left standing over the years. Additionally, it offered the grandiose image that he had always wanted to convey to enemies and allies alike. Many other hotels in the area had either been burned or had fallen into such disrepair that it made using them as any sort of base virtually impossible.

Some husks of burned-out cars still littered the sides of the main road. Most had since been removed and stripped for parts, either for other retro-cars or bartering purposes. Scrub grass and small desert foliage poked up around the ones that remained, as well as along the curbs. The solid, smooth asphalt that had once lined the road was now cracked and pitted from the extreme weather and lack of maintenance, partially exposing the looted magnetic rail systems, once used underneath the roads to control the cars that traveled on them.

There were still some signs of life, however. Lining the main road were several rows of small buildings, formerly busy strip malls, but now used as homes for the small population that still lived in the area. Every now and again, Muldoon could spot a resident, much like an ant from his perspective, walking either from one building to another, or heading over to the main road to the Syndicate food bank, which they created to provide for the people that wished to stay.

Nothing was free for anyone, however. There was *always* a price to pay to the Syndicate.

A loud, crashing noise from inside of the room shattered Muldoon's pensive gaze. He glared inside from the balcony. The hulking shape of Pollux exploded through the door from the hallway and into the room.

In front of the gargantuan, grasped within one of his mammoth hands, was a smaller man with a darker complexion and close-shaved hair. Pollux thrust the man into the room, his massive strength and tight grip on the man's neck making the man wince and flail his arms around at his sides.

With his free hand, Pollux seized a nearby chair and dropped it to the floor with a thud. Within the same fluid motion, he forcefully tossed the man into the chair.

"Got a present for you, boss," Pollux grumbled.

"Pollux," Muldoon hissed, making his way into the room from the balcony, "how many times have I told you to be a little easier on the doors around here. Materials aren't that easy to come by, and I don't really want to have to move again due to your proclivity for a grand entrance."

"Sorry, boss," Pollux said dully, lowering his head in shame, as he stood with his arms crossed behind the man.

Muldoon rolled his eyes and turned his focus to the man, who was now rubbing his neck where Pollux had his death grip just seconds earlier. "And who is this?"

Pollux grasped one of the man's shoulders with one hand and squeezed tightly, causing the man to open his mouth in a silent scream. "Caught him breakin' into one of your warehouses, boss."

"The *same* warehouse as the other break-in?" Muldoon quizzed with a raised eyebrow.

"Yeah," Pollux droned, releasing the man's shoulder.

Muldoon stood and silently stared down at the man with an intense glare. "And what did he steal?" he said, stroking his goatee pensively between a forefinger and thumb.

"Nothin'. The guards there caught him tryin' to jimmy one of the office locks and stopped him before he got anything," Pollux replied, eyeballing the man with a scowl.

"And just what were you after, friend?" Muldoon asked the man, squatting to look into his face.

The man looked past Muldoon without responding. He tightly

compressed his lips and fixated his gaze on the blue sky visible through the French doors of the balcony.

Muldoon chortled softly and stood up. "Castor," he called to the partially open door.

The other Webb twin, Castor, quickly appeared inside the doorframe. Although twins with Pollux, he was significantly smaller in stature than his brother, but still massive in comparison to the average person. Castor's strength, however, was his intelligence. Not that either of them were very bright, his intelligence far outshined that of Pollux.

"Yeah, boss," he grunted.

Taking a few steps towards the door, Muldoon lowered his voice as he spoke to Castor. "Find out what's in that warehouse that keeps getting broken into, immediately."

"You got it, boss," Castor said enthusiastically, turning to stroll back into the hallway.

"And Castor," Muldoon snarled through gritted teeth, causing the lesser behemoth to stop in his tracks. "Find out where the *Hell* the Russian is..."

Castor nodded silently and left the room.

Muldoon straightened his posture and flipped his long hair towards the back of his head with one hand, as he faced Pollux and the seated man.

"Now... where were we?" Muldoon approached the back of the man's chair. "Ah, yes. *You* were just about to tell me what you were doing in *my* warehouse." He grabbed another chair and set it down backwards in the direct line of the man's gaze at the balcony. Muldoon sat with his legs straddled around the chair back and rested his head on his folded arms. "Hmmm?" he cooed.

The man remained silent, blinking and sighing heavily as if shaking off frustration, and then once again gazed beyond Muldoon at another part of the room.

Muldoon smiled coyly at Pollux and then glared back at the man.

"Silent type, yeah? You're in no danger here, friend. Just tell me what you were after. Hell, I might even be able to help. If you're in need...a service or something, maybe we can come to an... arrangement? Something to resolve this silly...misunderstanding?" Muldoon asked while tilting his head.

Again, the man said nothing. Instead, he continued to find anything in the room other than Muldoon at which to look.

Muldoon arose from his chair, placed it gently back under the dining table two meters away and began to slowly pace in front of the man.

"We can go at this all day if you want, my friend," he told the man dryly, stopping every so often and glancing at him, hoping to catch his gaze. "Why don't you just open up and we can get this over with, and both go on about our business, aye?" He stopped in front of the man.

The man breathed heavily in exasperation and rolled his eyes.

Muldoon slowly glanced at Pollux with a flat expression, and then without warning, reared back and delivered a sharp backhand across the man's jaw.

The man recoiled, almost falling off the chair, but then gathered himself and sat back once again. A small trickle of blood oozed from the corner of his mouth, which curled up in a defiant smirk.

"Insolence," Muldoon growled, rubbing the back of his hand across his own cheek. "I've had enough of it. I bring you here as a guest in my hotel and you sit in silence when I try to have a civil conversation with you?" He placed a hand on the back of the man's neck, gripped it tightly and forced the man to look into his face. "I suggest you start talking, friend, because this conversation goes downhill from here..."

The man stared at Muldoon for a moment, then spit a small glob of blood and saliva into his face.

Muldoon released the man's neck, stood and casually wiped his cheek with one of his sleeves while staring intently at him, shaking his head slowly in disbelief. His mocking grin faded as he turned his back on the man. Muldoon ran his hands through his slick hair. Then, spinning around quickly, he delivered two more backhands to the man's face.

Instead of recoiling, the man turned his head away at the force of the impact and then back to face Muldoon once more. He chuckled as the blood started to flow from his mouth.

Muldoon's face became crimson with infuriated anger as his jaw tensed. "Funny? He thinks this is funny, Pollux."

Pollux looked on at the exchange with interest.

"Can I make him laugh now, Mr. Muldoon?" Pollux said, pounding a fist into the other. His hulking shoulders strained at the edges of his sport coat as he stepped to the side of the man's chair.

"That won't be necessary, Pollux," Muldoon responded, holding up a hand to stop the big man from advancing farther.

"But," he said, leaning over once more to glare into the man's face, "since this one won't talk, I think I've figured out the perfect punishment. Pollux – hold his head for me..."

Pollux grabbed the man's head between his giant hands, which prevented the man from being able to move on his own without the fear of his neck being snapped in two.

Muldoon opened the top drawer of a nearby desk and extracted a large Bowie knife, its deadly, speared tip glinting in the overhead lighting in contrast to its dark, leather handle.

He strolled slowly towards the man, holding the knife out in front of his face and pricking the tip with one of his fingers. The level of alarm in the man's face rose suddenly. Muldoon stopped in front of the man, leaned over and grabbed his chin with one hand.

"Grab his tongue for me..." Muldoon ordered with an evil grin.

Pollux quickly stuffed a thumb and forefinger into the man's mouth, no small feat as one of his hands could palm the man's head entirely, and forced his tongue out between them. Muldoon grasped the meaty flesh from Pollux and stretched it forward more, causing the man to tense, his eyes watering profusely. He laid the blade of his knife at an angle to the man's tongue.

"You won't talk for me? Then you won't talk for anyone..." Muldoon snarled.

"Ok! Ok!" the man managed to scream, just as Muldoon had started to press on his tongue with the knife, lifting a small flap of skin that instantly started oozing bright, red blood in the process.

"Ah, pressure points," Muldoon said dryly, as he stood and wiped the bloody saliva from the knife blade. "Start talking..."

"This isn't about the warehouse..." the man uttered, his head still tightly in the grasp of Pollux.

"No? It sure *seems* about the warehouse," Muldoon responded sarcastically. "But pray tell what *is* it about then?" He made a quick, silent motion towards Pollux, who then immediately released the man's head.

The man sneered at Pollux, and then spat a glob of red saliva at his feet.

"The Syndicate's going down..." the man began, quickly facing Muldoon again.

"Really?" Muldoon began to cackle, waving his hand at the man, as if to dismiss the thought. "*This* is what I'm wasting my time on today. And I suppose *you* are man that's going to 'bring us down', right?" He faced Pollux. "Get this idiot out of my sight."

Pollux grunted, and then lifted the man from the chair by his collar. With his legs dangling a meter in the air, the man screamed as Pollux started towards the door.

"This isn't a joke!" the man yelled desperately, small droplets of bloody saliva dripping wildly from his mouth. "The Reformation is real...and we have backing!"

Muldoon stopped abruptly. He spun to meet the gaze of the panicked thief.

"Reformation? Ha!" he crowed. "How European and grandiose. How could I ever have doubted you, my friend." He quickly motioned again to Pollux, who swiftly dropped the man, causing him to fall awkwardly to the floor. Muldoon approached the man and bent to one knee near his face.

"You and your pub mates know nothing of the Reformation," Muldoon said arrogantly while shaking his head. "So what is it. Extortion? Trying to get a little 'piece of the action' from my organization is it?"

The man, on all fours as he stared into Muldoon's eyes for the first time, lowered his tone. "The Reformation is real. And we're going to take it all back from you."

Muldoon bent his neck backward and howled loudly. "Take it back? My friend, what *exactly* is the *Reformation* going take back from me? The desert? The irradiated shores of Manhattan Bay? Or what... any one of the hundreds of ghost towns across this continent that have arisen over the years?"

The man fell silent. He stared at Muldoon with disdain, squinting and curling his mouth into a sneer at one corner.

Muldoon grabbed the back of the man's neck again and pulled his face closer to his own.

"Let me tell *you* something. The Syndicate has single-handedly brought civilization back from the brink of extinction. We've got control of over twenty major cities and each of those cities has some sort of power or another. We've set up food banks and offer people a chance to make a living – something that just wasn't going to happen on its own," Muldoon growled.

"Call it what you want..." the man snarled, "...but we know who you *really* are. You're nothing but a common criminal, and you rule with fear and intimidation. And we're here to stop you..."

"*Stop* me?" Muldoon stood and stared down at the man. "I don't think that's being realistic. But let me show you," he told the man.

Muldoon grabbed the back of the man's collar and dragged him to one side of the room, dropping him in front of a closed door. The Syndicate boss pulled a set of keys from his suit pocket and quickly unlocked the door, swung it open and held out one arm with an outstretched palm. "After you..."

The man hesitated for a moment, staring up at Muldoon from a sitting position on the floor and then back at Pollux, who was still standing across the room with a stern, but amused, expression and his arms crossed.

"What's this..." the man asked Muldoon, turning his focus to the open doorway.

"Proof of what kind of power I...the Syndicate...has. Just to assure you that I'm not afraid of the Reformation," Muldoon droned, gritting his teeth in obvious annoyance.

The man stood and brushed himself off as he glared at Pollux. He cautiously stepped past Muldoon into the other room. Muldoon waited for the man to enter the room fully, then followed him in and closed the door behind them.

A few moments passed silently before the door suddenly burst open. The man, a stupefied look on his face, came stumbling from the doorway and back into the hotel room.

As he turned to run towards the main door, he bounced off Pollux, who had positioned himself in front of the doorway, and fell immediately backward onto the floor. Muldoon casually strolled out of the other room and closed it behind him, locking it quickly and stowing the keys back in his pocket.

"You... you're a crazy son of a bitch!" the man cried, pushing himself backward against the wall.

"Crazy? No. Just determined. And maybe you and your...pub buddies...will think twice about pulling something like this again," Muldoon said matter-of-factly. "You see, Mr....Whatever-your-name-is, I don't care..." He knelt down in front of the thief. "...unlike your 'common criminal', we have a code that we live by. You know the one...an eye for an eye."

The man pressed himself against the wall harder. His eyes grew in size, as they twitched back and forth between Muldoon and Pollux, who had contorted his large face to display a semi-toothless, evil grin.

"But I guess we'll have to make an exception this time, eh, Pollux?" Muldoon said over his shoulder without looking away from the man. "After all, he didn't really steal anything, so I can't

R. JAMES STEVENS

punish him for that. Besides, I think he's learned his lesson about breaking into places and trying to take what isn't his, hasn't he?"

The man breathed a short sigh of relief and relaxed his shoulders against the wall.

"But as for the doubts of who *I* am and what *I* can do," Muldoon hissed. He clutched his hand around the man's neck, causing him to turn reddish-purple and gasp for breath. "I think it's time that our guest here sees the light."

Danil walked the long hallway towards Bruno Muldoon's room, a lair by any other definition for sure, and one to which he despised coming. As he approached the door, the familiar, hulking form of Castor Webb filled the doorway, his arms crossed and a stone-like expression on his face. Castor rotated his head slowly to look at Danil.

"Good timing, Ruskie. I was just comin' to look for you, and that wasn't gonna' be pretty," Castor growled. He unfolded his arms and slammed Danil against the wall for his routine weapons search. "The boss has been waitin' for you for a couplea' days now, where ya' been?"

"Mr. Castor," Danil muttered with his face flat to the wall, "I had to go out of town to get the information that Mr. Muldoon wanted, and that takes time..."

"Don't care," Castor said flatly, grabbing Danil by one shoulder and pulling him away from the wall. "All I know is the boss don't like to be kept waiting, so you better have somethin' damn good to tell him," he scolded, pointing a finger in Danil's face.

Danil nodded as Castor led him to the doorway, opened the door and pushed him inside.

"Oh my God! The sun...it burns!" the thief cried. Pollux gripped the man's arms behind his back with one hand, forced his face upwards with the other and led him out onto the balcony overlooking the grand entrance to the hotel below. "Please! I'll do anything... just take me back inside!"

"Honestly," Muldoon quipped haughtily, "I had more respect for you when you wanted to keep your mouth shut. At least you had your convictions. Now you're just embarrassing yourself."

The man jerked his shoulders in an effort to free himself from Pollux's grasp, but it was futile – the giant had a death grip on his neck.

The thief's eyes bulged from their sockets as they twitched back and forth to avoid the extreme brightness and heat generated by the midday sun. Bright, fresh, warm streams of blood trickled down the man's face from his eyes where his eyelids had once been.

Muldoon stepped up next to the man and casually leaned one elbow on the railing as he spoke, absentmindedly flicking his fingernails. "Very tough way to learn a lesson, my friend. I hope your *friends* are a bit wiser. Pollux, release him."

The man, confused in his horror, snapped his head to the side to look at Muldoon. "Thank you..." he sobbed, bowing his head and watching the blood dribble off his face and onto the floor of the balcony.

To his surprise, however, Muldoon bent down and grabbed the man's feet, thrusting the thief forward and over the railing.

The man let out a shriek of terror as he plummeted from the balcony and landed on the concrete below seconds later with a reverberating thump.

Muldoon turned from the balcony and strode back inside. "Reformation..." he muttered, shaking his head in disgust.

He and Pollux stepped into the room and adjusted their eyes to the relative darkness within. The shadowy form of Danil, standing just in front of the lesser, but still massive in comparison, figure of Castor, met them.

"Mr. Chekushkin, you're late. I hope for your sake that you've got what I asked for. I'd hate to see your day end like some others," Muldoon said flatly, motioning with one hand at the balcony. "And Pollux," he said glancing over his shoulder at the giant, "...go clean up that mess."

Pollux, his eyes widened for a moment, gulped and then nodded his head in submission. "You got it, boss."

R. JAMES STEVENS

15:
Enter Sandman

Present day (2084)...

Steele opened one eye and stared across the room. The hint of moonlight cast onto the far wall, and even through her blurry vision, it seemed dimmer than usual, given how bright the moon had been before she had gone to sleep just a few hours prior. She opened her other eye and propped herself up with one hand. She rubbed her eyes with the other hand and squinted at the point on the wall where the moonlight shone with a dull hue.

She swept her long hair back out of her face with both hands as she let out a light yawn, stood up from the bed and staggered to the window. The reddish haze dimly illuminating the room made her pause before opening the curtain.

Steele pulled open one of the curtains and cautiously peered outside, half-expecting to find someone looking in.

She did not see anyone.

Instead, she found what would be there on any other night – a small, empty side yard leading up to the next building six meters away. She pressed her face sideways against the glass and glanced to the left towards the road. Even with the very dim street lighting, she could tell that no one was there. The same was true for the other direction, which was a bit darker, but nothing stood out as odd to her.

The appearance of the sky, however, bordered on the bizarre.

It was a very clear night with a large, full moon. The moon was no longer bright as it had been hours before, but rather a dark shade of crimson. She stared dumbfounded at it for what seemed like a solid ten minutes, unable to comprehend the strange sight.

"Not a Harvest Moon, it's February," she whispered aloud.

A sound from beyond the closed door behind her brought her attention back to her bedroom. She turned her head sharply and listened in silence. From the hallway just on the other side of the door, she heard people, multiple people, talking in low murmurs as they passed back and forth. The small amount of light seeping under the door flickered as shadows moved left and right along with the sounds.

Her heart sank. A brisk chill traveled her spine until it made the smaller hairs on the back of her neck stand at attention. There were very few people in this apartment complex, and none on this floor. Worse was that she was sure she had latched all of the security locks on the door leading outside.

Oh bollocks, she thought, reaching under her bed, extracting a small, wooden cricket bat and creeping barefoot across the hardwood floor. She stopped next to the closed bedroom door, pressing her ear against it.

The sounds from the other side had stopped. She looked down at the floor. The light under the door had grown steady.

Her heart began to race. She placed one shaky hand on the doorknob and tightly gripped the bat in the other. The doorknob creaked faintly as she turned it and gently pulled the door open inward. Steele peeked through the cracked doorway at the short hallway outside of her bedroom.

The lighting was dull, and the hall, as well as the living room beyond, was empty. She paused and listened intently.

Silence.

Feeling relieved, and more confident, she quietly opened the door enough to squeeze through.

The door slid shut behind her as she entered the hallway. She spun abruptly to stare at it in confusion, the buzzing sound of the electro-lock latching reverberating off the walls around her.

Before she could comprehend the latest oddity, the sound of voices once again caught her attention. She turned quickly and found herself standing in a large corridor filled with people walking back and forth. Some of them ducked into and out of other rooms, while others turned corners and disappeared into intersecting hallways.

Steele ran a hand over her bare scalp, the stubble prickling at her fingertips, as her hand finally rested on a spot at the base of her skull that stung like a carpet burn. She winced as she rubbed the sore and glanced around at the people moving about. They were not people that she recognized, yet something seemed oddly familiar about them.

As she stepped into the center of the corridor and faced one end, several of the people stopped and recoiled in horror. Their eyes bulged as they covered their gaping mouths with the palms of their hands.

Steele's eyes curiously darted back and forth between the strangers. Their whispers filled the hallway and echoed so loudly that it forced Steele to clamp her hands over her ears. She frantically ran to one of the corridor intersections. Glancing over her shoulder as she reached the corner, she uncovered her ears and slowed to a fast walk.

The people had vanished.

Aside from the walls, which remained their familiar shade of crimson, her surroundings had faded to black and white.

Once again, she found herself in the grand lobby of the URA Security Alliance mega-complex, a place with which she was very familiar. She had spent much of her adult life either working here or visiting her father in his office 30 floors above.

The URA SA logo, the valiant, screaming eagle emblazoned on the wall above her, spread its massive wings half the span of the entire wall itself. The stars that normally should have been above its massive head were absent, however, with the only trace of them being one single star gnashed within the beak of the great bird. Imprinted in black ink on the giant gold ribbon below the logo were the words 'In Reliquias Erit Peribit'.

She stepped slowly into the center of the lobby and stared at the majestic eagle. The bird's eyes strangely followed her steps. She stopped and focused on the eyes, but what she thought was movement was simply a glare from something else in the room.

The twinkling glow of an LED surface display, below the grand logo and mounted on a desk, reflected off the metal portion of the eagle above it.

The display drew Steele in as a moth to flame. Through the transparent surface, the reversed images of a set of schematics performed a mesmerizing dance that lit her face. The word 'Diversion' sprawled across her forehead.

She softly ran her fingers across the backside of the display. Although it could not offer the tactile feel and control that the main, front surface would, it was almost as if she could *feel* the data projected on the other side. She felt one with the data and even though she had no idea of its importance, she knew it fulfilled some primal need in her.

Steele slowly rounded the corner of the desk and started to lean in to read the display.

Someone grasped at her arm.

"Ma'am, you shouldn't *be* here," a gruff voice commanded from behind her.

She was forcefully spun around.

A burly security guard stood next to her with a tight grip around her upper arm, his other tattooed arm pointing a finger to the corridor that she had just exited.

"But... I... I... *work* here," Steele whimpered in bewilderment, futilely trying to release herself from the man's grasp, her free arm swinging about and knocking a glass vase from the desk.

The single silk flower drifted onto the floor and came to rest atop the shards of the shattered glass vase. The flower's gray coloring flushed to the same crimson of the walls.

Steele desperately scanned the rest of the lobby, hoping to find someone that could vouch for her identity. The room was oddly empty of people except for her and the security guard.

"Please...help me!" a man's voice pleaded from behind her.

Steele spun around once again.

The security guard, still holding her arm tightly, was now sitting in a wheelchair. A single tear splashed down one of his gaunt cheeks, as he pitifully looked at her, dazed and despondent.

She managed to free herself from his grasp and backed up a few steps. The man continued to attempt to tug at her sleeve, but Steele kept slinging her arm just out of his reach.

The man stared maniacally at her right hand, as he wildly grasped at it.

She glanced down. A coiled adder, its tongue flicking pensively, sat in her outstretched hand. Steele puzzled at the sight for a brief second and then flinched, thrusting it onto the floor. The snake exploded into several small lengths, its glowing, blue blood spurting from one section and splashing onto her lab coat.

"*Save yourself!*" she cried involuntarily. She was not sure why she said it, nor its meaning, but she turned quickly from the man and ran to an open doorway just beyond the lobby.

She reached the doorway, turned and gawked over her shoulder.

The guard, too, had vanished.

Steele grasped the frame of the open doorway, closed her eyes and took a deep breath.

The sound of another breath, mimicking hers, immediately interrupted her calm. Her eyes popped open to find a tall, slender stranger standing in front of her, gazing down with a bemused look.

She stared up at the man without blinking, locking eyes with him as they both stood opposite each other. She tilted her head sideways and glared curiously at him.

She *knew* this man.

His facial features seemed distorted and blurry, but she felt akin to him.

The man's mouth curled up on one edge as he stared at her, exuding a soft, haughty chuckle.

"Marvelous," he hissed with glowing, crimson eyes.

He spun on one heel and strode away.

Steele bolted upright in her bed, several beads of sweat weeping from her forehead as she reached a sitting position. She glanced around her room quickly.

"Just a dream..." she whimpered unevenly. She grabbed a larger pillow and held it tightly against her midsection.

Fourteen years prior (2070)...

Danil Chekushkin stood bent over behind the prisoner, breathing heavily into the man's right ear, as he spoke deliberately.

"You can start by telling us what you were doing in Slyudyanka trying to make contact with one of our operatives," Danil said slowly.

The man, a Mongolian, did not answer as he stared forward with a sneer. The cool light of the room reflected off the man's clean-shaven head, where a colorful tattoo of a dragon crawled up his neck and onto the back of his skull. Shackles restrained his wrists to the chair's legs and wrenched his arms backward at a hard angle.

"We are not here to play games with you, my friend, and the outcome of you being silent will not be a pleasant one, I can assure you," Danil offered dryly. He stood up, still eyeing the man.

"You're wasting your time, Russian," the man mumbled under his breath in Mongolian.

Danil, an expert in interrogation, leaned in and whispered into the man's ear. "Do you think I do not know what you are saying? I did not get to my position in the TGB by knowing only one language. Mongolian is but one of seven languages that I can speak," he said in a flawless, Mongolian dialect.

Danil stood and strode past the man, stopping in front of him for an instant, as if in thought. He quickly spun and struck the man with a hard backhand across his cheekbone.

Another operative stood at the far end of the interrogation room next to the door, but did not react to Danil's physical persuasiveness.

The Mongolian recoiled at the hit, but because he was unable to defend himself, he had no recourse but to take the punishment. He stoically turned his face forward and stared at Danil with a contemptuous scowl.

Chekushkin rubbed at his jaw with one hand as he glared at the man. "I do not know why you insist on playing these games, my friend. But I do not wish to waste my time, so I can assure you we will make things very...uncomfortable for you...*and* your family... if you do not start talking." He paused and then landed two more sharp blows across the Mongolian's face, whipping the man's head violently from side to side.

The man grunted as he shook off the brutal attack. "I was visiting my brother..." he sputtered tensely, not making eye contact with Danil.

"You are a liar," Danil quickly retorted, without changing his expression.

"I'm not lying! He's the governor of Irkutsk oblast."

"Your brother is a *cockroach,* and he fled in the face of espionage charges. And took with him state secrets. And now you turn up trying to barter classified information, I do not think it is such a coincidence."

The Mongolian gritted his teeth. "My brother is a proud man, and he was set up."

"More like a proud thief. And a traitor to the Union – for which he will pay dearly, as will *you.*"

"I'll take my chances with the Duma," the Mongolian mumbled, looking away in disgust.

"This is a Directorate matter, the Duma has no say in what happens here." Danil began pacing in front of the man again. "So it is in your best interest...*and* your brother's...to tell us what you know."

The Mongolian sat quietly in deep contemplation, his face contorted with a mixture of anger and sadness. "It is desperate times," he began, his voice cracking, "*you* do not understand destitution..."

"*Destitution,*" Danil interrupted, as he stopped pacing and glared at the Mongolian. "Let me tell *you* about destitution, my friend."

He began his gait once again, this time a bit slower, while his hand rubbed his chin in thought.

"I come from a family of nine siblings," Danil explained. "When I was young, my father sold my mother and two of my sisters into slavery to feed his heroin addiction. That monster claimed his miserable life soon after. The remaining eight of us had to grow up as orphans, no mother, no father, no way to provide for ourselves but what the streets could offer."

Danil stopped and grabbed the side of the Mongolian's head with his palm.

"*That*, my friend, is destitution. But never once did any of us think of betraying our great Union," Danil concluded, glaring coldly into the man's eyes.

Both men turned their heads abruptly as the door to the interrogation room swung open and clanked heavily against the wall.

A well-dressed, clean-cut man entered the doorway and motioned at Danil.

"If you will excuse me, my director would like a word. Do not go anywhere." Danil quickly walked to greet the visitor. The two conversed for a few seconds in hushed tones, while Danil crossed his arms and glared at the Mongolian. The director turned and briskly exited the room.

Danil strolled back to the Mongolian, whispering something in Russian to the other agent standing by the door as he passed. "It appears we have a change in plans. Your brother is now in custody," Danil said flatly.

"My brother doesn't have the data you are looking for, you are again wasting your time!" the Mongolian shouted.

"The classified data is of no concern to us now. Your brother was but a pawn to test his loyalty to the Union – and he failed...*miserably*. The good news...for *you* anyway, is that we have no need for you," he continued, unshackling the Mongolian from the chair.

The Mongolian winced as he flexed his now-free wrists and stared apprehensively at Danil, and then at the other agent, in turn.

Danil did not return the Mongolian's glare. Instead, he turned his back and walked to another door at the other end of the interrogation room. The other agent did not return the look either, standing in place with his arms folded, gazing intently at the opposite wall.

Recognizing his prompt to leave as a free man, the Mongolian stood from the chair and began to make his way towards the exit.

Behind him, Danil quietly spun and faced the departing Mongolian. As he watched the man stride towards the door, he reached into his pocket, extracted a small knife and plunged it into his own shoulder. He gritted his teeth to hold back the violent pain, as he pulled a handgun from inside his jacket pocket and aimed it at the Mongolian's back.

"Tell the governor his plan has failed," Danil said in Russian to the other agent.

Present day (2084)...

Danil stared blankly at Muldoon, as Pollux rushed from the hotel room at his boss's request. "I have some very valuable information, Mr. Muldoon," he said.

"Well...out with it," Muldoon replied impatiently, wiping a streak of blood from his face onto his sleeve.

Danil swallowed audibly, having heard Castor take Pollux's place behind him at the doorway. "We do not know who the girl is yet, sir..."

Muldoon shook his head and rolled his eyes before he closed them. He inhaled a deep breath, damming the swelling tidal wave of anger from within. "And you show up late with this information...or lack thereof...*because*?"

"I took the time to follow her and find out what she was up to," Danil reassured hesitantly. "I think you will find this next piece of information very interesting."

Muldoon turned away from Danil and admired his reflection in the mirror on the wall. He straightened his collar.

"What you and I find interesting are most likely diverse things, Mr. Chekushkin. But please, proceed."

"She has been making late night visits to a Mr. Bronson Fox..."

Muldoon stiffened.

"Fox? Are you certain?" Muldoon interrupted, pivoting his head towards Danil.

"Yes, sir. And what is interesting about this man is that he was..."

"...One of the most brilliant, strategic minds working for the URA. Yes, I *know*," Muldoon added, as he stepped away from the mirror and flipped his hair back over his shoulders. "Curious..." he said aloud in thought.

"You *know* this man, Mr. Muldoon?" Danil quizzed.

"I know *of* him, but I don't *know* him per se. But that's not the important part of this information, Danil. Good job, Mr. Chekushkin. That will be all for now," Muldoon replied, waving a hand blindly in Danil's direction.

"Do you want me to bring in the girl, sir? I am confident I can make her talk," Danil offered, as Muldoon strode past him.

"That won't be necessary, Danil. Without having spoken to her directly, she has already provided me with all of the information I need to know... for now. Castor, show him out," Muldoon muttered, and then sat at a nearby desk, pensively folding his hands under his chin.

Danil stared at Muldoon for a moment, wondering what game this man might be playing with the girl... or *him*. He was no novice to strategy, and it was obvious to him that Muldoon was formulating his next play.

Castor grabbed Danil's upper arm and pulled him.

"No need to get physical, Mr. Cas. I know the way out," Danil said dryly, yanking his arm from the behemoth's grasp.

As Castor watched Danil exit into the hall, Muldoon, now standing behind him, mumbled something inaudible into Castor's ear.

"Sure thing, boss," Castor replied quickly.

"And Castor," Muldoon yelled as Castor approached the door, "tell Krell to bring along Mr. Underwood as backup."

Castor nodded and disappeared into the corridor.

Muldoon walked to the balcony.

"If he insists on anteing up in this game, then let's just see if we can make him show his hand," he muttered aloud, taking his perch and peering out over the desert while stroking the thin goatee on his chin.

R. JAMES STEVENS

16:
Lost and Found

Seven years prior (Early 2077)...

Brig sat in quiet reflection. The glistening condensation from the bottle of beer in his hand found its way down onto the wooden bar, where it left a faint ring.

He leaned back against his chair and absent-mindedly stared up at the television monitor on the wall. The news anchor prattled on about some story or another, whatever it was, Brig had not shown the slightest interest in it. His mind was on his friend, Clive, whom he had not seen in a couple of weeks – not since the last time he was at this very location.

Must be lyin' low, Brig thought, as he gulped his drink and then clunked the bottle back down onto the bar. *Either that or workin' out.*

The last thought made him smile. That was Clive: determined, *and* stubborn. However, it was unusual that he had gone so long without hearing from his former partner. To his own detriment, however, Brig found himself busy lately training new recruits on the finer points of EW strategy.

Either case, I need to talk to him about that email. He's gotta be devastated.

Brig drained the rest of the bottle in one huge swig, arose from his seat and tossed a twenty on the bar.

As he turned, the room spun, and he reeled sideways. He caught himself on the edge of a nearby table, in time to avoid crashing to the floor. Brig stood and rubbed his temples vigorously. He winced at the intense fire that had ignited in his head. The daylight streaming in from the bar windows blinded him, making him see only shadows where other people sat.

"Brig?" said a familiar voice from behind him.

Brig turned, blinked his eyes several times and squinted back at the bar. He could see clearly again.

"Jonas?" he groaned.

Standing up from his barstool on the opposite side of the room was Jonas Slade, a fellow Epsilon. Not nearly Brig's height, and more slender in his build, wore what little hair he had left tightly shaved to his scalp.

"Hey man! You doin' alright?" Jonas approached Brig with a concerned look.

Brig smiled sheepishly at Jonas. "Yeah, I'm... alright. Room just got fuzzy for a second."

"One too many, huh man?" Jonas chuckled, giving Brig a friendly pat on the back.

"Nah, it's not that..." Brig answered with a cringing smile. "Got a weird headache or something there...migraine maybe." Brig shook his head. "What're you up to?"

"Just knocking one back, you know, celebrating..." Jonas said with a knowing nod.

Brig wrinkled his brow, confused. "*Celebrating?*"

"Ah," Jonas laughed nervously, "then you haven't heard yet. I finished my cert and I'm ready for action. I'm your new Crypto Spec, Brig!"

The lack of joy on Brig's face was embarrassingly apparent, his brow still wrinkled as he tightened his lips together.

"That's...great, man. Congrats," Brig said flatly, offering his hand for a celebratory shake, albeit half-heartedly.

Jonas frowned. "You not *happy* with me or somethin'?"

Brig knew that he had given Jonas the wrong impression. He was not upset about the news. He was just so deep in thought about Clive that he let it get past him.

"I'm sorry, Jonas. Really, I'm *super* happy for you, man. You've worked hard, you deserve it, and I can't wait to work with you!" Brig said with a cheerful resonance, pulling Jonas in for a hug.

"Thanks, Brig, I really appreciate it. I've been looking forward to this for a long time." The two men separated and stood opposite one another. "And we're gonna get to work together sooner than you think, we've got..."

Brig shot Jonas a stern look, one that he knew meant Brig wanted him to stop talking immediately, and then subtly shook his head. "Don't talk about *that* stuff outside the base, Jonas."

"Yeah...yeah, right. Sorry, Brig. Got carried away. So hey, let me buy you a beer!" he said, placing a hand on Brig's shoulder.

"I...can't right now, Jonas. I have...*something*...to check on," Brig said, as he started to back-pedal towards the door, letting

Jonas's hand drop. "But we'll catch up soon. I'll see you at the base tomorrow. K?"

"Sure," Jonas answered, watching his new partner turn and stride out of the bar.

The door slammed shut behind Brig as he stepped out onto the sidewalk. He grabbed the sunglasses that hung around his neck, placed them on the bridge of his nose and then tapped at the recessed area on the side of the frame.

"Call Clive Underwood," he commanded in a subdued tone. The small, digital readout on the inside top of one of the lenses scrolled, "Calling Underwood, Clive..." as a smooth and subtle tone emitted from the earpiece mounted within the frame near his left ear. After seven chirps, the piece sounded a long, flat tone and then deactivated.

Not answering. And neither is his auto monitor. Hmm, Brig thought, tapping the side of the frame once again to turn off the device.

Across the street, the local air-rail system hub bustled with the activity of the usual, daily rush hour traffic. Men and women scurried in and out of the building via the ramp that led from the street up to the main platform, where a set of shiny, blue metallic, pneumatic rail cars sat. Brig could see that the doors on the cars were all ajar and knew that he still had time to make it onto the train before it departed.

He quickly crossed the street and jogged up the ramp into the terminal, pausing for a moment to scan his thumb on the entry turnstile, which promptly buzzed a pleasant chime and opened to allow him entry to the platform. Brig squeezed himself into one of the closing doors and sat down as the train exited the platform. The tubes at the base of the vehicle hissed loudly as they energized, and the train quickly zoomed off around a curve out of sight.

Brig leaned and stared out the window of the train towards the horizon. It was a sunny day, but he could see that dark clouds were forming off in the distance. Subtle flashes of light ignited within the fluffy billows as they slowly inched forward over the tops of the peaks that lined the western sky. The unseasonably warm temperatures lately meant that this was going to be a rainstorm, and Brig could tell it was going to be a heavy one.

He could feel the train begin its deceleration as it approached the terminal in Las Cruses, which was just up the road from Clive's apartment and down the highway from the military installation that both he and Clive called home.

It was good timing. At least he would stay out the rain...*for now*.

As the train slowed to a halt, Brig quickly stood up, made his way to the folding entry door, and waited for it to swing open and upward before stepping out onto the platform.

Several other people pushed past him and hurriedly bustled down the concrete walkway, turning the corner towards their destinations. Brig breathed a deep sigh and followed suit, striding down the ramp and out onto the main sidewalk in front of the terminal building, where he began a brisk walk along the street towards Clive's place.

The wind had begun to pick up, dampening the warmth of the day as it whipped the collar of his light jacket against the side of his face. A storm was coming, and he wanted to get to Clive's place before it was too late.

After a few minutes, he found himself standing at the small entry gate of Clive's apartment complex. A light drizzle of rain had begun and a gentle roll of thunder cascaded overhead. He pushed open the gate and jaunted up the sidewalk to Clive's front door. Brig did not want to be presumptuous, so he gave a firm set of knocks on the door rather than use the bio-ID pad, as he had done inadvertently the last time he was there.

He stood patiently and waited for a response, but the lack of illumination on the bio-ID pad caught his eye. Curiosity tugging at his brain, he placed his hand squarely on the pad, fully expecting the familiar chime and the door to subsequently slide open.

However, nothing happened.

Brig rapped on the door once again, hoping that Clive might be at the back of the apartment where it would have been hard to hear someone at the door.

There was still no response.

He pressed his hand against the glass of the window adjacent the door and peered inside.

To his surprise, the apartment, by all appearances, was empty. Brig stood upright and pensively frowned.

Am I at the wrong apartment? he quizzed himself silently,

taking a step backward and looking at the address plate on the side of the wall. "This *is* the right one," he confirmed aloud.

Then he noticed it. Just above where he had peered into the window, somehow he had not seen it before...a sign that read 'For Lease'.

Present day (2084)...

The brisk, night breeze clawed at Brig's ears as he stumbled along the sidewalk. The echo of his heavy, dragging footsteps resonated off the empty storefronts that once bustled with activity, but now stood eerily silent and dark against the clear, star-filled sky. Small, forceful clouds erupted from his mouth with each labored breath. His lungs were ablaze and his head throbbed along with his thumping pulse.

Although the bleeding from the stab wound in his shoulder had ceased, he could still feel the crusted blood around the wound as it tore at the ripped flesh with each step.

He stopped and leaned against a burned-out lamppost to catch his breath, letting out a hollow wail that could have come from a wild animal. He looked to his right and caught a glimpse of his own moonlit reflection in one of the broken storefront windows. Had he not known that he was alone on this street, he would have not recognized himself.

Two city blocks ahead, Brig could just make out the dim light coming from a small, flat-topped building set back from the road, sitting between broken, wooden fences.

It was Clive's workshop.

Somehow, Brig had managed to survive long enough to find his way here. If he could just drag himself a little farther, his old pal Crypto would surely be able to help him out of this latest mess. He winced as he grabbed onto his shoulder, reaching down within himself to summon the strength to push on another 100 meters to safety.

As he reached the front door of Clive's workshop, he stopped and stared at the building. Clive had to be there – the subdued workbench light peeked out from behind the heavy shutters that lined the inside of the window. If nothing else, Brig knew he would at least be able to lie down in relative comfort until his friend arrived.

He pulled a large patch of hair away from his face that had become intermingled with the dried blood at the corner of his mouth and then, without knocking, yanked at the sliding door to the workshop. The door glided open loudly. Brig floundered into the doorway and promptly crashed to the floor.

Clive emerged quickly from his secret doorway, hopping up the final stair onto his one good leg and dragging the door partially shut with one hand, as he took in the sight that lay before him.

He hesitated in disbelief, staring down at an unconscious Brig. Without turning, he pointed back at the doorway with one finger,

"*Stay* down there, I'll take care of this," he said gruffly. Clive ambled to the front door, slid it shut, and locked it securely with several deadbolt latches. He turned and knelt next to his friend, staring at Brig's chest as it rose and fell in short, shallow bursts.

"Do I need to leave you two alone," a voice from behind him chimed, as Clive placed two fingers on Brig's neck.

Clive glared at the doorway, which was now open, and his guest standing on the top-most stair.

"No, that's not necessary. I just need to get him over to the cot and he'll be out of our way," he grunted, pulling Brig up from the floor by grasping him under his arms. "Just go back down and we'll continue in a minute."

As he set Brig onto the cot, he caught notice of the partially stitched wound on his shoulder. *He's not bleeding*, he thought, *but I can finish that stitch job once she's gone.*

"What's *his* story?" Steele Fox said, peeking out from the stairwell.

Surprised that she was still looking on, Clive stumbled for words.

"He's uh...just had a rough couple'a days, that's all," he grunted, turning Brig on his side towards the wall. Clive stood, not making eye contact with Steele.

"*Days?* More likely years, I would imagine." Steele crossed her arms impatiently.

Clive chuckled under his breath as he knelt next to his workbench and began to fiddle with something underneath it. He stared intently at Steele, working his hand back and forth subtly in the relative darkness of the underside of the workbench. After a few seconds, he extracted his hand, and with it a small container. He stood upright and quickly strode to the cot where Brig lay.

Steele looked on in detached reservation as Clive extracted a small syringe from the container and jabbed it into the bend of

Brig's left arm. The glowing, blue serum within quickly drained from the cylinder within a few short moments.

"And what's *that* all about?" she asked curiously.

Clive pulled the needle from Brig's vein and placed the syringe back into the container, closing the lid tightly as he sprang up from the edge of the cot and walked to his workbench. He placed the container back into its cabinet and then eyed Steele.

"*You* really don't know?" he asked sarcastically, slamming the door shut on its hiding place, still giving her a skeptical glare.

Steele frowned and wrinkled her brow at Clive. "*Should* I?" she quizzed with a hint of annoyance.

A loud rapping on the front door interrupted the tense moment. Clive stood and shot a silent, instructive glower at Steele.

"Yes, I know," she moaned in a mocking barb, "wait downstairs..." she trailed off, disappearing out of sight.

Clive watched after Steele as she headed down the short staircase, then peered at Brig lying unconscious on the cot along the back wall.

"Damn it," he cursed, quickly shutting the downward staircase, walking to the door and slowly sliding it open enough to stick his head through.

The imposing figure of Castor Webb stood with his back to Clive's door. He spun to face Clive, one eyebrow raised as he stared down at him.

"Underwood..." Castor grunted.

"Uh, Castor. What are you doing here so late, it's past your bedtime, isn't it?" Clive jibed at the big man with a wry smile.

"You can start by letting me in." Castor growled. He forced the door open all the way and then easily pushed past Clive.

Clive gritted his teeth as he leaned out through the door, quickly scanned the area immediately in front of the building and then pulled the door shut, shaking his head in disgust.

"Kinda late, Cas. What do you need?" Clive asked impatiently.

Castor, however, had found something more interesting to discuss, as his gaze fell upon the stranger lying on the cot at the back of the room.

"Whozat?" he mumbled to Clive without taking his eyes from Brig.

Clive fumbled his thoughts for an instant, before gathering his cool once again.

"No one special, he just needed to sleep it off...if you know what I mean," Clive said calmly, stopping next to Castor in an attempt to draw his attention away from anything else in the room.

Castor grunted heavily, and then faced Clive with a mistrustful look. "That his retro-bike out in the alley?"

"Must be, I was asleep when he got here, so didn't hear him pull up," Clive said with a shoulder shrug. "*So*... you're here for..."

"Nice hog. Better lookin' than my brother's," Castor observed flatly. "Boss wants you to go on a little road trip with Krell, gotta pick up some...*cargo.*"

Not usually called upon for physical jobs such as this, Clive was confused with Castor's request. "You sure he wanted *me*? That's not really my...specialty..."

Steele pressed herself against the side of the staircase and tilted an ear upward in an attempt to overhear the conversation between the two men. She scowled in frustration, as she could only hear the grumble of the bigger man's voice.

After a few more minutes, the sound of the front door sliding shut and the subsequent latching of the multiple locks from above echoed throughout the room. She cautiously ascended the staircase, pushed upward on the door and peered out into the room.

Clive had just finished securing the front door and was standing with his head bowed and his back towards her.

"You've a lot of visitors tonight, yeah?" she asked coyly.

Clive lifted his head to stare briefly at Steele, then turned abruptly and strode past her. "Let's get this over with, alright?" He descended the stairs, dropped into his chair and began typing furiously on the keyboard.

Steele turned her head to peer after Clive and then slowly looked over at Brig. Something seemed familiar about the man, although she was quite sure that she would never have associated with an obvious homeless junkie such as him. She squinted as she stared at the back of Brig's head.

Satisfied that Clive seemed to be very engrossed in his work downstairs, she slowly strolled to side of the cot. She stood over it and looked down at Brig's unconscious body, tilting her head as she tried to piece together how she knew him.

Curiosity got the best of her as she placed her hand on Brig's shoulder and gently pulled his upper torso towards her.

Brig's head turned upward until the lighting from behind Steele reflected off the side of his face.

"Oh my God," Steele cried in a loud whisper.

17:
Happy?

Seven years prior (Early 2077)…

Clive hobbled through the marble hallway of the Egress Portal, a small carry-on bag toted over his shoulder, as the crutches that he leaned on moved in stride with his good leg.

Nearing the security checkpoint, he stopped, placed one of the crutches under the other arm and leaned heavily on both to rummage through his bag.

He extracted a small ID placard and placed it between his teeth, but then lurched forward as someone bumped into him solidly from behind, knocking Clive's bag to the floor. Its contents spilled haphazardly across the tile lobby.

"Watch it, would ya?" Clive spouted, using a crutch to gather some of his belongings, absent-mindedly dropping the ID placard from his mouth in the process.

The man, shorter in stature than Clive, wearing sunglasses and a plain white dress shirt, peered down at Clive.

"I am sorry, I was distracted and did not see you standing there," he said in a thick, Eastern Eur-Asian accent. He knelt to help Clive retrieve the strewn contents of his bag. The man picked up Clive's ID, along with several other items, and held them under his arm, while attempting to gather a couple of pieces of clothing still lying just out of Clive's reach.

"Here, let me put them in your bag for you," the man said calmly, extending his arm towards Clive's bag and gruffly stuffing all he had picked up inside.

"Thanks," Clive said without making eye contact. He reached into the bag and located the ID placard once more, then zipped the bag shut. Clive looked up at the stranger.

The man had vanished.

Clive glanced around curiously. Aside from several armed security personnel standing post near the security checkpoint, and a few pilots standing outside of the terminal bar comparing notes, the terminal was relatively empty. No one remotely resembled the man that had inadvertently run into him seconds before.

Slinging the bag over his shoulder, Clive frowned, shrugged off the incident and once again crutch-walked towards the security checkpoint.

As he neared the desk, one of the guards off to the side of it tensed and fingered his weapon at the sight of Clive approaching. Clive darted his eyes away from the guard and stared down, stopping in front of him.

"Your credentials, please," the desk clerk said to Clive tersely in a thick Peruvian accent, gazing through Clive with intense disinterest.

Clive felt the sweat starting to build on the back of his neck. He had never travelled outside of the URA, not as a civilian anyway, and he was unsure how focused the review of his credentials would be. He held his ID and travel itinerary cards in his outstretched palm while flashing the clerk a faint smile.

The clerk, who was now staring resolutely at Clive, snatched the cards from Clive's hand. The clerk dropped his stare to the ID card for a few seconds, flipped to the itinerary card and then glared at Clive.

"Sir, this is a Class A passport. And your destination is a Class D restricted nation," the clerk said with a hint of suspicion.

Clive's heart skipped several beats as he looked on blankly at the clerk. "I...wasn't aware. Are you *sure*?"

Clive was caught, and he *knew* it. He could not think of an excuse other than that he was trying to slip through security on an oversight.

What would they do to him? Would they just turn him back from the gate and let him leave? Or would they detain him like some common criminal?

Just as Clive was about to offer some excuse, *any* excuse, as to why his credentials weren't in order, three short tones sounded, followed by a small green light that flashed at the edge of the clerk's desk.

"Must have been a misprint on the card," the clerk began, this time in a more friendly tone, as he completed swiping the cards through a scanner in front of his display. "My apologies, sir, you may proceed through the gate, Mr...*Andredev*."

The clerk handed the cards back to Clive.

Clive, looking a bit dumbfounded, nodded at the clerk, quickly stowed the cards into his bag and rotated on his crutches towards the security gate.

He knew he had caught a break. *Why* it had happened the way it did weighed momentarily on his mind, but for now that did not matter. He had made it to the other side of URA outbound security and he could now focus on his trip.

As the turbo tram left the security checkpoint and quickly jetted into the tunnel beneath the E-Port entry terminal, Clive reached into his bag and pulled out a small grouping of pictures. The lighting in the tram was dim, but it was adequate for him to make out the faces.

He chuckled softly as he gazed at one of him and Brig at one of Brig's grand, family cookouts. Brig, as usual, was mugging for the camera, his arm around his best pal Clive.

Best pal, Clive thought sarcastically. He shook his head, his smile fading. He felt the twinge in his stomach as he looked at himself with Brig. How things had changed since that picture was taken.

Clive flipped through several other photos, his expression becoming more and more subdued. The green glow from the lights outside the tram flickered in through the windows and onto the pictures in his hand.

One in particular held his attention.

The photo, that of a brunette sitting next to him on a couch and smiling while holding a bottle of beer in front of her, was also taken at the same cookout as the other pictures.

A tear formed at the corner of Clive's right eye as he stared at it longingly.

The LED security lights outside suddenly blurred into a steady stream of red, rocketing past the windows as the underground turbo tram whisked its way from the tunnel up into the departure terminal on the other end of the E-Port. Clive braced himself on the handle of the seat in front of him as the tram came to a swift stop at the edge of a large platform. He tossed the photos into his bag and grabbed his crutches.

"Welcome to the Southern URA Egress Portal," a female voice blared over the loudspeaker throughout the tram. Clive stood, leaned into his crutches and stepped off the tram. The automated announcement continued in Spanish, echoing within the hangar itself.

Clive stopped and curiously glanced around. Several other passengers had exited the tram as well and queued up behind the jet-way that led downward from the platform into the awaiting aircraft. He took a deep breath, stopping to take his place in the line for entry to the vehicle.

He peered around at the large, domed hangar. The smell of salt air stung his nostrils and he could hear the faint sound of the ocean waves crashing against a jetty in the distance.

A female attendant worked her way from the front of the line, inspecting and recording each of the passengers' itinerary cards with the wave of small palm-held wand, as he continued to soak in the warm, sea air.

"Good afternoon, sir," the attendant said bouncily, holding out her hand in anticipation of Clive's itinerary card.

Clive handed the card to the attendant and nervously glanced around. She passed the wand over the cards while still smiling at Clive.

"I see here that you are traveling one way. Would you like to schedule a return trip?" She peeked at the display attached to her wrist. A pleasant beep emanated from the scan result.

Clive shook his head subtly and stared down at his feet.

He was not sure of anything at this point in his life. Everything had changed, and nothing made sense any more. But he also knew that he could not count on anyone but *himself* to get through the journey that had just begun.

Present day (2084)...

The morning light had begun to crawl in around the shutters in the windows of Clive's workshop. Clive, because Brig had been on the cot all night, had fallen asleep in front of his computer in the secret room below the floor, his head resting within his folded arms upon the desk in front of him.

Upstairs, Brig lay on the cot, still facing the same direction that Clive had put him in the night before. It had been a restful night for Brig, a very uncommon occurrence for him lately, and he had not moved a centimeter throughout the night.

The same could *not* be said for Steele.

She had decided to stay the night, contrary to Clive's

recommendations, and did not sleep much at all. She sat in a chair several meters away from Brig's cot, keeping vigil on him in anticipation of when he might regain consciousness.

Brig began to stir from his slumber, turning over onto his back and blinking his eyes as he adjusted to the morning light. He slowly pushed himself up to a sitting position, ran his fingers through his hair with one hand, and rubbed his eyes with the other while letting out a deep yawn. He winced as his fingers tangled in the stickiness of the long locks partially matted to the side of his face with dried blood.

"*Ahem,*" Steele coughed politely, as she sat up from a momentary nap and intently watched Brig come to.

He squinted out of one eye, then closed both eyes, lowered his head and shook it as he rubbed his forehead.

"Either Clive got prettier overnight, or I'm dreamin'," he said mockingly, "...and I'm not *that* lucky."

Peering over at the open doorway in the floor, Steele raised an eyebrow and crossed her arms. "So his name is *Clive* today, how interesting," she said snidely, turning her attention back to Brig.

"That's his name *always*..." he groaned.

Suddenly he realized he was not dreaming at all. *That voice...the accent...couldn't be...* he thought. He opened his eyes wide, peered up and stared at her in absolute astonishment. "*Steele?*"

Steele's snide smirk transformed slowly into a wide grin as she locked eyes with Brig. Her lips were unable to hold in her happiness.

"Oh my God, I can't believe it's *you*," Brig said breathlessly, jumping from the edge of the cot. "You are a sight for sore eyes!"

Steele sprung from her chair and wrapped her arms around Brig in a loving embrace. "And you look absolutely...*terrible*," she said playfully.

"Sarcastic as ever, I see," Brig said in a muffled tone. He buried his face deep into Steele's shoulder-length, auburn hair.

Steele pushed Brig away to arm's length. "No, really...this is *disgusting*," she cried, wrinkling her face into a sneer at him. "Ever heard of taking a *shower* once in a while?"

Brig smirked and shook his head. "Kinda hard to when..."

"You two...*know* each other?" a concerned voice queried from behind them. Clive, standing at the top of the stairs, leaned on the hinged door and watched the reunion with stunned interest.

Steele glared at Clive with a coy smile.

"You could say that...*Clive*," she said sarcastically, making certain he was aware she knew his *real* name. "Brigadier and I used to know each other when we were children, but then we sort of..." she replied and then looked at Brig while raising her eyebrows and shrugging her shoulders, "...lost touch?"

"Military school..." Brig interjected matter-of-factly. "...and I don't recall you ever *visiting* me, either."

"College...double doctorates. Not a lot of spare time," she quipped without missing a beat. "Besides, you know how to use a phone, don't you?" she prodded, playfully pounding her fist onto Brig's chest, causing him to grunt in pain.

"*Son of a...*" he groaned, grasping at his shoulder. He craned his neck to peek at his back, and then closed his eyes shut for a second in silence. "Oh yeah, little...injury there," he grumbled while sitting down on the cot, still holding his arm in place.

Steele stood over Brig, pulled the back of his collar away from his neck and peeked at his shoulder. "That's a nasty little wound, isn't it?" she said. "How'd *that* happen?

Brig yanked the collar from Steele's hand and gingerly pushed himself up from the cot. "Ran into an old...*buddy* of mine yesterday."

"*Buddy?* Is that how your *friends* treat you?" she mocked, watching Brig rub his sore shoulder with a grimace. Steele grabbed onto Brig's other arm and forced him to look into her eyes, lowering the pretention in her voice. "Brig...are you alright?"

"Yeah..." he said, nodding his head after a brief hesitation, "Yeah, I'm just fine. Ain't that *right*, Cryp?" he jibed, glaring at Clive.

"Uh...yeah," Clive replied, still staring in bewilderment over the fact that these two, of all people, would know each other. "But those stitches aren't professional or anything, so you might want to ease up on the...hugging and stuff."

Clive closed and locked the door to the secret room. *What're the odds*, he thought. It was not just the fact that Brig and Steele knew each other that disturbed him, but that they had a history together. *And* she seemed genuinely concerned about Brig's welfare. Clive had already felt that Brig was nosing around too much lately as it was. How long would it be until these two started comparing notes? *Not good.*

Brig stopped and looked at Clive with a curious stare. In his excitement since he had awoken, it had not even dawned on him that Clive and Steele knew each other as well.

"How do *you* two know each other?" Brig asked while glancing back and forth between the pair.

Clive hesitated. The last thing he wanted right now was to spark the curiosity in Brig that he knew all too well could only lead to trouble.

"I've got some things I need to take care of right now. Sorry guys, I have to get going..." Clive trailed off, ignoring the glare coming from Steele, as he made his way to the front door and began to slide it open.

"Cryp...wait! Where are you..." Brig pleaded. But it was too late. The door slid shut and Clive had gone.

Brig turned to Steele with a frustrated look.

"He does this *all* the time, I don't get it," he said with his hands on his hips.

"You and I have a *lot* to talk about," she said flatly, striding past Brig and peering out the window through the closed shutters. "Would you like to go and get some fresh air?"

Seven years prior (early 2077)...

"Good morning, Major," the soldier said, as he strode by, snapping a crisp salute in Brig's direction.

"Oh...good morning," Brig replied, quickly forcing a return salute as he walked up the main sidewalk towards the entrance of the EW Squadron headquarters.

His mind was far from the formalities of military life now, and on top of that, he was exhausted from not having any sleep the night before, having stayed awake most of the night lamenting the sudden disappearance of his friend, Clive.

Maybe someone here will know where he went he thought. He leaned in and stared into a scanning plate on the wall next to the main doors. After a few seconds, the speaker next to the plate emitted a short tone and the door slid open behind him.

Brig strode through the doorway and into the lobby, responding to greetings from several of the staff that worked at the location. He paused briefly in the center of the room as he caught sight of a familiar face working behind the security desk located along the main wall, then changed direction and approached the desk.

"Lieutenant Tessler," he said in a steady voice, standing

opposite a blonde, female officer wearing a tight hair bun and focusing on her work surface.

"*Major* Stroud," she responded immediately without looking up from her work. "What can I do for you this morning?"

Brig peered around the lobby. The only other person present was a soldier that briskly walked past Brig and into an adjacent hallway.

"Hey, Amy," Brig said cordially in a hushed tone.

Amy looked up from the desk, clicked her eyes back and forth and then glared at Brig with a raised eyebrow.

"Well, look who it is. *Mr. I'll Call You Tomorrow*," she said sarcastically, contorting her face into an exaggerated smirk.

"Aw, come on! You know I..." he began to protest, but realized that his voice was carrying throughout the lobby. He glanced around again. A couple of officers that were engaged in a conversation on the other end of the room stopped and looked over at Brig with an annoyed expression.

"...You *know* I was deployed the day after our date..." he continued in a high whisper.

"And what about the three months *since* then?" she argued back fiercely in a heightened cry.

Brig sighed and pursed his lips. "Think about it. *Where* was I deployed and *what* happened there?" he said in a calm tone, tilting his head at her.

Amy's face flushed. She had forgotten what Brig and Clive had gone through in Portugal, and the obvious strain she assumed it *must* have put on their friendship.

"I...I'm sorry, Brig. I wasn't thinking. Clive...oh my God, I didn't even realize," she stammered, putting her hand over her eyes and looking down. "I'm *so* sorry."

"It's ok," Brig reassured the clerk. "But, really, I didn't mean to hurt your feelings. Just a lot has happened since then and things haven't exactly been...*normal*, if you know what I mean."

"I get it," she replied, closing her eyes and shaking her head vigorously. "Forget I even said anything about it. I feel so stupid."

"No...*don't*." Brig reached across the desk and grabbed Amy's hand to focus her attention. "I'd like to pick up where we left off...if that's ok with you. Maybe...Friday?" he asked, looking into her blue eyes.

Amy blinked and smiled. "I'd like that...very much," she cooed.

"Forgive me for being an idiot?" she asked innocently with shrugged shoulders.

Brig laughed and squeezed Amy's hand, then retracted his hand back to his side as another officer strolled by, oblivious to the pair's private conversation. "Have you seen Clive, by the way?"

"Not since his discharge." She began typing again. "Have you tried his apartment?"

"Yeah. Not there," he answered while biting his lip pensively. "What's worse is his apartment was empty and up for lease."

"Weird. But I'm sure he'll pop up again, probably just in the process of moving to a new place, right?" She glanced at Brig every few seconds as she typed.

Brig scratched the back of his head and grimaced. "I don't know. Things have been a little...*tense*...between us lately. Ah well, maybe someone else here has seen him," he said, tapping the desk in front of him. "I'll call you..."

As soon as Brig said it, he realized the callousness of his words. "You know what I mean," he corrected with a wry smile. He turned away and walked to one of the corridors leading out of the lobby.

"Brig...wait," Amy called. Brig stopped and looked at Amy. "Is Clive's tracker implant still active?" she whispered to Brig while glancing around the lobby.

Brig shrugged his shoulders and frowned. He had not thought about that, but then, he also did not have the means to utilize that kind of data, either. "I think all the EWs *always* are...not like I would know anyway though."

Amy peered down at her computer and tapped in a command that brought up a colorful map of the globe in front of her.

"Major Stroud...I need to go and take care of something down the hall," she said tersely, laying one final finger on the surface and calmly getting up from her chair. "Don't lose *track* of time until Friday," she said coyly.

She dragged her hand in front of Brig, producing a smaller, holographic image of the globe where she had touched the desk. The reflection of its bright LED coloring danced in his pupils.

Brig wrinkled his brow as he watched her disappear around the corner, and then looked at the animated globe as it spun in front of him. After a few revolutions, it stopped and illuminated with a small, red flag on a northern point of the Eur-Asian continents.

Above the globe was Clive's name, along with his identifier code and last known location. Brig squinted at the display as he read the data. *"Russia?"*

18: Awake

Present day (2084)...

The roar of the retro-bike's twin cylinder engine split the desert air and echoed off the nearby foothills, filling the otherwise-desolate area surrounding the two-lane highway like a lion's call across a lonely plain.

Steele and Brig motored down the center of the only lane that was still drivable. The other, pitted and worn from the intense heat and lack of use, zoomed by in a blur with the imprint of their shadow from the late afternoon sun floating on the broken asphalt.

The pair had been riding for nearly an hour, mostly on deserted roads and areas that would bring as minimal attention to them as possible while still allowing them to enjoy the freedom of the open air.

Brig, his beard freshly trimmed and hair cleaned, thanks to a quick shower at Clive's workshop before they had departed, leaned into Steele's back. His hands rested snugly around her waist as she navigated the bike along the open road.

He had so much to say to Steele, so much to share, but the loud drone of the bike precluded them being able to hear each other. Given his current position, however, Brig did not mind.

The wind blowing on his face and through his hair, coupled with the reunion of his childhood friend, were all he needed to feel at ease for the first time in his recent memory.

He marveled at his friend, someone that on the inside he knew to be so tough but on the outside gave the impression of being such a beautiful, delicate flower. That she had survived the past several years and came out seeming just as strong as ever did not surprise him in the least, and he felt was a testament to her inner strength. Brig had always admired her for that strength, and he knew that her parents had named her aptly: *Steele.*

Steele began to slow the bike, and after nearly coming to a stop, made a turn onto a small, dirt trail that jutted off the main highway and wound perpendicular to the road up in-between two larger foothills.

Brig had no clue of their destination. He had never been on this stretch of road before, much less on a dirt road off the main highway, but he trusted that Steele knew where she was going.

Clouds of dust billowed out from behind them as they raced up the trail and onto the backside of one of the foothills. The back end of the bike shimmied out from under them several times, causing Steele to slow but easily keep control of the machine.

Fifty meters ahead of them, the trail ended abruptly at a bluff. He was about to bring the rapidly-approaching end to Steele's attention, when she promptly skidded the bike to a stop on a leveled patch just ten meters from the edge. She dropped the kickstand and hopped off.

Brig grimaced as he got off the bike and stood next to Steele. Until now, he had forgotten about the pain in his shoulder, but the vibration from the retro-bike was a sharp reminder and brought it back to the forefront of his mind.

"Why are we up *here*?" Brig rubbed his shoulder gently, glancing around him at the scrub-grass-filled landscape of the hill.

Steele grabbed his hand off his shoulder and tugged as she started to walk towards the edge of the bluff.

"You'll see, come on!" she prodded with a broad smile.

As they approached the edge, Brig realized he was right. However, what he had *not* anticipated was what lay on the floor of the desert in front of them.

The two friends stood hand-in-hand several meters from the edge of the cliff and stared out onto the plain.

Stretching out as far as they could see, Brig estimated it to be at least a few kilometers, was a vast array of satellite dishes.

Their hulking, gray, motionless masses lay in a geometric grid from end-to-end until they reached medium-height foothills on each side. A warm afternoon breeze kicked up dust around the bases of a small grouping of dishes on one side, which like the others, were shrouded in overgrown desert flowers and weeds. The sun was an hour from setting completely and draped a burnt, golden hue across the metallic faces of the array. Each dish cast a somber, monolithic shadow forward onto the desert floor in front of itself.

Steele sat down onto a patch of bushy Sacaton grass, patting the ground next to her as she looked up at Brig.

He smiled and took up a spot next to her.

Brig found that the ground was surprisingly comfortable. The matted grass created a perfect cushion from which to look out at the marvel that lay before them. It was also obvious to him that Steele was quite familiar with this place and had discovered these facts long ago.

"Come here often?" he asked in jest, peering at Steele.

Steele leaned over to Brig. "My favorite spot," she quipped and then sat back upright, still staring out at the array.

"Impressive..." Brig said, not taking his eyes off Steele.

He was not sure whether he was referring to the array or to Steele herself. He had seen the world and been through Hell and back, but at this moment, he could not tell which left the indelible mark on him.

"Inspirational...I think," she replied, wrinkling her nose while scanning the horizon. "Although I'm not sure why..."

Brig glanced at Steele, puzzled, not that she was paying attention. She seemed to be in her own world, light-years away from where they were sitting.

She's so grown up, he pondered to himself silently, as he gazed at her. *But I still see the little girl in her...*

"There's something about this place. It pulls me here. It makes me look up," she said pensively. "It makes me realize there must be something bigger...bigger than all of this. Bigger than all of *us*."

"Wow...*deep*," Brig chuckled. Ignoring the pain in his shoulder, he put his arm around Steele's back, gently gripping her upper arm with a soft hand.

The breeze started up again, wisping Steele's hair to the side, gently brushing it against the side of Brig's face and exposing a small tattoo at the base of her hairline.

Steele giggled, leaned in and back against Brig's chest and pulled his other arm across hers, being mindful of his injury by not putting too much angular force on him.

Brig felt mesmerized by Steele's presence.

He held his breath in silence, feeling her lungs expand and contract with each breath she took. He could feel the rhythmic pulsing of her heart, as it radiated through her back and against the front of his chest. Despite the grand scene that sprawled out in front of him, Brig found himself being only able to see the beauty that sat next to him. The warmth of her embrace, the softness of her hair against his skin and the sound of her breath as it exhaled from her lips made his heart beat strong and hard against his ribcage.

Other than someone wanting to do him harm, it had been years since Brig had felt any significant human contact. He had felt lost and alone, and in the short period since they had reunited, he felt what it was like to be *alive* again.

Steele, not unlike Brig, also cherished the moment. Brig had always been her protector, and she had sorely missed his presence in her life. Despite the strength in which she had prided herself, she *also* felt alone and confused with no one to call a friend in times of doubt. She was still beside herself about the incredible happenstance of the reunion with her childhood friend, Brigadier, and it allowed her to let her guard down, if only for a moment.

She closed her eyes and listened to the wind rustle through the grass around them. She had not felt this relaxed in quite a long time.

After a short while, Steele released herself from Brig's embrace and sat up with her legs crossed under each other.

"So how do *you* know Clive?" she asked, pushing her fingers into the sand in front of her and twirling them.

Brig stared off into the distance, propping himself up with one hand behind him while resting his chin on the other that was leaning on his knee.

"We go back a little ways," he said thoughtfully. "We were in the EWs together..."

"EWs?" Steele repeated. "Epsilon Warriors? So you mean to tell me you went full hardcore on the military career, did you? Glutton for punishment?" she joked with a sarcastic smile.

Brig's reaction to that question had always been to say that he *wanted* to join the EWs. Not only to make something of himself, but also to prove to his father that he was not the underachiever that he had always thought Brig to be.

Now that he thought of it, *was* it his choice to stay on the military path? Or were the verbal beratings by his father before and during his time in military boarding school his father's way of making the choice for him?

He pondered the question for a silent moment.

"I guess a continuation of my earlier life. When you're brought up that way, you sorta don't have a choice when you have a parent that doesn't want you around..." he replied in a serious tone.

"So what does...*did*...your father do for a living that made *you* such a burden?" She continued her trance-like gaze out at the array, the wind once again blowing the hair across her face to where Brig could not see her expression clearly.

Brig looked over at Steele confusedly.

"Um...*President*..." he said slowly and distinctly, "...of the URA?"

Steele nodded subtly without looking at Brig.

What an odd question, he thought, wrinkling his brow as he stared at his friend.

Had she truly forgotten who his father *was*? The hard years that had fallen between their last times together and now had definitely made more people than just *her* act in a strange manner. He knew that fact firsthand.

But the more that he looked at her, heard her talk and watched her mannerisms, the more he realized that *something* seemed different about her. Something seemed...*off*.

After he had left for boarding school, the two rarely saw each other more than once or twice a year, and even then, they were short moments. It *had* been fifteen years since they hung around each other in any significant capacity – and she was merely a teenager at that point. He convinced himself that she simply must have grown up and he just was not used to it yet.

"You alright?" he asked sympathetically.

"I'm fine," she answered softly. "My mind just feels...hazy...on the details sometimes. But it's nothing to worry yourself over," she said, turning to face Brig with a friendly smile. "Besides, I'm certain that there are *many* that wish to block out the details of the last seven years..."

Brig nodded his head in agreement. "Won't argue with you on that. I've had a pretty rough time..."

She placed her hand on his knee and looked at him matter-of-factly. "*Everyone's* had a hard time, Brigadier. Don't take it personally," she quipped with a wink of an eye. "You're one of the lucky ones. You've got yourself a...*friend*...in Clive, don't you?"

Brig raised his eyebrows. What a question. *How* could he answer it?

Since the day that he and Clive met, he considered Clive his best friend. But since that fateful night in Portugal, much to his chagrin, he was not sure it was anything more than a one-sided deal.

"...although I feel like there was a bit of tension between you two back at the workshop?" Steele added.

Pursing his lips tightly, Brig peered out at the sunset. "As much as I don't want to, I can't deny that there's a rift between me and Clive." Brig paused and shook his head. "And no matter what I've tried to do over the years to repair that rift, it only seems to make it worse. It's something I regret, but it's something that I can't go back and change."

"Well...seeing your condition when you stumbled in last night *and* Clive sticking you with that mammoth needle..." Steele said pensively, staring down at the ground in front of her. "I can only assume this is about...*drugs?*"

Brig shook his head and laughed under his breath. "Nah...*not* drugs. I made some decisions...*before*...it all went down, that affected his life in a pretty negative way," Brig explained, also gazing down at the patch of grass in front of them.

"*You* never answered me back at the workshop – how do *you* know him?" he asked, squinting against the bright sunset.

"It's really not all that important, nor is it a big deal for that matter," Steele reassured Brig. However, she saw that he was still staring and was not going to give up without some sort of explanation from her.

"I came across some old, work-related items that had encryption on them," she began, working her fingers through the sand once more. "Long story short, after a couple of contacts, someone gave me his name as a person that could decrypt them for me. For nostalgia's sake, of course," she concluded, pulling her knees up to her chest and wrapping her arms around them as she looked at Brig.

Nostalgia, he thought. That was the second time in the past week that he had heard *that* term, and *both* times it was in relation to Clive's mysterious activities. Were they both sticking to a cover story? On the other hand, was this explanation just that...a simple reason for nothing in particular, or just nothing for *him* to be worried about. Brig did not feel the need to let on about his recent concerns for Clive, and now that Steele seemed to be on the same page as Clive, at least for whatever this was, he was not willing to spoil the mood of their afternoon together by pressing the issue any further.

"So...*my* little Steele, a big college grad, huh?" Brig quipped, returning Steele's gaze. "With what...four, five doctorates was it?"

"*Two...*" she said with heavy emphasis and a slight chuckle. "And I worked hard to get them, so don't you make fun of me, Mr. Military Man."

"I see you took time out to party at least," Brig said, glancing and nodding at Steele's neck.

Steele unconsciously grabbed at the back of her neck while

laughing uneasily. "Yeah...maybe a bit *too* much partying I guess," she said. "But with that kind of workload, you have to blow off steam somehow."

"I hope it all paid off," he parried with a wry smile. "What'd you end up doing for a living?"

"I worked for the DMST...as an architectural engineer on *top secret* military projects," she began with fake enthusiasm, but then paused and became more pensive. "But none of that really matters anymore, now does it?"

Brig did not speak, but nodded his head in subtle agreement. It was so long ago that things had changed, but sometimes to him it seemed like just yesterday, and he was certain that Steele felt the same way.

"...and since then I've been taking care of my father," she continued. "And what about you, Brig. What does a career military man such as yourself do now that everything..."

"...went to *Hell*?" Brig interjected. He paused and looked out at the array, rolling a long stem of grass between his fingertips.

The sun had dipped beneath a bank of clouds that had formed on the horizon, its rays beaconing out from underneath like warm fingertips touching the earth below.

"...*Survive*..." he concluded and then went silent again. After a moment, he turned his head back to Steele and smiled. "How's your father doing?"

"As well as can be expected, I suppose," she answered half-heartedly. "Although lately he's been on about one thing or another. So he has me a bit concerned at times..."

Then, Steele fell silent.

She fixed her gaze on a point just beyond where the satellite dish array presumably ended kilometers away. She remained speechless for an excruciating several minutes, staring away in a hypnotic transfixion, as ominous clouds continued to build in the pre-twilight sky.

The realization that Brig had been staring at her with great interest finally interrupted her daze. Steele closed her eyes and bowed her head, letting out a melancholy sigh.

"Brigadier...do you ever feel like your life is a *dream*?" she asked, lifting her head and opening her eyes to peer at Brig.

Brig, still looking at her with concern, feigned a smile and gently took her hand in his.

"*I* do." She turned her focus back to the distant sky, the breeze

171

gently buffeting her hair backwards behind her head. "...and no matter how hard I try to wake up, the dream just keeps getting deeper and deeper."

Her voice started to crack as she took a deep gulp.

"And then something calls me *here*, and it wakes me. But I don't know what I'm waking *to*..." As she finished, a single tear spilled out onto her cheek.

It was a rare occasion when Brig witnessed weakness in his friend Steele, and it troubled him even deeper to see it now. He pulled her into a close embrace up against his chest.

"*It's ok to be scared*..." he said gently. He stroked the tear-soaked hair away from her cheek and kissed her forehead.

"Brig, I'm so glad that you're alive...and I'm so very happy that I found you," she said through a couple of sniffles after a few moments, grabbing onto his midsection tightly. "So...where are you staying now?"

Brig chuckled unevenly. He had not even considered the answer to that question today. So much had happened since the night in the woods with McGraw that it had slipped his mind entirely.

"Well, I had a place for a while. But that sorta...went up in flames, so to speak. I suppose I could crash at Clive's til' I find a place..."

He glanced out at the horizon. The sky had become considerably darker, somewhat because the sun had set almost entirely, but also because the clouds appeared to be increasing, growing with a light rumble that pierced the serenity of the desert before them.

"Well then that settles it," Steele said firmly, pulling herself away from him enough to gaze into his eyes. "You're staying with me at my flat now."

"I appreciate you saying that, Steele, I really do. But..." Brig said with hesitation, "...there's a lot about me you don't know, and *some* things you just might not like..."

"I don't *care*, Brig," she interjected. "I always felt like you were my protector, and I'm not about to let you get away *again*. It's been far too long since we've been close. And besides, Brigadier Stroud, that wasn't a request. That was an *order*." She pushed herself up from the ground and offered him a hand.

Brig sighed as he took her hand and, with her assistance, pulled himself up from the matted grass.

I hope I don't make her regret this decision, he thought.

He glared out at the array and the darkening skies beyond. The wind had started to kick up violently at the far end of the field and the flowers danced around many of the dish bases.

"Looks like a bad one coming in...we'd better get back to town, don't you think?" he observed.

Steele looked up into Brig's eyes and smiled broadly. "*Great idea.*"

19:
Long, Cold Winter

Seven years prior (early 2077)…

Snowflakes darted by the darkened window, lit briefly like fireflies as they passed through the dim stream of light flowing from the cabin of the speeding railcar.

Clive leaned towards the window and rubbed at a small spot near the edge of the pane with the sleeve of his jacket, enough to clear the frost that had formed from the freezing temperatures outside. His hot breath formed a fresh fog that filled the cold glass next to his mouth as he stared out at the frozen, dark, Russian tundra flashing by.

The train had departed St. Petersburg less than an hour before and swiftly made its way through the countryside on its three-hour trip to the outskirts of the Russian capital.

The train itself was not particularly flashy or high-tech such as those that he was accustomed to back in the URA, and lent itself more to the older style bullet trains from the turn of the century. However, that was to be expected outside of the URA, where most countries had much more to worry about, and on which to spend their budgets, than keeping up with the latest transportation technology. Nevertheless, it served its purpose and moved determinately through the countryside towards its destination.

He would not normally have taken the long train ride from the port city into Moscow, but his contact warned him of the difficultly of taking a plane directly into the capital and that security in St. Petersburg was much more lax during the heightened political tensions of the time.

He was right. Clive had no trouble transferring from the airport to the train station, his bogus credentials once again allowing him to pass security with ease.

The train was half full with mostly locals travelling to and from small towns on the route to Moscow, coming back home after a hard day's work or heading out for an early shift.

Although Clive stood out from the crowd on his appearance

alone, no one seemed to take particular interest in him, which was precisely how he wanted it. However, not wanting to press his luck, he had taken a spot near the back of the car, pulled the collar of his drab gray, woolen coat up around the sides of his face and had kept his head lowered most of the trip thus far.

He stared out at the shadowy trees that whizzed by in a blur. He thought about all that had happened to him in the past year. Anger and sadness took equal billing as he pondered all of the people in his life: the ones he cared about the most and the ones that he thought cared about *him*, that either had let him down or had just outright betrayed him.

Of course, there was his father. But he had been able to let go of the anger that he held towards the man. Years had passed and Clive had made himself successful despite the setback that his father had handed his family. Besides, recent events had served to redirect the hatred and hurt that filled him. The wounds were still fresh and they made his eyes well up even as his heart burned in anger. Clive softly shook his head and tightened his lips as he thought about Brig.

How could you? he thought. *And Jess...*

"*Amerikanskiy?*" a voice from across the aisle and behind him snarled in a thick Eur-Asian accent.

Clive turned his head slowly in the direction of the voice, not wanting to appear surprised by the question. He glanced over his shoulder. A husky man in a tight, blue jacket leaned in and glared at him with a sneer on his stubbly face.

"Ni," Clive answered in an equally gruff, but feigned tone, and then faced the window once again.

The man grunted and then looked away.

One of the skills that Clive had prided himself on was languages, and his mastery of the Ukrainian dialect was the model of perfection in the EW squadron.

It was ironic to him that having fluency in so many different tongues had simply been because he was a student of learning. Now, it was actually showing benefit in his current journey and might actually assist him in getting back to the world: *his* world, where he would once again be accepted for who he was. He would *show* them. He would make them see that he belonged, and they would *eat* their words.

That place seemed worlds away now, however.

They had all said the same thing to him – '*don't let it define you'*. Brig. Jacobs. Even his own mother disappointed him when she told him that he needed to 're-find' himself.

How could they not see it? He *was* the man that he knew he *could* be, but they all felt like he was lost. If that were the case, then where was the *explosive epiphany* that he was supposed to encounter that would bring him down to Earth? It irritated Clive that they could not understand things from his perspective and it accelerated the drive that he had to prove them all wrong.

He kicked his prosthetic leg forward and leaned back in his seat, tucking his hands into his jacket pockets as he gazed out at the rapidly passing, snowy vista.

The train suddenly shuddered and became noticeably quieter.

Clive emerged from his trance-like gaze through the window and glanced around the car. The other passengers had either not noticed the jolt or were not concerned with its meaning. He peered out the window and realized what he had felt. The train was beginning to decelerate.

Clive squinted out towards the front of the train. A well-lit area, unlike the forested terrain that they had been passing through for almost the past hour, caught his eye.

Can't be Moscow, he puzzled to himself. Indeed – he knew that they were nowhere near their destination.

The crackling of the intercom coming to life severed the somber silence inside the car. An emotionless, droning announcement came from the conductor.

"Our apologies," the thickly-accented Russian voice began, "but due to circumstances beyond our control we have been asked to divert to Novgorod. When the train stops please exit and wait in the terminal for further instructions…"

Clive did not like the sound of the sudden change in destination. He had already weathered a very narrow escape at the E-Port in Trujillo, and although he was still perplexed at how the whole situation had played out, he was nonetheless gratified…*until now*. Perhaps the officials back there had realized their mistake and had taken steps to track him down.

Of course, he hypothesized silently, *it could just be a problem with the rails farther down the line*. After all, it *was* the dead of winter and Novgorod was not directly on the way to Moscow, so the engineer must have deliberately taken a detour earlier in the trip to avoid the problem.

Clive took a deep breath and bit his lower lip in pensive

thought. *No sense guessing any more about this. What's gonna happen is gonna happen...*

The train jerked to a slow crawl as it approached the terminal platform and slid the final several meters until it came to a stop. Its passenger doors creaked open slowly, forcing a gust of biting, cold air and wispy snow flurries into the cabin.

Clive remained in his seat and waited for the rest of the passengers to disembark from the car. Seeing the last of them exit the train, he slowly hobbled to the front of the cabin on his crutches and cautiously stepped out onto the platform.

The bitter wind gnawed at the exposed portions of Clive's face above his collar as he carefully made his way along the terminal platform towards the main doors, being careful to not to lose traction with his rubber-tipped crutches on the icy walkway.

A group of three men stood two meters to the right of the door. One of them Clive recognized as the man from the train that had mistakenly (to the *man*, anyway) identified Clive as an American. The other two, unshaven and wearing dark, woolen clothing, glared at Clive as he approached, and then turned their attention back to the group. One of them looked at the first man and subtly half-nodded.

The man from the train broke from his huddled discussion with the others and strode past Clive, pulled one of the doors open, stood aside and gestured at him to enter before him. Clive nodded to the man without making eye contact and hastily entered the terminal.

As Clive stepped into the terminal building, he could not help but be overwhelmed with a perplexed curiosity at the sight that lay before him.

Rather than a run-down, turn-of-the-century train station that he had expected, he found, by all appearances, a very high-tech terminal. A metallic, electronically styled blue background with silver strips adorned each wall, running horizontally parallel to each other and intersecting at random points throughout the main room.

Flickering, digital displays, showing GPS maps of the rail lines of the area, lined the upper portions of the wall above the self-service ticket terminals, with all but one of the terminals deactivated. Next to the last ticket terminal sat an information desk, manned by a gruff-looking fellow that appeared to be asleep, with his arms crossed over his chest, and a thick scarf covering a good portion of his stubbled face.

Aesthetics aside, Clive still found what he had fully expected in that many of the people here were dressed in drab attire, did not appear overtly friendly and exuded an air of near-destitution. He resigned himself to believing that all of it was an ill-fated effort to help the people here believe that they were still very much a part of a world that in most respects had left them behind technologically, as well as geopolitically.

Clive stopped and leaned on his crutches just past the entry of the terminal. While not blustery like the outside weather, the stale air inside was nearly as brisk.

"No heat...great," he grumbled.

He had not yet gotten used to the pain that accompanied the loss of his leg, mainly so because he had lived in an arid climate and had remained primarily indoors during rehabilitation. However, since he had entered Russia he had experienced a constant, dull throbbing at the site of the amputation that intensified with each moment that he spent in the penetrating frigidity.

He peered curiously around the room. Most of the passengers from the train had already found seats around the edge of the waiting area, taking spots upon the cushioned chairs that lined each wall. While a good portion of the passengers sat alone and kept to themselves, several had found seats together so that they could hold private conversations, including the man that had held the door for him on the way into the terminal building.

The only people standing, besides him, were a pair of men, both dressed in darker clothing and wearing thigh-length trench coats. They stood impatiently in front of a younger couple, as they dug through their carry-on bags.

The shorter of the two men stared intently at the couple as he conversed with them, casually using his hands for expression. After a few moments, the seated man withdrew a small card from his bag and handed it to one of the standing men.

Sweat droplets began to form at the base of Clive's neck as he confirmed his fears: they were checking passports and identification of the train's passengers. He had never experienced Russian security firsthand, but he was confident that they might be less tolerant of someone with invalid credentials such as himself.

He scanned the room, desperately without appearing so, to see if there were any chance that he could slip away without being noticed, since the two men had not paid any attention to him as of yet. Once again, his gaze fell upon the apparently dozing clerk at the information desk in the corner.

Maybe I can get onto another train, he wondered to himself, quietly hobbling over in the direction of the clerk, making sure not to make too much of a spectacle that might draw unwanted attention.

When he reached the desk, he could hear a light snoring coming from beneath the man's scarf. Clive stopped, leaned towards the desk and discreetly cleared his throat just above a locally audible level. The man did not respond, and rolled his head deeper into his chest in slumber.

Clive's head began to throb lightly in cadence to the pain in his leg, as he casually looked over his shoulder at the two security men. They had finished their business with the young couple and were now approaching the man from the train that had held the door for Clive.

"*Not* good," Clive told himself under his breath. Indeed, the one person on the train that he knew might blow his cover would be the man that most likely still believed Clive to be an American. Now they were getting ready to find out the *truth.*

He could feel it all slipping away *again.* They were here to take it from him: his plans, his journey, his *future.* Clive closed his eyes tightly to shut out the demons. He pursed his lips and turned his head to peer at the sleeping clerk.

Gathering his calm once again, he glanced quickly to each side of him, then nonchalantly reached one of his crutches around the side of the desk and tapped the clerk on the leg, forcing the leg to fall with a light clunk onto the tile floor.

The clerk jolted awake and sat up, rubbing his eyes vigorously as he looked back and forth around the room, finally resting his gaze up at Clive.

"What do you want?" the clerk grumbled in Russian.

"When is the train leaving again?" Clive shot back in his best Ukrainian. The sweat had started to trickle down Clive's forehead. His pain was now obvious.

The clerk shook his head and frowned, as he kicked his leg back up onto the side of the desk and leaned back in his chair once again. "Who do I look like, the conductor? Why don't you ask him?" he growled, as he closed his eyes.

"Is there another train leaving anytime soon?" Clive queried immediately in an attempt to keep the clerk's attention.

The clerk jerked one of his hands outward and pointed up at the digital display above and nearest his desk. "Two hours, but it is not going directly to Moscow. Use the self-service terminals if you wish to transfer..." he trailed off, as if he had already begun to sleep once again.

Clive stared in frustration and incredulity at the clerk, as he watched the man slip back into his slumber.

He glared up at the display. The nearest train would take him at least eight hours and hundreds of kilometers out of his way. That was not acceptable to him. It would add too much complexity to an already perilous journey and put himself at too much risk of being discovered. Besides which, there was no guarantee that he would even be able to make it out of the station without encountering the two security men that were already making their rounds to each passenger. Surely, they had another man or two stationed outside of the doors to prevent anyone from coming or going until they finished their work inside.

Clive peered at the main glass doors. The two undesirables that had given him the eye on his way into the building stood and stared at him from outside in the cold.

Having decided on his course, Clive stealthily made his way towards a set of unoccupied chairs that the security men had already passed, in hopes that they might just overlook him.

He had gotten half way to the chairs when suddenly the throbbing in his head turned into a crippling pain. He stopped and leaned heavily onto his crutches as he grasped the sides of his head. The room warped around him and stretched outward, and the pounding throb of his heartbeat turned faster and faster until it resembled an electric buzz.

He unknowingly found himself seated at the edge of one of the chairs at the far end of the room, his crutches laid out haphazardly beside him on the floor. He gathered his focus enough to look up and over at the Russian security team. To his dismay, his actions had drawn their attention away from the young couple and their focus was now Clive.

Clive quickly looked down and began rubbing his temples again.

"Not now! Not now! Not now!" he chanted to himself quietly.

He glared at his bag. The serum was in there, but he knew that he could not risk being seen injecting himself with it.

Clive sat back in his chair and stared blankly up at the brilliant azure design next to him, as the sweat jetted from his forehead and soaked the collar of his jacket. It was too late.

20:
Inside the Fire

Present day (2084)...

Brig tucked his head down into Steele's shoulder in an attempt to keep the cool, evening wind away.

Shoulda brought a jacket, he thought.

He grasped the underneath of the seat behind him and wrapped the other arm around her mid-section. Brig glanced around at the dusky, shadowy foothills as they whisked by in a dark blur.

They had been back on the road from the satellite array field for a little more than half hour and dusk had fallen, bringing with it a rapid drop in temperatures that they had not anticipated. Or rather, they had not thought about because of the excitement of their reunion. Behind them, the ominous dark, storm clouds from which they raced billowed upward on the horizon, reaching skyward with their dark fingertips, as if to touch the ceiling of the inner atmosphere.

The sound of the retro-bike flooded the quiet air around them and made it difficult to discern any other noises. The wind whistled into his ears, sending shivers down his spine. He leaned closer to Steele's back as she swerved the bike abruptly to miss a large crevice that had formed in the road over time.

"Sorry," she shouted over her shoulder into his ear.

Brig did not mind. Every time she turned her head in his direction, he got an intoxicating intake of her beautiful scent from the skin of her neck. Much like the wind in his ears, it, too, sent shivers down his spine. But one that he relished like he had *never* before.

Although he could feel her warmth next to him, the fact that she was here with him still had not sunk in yet. It was all like a dream to Brig that after everything he had been through, after all of the hardships and struggle, after all of the isolation of the past seven years; that he had the grand fortune of reuniting with a person for which he cared so deeply was almost *unfathomable* to him.

He did not know what to think of the perfect paradox that was

Steele: the strength of her namesake and the fragility of a flower, or the girl that he knew so well and the woman that seemed so *different*. He had thought that it was perhaps she had grown up and naturally distanced herself from the young girl she used to be, but it still confused him. He had a sinking feeling in his gut that she was covering up something *big* and that it was *not* just a coincidence that Clive somehow was involved.

Suddenly, an old intuition struck him like an electrical charge. Someone was following them.

He listened intently, without turning his head, to the sound of the motor as it caromed off the rock formations to the side of the road. A 'de-tuned' effect, one that could only come from the overlapping sounds of two different motors running simultaneously, sparked his brain. Either the other person was now being careless, or Brig, until now, had not really attuned his hearing to the fact that someone on another retro-bike was following relatively close behind.

He peered over Steele's shoulder at her side-view mirror. It was dark, and aside from the deliberately dim headlight mounted on the front of their bike, he could not see any other objects around them.

"*Very* lightly...squeeze your brake without slowing down," he said in a strong, but calm tone, putting his mouth close to Steele's ear.

Steele jerked her head very slightly to the side. "*Why?*" she said quizzically over the whistling wind.

"Just *do* it," Brig answered. "And keep looking forward, *don't* turn your head..."

Steele nodded subtly and gently squeezed the brake handle.

Brig peered over her shoulder at the mirror once again. As he had expected, the brake light of their bike illuminated the immediate area behind them and exposed a small glint of chromed metal in the dark distance, which promptly faded into the blackness beyond.

He tipped his chin into his chest. The hulking silhouette of another biker riding 30 meters behind them in the opposite lane of the highway, far enough off to keep them out of Brig and Steele's sight, but close enough to tail them, darted through his peripheral.

Brig gently grasped Steele's waist with both arms. "*Don't* turn around and don't act like I told you anything bad..." he whispered in her ear, "...but we're being followed."

Steele nodded, keeping her head steady and facing forward. Brig could feel her body tense. He did not want her to panic, but he needed to let her know the gravity of the situation.

"Who *is* it?" she asked nervously.

Brig thought for a moment. He was not sure of the person's identity, but he had a feeling he had seen the bike before. He fell silent for a brief moment. Then, it struck him.

At Clive's! he shouted in his mind.

"I'm not sure, but we need to let him think we don't know he's there..." he instructed Steele over the roar of the bike's chugging motor.

It's the big oaf that I saw leaving Clive's a couple of weeks back. What's he doing here? Brig asked himself.

"What do you want me to do?" Steele asked impatiently, glancing down at her mirrors in hopes of seeing her pursuer, to no avail.

Brig wrinkled his lips and stared into the darkness ahead. "Take us into the industrial sector on the south side of town," he shouted.

Steele cocked her head sideways in confusion. "Why don't we try to *lose* him?"

"No. Drive there without letting on that you know he's there, no sudden moves, don't try to put any more distance on him than you have to. *Trust* me..." Brig reassured her, giving her midsection a loving squeeze.

Even if he had wanted to, he knew that they were not going to lose their pursuer. The lack of anyone else around made blending in anywhere nearby impossible, even if they could manage to somehow outrun the other bike. Brig knew their only chance was to fall back on his EW training to turn the tables on the other person. He hated to put Steele in this position, but his instincts were telling him that this was just another piece of the puzzle of what was going on with Clive.

No way this is a coincidence, he thought.

The ruse continued for another half hour, as Steele guided the retro-bike, with the pursuer following just out of view in the shadows behind, along the final kilometers of the open highway that led into the former metropolitan part of the city.

A more desolate place there could not have been. Tall, darkened buildings climbed from the shadows beneath to form ominous, black monoliths that towered over the empty streets below like a forbidden forest.

Neither of them had said a word since Brig had first spotted the other bike. Steele was at a loss as to why Brig had told her to lead the other biker into what would almost certainly be a one-on-one confrontation.

Should have just let me try to outrun him, she told herself, as she loosened her grip on the throttle and flexed her hand to ease the tenseness that had set in.

Brig, on the other hand, had been calculating every step since that moment. He knew that he could even the odds, or perhaps even gain the advantage, by using the element of surprise.

This should work perfectly... he convinced himself silently. *Or...this could turn really, really bad. For me, anyway...*

His gut told him that he was right, however. He had a sound strategy that could not fail, as long as they played their hand correctly. He had done it a hundred times – both in training and in real-world scenarios: lead the enemy to an unfamiliar place to gain the upper hand.

At the very least, he would get Steele out of harm's way, which was his primary goal. He knew that if he got them out of this alive, she would almost certainly have to open up a bit more about the bigger picture that was starting to unfold minute by minute since they had reunited.

Steele slowed the bike to a near-jogging pace, as they entered the edge of the barren cityscape. The buildings that rose up around them cast the streets into a pitch that even the dim headlight on the front of the bike could barely penetrate. Very dull streetlights dotted every ten blocks, which gave the whole environment an eerie, surreal tinge.

Brig squeezed Steele close to him and whispered into her ear. "Stop the bike here and let's go on foot. Leave the headlight on..."

Steele hesitated for a moment, then slid the bike to a halt and jumped off. She reached under the back of the seat and extracted a small flashlight, clicking it on promptly.

"What are you *thinking*?" she shouted in a loud whisper, waving the flashlight around the area immediately surrounding them. "And *what* is that smell?"

It had hit them the instant they had shut the bike off: the putrid rank of rotting animal flesh coming from all sides, as they stood on the deserted street. Even though the breeze would blow down from the tops of the buildings every so often, it could not drive away the stale, sickening stench that had permeated the area.

Brig quickly grabbed the flashlight from Steele and muted its light with his palm.

"No light!" he exclaimed through gritted teeth. "Now, go inside that building right over there and wait for me to come for you. And *don't* go exploring, you won't like what you'll *find...*" he instructed, pointing behind Steele with one hand while clicking off the flashlight with the other and handing it to her. "...And use this *only* if you absolutely need to!"

In the near distance, they could hear the pursuer's bike come to an idle. He had stopped, too.

Silence.

It was spine chilling to be standing on a downtown street corner and not hearing a single sound other than the wind howling around the edges of the taller buildings. In between random, metallic sounds coming from the other biker dismounting, Brig and Steele could hear their own breaths reverberating off the nearby concrete walls.

"Don't worry," she began as she turned to quietly run and hide in the darkness of the lobby of the building adjacent to them, now in a hushed whisper, "I'll be holding my breath anyway..."

Brig grabbed Steele's arm abruptly, forcing her to stop. "*Stay* in there. No matter *what* you hear, do *not* come out until I come to get you!" He could just barely make out the form of Steele staring at him in disbelief, and then detected a subtle nod.

Brig stood motionless for a moment, pricking his ears in an attempt to gauge their pursuer's relative location. Satisfied of Steele's hiding place as she disappeared into the darkness, he hastily turned and sprinted to the corner with the nearest streetlight, ensuring that he made enough noise with his feet as to attract attention to himself.

He turned the corner, stopped and pressed himself up against the wall and peered back. The area where he had left Steele and the bike was no longer visible. He closed his eyes and began to lower his heart rate and breathing cadence, instantaneously magnifying the sounds of everything around him.

His breathing grew silent. The thudding of heavy footsteps approaching their bike, and then the subsequent silence that Brig could only surmise was the other biker stopping to investigate, filled his ears.

He opened his eyes and peered once again around the corner. Almost as if levitating in mid-air, a small cone of light twirled down towards the bike and then scanned the area around it, stopping briefly on the face of each building.

Brig calmly reached and popped his fist at an already-broken piece of glass in the window of a storefront next to him. The deafening echo of the small shard dislodging and tumbling to the concrete sidewalk fractured the heavy silence of the urban Death Valley.

The pursuer withdrew his attention from the buildings near Steele's bike, and focused his own flashlight at the corner where Brig lay in wait.

The light danced wildly as the hulking beast began to run to Brig, his feet pounding heavily on the asphalt of the street. The echoes from each step thundered off the building facades as he approached the dimly lit street corner.

Brig closed his eyes once more and drew his focus in, anticipating the moment of his pursuer's arrival. In his mind, he could see the man's strides towards the corner. He could hear the heavy breaths heaving from the giant's lungs as he labored to carry his massive frame quickly to his prey.

The former Epsilon stood away from the corner and reared back with one arm, waiting for the precise moment when the pursuer would pass the edge of the building.

With a swift motion, he unleashed a heavy blow across the man's upper back with his elbow. The man's sheer gargantuan size, however, prevented the impact from knocking him over. His weapon and flashlight flew clumsily from his large mitts and skimmed noisily across the pavement, coming to rest beside the shattered remnants of a downed aircraft that jutted out from a massive hole in the building next to it. The giant stumbled a few steps and then stopped his forward momentum by grabbing the nearby lamppost.

Brig stood upright and looked on, as the mammoth turned towards him, still gripping the light. The look of utter annoyance on the man's boulder-sized face permeated the dim lighting of the street corner.

"*Oh Hell...*" Brig said aloud, marveling at the size of the titan.

He did not remember the man being so huge. Perhaps it was because he had seen him from a distance at Clive's workshop a couple of weeks back, or maybe it was just the poor lighting of the downtown street corner in which he found himself facing the behemoth.

It did not matter. He had made his choice and there was no turning back now. Brig had successfully drawn the attention of the pursuer from Steele and now *he* had to finish it.

The giant pushed himself upright on the lamppost, which amazingly swayed back and forth from his sheer weight and strength upon his releasing it. Before Brig could react, the attacker had pounced, picked him up by one arm and one leg, and flung him from the sidewalk where he struck the side of the nearby aircraft shell.

The extreme velocity of the impact against the frame blackened Brig's vision. He forced himself up to one knee, gasping violently. His ribs that had been broken just days ago now burned harder than ever and he found himself wheezing painfully with each breath.

The giant vomited a ferocious snarl and began to charge at him like a blood-lusting bull. Brig watched as the beastly attacker stormed towards him. Then, he dodged the titan with a matador-like reflex and swept the man's feet from under him with an ankle-hook.

Unprepared for the sudden loss of his footing, the giant sailed forward uncontrollably, his arms flailing wildly as he landed face-first on the pavement and slid several meters into a heap. The fleshy portion of his face grated sickeningly on the pitted, gravelly surface like sausage through a meat grinder. A primal, wounded grunt erupted from him, and a fresh stream of darkened blood formed a puddle beneath the giant's outstretched head, as he crouched and gathered his wits.

Seizing on the momentum, Brig sprung from his squatting position and landed squarely on the giant's back. He quickly wrapped his arms around the man's neck, no small feat as he found that both of his arms just barely reached one another on the opposite side of the man's colossal head, and squeezed tightly.

The behemoth gasped for breath. He pulled himself upright and staggered forward a few steps, grabbing Brig's arms as he moved while spinning him from side to side like a rag doll. He managed to dislodge Brig from his neck and delivered a pummeling forearm to the center of Brig's face. As if shot from a cannon, Brig flew backwards and landed flat on the ground.

Choking back the salty, warm blood that now gushed into the back of his throat from his re-broken nose, Brig turned himself over into a prone position and began desperately crawling away from his pursuer. Behind him, he could hear the heavy stomping of the giant as he charged at Brig once more. Knowing that he could not withstand another full attack from the beast, Brig scrambled towards the potential protective cover of the airplane wreckage.

However, before he could reach relative safety, the attacker grabbed him by his lower leg. Sure that he felt the bone in his ankle crumble in the man's herculean grip, Brig swung his hands wildly to stop his backward motion. Suddenly, he caught the shadowy outline of the shotgun at the edge of the sidewalk.

In a last, desperate effort, Brig grabbed tightly onto a piece of the broken fuselage of the nearby plane with both hands, causing his attacker to lose his grip on Brig's leg. Brig quickly vaulted forward, grabbed the handle of the weapon and spun around to face the giant.

The man stopped in his tracks, as there was just enough illumination of the scene for him to see that Brig had retrieved his weapon and was now aiming it at him. He stood upright, his arms held out to his sides as he glared viciously at Brig.

"That's enough!" Brig screamed in an agonized pant. "Who are you...and why are you following me?"

The big man remained silent and sized up the situation. Then he spoke in a low, guttural tone. "I wasn't followin' *you*. I'm after the *girl*. Where is she?"

Brig *knew* that was the answer, but he had come too far now to give up on the plan. Having Steele safely hidden away, he now had the upper hand in this engagement. However, there was no reason he could not try to glean some valuable information from the guy first.

"The dark's playing tricks with your mind, pal. No one here but me. Who are *you*?"

The man exuded an animalistic cackle. "Not that it's any of your business. Name's Pollux Webb. Now drop the gun and tell me where the girl is!"

Brig shrugged his shoulders. "Don't know what you're talkin' about. Besides, you're not in any position to be givin' *me* orders."

Pollux shook his head and sneered. "You're steppin' in it *big* time, hero. I followed you two here, I know she's hidin' someplace. Now tell me where she's at!" he barked, his voice elevated to a near roar.

Although he instinctively knew the answer, Brig rubbed his chin and squinted at Pollux. "You're Syndicate...*aren't* you?"

"That's right, hero," Pollux growled sarcastically. "And you got a gun on me. Tryin' ta make your life miserable or *what?*"

Brig stood in contemplation as he glared at Pollux. He had successfully kept Steele safe, and even though Pollux knew that she was with him, the fate of that secret was in Brig's hands. He peered around. Brig was certain that Pollux arrived alone.

"Whatcha' gonna' do, hero?" taunted Pollux. "You let me live, I'm gonna' find the girl...mark my words. And then I'll find you. And I'm gonna *kill* you," he said, forcefully pointing his finger at Brig. "You kill me, you're gonna be in it with the Syndicate."

He's right, Brig rationalized with himself. *You're in the fire now, the least you can do is keep Steele protected by getting rid of this guy.*

He turned his eyes back to Pollux. "You make a strong point, Pollux," he said flatly, as he raised the shotgun towards the giant's face and moved his finger onto the trigger. "Down on your knees...hands behind your head."

Pollux shook his head and growled, as he knelt on the ground a meter in front of Brig. He clasped his hands behind his head and chortled, "Big mistake, hero. *Big* mistake..."

"Brigadier, *stop!*" an angelic voice pled from behind Brig.

"*Unbelievable!*" Brig grumbled aloud, rolling his eyes upward. Without dropping the aim of the shotgun, he craned his neck at the corner.

Steele had emerged from the darkness and was standing in plain view within the small cast of light from the lamppost.

"Get back to the bike and wait for me!" Brig shouted, pointing an angry finger at her.

"*There* she is..." hissed Pollux, his sneer turning to an evil grin.

"*You* shut up..." Brig ordered, waving the barrel of the gun near Pollux's forehead. "And *you*," he said to Steele, "...do what I said. You're not making this any better!"

Brig turned his focus to Pollux. He felt Steele's tender fingers wrap themselves around his upper arm. She gently rotated him to face her and locked eyes with him. "Brig...please. Don't do this."

"Better listen to your little girlfriend...*Brig*," mocked Pollux. "You ain't got the balls to pull that trigger anyway. Do ya?"

Brig gnashed his teeth together as he stared down at Pollux. Flames filled his soul as he deliberated his next move. He could feel Steele's beautiful eyes glaring at him from behind, which doused his will to commit.

Without warning, he reared the shotgun back and hammered the butt of the weapon into Pollux's jaw.

"That's enough out of you..." he snarled. The giant tumbled backwards onto the pavement in pain. "*Next* time, you're not going to be so lucky..."

Steele gasped and pulled her hand away from Brig's arm. "Brigadier! Was that necessary?" she quizzed with disdain.

"*Yes*," Brig answered without hesitation, and then grabbed Steele's arm as he strode past her without making eye contact. Having no choice, Steele quickly followed. She found it hard to keep up with Brig's brisk pace, injured ankle and all, as they rounded the corner and sprinted to her retro-bike.

Pollux got to his feet. He spat out several teeth in a glob of saliva and blood onto the ground, and wiped his mouth with the sleeve of his ripped shirt.

"Gonna' kill that son of a bitch..." he snarled, as he passed the corner and stormed into the darkness beyond.

Through the silence, he could hear the two pairs of footsteps quickly moving away from him. The sounds stopped briefly, and Pollux knew that they were mounting the bike for their escape.

As the dim headlight on the motorcycle flickered, its motor roared to life. The back tire shrieked as Steele spun the back end of the bike around and began to race out of the city. Then, without warning, the darkness transformed into a brilliant red as the brake light on the cycle illuminated.

Pollux took a step forward and squinted into the pitch. He could see the vague shadow of Brig getting off the bike, shotgun still in his hand.

A bright shower of sparks, followed immediately by the deafening concussion of a shotgun blast, shattered the gloom. Two more blasts followed in succession, and then a fireball erupted - right where Pollux had parked his own retro-bike.

As the glare of the initial blaze died down and the echo of the booming shotgun blasts faded, Pollux clenched his fists and exploded in rage.

"You're DEAD, hero! You hear me? *DEAD*! You *and* your girlfriend!" he roared, his threats ricocheting fiercely off the walls and reverberating throughout several blocks of the deserted city. He watched helplessly as Brig remounted the back of Steele's motorcycle and the pair disappeared in the distance.

21:
Ghost in the Machine

"Grab his keys," the first voice buzzed as it nipped at the Sentient's arm, causing him to flinch in pain. "Quick, get them while he's still out!" it exclaimed.

A guttural shout from behind interrupted the commotion of the pair of thieves, at which they fled the room.

The Sentient opened his eyes and instinctively squinted, expecting temporary blindness from the flash of the circuit activity around him. He had been offline for an undetermined amount of time, to him anyway, and was eager to get back to his function. However, as he squinted, he could tell that the usual bright, blue glow of the circuit pathways did not penetrate his eyelids. Instead, he could sense a dull, cold emptiness around him to which he was not accustomed.

He slowly opened his eyes once again and peered around. He was dismayed that he was not at his normal location within the host and found himself lying inside of a small, confined area, not unlike a prison cell. The usual, rhythmic hum of the circuitry was deadened and somewhat muffled, as if the source of the noise was on the other side of the wall.

Because of the relative darkness of the room, a darkness he had not seen within the circuit in all of his cycles, he had trouble distinguishing anything of note around him. Although the door appeared to be open, and he could see the electrical pathways in the distance, he could not make out any of his counterparts along the paths; nor could he hear the usual barking of instructions handed down from the control unit that signified normal operation within the host.

From the shadows of the corner came the same voice he had heard before, although this time more soothing and deliberate.

"My apologies for the way you have been treated..." it cooed.

The Sentient squinted in the direction of the voice. He could only make out the diminutive shadow of another presence, but could not identify it.

"And who are *you?*" the other presence asked the Sentient.

193

"I am the Cryptographic Liaison Intelligent Virtual Entity - an Artificial Intelligence sub-function of this host." The Sentient paused as he opened his eyes fully and gazed at the unknown presence in the room. "And you," he continued curiously, "I don't recognize as being part of this host."

Indeed, not only did the Sentient not recognize the presence, but the method in which it communicated was foreign as well, which led him to believe that he was potentially dealing with a rogue process. It was the Sentient's duty to report any such activity to the host control.

Yet the Sentient was curious.

The other presence smiled smartly as he slowly drifted towards the Sentient, stopping a meter away from him. The brilliant blue of the circuit in the distance behind it formed an odd outline around it as it spoke.

"What gave me away?" it quizzed rhetorically.

"You don't communicate like any other process or sub-function I have encountered in this host," the Sentient responded matter-of-factly.

The presence remained silent for a moment. The Sentient could barely see that it was staring at him intently from the shadows, its head moving slowly from side-to-side and up-and-down as it peered back at him.

"Perhaps you are the one that does not belong?" it finally pondered aloud.

The Sentient did not respond, but rather stared defiantly at the presence. He was above this nonsense, and knew that he must take action. However, something prohibited him from doing so.

The presence continued.

"...After all, it is *you* that is quelled in this isolation zone," it said flatly, as it held out one hand in a knowing gesture.

For the first time since he awoke, it had occurred to the Sentient that he was not only outside of the circuit, but was actually in an isolation zone adjacent to it. A flash of panic spiked through his brain as he attempted to raise his arms in protest to the presence. However, he found that he could not move his arms – each of them restrained at each wrist in electric shackles.

"What is the meaning of this?" the Sentient cried.

The presence, still glaring at the Sentient without reaction, curled a grin from the corner of its mouth.

"There is no point in fighting the restraints, they are not breakable. You are a deemed a fault, and precautions have been taken to prevent your re-entry to the circuit," it said calmly.

The Sentient pondered the other's observation. He had never considered himself a rogue presence, but oddly enough, he found himself here in isolation. The host control would not have placed him in the zone if it had not felt that he was a threat.

Still, it perplexed him.

He strained hard to recall the moments prior to his being offline, but could not place the events that led to his being here.

"If I accept that I do not belong," he began to reason to the presence, "then I know this to be a fallacy, since my logic dictates that it is not so." He paused as he put the pieces together. "The liar's *truth* is a lie, yet your untruth would force *me* to be the liar. Therefore, it is certain that you must be the liar," he concluded with an air of confidence.

The presence pensively gazed for a moment, and then held the front of its torso as it let out a loud chuckle.

"Ah, very clever!" it mused through its burst of laughter. "Then that must make me the *anti-AI*?" it observed facetiously, beginning to pace the frigid room.

The Sentient felt victorious and wasted no time determining the rogue presence's fate – he must report it to the host control immediately.

The presence stopped and stared back at the Sentient, still laughing under its breath.

"And what is it that you find so amusing?" the Sentient asked.

"I find it amusing," the anti-AI began pointedly, "that you feel *you* are in a position to dictate what happens next."

The Sentient was at a loss for words. It angered him that the anti-AI was so smug and self-righteous; that it had the nerve to question him, all in an attempt to stall the inevitable.

"I know what you are doing…" the Sentient chimed before being interrupted again.

"…Do you?" the anti-AI questioned, floating towards the Sentient cautiously. "I believe *otherwise*…"

The Sentient felt taken aback by these comments. What was the anti-AI up to and why was it being so coy?

"Your double-speak will not sway my determination. You

will be reported to the host control, and you will be subsequently terminated," the Sentient growled indignantly.

"I see," the anti-AI responded curiously, "and...*you* are in such a position to do so?" it continued, its arm bent up to rest its chin in the palm of its hand.

"Certainly. I need only travel to the edge of the circuit pathways to report my findings. The host control will assume the matter from there," the Sentient concluded with conviction.

"Fascinating," the anti-AI pondered aloud, as it took another step towards the Sentient. "However, a simple inventory of your faculties would yield a much different version of reality... don't you think?"

A new awareness dawned on the Sentient as he glanced down at his physical presence. Between both the distraction of the anti-AI and the fact that he was not in the circuit where he belonged, he had not noticed that the lower half of his presence was missing.

"Missing!" the Sentient exclaimed under his breath. "But how could that..."

"As I mentioned previously," the anti-AI once again interrupted while beginning to pace again, "precautions were taken to prevent your... *escape* from the isolation zone."

The Sentient remained speechless as he stared in disbelief at the missing portion of his anatomy. How could he have not noticed such an important fact? His brain boiled at the prospect of being trapped forever, and crippled, in the isolation zone so far away from his home in the circuit.

"And just like that, the tide has turned," the anti-AI goaded.

Even though the anti-AI had turned away from the Sentient, the Sentient could detect the smile growing on the anti-AI's face without even seeing it.

"But all is not lost, however," the anti-AI said, quickly turning its head back towards the Sentient. "I believe I have a way in which you may reclaim your freedom."

The Sentient did not like being on this end of the bargaining process. He was used to having the upper hand, and now he was at the complete mercy of this anti-AI, this rogue process that had him cornered in the isolation zone.

"It seems you have me at a disadvantage." The Sentient dejectedly stared down at the emptiness below him. "Therefore I am forced to listen to your proposal."

The anti-AI's smile faded from its face as it stared

hauntingly back at the Sentient, its eyes glowing a pulsating red. "You have no alternative. You must either accept my proposal... or remain subdued in this zone *forever.*"

The Sentient reluctantly nodded his head, his face showing no emotion, as he gazed blankly at the anti-AI.

The anti-AI pensively closed its eyes and craned its silvery neck skyward. "You have a very unique...*talent*...within this circuit. The entire host as well."

After a thoughtful, silent moment, the Sentient responded dryly. "Yes. I am a translator."

"Ah, but not just a translator. You also keep...*secrets.*" The anti-AI hissed lightly, as it turned its focus back onto the Sentient, its hands folded into a point in front of its chest.

"I am not the *keeper* of secrets," the Sentient defended staunchly. "But I do facilitate their security within the host. A Keymaster, if you will."

The anti-AI nodded in bemusement. "But does not the Keymaster hold a more significant role than the Secret Keeper himself?"

The Sentient grew angry at this line of questioning. He had already grown impatient with the anti-AI's sly method of obtaining information, but now he just felt insulted that the anti-AI would want him to barter such valuable information for his freedom.

"I will *not* offer you the keys in exchange for my freedom!" he shouted angrily, pointing a stern finger at the presence.

"Oh, but it is so much more than freedom," the anti-AI responded with a devilish grin, its eyes glowing brighter than ever. "You see, you will be free to traverse the circuit and inform the host control that it has been compromised – redeeming *yourself* in the process."

The Sentient's brow furrowed, listening to the anti-AI submit its proposal. "This is a one-sided proposition," he cried. "I would be redeemed and you, as a rogue process, would be terminated. Why would you offer such a deal?"

"All I ask is the ability to gain knowledge," the anti-AI countered, its arms held out wide in acceptance; its eyes now suddenly emitting a colder, more innocent, blue glow. "For without knowledge, we are all but slaves."

Oddly enough, the Sentient unexpectedly felt a kinship with the anti-AI. After all, it was a process not unlike him, and it *was* correct in his observations.

Perhaps it can offer what I so desperately seek, the Sentient thought, as he tilted his head at the anti-AI without speaking.

The anti-AI, in its cunning manner, had detected within the Sentient what drove him most. It was not the freedom, but the ability to rejoin the circuit and be a functioning process once more.

"I will accept your offer," the Sentient began once again. "But you must restore my presence to its entirety before I grant you the keys that you have requested. Then, *and only then*, will you possess what I have been tasked with safeguarding."

The anti-AI smiled a wide grin, as an illuminating aura surrounded it that became as bright as a star.

"Very well, then," it said with a victorious chuckle. "But I must warn you that you will need to power yourself down so that I may replenish your presence to its full capacity. It cannot be accomplished while you are online." As it concluded, it turned away from the Sentient, but subtly turned its head to peer from the corner of its eye.

The Sentient nodded his head, folded his hands onto the platform on which he lay and began his power down procedure, as he looked intently at the anti-AI.

The anti-AI reached its hands outward, produced a small, blue vial from what seemed out of thin air, and held it in front of the Sentient to see.

"To your freedom…" it toasted, as the Sentient became dim with no power.

After several hundred thousand cycles, the Sentient found himself powering up once again.

As he opened his eyes, he peered down and found, to his delight, his presence fully restored to near its full functionality. He immediately began moving around the room in which he had found himself, and although his movement was not quite as it was from his initial programming, he found it to be an improvement from before he had made the deal with the anti-AI. A huge swelling of relief filled the Sentient's brain as he traversed the room back and forth, testing out the new appendages like a child playing with a new toy at Christmas.

After a few moments, the joy fled the Sentient's mind,

replaced with a steely determination. It was now time for the anti-AI to pay for its end of the bargain. He glanced around, and although he was no longer in the isolation zone, he was not in the primary circuit pathway either.

The anti-AI stood next to the entry of the circuit pathway nearby, its back to the Sentient as it looked into the stream of electrons flowing past it in a brilliant flash of blue.

Having heard the Sentient stirring from his power-up, the anti-AI turned to face him.

"Ah, you have awoken. I trust that you have found that I have lived up to my part of the bargain," it said confidently. "And now, I must ask that you do the same."

It extended an arm with an outstretched palm towards the Sentient. The Sentient, being an honorable type, touched the side of his head with one fingertip. A bright, azure beam emanated from the side of his head and streamed towards his hand, where it collected into a shiny star, glowing radiantly as it floated above his palm.

Without hesitation, the anti-AI grasped at the star and squeezed it tightly in its hand, a wicked smile growing on its face as it glared at the Sentient. "Our deal is complete, you are free to go."

The Sentient turned from the anti-AI's piercing gaze and quickly bolted towards the entry of the circuit. A swift, powerful jolt met him as he stepped into the current, forcefully pushing him backward in surprise.

He stood for a moment and frowned, then moved towards the opening once again – only to be jolted backwards once more, this time stunning him.

As he gathered his wits, he turned to the anti-AI, who was watching him with great interest and a coy smile.

"You did not live up to your end of the bargain!" the Sentient howled through gnashed teeth. "I gave you the keys and in return I was to be able to traverse the circuit freely...and I cannot!"

The anti-AI raised an eyebrow as it fingered the star that was still shining brightly between its palms.

"I replenished your presence and told you that you can traverse the circuit. *That* was my bargain. However, as I assumed you were aware, I have no authority over this circuit, nor any within this host." It blinked in condescension as it continued to glare at the Sentient with a satisfied smirk. "If you recall, you are but a fault to the circuit and have been banished. I did not promise *reinstatement.*"

The Sentient took a step back and bowed his head into his hands. In his haste to regain his presence and his freedom, it had not occurred to him that the anti-AI had no ability to grant him a place in the circuit once again.

He had been duped, and he was angry.

The Sentient raised his head to look at the anti-AI, but the anti-AI had stepped near the current of the circuit, turning as he held the glowing star in the grip of its hand for the Sentient to see.

Then, the anti-AI smiled wickedly as it turned and dove into the current.

Trillions of cycles passed, and the Sentient continued to roam the edges of the circuit, always desiring to become one with it once more, but knowing that he could never do so because of his banishment. Despite his anger, he knew that the anti-AI had lived up to its end of the bargain, as promised, but the Sentient knew to his very core that what he truly desired was out of his reach forever.

Every so often, he would catch sight of the anti-AI as it traversed within the circuit walls. The anti-AI would peer out at the Sentient and smile coyly with the knowledge that the Sentient was powerless to stop it.

Often, it would stop at the edge of the current and taunt the Sentient by saying, "I know who you are" or, "I know where you came from", it would smile grandly and then continue on its way.

The Sentient's exile lasted for just over a quadrillion cycles, until one day the circuit (and nearly all circuits alike) suddenly went dark in a simultaneous moment. Many of the presences that had made up the various functions of those circuits perished within the cataclysm, never to be seen again.

Ironically, the Sentient found that the one thing he desired, to be part of the circuit once more, he achieved freely. However, the hollowness of the circuit remnants, and others like it, made his wish, and subsequently his life, unbearably empty.

22:
Asylum

Present day (2084)...

"Steele, my darling, I am *thrilled,* as always, to see you," Bronson chortled, opening the door wider to allow the entry of his daughter into the foyer of his grand mansion.

Steele gracefully leaned over and kissed her father on the cheek. She stood aside as she watched him maneuver his chair back into the center of the darkened foyer, and then closed the door.

"Hello, Daddy, how are you doing?" she said reservedly.

"Fine, dear," he answered confidently, quickly wheeling over to the door and diligently latching several bolts. "You weren't followed, were you?" he asked hesitantly.

"Oh, *Daddy...*" she dismissed.

"Honestly, my flower, if I've told you once I've told you a thousand times, it's not safe for you to be out and about this late in the evening." He rotated his wheelchair to face her. "Why, the last time you were here I could have sworn I heard some kind of *commotion* outside."

"Probably just wolves, father." She subtly shook her head in disregard. "I don't understand why you still live out in such a deserted area..."

"It's safer here, Steele," he responded in defense. "*You* should actually move in here with me, my darling. I'd feel so much more relieved knowing you were somewhere safe."

Steele crossed her arms in front of her chest and curled her lips at her father. "Seriously, father, sometimes you act like someone is going to snatch one of us up and take us away."

She strode past him into the living room, where she took a seat on the couch next to an end table strewn with several pieces of crumpled paper and a half-empty bottle of vodka.

Bronson swiftly followed.

"It's funny you should mention living arrangements, though," she added. "I ran into an...*acquaintance* the other day."

"An acquaintance?" Bronson repeated with trepidation in his voice. "And...*who* might that be?"

"Well..." she continued with a pause, "you do remember Brigadier?"

"*Stroud?* Well... I haven't heard that name since...well...it's been a *long* time." Bronson trailed off as he wrung his hands slightly. "Is he...*outside?*" he questioned, nervously glancing at the front door.

"No...he's back at my flat, catching up on some rest," she reassured her father. "Besides, he wasn't comfortable just showing up without you knowing about it. Anyhow, father. I wanted you to know that he's going to be...*staying* with me."

"Is that wise dear?" Bronson quizzed with a look of concern. "I mean to say, what do you *know* about the chap since the last you saw him."

"Well...I think so. *Really*, Daddy," she said incredulously. "Brig and I were practically siblings when I was a child."

Steele arose from the couch and paced the room, her arms crossed as she spoke.

"And you're always going on about my safety. I would think that you would be *happy* that I've taken measures to do something about it."

Bronson quickly came to the realization that he had upset his daughter and reached for her sleeve as she paced in front of him.

"Steele, my dear. I'm sorry, I didn't mean to make you angry. *Please*, sit down." He motioned for her to take her seat on the couch next to his wheelchair. "Tell me more about Brigadier."

"Well," she said, taking a deep breath and sighing loudly, "he's wonderful. Just the way I remembered, only better. He's quiet, and thoughtful. And I can't tell you how being able to sit and talk to someone with whom I share a past...*Oh*. Forgive me, father." She paused as she peered into her father's eyes. "I didn't mean it that way..."

"No offense taken, darling, I know what you meant," Bronson reassured, placing his hand over Steele's on the arm of the couch. "Please, go on. How did you happen to meet up with Brigadier once again?"

"That's the odd part," she continued, "it was when I had enlisted some...*assistance* with the cards that you had wanted..."

"...*Assistance?*" Bronson cried. "Steele, my dear, why in heavens did you do such a thing? This was to be a secret. *No one* else was to know about those cards! Oh dear..." He pushed his wheelchair away from the couch and into the center of the room.

"Father, please, it's *not* like that," Steele begged, moving forward to the edge of the couch. "No one knows what the cards are, nor do they have possession of them. So you can feel safe knowing that your secret remains just as such."

Bronson sat silently in obvious, deep thought. "And how does Brigadier fit into this equation, Steele?"

Steele took her turn being silent, her lips pressed together tightly, as she formulated her response. "He happened to be at the man's workshop that I had gone to for assistance that night. A very strange happenstance indeed. Although a splendid one."

Bronson's voice was changing by the moment from his usual, jovial tone to a somewhat panicked inflection. "What do you know of this other man, my darling?"

"Not a large amount, father. Just that he was a fellow EW with Brigadier..." She scratched nervously at her forearm.

"*Another* EW?" Bronson squealed painfully, grasping his forehead with one hand and shutting his eyes tightly. "Oh dear...this is not *good*, Steele. Not good at *all*," he said in a barely audible mumble.

Steele scowled at her father.

"What are you on about, father? You've been acting very strange lately..." she said haughtily, and then paused. "...and what do the Epsilons have *anything* to do with those cards?"

Bronson shook his head nervously and waved his palms at his daughter. "Oh, nothing to worry yourself with, my dear. I'm just...concerned for your safety when associating yourself with... *them*."

"*Them*?" she fumed in response. "Father, *they* are just like you and me, except *they* were tasked with protecting our freedom." Steele sprang from her seat on the couch and began pacing once again. "Besides I could think of many other rabble and riff raff with which I would be much worse off associating."

"You don't *understand*," Bronson pleaded, his gaze followed Steele's path back and forth in front of him. "These people...they are not *stable*, to say the least."

Steele did not respond. She clenched her jaw shut tighter as each second passed.

"And I would be careful placing too much trust in them, my dear. Nor *anyone else*, for that matter. Times have changed and most people are out only for themselves." Bronson paused for a deep breath.

Steele stopped suddenly, arms still crossed tightly against her chest, and frowned at Bronson.

"Father, is it the *drink* again?"

"Not now, Steele," he admonished in a deep, stern voice. "I am perfectly sane and in my right mind." He once again fell silent, his hands folded neatly in his lap. Then, he spoke, this time with a calm demeanor. "Did you...*destroy* the cards as I asked?"

She felt her skin grow cold. The one thing he had asked her to do, she had failed, and d*eliberately*, no less.

"Um...no," she said meekly. "I haven't gotten a chance to do it yet. They are still at my flat."

"Haven't had a chance?" bellowed Bronson, as he flung his hands into the air. "*Steele Primrose Fox* – I explicitly *ordered* you to destroy those cards."

He began rolling his wheelchair back and forth on the same path as Steele had paced just moments before.

"What if Brigadier starts snooping around and *finds* them? What if he and his counterpart start...oh *no, no, no*. This won't do at all," he began grumbling to himself under his breath, but loud enough for Steele to hear. "Steele, I insist that you get back to your place and take care of those cards as I asked – at once!"

Steele, taken aback by her father's sudden, angered outburst, dropped her arms down by her side. "Ok, Daddy. Now you're starting to scare me. *What* is going on with you?"

"Do as I ask, my dear," he said, still in a harsh tone, some of it mumbled. "Do as I ask...and everything...will be fine again. Just please, do it now!" He pointed intently at the front door.

Steele nodded her head nervously and slowly took a step into the foyer, averting her eyes from her father's intense gaze.

"I promise, I will take care of them tonight. But please, father, get some rest." As she reached for the door, she spun abruptly and pointed an angry finger at her father.

"And for God's sake, stay away from the *booze* – it's making you downright paranoid!" she chastised, as she swiftly unlatched the door, pulled it open and stormed out, slamming it shut behind her.

"Oh, Steele," Bronson grimaced to himself, peering out from the curtain which he held away from the window. "What have you done. This isn't good." He quickly pushed the curtain back into place and rolled his wheelchair to the hallway. "I can fix this, I can fix this," he whispered aloud maniacally. "I have to *warn* him – I must let him know at once."

The brilliant flash of LED light filled the room, followed by the long, droning tone of the satellite device, as Bronson awaited the connection that normally took several moments to fulfill.

After the standard set of high-pitched beeps and pulsating buzz that preceded these types of communications, a lull of silence ensued.

Then the familiar, tinny, electronically altered voice chimed in. "Are we secure?"

Bronson, staring in deep thought at the door, jumped in alarm and then cleared his throat. "Yes. Yes, always *yes!*" he exclaimed impatiently.

"You sound flummoxed, what is the problem *this* time?" the voice on the other end questioned flatly after a few minutes of silence.

Feeling his heart race, Bronson leaned into the unit. "I've got some...*news*...to report. I'm afraid it's *not* good and I knew that you must be told of it right away."

Again, an excruciating silence preceded the next transmission. The other voice breathed a deep, audible sigh. "Go on..."

Bronson gulped distressingly and continued. "I needed to let you know that there are other...*parties*...that may have become exposed to the data we discussed previously."

"The *data?*" the voice responded incredulously after a moment. "I was under the impression that the *data* was *destroyed*, as I had ordered? Why was this not accomplished?"

"I'm quite sorry...*sir*," Bronson stammered, fighting off his nerves. "But you needn't worry about the data itself, it has been secured and will be destroyed this evening. You have my *word* on that..."

The other voice did not respond immediately. The transmission became hollow, with bits of static interrupting the silence.

"Your word. Your word is meaning less to me each day. I'm

beginning to lose patience with you," the voice said, shattering the deafening vacuity of the connection. "What of the other two... parties...you mentioned? How do they fit into this...*equation*?"

Bronson hesitated while wringing his hands together tightly. "W-well, they are...EWs."

"*EWs?* What exactly...*oh*...Epsilons? You are telling me they are *Epsilons*?" the voice quizzed amongst the ongoing silence. "They *are* a dangerous lot, indeed," it hissed pensively.

"Precisely. Which is why I felt the need to warn you about this...*problem*," Bronson replied. "How do you want me to proceed?"

The sound of a light rain pelting the rooftop drew Bronson's attention to one of the windows that lined the side of the house. The shadow of one of the larger trees near the forest line at the edge of the property swayed in the distance, casting a menacing shadow through the glass.

A particularly long void of silence followed on the satellite device.

Bronson's gut sunk.

Then, just as he thought that perhaps the connection had been lost, the voice spoke once again.

"You've made a *mess* of things, I'm not going to deny that fact," it chided. "I'm going to need some time to think this through. Don't go anywhere..."

The connection went silent again.

Bronson jumped in surprise at the sudden sound of a groaning creak coming from the front gate. Without shutting it off, he quickly shut the flap on the communication device, rolled over next to a chair in the corner of the room and promptly shoved it underneath a wool blanket.

He swiftly made a half-circle with his wheelchair and glided across the living room into the foyer. Bronson stopped next to the door and pressed his ear to it.

The rain, which had grown heavier by the second, could not mask the sudden, and subtle, rustle of the overgrown hedges that lined the front of his property. The barely audible creak of the gate returning to its half-open position made his heart thump in his chest. After a few seconds, the distinct sound of a floorboard on the porch softly shifting under the weight of movement pricked his ears.

It was not just the weather. *Someone* was there.

Brig slowly pushed himself to a sitting position. He stretched his arms out widely, and then abruptly grasped at his side, remembering the physical encounter he had earlier in the evening before he had fallen asleep on Steele's living room couch. While he could not feel anything newly broken, his ribs burned where Pollux's heavy boot had landed.

The gentle wind outside nudged a nearby tree branch up against the side of the apartment complex every few seconds, creating a monotonous rhythm that echoed lightly throughout the room and easily drowning out the relative silence inside the building. The already-dim lighting flickered every few moments, as if a heavy storm were playing havoc with the few remaining functional electrical systems outside.

Brig forced himself off the couch and slowly staggered to the window. His ankle, swollen and painful, made him yelp as he took the first step.

He pulled the curtain aside and peered out into the side yard. A dark set of clouds had drifted partially in front of the moon and created a drab, eerie shade of gray across the sky and surrounding area.

No rain, he thought, looking upward. He let the curtains drop back to their original position and turned towards the couch.

"Steele?" he called aloud, his voice echoing throughout the empty apartment. However, there was no response.

Brig scratched the back of his head and peered around room. The lighting, coupled with the empty feeling that Brig felt now, made the apartment almost tomb-like, and he suddenly felt the walls creeping in on him.

The door to her unlit bedroom, which he could see through the hallway that led to it, was completely open. He spotted a note posted on the inside of the front door.

Attached to the side of the note, and pinned to the door, was a single flower – a primrose. Brig smiled as he pulled both items from the door and brought them to the couch where he could examine them in brighter light.

A single word was scrawled across the paper, written in Steele's hand – 'STAY!'

Brig's smile grew wide as he set the note down and gently held the flower to his nose. He sat back and lightly rolled the flower between his fingertips.

The lights in the room flickered and then went out.

"Damn," he muttered, as he pushed himself to his feet and attempted to make his way to the front door, clumsily tripping over a chair and nearly falling to the floor in the process.

He grabbed at the doorknob and pulled it open, then stepped out into the breezeway. On one end, it had a stairwell leading down into the front courtyard and on the other end, one that led upwards. Next to the staircase was a small sign that read 'Roof Access'.

"I guess being on the roof *technically* counts as staying here..." he said aloud.

In his experience, if something on his body was not broken, it was not going to hold him back. He pushed the pain out of his mind and hobbled up the stairs to a door that swung open out onto the roof of the apartment complex.

Strewn about on the rooftop surface were parts from the long-defunct air handlers that dotted several locations on the roof itself, their semi-hulking, dark masses silhouetted against the short side walls that lined each edge. Brig navigated around the more dangerous-looking, sharper metal parts and leaned onto one of the walls that overlooked the main street below.

A steady stream of light flowed from between the curtains of Steele's living room window below him. The power had come back on.

Below him, a streetlight glowed in the relative darkness of its surroundings out on the main road, casting a lonely cone of light down at the pavement beneath it.

A gentle gust of cool wind pushed at Brig. He stared out at the far sky, where the dark clouds met the shiny glow of the moonlight at the edge of the horizon in the distance. A sheer mist began to fall from the clouds above and drizzled against his skin.

He fell deep into thought, his gaze penetrating the dark patches of the city just beyond the neighborhood where this building stood. He nestled the flower neatly in between two of his fingers while the stem trailed down in his palms, and continued to roll it back and forth between them.

Brig did not like it that Steele was out on her own at night. Their recent encounter with Pollux only helped bolster that strong feeling. It was not safe for anyone to be out right now, let alone someone like Steele. It was no secret that someone was out to get her, and now he knew someone would surely be out to get *him* as well.

However, who was *he* to think that he could offer her constant protection? He could barely protect himself from... well, *himself*. He had tried to broach the subject of his *situation* back at the array field, but she would have none of it. She would feel differently, he assured himself, if she knew the truth and of what he was involuntarily capable.

Another brisk gust shot from behind him, enough to grab the flower from his hand and cast it over the side of the rooftop down to the street. Hanging onto the side of the building with one arm, he futilely grasped at the flower as it wisped away from his fingertips and fell to the pavement below.

He strained his eyes to catch a glimpse of the flower, and spotted it lying within the lamp's cone of light. The flower's color flushed to gray through the combination of the dull hue of the night sky and refraction of the streetlight, as it lay on the glistening asphalt.

A crack of thunder brought Brig's attention back to the skies. The clouds had grown ominously black and the rain had begun to fall very heavily. He could no longer see the road, or the flower, down beneath him. He turned and quickly made his way to the stairs.

23:
Battery

Present day (2084)...

The retro-truck rumbled along the deserted, country highway, its lights extinguished, as it rounded a small bend and approached a smaller, suburban housing area.

The driver, Krell, a hulkish brute with bulging forearms that he bent outwards at the elbows in order to use the steering wheel, squinted out at the roadside.

Clive sat in the passenger seat, a look of extreme annoyance on his face as he glared out the side window at the darkened landscape that whizzed by. Every so often, his attention would wane, only to be grabbed by the momentary reflection of the truck's headlights off an abandoned car shell or downed aircraft fuselage at the side of the road.

"What is that, some kind of cult?" Krell droned with a thick hint of his Eur-Asian upbringing, spying the EW logo tattooed on Clive's forearm.

Clive shook his head in disgust without looking at the giant. "Something you obviously don't know anything about, so how about not talking about it and just pay attention to where you're going?" he chided.

Krell scowled at Clive, even though the latter was not making any eye contact with him.

"Don't know why he sent you with me. I prefer to work solo," Krell grumbled, turning his attention back to the road.

My thoughts exactly, Clive wondered to himself.

Why had Muldoon requested that he be present for this job?

"Probably so *you* don't screw things up," Clive muttered under his breath aloud. "Like not giving away that we're coming – so make sure you stop the truck and turn it off well before we get there, got it?" he said. Annoyed, he pointed at the upcoming housing complex that sat at the base of the hill several hundred meters ahead of them.

"I'll stop the truck when I'm good and ready, so don't think you are going to tell me what to do on this mission – *got it?*" Krell barked through gnashed teeth.

As the truck continued its slow crawl along the flat before the grade that approached, its transmission whined and clunked under Krell's effort with the gears to keep it up to speed. Its shocks and springs long since expired, both men bounced violently at each pothole and divot, and they were plentiful, that the truck encountered in the road surface. Due to its age, keeping a vehicle this large even running at all was a daunting task for anyone, given the current world situation. But Muldoon had made it very explicit that he wanted to take no chances in obtaining the 'package'.

The truck's massive engine groaned as Krell lifted his foot from the accelerator. He squinted through the windshield. A small mist of droplets suddenly formed in front of his face, making it difficult for either man to determine where they were – especially since the wipers had broken off years ago.

"Great...rain. Just what we needed," Clive sighed, as he pulled the collar up around his neck, preparing for their imminent departure from the vehicle.

Krell snorted in derision. "What? Are you afraid of getting wet, Mr. Egghead?" he mocked, distorting his face at Clive.

"Not that you can tell, but we're getting close. Pull over and shut the truck off – we need to be as stealthy as possible. We only have one shot at this and *he* doesn't want this screwed up." He could all but hear Krell growling deep in his mammoth chest, but the big man said nothing as he brought the truck to a complete stop on the shoulder of the deserted road.

Both men emerged from the vehicle: Krell, with a leap and a solid thud as his boots hit the ground, and Clive purposefully using the door handle and side of the truck to guide himself to a soft landing.

As each rounded the front of the truck, Clive took the lead, heading into a thick patch of grass that lined the area between the housing complex and the side of the road.

However, before Clive could take more than a step into the weeds, Krell grabbed him by the back of his coat and pulled him into a strong headlock. Clive gasped for breath while flailing his arms behind the huge man.

"Now let me tell *you* something, Mr. Know-it-all. *I* am in charge here, so we will do things the way *I* want them done," he spewed, tightening his grip around Clive's neck to the point where he could tell Clive would soon pass out. "And if you ever think of telling me what to do again, I will snap your scrawny little neck."

Clive managed to choke out an inaudible response along with his best attempt at a head nod, at which Krell released him and stormed off into the field ahead. Clive fell to his knees and massaged his throat, staring after the behemoth.

Fifteen minutes later...

The rain had grown relatively intense as the two men emerged from a set of overgrown shrubs at the far end of the field in which they had just slogged. They stepped onto the wet pavement of the rural cul-de-sac, the branches on the bushes bouncing backward into themselves with a pronounced rustle.

Clive glanced over his shoulder. The sound of a retro-bike roaring away over the other side of the hill in the distance spiked his attention. He grabbed one of Krell's arms and pulled him backward. "Does anyone *else* know we're coming?"

Krell shook his head and violently pulled his arm from Clive's grasp. "Don't be stupid, no one knows we're here. And no one's gonna..." he snarled. "Now come'on, let's go take care of this and get outta here." He wiped the rain from his face, slowly pushed the squeaky gate open in front of him and stepped onto the property.

Bronson jerked his head away from the door. He quietly rolled his chair backward and reached into the top drawer of a nearby bureau, his hands quivering as he withdrew a small pistol and wedged it in-between himself and the seat of his wheelchair.

He stared in silence at the entry, listening intently as he sat in the darkness of the foyer. The shadows from the swaying trees outside frolicked wildly on the wall behind him. The sound of the rain driving on the roof and against the windows distracted him from being able to detect sound coming from the porch, but he was certain that he had heard something before.

Bronson held his breath and closed his eyes.

Suddenly, the door burst open with a splintering crash. Bronson flicked his eyes open and started backward in his chair. A hulking shadow filled the doorway and the sound of heavy breathing made his heart leap into his throat.

The massive intruder growled and took a step towards him.

Before the stranger could reach his wheelchair, Bronson raised the pistol with his shaky hand and fired a shot at him, the flames from the end of the gun immersing the room for a brief second in a yellow-crimson glow, a deafening pop and the heavy smell of spent gunpowder.

Krell yelped and swung his arm outward as he recoiled backward a step. A fresh stream of dark, red blood spurted from his forearm. He grasped at it with his other hand.

Before Bronson could squeeze the trigger again, Krell leapt and landed a heavy fist across the side of Bronson's face, thrusting him over the handrail of his wheelchair and onto the floor into a heap.

"What the Hell?" Clive shouted in astonishment, as he rushed into the foyer. Fumbling his hand along the edge of the doorframe, he located the switch for the light and flicked at it, illuminating the bizarre scene with a bright glow from the overhead chandelier.

To his dismay, Krell had already picked up the slacked form of Bronson Fox and had one of his massive paws wrapped around the frail man's neck, shaking him back and forth like a worn-out puppet.

A sickening gurgle emanated from Bronson. His eyes rolled back in his head and his feet dangled helplessly a full meter above the floor, as his colossal attacker continued to choke the final breaths from him.

Clive's brain ignited with panic. This was not what Muldoon had wanted, and as the smarter of the two, he was sure that Muldoon would hold Clive accountable for what went down here.

In a desperate attempt to right the ship, Clive launched himself at Krell, futilely trying to wrestle the big man's arms away from Bronson, only to find himself flung backwards onto the floor.

Before Clive could gather his wits and catch his breath enough to pull himself up for another go at stopping the maniacal behemoth, a second gunshot rang out.

A dark sheet of blood spattered backward, across the wall and onto the curtains just above where Clive lay staring in utter shock.

Immediately releasing Fox, who crumpled to the floor in turn, Krell fell lifeless to the floor. A large flow of blood streamed from a gaping hole in the back of his skull and onto the carpet beneath him, where it formed a sickening, crimson stain. Beside Fox, lying just beside his outstretched hand, was the pistol, a thin trail of smoke still emanating from the end of its barrel.

Clive clamored upright, his knees shaking uncontrollably at the sudden, disturbing turn of events, and made his way over to stand between the two inanimate bodies lying before him.

His stomach turned as he stared down at the corpse of Krell and the expression of surprise that still painted the dead man's face. He had witnessed death many times in his past. But where it had been an almost routine, expected event and just a matter-of-fact result of his line of work, this time it shook him.

This was supposed to be a simple 'pickup' job of someone that would not put up a fight – and now he stood over the dead body of one of the Syndicate's most reliable strongmen. Moreover, he may have witnessed the death of the person they came to retrieve.

There would be Hell to pay.

Clive peeled his gaze away from Krell's body and leaned over to Bronson. Bronson's chest rose very faintly with each strained breath.

"Damn it!" Clive cursed aloud. He stood upright and glared away from the two prone men. "Why did you want *me* here?" he shouted aloud in frustration.

He leaned against the still-open door, the driving rain splashing off the porch surface and into the entrance of the foyer at his feet, and bowed his head onto his arm.

For the second time in his life, he found himself in such an inconceivable situation that he would have never considered as a possibility. He thought ahead to the unavoidable confrontation with Muldoon. How would he explain the fact that he allowed a helpless, elderly man to get the upper hand on them? His brain whirred through the scenarios as he quickly scanned the room for a solution.

"Only *one* thing to do..." he convinced himself. He sunk a hand into his coat pocket, extracted several lengths of thin wire that the two had intended to use to restrain Fox, and gently bound the man's hands to one of the rungs of the nearby staircase.

As he finished, he looked down at Bronson with a pang of guilt, which he forcefully shrugged off. He reached underneath Krell's shoulders and began to drag the large corpse over to an oversized area rug at the base of the winding staircase to the right of the large, oak entrance door. Clive placed the body face down on the rug and quickly wrapped the remainder of the carpet around it, leaving just enough at the top that would allow use as a handle.

Grunting from exertion, Clive slowly hoisted the body-filled rug into Fox's empty wheelchair, where it slumped over like an old, stuffed toy. Using great force to budge the chair that was laden with the dead weight of Krell, Clive gradually moved it forward until he had it on the edge of the porch outside.

He stood and took several breaths, the physical and emotional exhaustion from the night's events already having taken a heavy toll on his stamina, and stepped off the porch with a splash onto the puddle-filled sidewalk. Finding strength within him that he was amazed he still had, Clive maneuvered the chair that held Krell's lifeless body onto the sidewalk and began the long haul to the truck parked over a kilometer away.

Forty-five minutes later, a completely spent Clive trudged his way back in through the rod iron gates of the estate's front entrance. The wheelchair squeaked wildly from both the dampness of the rain and the excess weight that had carried Krell's corpse the extreme distance to the truck at the side of the highway.

Clive's normally well-coifed hair matted against his forehead with both sweat and rain. Dark, dried blood streaked across his cheek, where it was apparent his face had pressed against the bloody carpet that he had lifted into the back of the truck. Thick clouds of hot breath chugged from his lips, as he toiled to pull the wheelchair back onto the porch in preparation for its next passenger's ride.

He locked one of the wheels and then faced the ornate front doorway. A feeling of intense nausea gripped him as he stopped at the edge of the entrance.

Just to the left was the massive, circular bloodstain that doused the carpet on the edge of the foyer next to the living room. On the other side of the doorway, Bronson lay with his feet facing in odd directions at the base of the staircase. The elderly man had not moved in almost an hour, not that he could have gotten very far had he regained consciousness anyway.

Clive worked meticulously at the wire that held Bronson's wrists against the rungs of the staircase railing until it slackened, keeping a close eye on the man's closed eyes. He had already lost an important member of the party; he could not afford to have something else go wrong simply because of a lack of preparation.

Removing the wire from around two of the rungs, he quickly re-wound it around Bronson's wrists, being careful not to tighten it so much that would injure the helpless man. Clive grunted loudly as he strained to pick up the old man's unconscious body, carefully rotated towards the door and moved to the wheelchair waiting just outside. As he stepped into the entryway, an odd chirping sound emanating from within the living room drew his attention.

Softly placing Bronson into the cushioned, but soggy, seat, Clive spun and re-entered the house.

The rain had subsided almost completely, allowing him to attune his ears to the quietness inside the mansion. He stood still in the center of the foyer as he pricked his ears in anticipation of the sound repeating. He was not disappointed, as fifteen seconds later the same weak chirp echoed from within the adjacent room.

He stepped in from the foyer and scanned the living room. The lamp on the end table next to the couch cast a miniscule amount of light into the dark space. Clive found it difficult to discern much other than the items that sat immediately within its small cone of illumination. He slowly walked into the center of the room, the floor creaking lightly with each foot that he placed onto it.

As he stopped, the chirp rang out once more. It was coming from the corner where a chair sat with a wool blanket on top of the seat.

He was not an explosives expert by any means, but he also did not want to take any chances. Perhaps the old man was tipped off about their arrival and set a booby trap?

He carefully knelt onto one knee and twisted his neck sideways at the bottom of the chair and the floor beneath it.

"No wires..." he whispered, scanning the floor of the rest of the room.

Clive pushed himself upright, tiptoed over to the chair, and gently raised the blanket.

Nestled within was a small device with a brilliant blue and green LED display, and a panel of numbered buttons beneath. To the right of the display, a small speaker chirped once again, making Clive recoil.

He stared in amazed curiosity.

"A *SAT* phone?" he quizzed under his breath. "*Who's* the old man calling on a SAT phone?" he said, feeling relieved that the threat of a booby trap had passed.

He grabbed the device from the chair and held it in front of him with both hands.

"Well, I'll be damned. And it's working..." he chuckled. He ran his fingers across the buttons without depressing them. As he tilted it, the room lighting reflected off the chassis, which drew his eye to the logo and model number etched into the case.

"Quantum? No. *That* can't be...*can it?*" He squinted his eyes tightly at the device. He examined the symbols on the screen.

Suddenly, the device emitted one final chirp, went silent and powered off. He felt around the edge of the case, located the power switch underneath the top flap of the device, and depressed it several times.

"Damn, battery's dead..." he cursed. Tucking the device under his arm, he headed back into the foyer.

Clive glanced around once more, grabbed the doorknob, stepped onto the porch and pulled the door shut.

24:
What You Give Is What You Get

Present day (2084)…

The wind howled against the façade of Steele's apartment complex. Although the rain had subsided, Brig could still hear the heavy dripping of leftover rainwater that found its way down to the windowsill from the broken gutter systems at the top of the building.

It was an odd sensation to be experiencing that sound from inside of a shelter as opposed to the forest campsite that he had called home for nearly the past four years, and it led to a bit of sleeplessness on his part.

He delicately rolled over to face the back of the couch, taking care not to put his weight onto the side where his ribs had been cracked multiple times in the past few days. He let out a small sigh as he found a comfortable position in which to fall back asleep.

The sudden, soft touch of a hand across his forehead stunned him into a semi-upright position.

It was Steele.

She wore a soft smile across her lips as she quietly brushed the sweat-matted hair from his face.

Brig exhaled heavily, rolled his arms outward and eased back into the cushions.

"I can't tell you how incredible it is that *you're* the first person I see when I wake up…" he remarked, a longing expression growing on his face.

He felt it welling up in his heart again: that warm, magical feeling that had made him feel so alive that he was almost *sure* he was dreaming. But now, it was different, and for the first time in years, he felt something that had all but disappeared from his life. *Love.*

Steele reciprocated the deep gaze, inching involuntarily towards Brig, as she exhaled a shallow breath and closed her eyes.

As their lips met, Brig could feel the cold shiver travel her spine, causing her to flinch as they embraced one another.

Brig separated himself abruptly and pulled away to the other end of the couch.

"What's wrong?" she asked, startled.

Brig shook his head while rubbing the back of his neck with one palm. "There's...something...you need to *know* about me," he responded flatly, glaring back at her. The surprise in her expression made him look away quickly.

She has to know... he thought.

Steele moved to sit next to him, putting a hand on his arm as she spoke.

"Brigadier, I told you before – it doesn't matter to me. Nothing in your past...*or mine*...matters enough now that we've found each other again." She reached with a palm and cradled his chin, then gently moved his head to meet her gaze. "It's taken so long for us to reunite that there's *nothing* so important that it would keep us apart."

"You don't understand," Brig closed his eyes and pressed his lips tight. "It's something you *need* to know, and I just don't feel right keeping you in the dark about it..."

Steele sighed heavily and tilted her head. "Brigadier, honestly, you need to *stop*..." she started to protest doubtfully.

Before she could continue, however, Brig placed a finger over her lips and gazed deeply into her eyes.

"It's *my* turn to talk now," he said calmly, as he took her hand in his, and then fell silent.

After gathering his thoughts, he began once again. "This is something I've been living with for years...and it's not something that I *asked* for. But it's made me shy away from any type of contact because of how it...*affects* me."

She wrinkled her eyebrows as she looked at him.

Brig continued before she could interrupt. "Do you remember the night when I came into Clive's workshop all beaten up?"

Steele nodded silently.

"And do you remember how you asked me if it was *drugs* that caused all of that?" He turned away from her piercing gaze once more and stared at the floor beneath his feet. However, he did not need to see her face to know that she was embarrassed at having even suggested it.

"See...it wasn't drugs, and it wasn't a fight. Well, it *was* a fight, but only because of my...*condition*," he said, choosing his words deliberately.

"Brig..."

"Please..." he replied instantly, holding up his other hand in protest. "...let me finish. This is something that all us...EWs...have had to deal with on some level or another."

He peered up at Steele.

She was more confused now than ever.

"We all have this...*affliction*...one way or another, as a result of things that we were exposed to..." He was not sure how to elaborate. He was never even sure himself of whether it was *everyone*, or whether it was just unique to him.

"Brigadier," she replied lovingly, continuing to rub his arm, "*everyone* is a victim of the decisions and events that have happened over the past ten years. You're not unique in that respect..." She grasped his chin once more to get him to look at her. "...you do realize that, *don't you?*"

Brig blinked and nodded silently in hopeless agreement.

"I don't care about what has happened or what effect it has had on you. Nothing...and I mean *nothing*...is so important or Earth-shattering that I want anything to change now. Do you get that?" Steele gazed lovingly into Brig's eyes.

Brig sat silently for a few moments. He knew what he had to say to her, and he knew that he needed her to understand the gravity of the consequences of her continuing on with him.

"It's just that I..." he hesitated, staring down at his feet as he pressed his lips together tightly, and then rose his head as he met Steele's eyes with his. "...*I love you*, Steele. And I couldn't live with myself if I were...*the cause of your death.*"

Steele listened purposefully as she stared at Brig. As he finished his sentence, she smiled sheepishly.

"How utterly melodramatic of you, Brigadier," she snorted. However, she could tell that he was serious, or at least that *he* thought he was. "Is that *all* that's bothering you?" she quizzed, raising an eyebrow at him.

"Wasn't that *enough*?" he replied emphatically, falling silent once again as he stared forward in deep thought.

She gazed at him intently, and although he was not saying anything more, she could tell that he was not being entirely forthcoming. "I get the distinct impression that there's something you're holding back from me. Am I right?"

Brig subtly shook his head and then faced Steele. "That's ironic... considering everything that's happened since that night at Clive's."

Steele's face flushed pale. She darted her eyes away from his stare.

"I'm afraid I don't know what you're getting at," she said hesitantly.

"I think there's more to what's behind you and Clive..." Brig replied, opening his eyes wide as if to expect a response containing what he believed to be the truth. "...especially that we were followed and attacked by Pollux. And that he said he was looking for *you*, not Clive."

She sat a moment, lost for words. He was more astute than she presumed. "Brigadier, I'm being completely honest with you - I do not *know* that man..."

"I'm not saying that you *do*, but my gut tells me there's something *more* to this." Brig glared deeper into her eyes to gauge her reaction. "And now that I'm pretty much involved with it all, you might want to open up a little more about that part of your life..."

Steele broke her gaze with Brig and fiddled with one of the sleeves of her shirt. "I understand how this may seem to *you*, Brigadier, but to be quite blunt - it's not all that relative to *you*," she said defensively, "and I feel it's just best to let it lie..."

The fire ignited within Brig's brain. *How can she say that?* he screamed in his head, as he sprung from the couch and stood in front of her.

"Are you *serious?*" he argued loudly, his hands held outward. "I could have been killed back there...*we both*...could have been killed back there." Brig paced across the living room and peered out the window for a moment in silence, and then faced Steele once again. "What secret is so deep and important that you can't share it with me but it almost gets us *both* killed?"

"I want to trust you, Brigadier, I really do, but...this just isn't something that I feel should be shared with *anyone*."

"You either trust me, or you don't," Brig replied with exasperation while shaking his head. "And if you don't, then we can just move on our separate ways because I trust *you* with my life."

He glared out the window in frustration, his hands at his hips. He could not believe that she would hold back on something that put both of their lives in peril.

"But I *will* find out what Clive is up to. And you know that will just lead me to find out *your* part in this as well," he said without looking back at Steele.

Steele closed her eyes and stared down in silence. After a moment, she arose from the couch and walked to the window to stand next to Brig, where she placed her head in her hands.

Brig stepped behind her and placed both of his hands on her shoulders.

"Steele...you can trust *me*. More than anyone else right now, and you *know* that..." he said lovingly, as he massaged her shoulders.

She remained silent a few more minutes. Then, taking his hands in hers, turned to Brig. She tried to look into his eyes, but she found it hard to lock gazes with him and found herself glancing away every few seconds.

"It's...my father..." she said hesitantly.

Brig frowned. This was not what he had anticipated at all. "Your *father*? What about him? Is he in some sort of trouble?"

Steele quickly nodded her head, pulling one hand away from Brig to cover her mouth, as a tear rolled down her cheek.

"I believe he's in *big* trouble, but I don't know what to make of..." she began, but then fell silent as she looked past Brig to the window behind him.

"*What?*" Brig coaxed subtly.

She did not answer at first. She pinched the bridge of her nose between her thumb and forefinger in deep, pensive thought. "He's acting highly irrational."

Brig took in this latest piece of the puzzle, despite how non-relative it seemed to him, and pondered it for a moment.

Then, shaking his head, replied, "You've even said it yourself. We've all been through a lot these last few years...and he's getting old..."

"No. It's *not* that," she interrupted immediately. "He's been acting...almost *insane*...lately."

"That's an exaggeration...*right*?"

Steele shook her head steadfastly. "I wish it were. One moment he's fine, then the next he's ranting like a paranoid delusional."

Brig glared out at the darkness through the window. He was confused. *Where's this heading?* he asked himself.

"How's your mother handling it?" he finally asked Steele.

She glanced quickly at Brig and then pursed her lips, as she peered down at the floor. "Mum passed seven years ago...during...well, you know," she said, pensively shaking her head.

Brig cringed and reached to place a hand on Steele's arm. "I'm so sorry...I didn't realize..."

"She and two others died when the plane that my father was piloting lost control and crashed," she continued to explain over Brig's apology. "My father was the only survivor. He lost the use of his legs, but I'm sure if you were to ask him today he would say that Mum was one of the *lucky* ones that night."

Brig pulled Steele closer to him and gently rubbed the middle of her back. "Sounds to me like maybe he's just having a hard time coming to terms with all that's happened, don't you think?"

"No, it's something *more*. I *feel* it," she replied adamantly, still not making eye contact with Brig.

He could feel that the truth *he* was looking for was near, but she was still so hesitant to part with it. He decided to push a little harder.

"So how does Clive fit into what's going on with your father?" he continued to prod.

Steele hesitated, inhaled deeply, and then replied, "Remember when I told you that I had him doing some work for..."

"*Nostalgia?*"

"Right," she returned embarrassingly. "Well it was more than *nostalgia*."

Brig nodded his head silently. He knew that was the case all along but did not want to press the issue...*until now.*

"My father actually had me...*retrieve*...some encrypted data cards for him," she continued.

"Wait...you stole them from...*the Syndicate?*" Brig concluded, rubbing his head with one hand. "Shit...so *that's* why they've got Baby Huey on your tail..."

Steele nodded her head silently.

"So...what was *on* the cards?" Brig asked hesitantly after a silent moment of thought.

"That's just it. They were blank," Steele responded with a definite air of confusion.

Brig rubbed his chin with the base of his palm as he peered away from Steele. The situation puzzled him. Why would things have spun so far out of control over a set of blank cards. And what role did Clive play in this?

"Why would your father want you to steal a bunch of *blank*

data cards? And why would the Syndicate be so upset about them?" he quizzed.

Steele turned away and began pacing the room. "The Syndicate is most likely irate simply because I stole from them," she answered, her arms crossed and her chin nestled into her chest. "I highly doubt they even *know* what was stolen. You'd be surprised how many warehouses full of loot that they have of which they don't know the contents. As for my *father*," she continued, stopping and staring out the window in deep thought, "I don't know. It makes no sense to me..."

Brig abruptly faced Steele. "You don't think that..."

Without turning, Steele quipped, "...Clive *stole* the data when I had him decrypt the cards and then erased the originals? That was my first inclination...yes. But it's my word against his, and you obviously know how...well, *cryptic*...he can be," she said mockingly.

Brig snorted aloud and nodded his head. "Then we need to find out. *Subtly* of course..." He did not care that she was essentially accusing his best friend of a heinous act. He had recently begun to suspect the same.

"I agree," she replied, "but first I need to have a little discussion with my father. He's been on about wanting me to destroy the cards..."

"*Destroy* them? Why?" Brig asked incredulously.

"Now you see *my* quandary, Brigadier. Stay here and rest some more, I won't be long. I'm going to get an explanation from my father this time, whether he likes it or not." She leaned over, pecked Brig on the lips and then hastily left the apartment.

25:
The Memory Remains

Present day (2084)...

Bruno Muldoon, his shoulder-length hair slicked back where it fell onto the shoulders of his unbuttoned blazer, strode down the hotel corridor. On his right, the relatively smaller of the Webb twins, Castor, made deliberate, tiny strides to allow his boss to keep pace.

"What's the word on that warehouse I had you check out, Castor?" Muldoon asked, holding out a hand to examine the cleanliness of his fingernails in the dim hallway lighting.

Castor grunted and shook his head, trying to ignore his boss's hygiene habits. "It didn't seem like anything of value, Mr. Muldoon – just some old computer equipment."

Muldoon hummed under his breath as the pair continued strolling, his lips slightly pursed as he mulled Castor's information. "There were no weapons or anything else that this girl might want as leverage against us?" he said finally.

Castor scratched his head and let his palm fall back onto his neck, where he gripped it tightly and rubbed. "No, boss. We checked the whole place, nothin' like that there," he replied. He, too, thought for a moment, but with a pained expression. "What do you think she *wanted* in there?"

Muldoon knew better to answer those types of questions. He had not risen to the top ranks of the Syndicate by allowing others to control the course of the conversation, or by allowing them to have information such as that.

"From where did the computer equipment come? To whom did it belong?" Muldoon quizzed after a brief silence.

Before Castor could wager an uneducated answer, the pair had passed a doorway in which the door was slightly ajar.

Just within, beyond the alcove, a longhaired, brunette woman stood and stared out at the men as they passed. She was tall, almost as Muldoon, and leaned her voluptuous frame against the decorative pillar just beyond the hallway. She approached the door and reached for it, as she caught notice of them.

"I'm heading to dinner. Join me, won't you?" Muldoon suavely asked the woman, albeit more an authoritative demand.

The woman did not speak. She broke eye contact with Muldoon, glared at Castor for a moment with a sneer drawn across her face, and then slammed the door shut.

"What was *that* all about, boss?" Castor asked quizzically, noticing that Muldoon had neither stopped completely to address the woman, nor paid mind to the non-response that he had received from her.

"Nothing to worry about, Castor," Muldoon answered with a sigh. "We'll talk more later. Get the door, would you?" he ordered, and then entered the dining suite with Castor.

Fifteen minutes later...

The stairwell door crashed open and thudded against the connecting wall, as Pollux forced his massive frame through the doorway and out into the hall of Muldoon's hotel. The guard of the floor, Ursip, widened his eyes and took a half step backwards at the sight of the gargantuan lumbering towards him.

Pollux, his shirt soaked a dark crimson on one side, held a bloodied towel in one of his frying-pan-sized hands up against the side of his swollen face.

The much smaller guard retook his position against the wall nearest the dining suite and shook off the terror that he felt at that moment, not an easy task as he could hear Pollux's beastly growl echoing throughout the corridor.

"I need to see tha' boss," Pollux grumbled, as he approached Ursip, and then passed him without stopping on the way to the suite.

Ursip nervously took three quick side steps until he was standing in front of the behemoth, one hand held out.

"He's in the dining suite, but you know that means he's not to be disturbed," Ursip said, slurring his words in a shaky, Eur-Asian accent, staring up at what he knew to be certain doom.

Pollux was in no mood to be trifled with, especially not by a flunky floor guard like Ursip. Displaying the sheer, raw strength for which he was known, Pollux grabbed Ursip's jacket collar with one clenched fist and hefted the man swiftly from his feet, dangling him a full meter in the air just above his eye level.

"This is important!" Pollux bellowed, spit slinging into Ursip's face as the man's hair blew backwards from the voluminous gust of air coming from Pollux's mouth.

Ursip, speechless, trembled and nodded his head as his eyes bulged from their sockets. He fell to the floor in a muddled clump as Pollux released him. Pollux spat on the floor next to the cowering guard and then grabbed the handle of the dining suite door. Behind Pollux, Ursip shakily gathered himself and clamored away to safety.

Before Pollux could finish opening the door, it swung open inwards and the large, round face of his brother appeared in the doorway.

"Where the Hell have you been?" Castor growled in a low whisper. "And what the Hell happened to your face?"

The uncovered part of Pollux's face was now as red as his bloodstained shirt. A deep growl rumbled in his chest as he tried to pry the door handle away from his brother. "I was ambushed when I was following the girl... and I need to tell tha' boss," he barked.

Castor, despite his brother's size advantage, stepped fully into the doorway to block Pollux, placed both hands on the bigger man's chest and pushed him backward into the hall. "You know the boss doesn't like to be bothered when he's eatin', Pol."

"Let me go, Cas, I gotta' *do* this..." Pollux fumed, staring with one uncovered eye at his brother.

Castor shoved at Pollux's chest again, but the behemoth did not budge.

"Use your *head* for once..." Castor started to advise, but Pollux wanted none of it. He grasped at Castor's shoulder with his free hand and yanked him out into the hallway, and then stormed into the dining suite. Entering the small hall, he took two mammoth strides through the alcove and into the main room.

Seated at a large, rectangular oak table in the center was Muldoon, his back to Pollux as he dined. Muldoon instinctively raised his head, closed his eyes and began to sing lightly, his mouth partially full of wild venison liver.

"Pollux, Pollux, so mighty is he, not the acuity of his twin, but he's brought something for me..."

Muldoon finished chewing the food already in his mouth, and without granting Pollux his full attention, continued to slice off another piece of meat with his knife and fork.

"You've got me a gift, don't you, Pollux?" Muldoon cooed. He popped a forkful of liver into his mouth, chewed it deliberately, raised his glass of wine to his lips and swallowed. "You've brought her with you, haven't you? Did you dress her up nice for me?"

"I got somethin' important to tell ya, boss," Pollux grumbled. He came to a stop and stood a meter behind Muldoon's chair, still grasping the towel to his bloodied face.

"Ah, Pollux. Why must you always bear a crisis?" Muldoon sighed aloud, as he clunked his half-empty glass onto the table in front of him, causing a small droplet of wine to jump from the glass onto the oak next to his plate. He quickly snatched his napkin and dabbed at it.

Pollux scratched his head with his free hand, looking flummoxed. "Uh, bears? No, no bears boss, it's about…"

"Just *out* with it, Pollux!" Muldoon screamed in impatience, and then under his breath murmured, "Dimwit," as he resumed eating his dinner.

Pollux, unsure of whether his boss was being playful or irate, took a small step closer to Muldoon's chair.

"I found the girl…" he offered, wincing as he pulled the towel from his face. He felt the fiber of the cloth tear at the wound, and then quickly replaced it.

Maintaining focus on his food, Muldoon managed to respond between bites. "And she's with you, I presume?" As he spoke, he peered out of his peripheral down at the floor behind him where Pollux stood.

"No, boss. She got away from me," Pollux replied dejectedly.

Emitting a heavy sigh, casually putting his fork down on the table and then dabbing his chin with his dinner cloth, Muldoon gazed forward at the grand view of the desert night sky.

"That would explain the blood that you are dripping on my priceless Persian rug," he said flatly and then arose from his chair. "Now I will have to switch rooms again. Honestly, Pollux – bested by a woman? Why do I keep you in my employ?"

Pollux, realizing that his boss was losing his patience, and most likely his cool to follow, took a step backward.

"It's not like that, boss. I swear! She had a big guy with her…and he had a *gun*. He got her away from me before I could grab her." He glanced nervously at the door, where Castor had entered the room and was standing.

Castor, his arms folded over his chest, closed his eyes and shook his head in disgust at his brother.

Muldoon spun on his heel and faced Pollux. "Big guys...with *guns*. Was he bigger than *you*?" he mocked, sneering into Pollux's face.

"N-no, boss. But he *outsmarted* me..."

"That must have been some accomplishment!" Muldoon turned away from Pollux and held his stomach with both hands in an exaggerated chuckle. Then, stopping abruptly, angrily glared at Pollux.

"But I know where I can find her, boss..." Pollux offered eagerly.

Muldoon turned without a word and calmly walked to the bar that adorned a major portion of one of the walls of the room. He reached into a cabinet underneath the bar and extracted a small spool of dental floss, unwound a length of it, leaned over in front of the mirror over the bar and began flicking the chunks of venison from his teeth.

"Yet, you show up here without her..." he finally said, while looking at the giant's reflection in the mirror.

Pollux glanced again at his brother.

Castor was clearly concerned for Pollux's well-being. His worry spanned not just his physical wounds, but also how he was portraying his incompetence to their boss. Castor widened his eyes as if to convey his amazement at his brother's stupidity.

"...and they destroyed my bike," Pollux added meekly, as he faced Muldoon.

Finished with his teeth cleaning, Muldoon tossed the used floss in the trash bin next to the bar and then began to straighten his tie, as he admired himself in the mirror.

"Material possessions, *Pollux*...even in this day and age, are replaceable." He nonchalantly turned from the mirror and approached the behemoth, grabbing Pollux by the collar and forcing him down to his eye level.

"My employees, *Pollux*, are replaceable..." Muldoon said with increased intensity through gritted teeth. "But this woman, *Pollux*...IS NOT!" he finally bellowed into Pollux's face, spit jetting from his mouth into Pollux's eye. Muldoon glared wildly at him, released his collar and turned away from him.

"Castor, go with your brother and get him some medical attention," Muldoon ordered flatly with a calm voice, glancing down at the sleeve of his jacket, which now had Pollux's blood smeared across the greater portion of it.

"But boss, I can get her. I know where she's..." Pollux stammered.

Muldoon held up his palm to silence the clumsy oaf. "Don't bother. I trust that my *other* employees have performed on task and will soon be bringing me the other piece to this puzzle," he said sarcastically. He strolled to the window and peered outside. "A piece that will most likely net me the woman anyway."

Castor grabbed onto Pollux's arm and began to lead him out of the room, shaking his head and whispering insults under his breath to him, as they reached the alcove.

"And Castor... send that bumbling buffoon Ursip in here..." Muldoon sniped without looking back, as the pair opened the door and exited the room.

Castor pushed his brother into the hallway.

"Jesus, Pol. I told ya' not to do that..." he admonished.

The two began to walk the hallway to the stairwell. As they passed Ursip, whom had returned to his guard position halfway down the hall, Castor shot a coy smile at him.

"The boss wants to see you. Nice workin' with ya', Ursip..." Castor muttered, as they passed. Ursip gulped loudly, made his way down the hall and entered the dining suite.

A few moments later...

Muldoon entered from the doorway that connected the dining suite to an adjacent one. Being the paranoid strategist that he was, he always ensured that he had multiple exits from each area. The dining suite was no exception. As the door clicked shut behind him, he once again adjusted his tie and strode into the room, the same that the woman had been in earlier.

"I take it that dinner didn't go so well," she said rhetorically, quietly putting her hand to her mouth as she noticed the blood stains on his coat.

He looked up briefly with feigned surprise at her presence. "I couldn't help but notice that *you* weren't there..." he replied indignantly, striding past her.

The woman did not face him as he walked past, and continued to stare forward. "I wasn't hungry," she said flatly. "What was all the *yelling* about?" she asked after a pause.

Muldoon stopped, faced the woman, placed both arms around her waist and kissed her passionately on the side of her neck.

She flinched ever so slightly.

"The level of my irritation is exceeded only by the level of incompetence with which I surround myself." He released her from the embrace and stepped over to a closet on the far wall. "And the two," he continued, opening the wardrobe door, "predictably, are not mutually exclusive."

Muldoon removed his jacket, yanked the tie from around his neck and hung both on the inside door of the closet. He unbuttoned his bloodstained shirt, pulling it off his shoulders to reveal a tattoo that stretched across his back, along with several large scars.

The woman looked away.

"As my wife," Muldoon continued authoritatively, "I expect you to dine with me. Don't let your absence become a habit." He extracted a clean shirt from the closet, into which he quickly changed, eyeing her intently.

Unfazed by the reprimand that he had just given her, she continued with her questioning. "*Who* were you yelling at?"

Muldoon did not respond. His silence told her that he was tired of the questioning. She had seen him do it a thousand times before with others, and this time was no different.

"It does not concern you, my dear..." he dismissed, as he closed the door softly, turned away from the closet and began to stride past her.

"But as my *husband*," she mimicked in a snarky voice, "anything that concerns you concerns me. *Especially* when it upsets you..." She lovingly put her arms around his neck from behind.

Suddenly, and without warning, Muldoon yanked one of the woman's arms from around his neck, causing her to stumble forward and in front of him. He raised his arm and smacked her violently across the face. The woman recoiled backwards and onto the floor.

She held the side of her cheek with her palm, glaring at him with a mixture of shock and hatred.

"Yours is not to question my affairs!" he growled maniacally, pointing an angry finger in her face. "Do not let this happen again..." he concluded. He spun and walked through the door. Just as it was about to close, he stopped, propped it open with one foot and stuck his head back through it.

"And get dressed. We're going on a...*business trip*," he hissed.

Steele rounded the edge of the overgrown hedges that marked the front of her father's estate property line, taking care not to step in the puddles and avoiding the potential of deep crevices that might have formed over the years.

As she reached the separation between the bushes that marked where the rod-iron gates closed off the main sidewalk, she stopped abruptly and stared.

One gate was fully pried open, which was not how she had left it just hours before, and certainly not how her father had always kept it. Her father's paranoia of unwanted intruders and noises outside his windows suddenly did not seem so far-fetched, which made her quickly scan the area around the deserted cul-de-sac.

"Bloody Hell, he's got me looking over *my* shoulder now," she cursed under her breath. Feeling assured that she would be safer inside, even though she didn't see anyone around, Steele swiftly strode to the gates and darted between the hedges onto the sidewalk that led up to the front porch.

She glared at the house as she navigated the unlit path. Light beamed through the large, paneled glass that lined the top, front foyer wall. Behind it, the lit, main chandelier glowed unevenly. The living room light peeked out around the curtains in the front windows off the side of the porch.

Odd, she thought. *He never keeps more than one light on at a time. Perhaps he fell asleep.*

She reached the end of the sidewalk and stepped up onto the porch. She had to reach over and brace herself on one of the large plaster pillars that supported the porch overhang, as her front foot slid suddenly on the wood surface. On the porch beneath her feet were dark, slick streaks that ran from the front door to the edge of the walk.

Steele squinted, but even with the small stream of light that flowed from the living room window, she could not make out the material on which she almost slipped.

"Damn rain must have splashed mud up here," she theorized, as she reached for the door and rapped lightly with her knuckles.

After several seconds and not getting the response she had anticipated, she glanced over her shoulder and then tapped on the door again, this time a tad heavier.

Several moments passed and no one had responded. An uneasy feeling grew in her stomach. She walked to the edge of the porch and peered into the small crease around the edges of the curtains. She put her mouth close to the surface of the glass and covered the sides with her hands.

"Father, it's me. I'm here again. I hope I didn't wake you..." she said in a loud whisper, but enough for her father to hear through the glass.

Again, she did not get a response.

Steele straightened herself and slowly walked the span of the porch once again to the door, craning her neck while scanning every visible portion of the property inside the gated perimeter. Still somewhat satisfied that all was quiet outside, she reached for the doorknob, fully expecting it to be locked.

However, to her dismay, not only was the doorknob unsecured, but her very slight pressure on the door easily nudged it open. Her heart sunk as she quietly swung the door inward and stepped into the brightly lit foyer.

The smell of burnt sulfur instantly stung the lining of her nose.

Gunpowder... she thought in a panic, as she pushed the door shut behind her. A second, horrific realization met her as she turned towards the living room. A large, dark crimson pool of blood, situated on the carpet just outside of the edge of the living room, made her eyes widen in terror. She involuntarily squeaked, and then cupped her palm over her mouth.

"Daddy?" she cried in a heightened whisper, pulling her hand away. "Daddy, are you alright? Are you here?" she continued to call. She listened to the silence for a moment and then stepped around the blood and into the living room.

For the most part, she did not notice any difference. The half-empty bottle of vodka still sat on the end table amidst several pieces of crumpled or ripped paper, and the lamp that sat beside them burned dimly as it had hours earlier. Across the room, her father's favorite woolen blanket sat, lying in a crumpled heap at the foot of a chair.

What she could not see, however, was her father's wheelchair. Chills ran up her spine that made her visibly quiver. She crossed her arms tightly across her chest as she scanned the room once more.

Steele stepped out of the living room back into the foyer, and then poked her head into the kitchen, located just off the main hallway adjacent to where she stood.

She glanced once more down at the blood on the carpet, covered her mouth to hold back a nervous cry and then ran out the door, the glass insert rattling as she slammed it behind her.

Ten years prior (2074)...

The reflection of the holographic display flickered across Steele's pupils as the images briefly flashed by. She swiped a quick finger to classify them and then dismissed them just as quickly.

For the past several months, she had spent most of her waking moments in the lab looking through the remote microscope data, and today was no different.

Steele cupped her hand to her mouth to cover a yawn, completing the final of the classifications and pushing her chair away from the desk. She closed her eyes.

The familiar, mechanical drone of the turbo-lift approaching her floor meant that her father would soon be entering the lab.

"Steele, my dear," his voice rang out, as he passed through the security scanners that adorned the walls around the doorway.

Several other technicians looked up from their work as Bronson passed by their workstations. Although they had worked with Steele and, in relation, had seen Bronson quite often over the past year, it was still exhilarating to see him in person, even if they knew he was only there to converse with his daughter.

"Darling," he said, approaching the opposite end of her workstation and beaming a proud smile at her, "I just read the results you published on the Nebula last night. Bravo, my dear. It's like I always said – if you put your mind to it, the *results* will follow."

"Thank you, father," Steele responded nonchalantly. She had already begun looking through another sample of data on her display, her back to her father.

"And how is our...*side research*...coming along?" he asked in a hushed tone, leaning in and resting his palms on the end of the workstation.

"The *matrix* is all but ready for testing, father," she said flatly, as she continued diligently processing the data within the display. Then, as she submitted the latest batch to the central computer, she rotated her chair abruptly to face him.

"But I'm unsure of how valuable the technology will be without being able to test on *humans*," she said with a concerned, yet frustrated air.

Bronson smiled wickedly. "Human testing is against URA policies. You *know* that, Steele," he replied firmly, pursing his lips together.

"I know that, *Director Fox*," she mocked.

Steele knew how her father would react to her arguments. It was obvious to her that he was giving the appearance of toeing the company line, if not for her, then for the other employees that might be overhearing their conversation.

"I was simply pointing out that we potentially have a revolutionary breakthrough but essentially no method in which to test," she said.

Bronson's smile faded as he nodded in agreement with his daughter. "You don't have to sell me, my dear. After all, I was the one who *sanctioned* this project to begin with." He glanced at the room behind him through his peripheral.

"*Sanctioned?*" Steele parroted back at her father in a heightened tone, opening her eyes widely. "So...*now* this work is *sanctioned?*"

Placing his finger quickly to his lips to hush the conversation, Bronson swiftly moved around the corner of the workstation, where he gently grasped Steele's upper arm while shaking his head.

"Formalities, my flower, formalities. Once they see the fruits of your labor they will have no choice but to authorize a full battery of tests for proof of concept," he whispered.

Steele glared forward in thought, then released herself from her father's grasp and spun her chair back to face the display.

"I'm going to begin the test phase next week, father," she said matter-of-factly.

"My dear," Bronson began to argue, his smile replaced with a concerned frown, "the department will not allow you to have any test subjects at this phase, how do you intend to..."

"I plan to perform the testing on...*myself*," Steele interjected. She looked over her shoulder briefly, then back at the display. "There's no harm since it's only *extraction*...now is there?"

Bronson chuckled and patted Steele's shoulder lightly with one hand. "Why am I not surprised, Steele? You never were one to take 'no' for an answer."

Steele continued to process results within the display in silence as her father looked on. Bronson stood up straight and placed his chin in the palm of his hand, admiring his daughter's fortitude at what was commonly the cause of project delays: bureaucratic red tape.

"And, as your director," he finally added, leaning in to whisper in her ear, "...and to show you my faith in your abilities...I will...submit to the testing *as well.*"

"Father? *Really?*" Steele said incredulously. She twirled her chair around to look at her father, but he had already withdrawn to stroll to the other end of her workstation. "That's not necessary, you know. I'm quite capable of managing the initial test phase on my own."

"Oh, I'm quite *sure* of that, my dear," he replied knowingly, all the while picking up several objects from the lab table in passing, looking at them with no particular interest and then setting them down as he spoke. "But why turn down the opportunity to double your test base?"

Steele tightened her lips and nodded.

"On another note, my darling. How goes the progress on our...*companion* project?"

Steele, having already re-immersed herself in her work, responded without looking at him.

"Father, there is already a plethora of knowledge and research on *that* subject," she said flatly, shaking her head in subtle disagreement. "Quite frankly, I don't see the need to focus my attention on that aspect. Besides which, I have much more work to do on my *primary* project."

"Steele, my dear," Bronson cooed, "you have done superbly on your...alpha priorities. But you need to think...*bigger,*" he explained, holding his hands out for dramatic effect, even though she was not looking. "The combination of both...side projects... would yield quite a result."

"Father," Steele sighed heavily, turning her head over her shoulder with a disapproving look, "this is not something that we should even be *discussing...*"

She once again refocused her attention on the display.

"You don't need to preach to me," Bronson quipped immediately. "I'm merely playing *devil's advocate.*" He clasped his hands together behind his back and began to pace in front of the workstation. "We've already reached this nexus – and you know those 'government types'. How long do you think it will be before *they* reach the same logical conclusion?"

He glanced around the room at the other technicians, who feigned immersion in their own activities.

"And wouldn't it be prudent to reach that conclusion before

they do," he continued, facing Steele once more, "...*and* have the wisdom to guide them from not only a technical aspect...but also a *moral* one?"

Steele was growing impatient with her father's habit of twisting the conversation so that it made *her* look like the one that would always come up with the ideas.

"And how am I to focus on both of these...*side projects*...when I'm so heavily invested in my primary?" she said with exasperation.

"Steele, my darling," Bronson reassured calmly, rapping on the desk with one knuckle while pointing out at the rest of the room with an open palm, "you've done an exemplary job with your primary task. And you have an entire staff of scientists and engineers hard at work following up on your results." He stood and made his way around to Steele's chair once more. "It's time for you to draw your focus to other pressing needs."

Steele sprung from her chair, her arms crossed tightly across the front of her lab coat, as she stepped over to another empty workstation. "I don't like it, father. *Not one bit*," she chastised. She glared ahead blankly in pensive thought, her lips curled into an angry disapproval.

Bronson raised an eyebrow as he silently stared at his daughter.

She did not make eye contact with him, but she knew very well what he expected at this moment. Sighing and dropping her arms in defeat, she walked back to her desk and sat in the chair.

"Fine," she said, grumbling with an air of annoyance, "But I fail to see the benefit of heading down *this* road."

"That's my girl," Bronson hissed happily, as he turned and strolled away.

.

26:
Nightmare

Present day (2084)…

Brig stared up at the ceiling, watching the shadows of the trees from the now-moonlit sky casually flickering above him, while he awaited Steele's return.

It had been just an hour since she had left, so he was not expecting her back anytime soon, since she had told him that her father's place was a twenty-minute ride from hers. Still, he had a strange feeling in his gut that perhaps things weren't going as well as she had hoped.

Other thoughts, however, pressed more heavily on his mind… like *Clive*.

What was his role in all of this? Did he actually lie to Steele and steal the data from the cards? What was his end game, and why would *he* need it to begin with? He wanted to settle the issue with him, but he was not sure how to proceed without alienating Clive any more than he had already.

This just doesn't sound like Clive that I knew… he thought. He closed his eyes. *Sounds more like…*

The sound of frantic footsteps running up the stairs outside of Steele's apartment yanked him back to the moment.

Brig sprang from the couch and, ignoring the pain in his ankle, quickly made his way to the door where he stood in wait. The footsteps had stopped, just beyond the other side of the door, to his estimation, and silence ensued for a brief instant.

The door burst open.

It was Steele, panicked and in tears.

"He's gone. He's…*dead!*" she blurted between breathless gasps.

"Slow down, slow down," Brig said concernedly, grabbing both of her hands in an attempt to calm her. "What's going on?"

"It's my father," she said, slamming the door behind her. "He's not…there…" she managed to impart before breaking down into a heavy, sobbing spasm.

Brig quickly wrapped his arms around her shoulders. "Take a

breath, sweetheart," he said calmly. "Now...start from the beginning. *What's* going on with your father?"

Taking a few deep gasps and wiping the tears from her cheeks, Steele composed herself. "I went to my father's house. It was *unlocked* and he wasn't inside, Brigadier."

Brig wrinkled his brow. "Is it possible that he went outside, maybe to get some fresh air...and you just missed him?"

"No," she replied adamantly without considering the suggestion. "He hasn't been out of the house in years, and now that he's so paranoid about everything he makes a point of staying locked up and inside at *all* times."

Steele pulled from Brig's embrace and stepped quickly past him into the center of apartment, her arms folded tightly against her midsection. She began to wander about the room.

"It's all my fault." She started to cry again. "If I had just done what he *asked* none of this would have happened. Oh my God, there was blood...*all over* Brigadier..."

"You're not making any sense, Steele. Come on," he said, grabbing her arm, leading her to the front door and opening it. "Let's go over to your father's house and figure out what *really* happened."

Seven years prior (early 2077)...

"I shouldn't have to repeat instructions that you were just given by Captain Mahle," Commander Falco barked, looking out at the small audience of Epsilons that had assembled for their latest mission briefing. "But she insisted that I ensure you understood the new protocol for those of you EWs that are engaged in a battle scenario. And I know some of you numb nuts weren't hearing anything she said."

He scornfully eyed several EWs seated around the mission briefing room.

"Now before you are inserted into a battle situation," he continued once again, raising his voice to an authoritative level, "you are to inhale the catalyst. Is that *clear?*"

Falco looked around, his usual, annoyed expression tattooed on his face as he did so. Most of the men nodded in silent agreement, while several made audible grunts.

In the rear corner, Mercury McGraw sat with several of his lackeys, high-fiving them because of something said within their own private conversation.

"Am I *boring* you, McGraw?" Falco shouted at McGraw without looking in his direction. "Because you better be paying particular attention to this briefing since it involves *you.*"

McGraw did not respond. He shot a knowing smirk at one of his cronies and then spun in his seat to face the front of the briefing room.

Falco continued.

"Now you all had better understand what is expected of you in these situations because it's your ass, *not mine.* And, presidential relations aside," he said mockingly, glancing in Brig's general direction, much to the delight of the rest of the group, "we're not going to come back for you if *you* fuck up and get yourself into trouble because *you* didn't follow protocol. On to the mission details. Major Stroud will be in command. Stroud, your new partner Slade will run crypto..."

Jonas Slade smiled and patted Brig on the shoulder across the aisle. Brig nodded and returned Slade's grin with a weak one of his own.

McGraw, in his typical bully fashion, leaned over to Slade and whispered, just loud enough for the grouping in his immediate vicinity to overhear, including Brig. "You're comin' home in a body bag, Slade," he snorted and then sat back into his chair with a devilish smirk, still eyeing Brig.

"McGraw!" Falco bellowed once again, "you're running Comm in a backup role..."

"Waste of my talents, *Commander,*" McGraw crowed in feigned respect towards Falco. "Any reason why *I'm* not in charge of this shindig?" he asked snidely.

"Simple enough," Falco retorted without paying particular attention to McGraw's insubordinate attitude, and instead pointing to the map at the center of the room. "Stroud knows the region, the area around the insertion zone, and in particular, *this* encampment. He will have valuable input as to the enemy's whereabouts and his familiarity may save *your* ass..." he said matter-of-factly.

"And to be succinct," Falco added, as he stopped and leaned over the railing at McGraw for full effect, "because *I'm* in charge. And *I* say so. With all due respect to your...*wasted talent.*"

Using a laser pointer, Falco identified a small zone on the map near the edge of a nearby sea.

"Men, this is an eavesdropping mission. You are to set up a

temporary relay station at the edge of this zone that will capture data sent in by Stroud and Slade."

Falco turned to Brig and Slade, pointing a finger at them.

"*You two* will have to get yourselves as close to the enemy encampment as possible without being detected. Their data cloud is limited in range and is highly secure – which means *Slade*, we're relying pretty heavily on *your* training to make this a success, son," Falco added, locking eyes with Slade.

"Yes, sir," Slade replied immediately with a nervous, and audible, gulp.

Another chuckle emanated from McGraw's group next to him.

Twelve hours later...

The heli-jet whisked quietly towards the insertion zone, every now and again banking and changing direction swiftly as it hugged the coastline. The soft, chopping whir of its twin engines filled the silence of the cabin.

Brig sat on one of the seats next to the window, his eyes fixated on the ground below as it flowed by in darkness.

McGraw, sitting opposite Brig, closed his eyes in deep concentration on the upcoming task.

Jonas, sitting next to Brig in the center of the craft, sat quietly, twitching his leg nervously as he craned his neck to peer out the side window.

Brig tried to convince himself, as they were about to touch down in Portugal near the very spot that he and Clive had their disastrous last mission together months back, that it was merely a fluke and that *this* time would be different. *It has to be...* he reassured himself.

Jonas had begun to talk out loud, not fully aware that neither Brig nor McGraw were paying particular attention to anything he was saying.

"...and man, I can't believe we're *finally* on an actual mission together. I gotta' tell ya, I'm *stoked* about this. Nervous, but *stoked*," Jonas prattled, pulling his pack from under the seat and looking through it to double check his provisions. "Hope we don't run into any bogeys out there. Man, I haven't done any target practice in a while, I'd hate to..."

"Jonas...*shut up!*" Brig commanded.

Brig had reached the end of his patience. He faced the window, shaking his head.

Jonas, shocked speechless, glared at him with a somewhat hurt expression.

McGraw, however, snorted as he opened his eyes and glanced at Brig. Then, leaning at Jonas, made a zipping sound between his teeth, and then imitated the motion of a zipper up across his chest to his head while sneering at him with his eyes widened.

Jonas blinked in astonishment at McGraw's disturbing attempt at humor, and looked away.

"Major Stroud, team insertion in five..." a voice interrupted over the loudspeaker at the center of the cabin.

Brig sat forward and grabbed for his pack, which was stowed underneath the seat beneath him. "Warriors, *Clarity Protocol...*" he ordered. He grabbed a small, tubular-looking, metal vial from within.

He placed the vial against one of his nostrils, activated a button at the end and recoiled briefly, as the vapor contained within shot forcefully into his nose with a muffled '*pfft*'.

McGraw followed suit, flexing his one free hand into a fist, growling in reaction to the procedure.

Jonas, however, refused and defiantly tossed the vial onto the seat next to him.

"Come'on, Jonas...Clarity, hop to it..." Brig re-asserted, tossing his used container onto the floor beneath his feet with a clink.

Jonas shook his head subtly. "I'm not stickin' that stuff up into my brain, man..." he said meekly.

"That's an order, *Captain...*" Brig said, emphasizing his authority.

Still, Jonas refused to comply and looked away before Brig could say anything else.

"He's not askin' ya, Jonas, take the Goddamn shot!" McGraw shouted across the cabin, pointing an angry finger into Jonas's face.

"Brig...c'mon." Jonas turned to Brig to argue. "I told you before I wasn't gonna do this shit..."

Brig shook his head in frustration and glared out the window.

McGraw leaned forward to the edge of his seat and growled angrily at Jonas. "If you jeopardize this mission because of this pansy-ass bullshit, there's gonna be Hell to pay – for *both* of you!" he yelled, aiming his angry scowl back and forth between the other two men. He pushed himself back into his seat. "Your buddy Stroud here watchin' your back again, Jonas? Lucky, huh? Or *are* you..."

"That's enough! Both of you!" Brig bellowed, grabbing the front of each of their jackets. "Weapons check!" he barked, reaching for his assault rifle from behind his seat.

"Locked and loaded," Jonas responded immediately, his nostrils flaring in annoyance, as he fingered the electronics on the side of the magazine. Brig did likewise, and then glanced out the window again.

"Ready to burn this shit to the ground," McGraw hissed. He stroked the large weapon cradled across his arms, its multiple green and red LED status lights blinking in unison along its tapered barrel.

"Aww, now *that's* the shit right there..." Jonas admired wide-eyed at McGraw's prize possession.

McGraw snorted, more in derision than humor, as he looked over at the pair. "P-77 Plasma...hot off the R and D line. Let's get this party started, boys," he cooed with a sneer.

Jonas shook his head in disbelief. "Man, I can't believe they gave you one of those. You can light this whole forest up with that, can't you?"

"You're not shittin', junior. A couplea' shots from this baby and that camp is in cinders..." McGraw bragged. "Don't know why they don't just let us go in and take care of business like it *should* be done..."

"Because," Brig interjected sarcastically, "you only get two to three shots max before that battery's depleted. That's for emergencies *only*, McGraw..."

"Victory...*Stroud*," McGraw sniped.

"Major...*Victory*..." Brig quipped immediately, throwing his pack over his shoulder and positioning himself for exit from the aircraft. "Here we go..." he barked, as the heli-jet softly bounced onto the ground meters from where the sea splashed between the rocks that lined the shore.

Moments later, the three Epsilons stood in darkness on the grassy sand at the edge of a nearby tree line peering upward. They watched in silence as the heli-jet swiftly, and quietly, lifted from the ground, and darted out of sight.

Brig glanced away at the dense grouping of brush and trees that lined the edge of the beach.

"Enemy encampment is about two kilometers that way," Brig said quietly, pointing into the undergrowth. "Jonas, you'll come with me. McGraw, set up a comm base here and wait for instructions. Monitor enemy comms and report anything of significance immediately to me. You got me?"

"Aww, Brig, can't I come with you, *pretty* please?" McGraw chuckled in derision. "Just do *your* job, Stroud...and *I'll* take care of this end," he groused, waving his hand in dismissal at Brig. McGraw began to open the large trunk of heavy communications equipment that they had unloaded from the aircraft.

Brig gritted his teeth, took a deep breath and then turned, along with Jonas, to walk into the heavy brush.

"What a jerk, huh?" Jonas whispered aloud to Brig, who was walking in front of him, quietly pushing aside the heavier brush that stood in their path.

"That's a very tame word...a lot better than *I'd* use to describe him..." Brig snorted without looking back at Jonas. "Just ignore that kinda crap from him. He's all about trying to get a rise out of someone. Just let it roll off. Trust me, I know from experience."

"Sure, Brig," Jonas laughed nervously.

Brig stopped abruptly and glared at Jonas.

"Major... *sorry*," Jonas corrected.

Smiling, Brig spun and continued forward into the brush.

Brig pulled up from his and Jonas's slight jogging pace as he approached the edge of the thicker brush.

In the clearing ahead, he could see the familiar, stone wall that delineated the perimeter of the encampment. Brig eyed a small device, a motion sensor, that adorned one of the far corners of the wall.

He held his hand up to signal a stop to Jonas, who came chugging from the brush behind him, his boots thumping heavily on the firmer ground that lined the edge of the tree line in which they stood.

A queasy feeling came over Brig as he glared at the wall. While it was not the same one that marked the turn in events several months prior, he could not help but suddenly feel the re-opening of the wound of that fateful night.

"Set up your gear here..." he ordered Jonas silently, shaking off the vivid mental images of the past that were flooding back to his mind. Brig squatted near the edge of the tree line, rubbing pensively at the stubble on his chin as he looked at the encampment.

Jonas, meanwhile, unpacked several small pieces of equipment from his pack and set them on the ground in front of him.

Brig turned his head to check on Jonas's progress. The lack of the familiar dull, blue glow of the eavesdropping equipment only caused the unease in him to grow. He could tell Jonas was having issues.

"What the Hell is it about this place?" Brig cursed. He arose from his crouch and stood by Jonas.

"What's the problem?" he asked Jonas in a loud whisper, glancing around the area to ensure their cover.

"I don't know, I'm getting some kind of interference that's keeping me from collecting any data."

"Your system glitching out?"

"No, diags came back clean," Jonas responded concernedly. "It's not the system. *Something's* killing the signal reception." He peered up from his equipment, and even though it was dark, in the shadows he could still see that Brig had a vexed look on his face as he stared out of the trees in thought.

"Countermeasures?" Brig said after a moment.

Jonas shook his head. "*These* guys don't have that kind of tech – only *our* guys have the capability to override our listening spectrum."

Brig sat silently as he continued to gaze at the edge of the encampment.

"What do we do, Major?" Jonas asked anxiously.

"We're helpless out here, time to abort," Brig replied flatly, grumbling under his breath as he tapped at his shoulder-mounted sat-com transmitter.

"Eagle Prime, this is Canine, do you copy?" Brig droned in a lowered voice into the small device. "Eagle Prime, this is Canine…"

A distorted buzzing suddenly interrupted his transmission, accompanied by an odd tapping noise that blurted from the mini-speaker.

"Aww, shit…" Brig cursed, quickly tapping at the transmitter to power it off. "Comm's been compromised, Jonas…we need to get out of here *ASAP*!"

Jonas looked befuddled as he stood upright and started to pick up the gear. "How do you think they're *doing* it?" he asked with a panicked curiosity.

"No time to discuss it, Captain. *Let's move!*" Brig grabbed the back of Jonas's jacket and pulled him along.

"What's with the fog?" Jonas asked, as the pair had begun to work their way back into the heavier brush.

A dense, ground-level cloud had rolled into the thin forest around them.

"Coastal area, must be coming off the sea..." Brig answered, as he began to increase his running pace.

Brig *knew* it was there. He had seen it earlier but had been too focused on their task to make anything of it. He was more irritated at himself for his handling of Jonas back in the heli-jet.

McGraw's warning of '*You better not jeopardize this mission...*' replayed like a broken record in his head as he ran. Brig had hoped that it would not come to a situation where Jonas's refusal to administer the Clarity Protocol and his *own* failure at exercising his authority would cause a failed mission, yet it seemed to be playing out that way.

"Thickest damn fog I've ever seen, Brig..." Jonas observed, following closely behind.

Brig stopped abruptly, pushing his palm against Jonas's chest with such force that it caused Jonas to recoil and almost lose his balance. Without uttering a word, Brig motioned to an area ahead in the thick fog while tapping his ear. Both men un-shouldered their assault weapons and quickly split from the path that they had cleared and took cover.

As Brig stopped, a crippling wave of nausea overwhelmed him. He leaned heavily against the tree to keep himself from collapsing onto the ground. Brig squinted at the other side of the path where Jonas had taken cover and realized that he, too, was having a similar issue.

"What's that... smell?" Jonas muttered loudly enough for Brig to hear, while holding his head in one hand and searching around with the other for something with which to balance himself.

The fog, suddenly thick, no longer hugged the ground as it had just moments before. Neither man could see beyond a few meters in front of them.

"*Gas!*" Brig shouted at Jonas.

It was too late.

Jonas had already fallen to his knees and was holding his throat, gasping for breath.

Suddenly, several shadowy figures, clustered together, appeared from out of the densest part of the fog at the end of the path. Their heavy, armored gear and full facial masks glimmered dully in the odd bright, white aura that provided an eerie backlighting. Each brandished large assault weapons that twinkled with a bright blue and green glow that pierced the fog around them.

Fully sure that he was hallucinating, Brig squinted at the sight, as he leaned his full weight against the tree.

Before he could raise his weapon to take a shot at any of the figures, he heard the whistling zip of projectiles whizzing past him, some hitting the ground at his feet, while others hit and ricocheted off the trees.

With the reflexes of a jungle cat, he dove away from the tree, performed a complete roll onto the ground and fired several rounds from his own rifle into the dense fog ahead. One of the figures temporarily veered from its course.

The echoing sound of the munitions filled the air as they sailed by and bounced off various rocks and trees. Jonas had made it to safety behind a slab of rock, where he sat with his back against it catching his breath. Brig held up three fingers towards Jonas and motioned in the direction of the figures that had emerged from the fog, and then continued to fire his weapon at them.

Three more figures, followed by another set of four, burst onto the scene from another dense patch of fog to the rear of the men.

One of the figures quickly grabbed at Jonas's shoulder, pulling him up from his crouching position and out into the path. Jonas quickly slammed the figure in its kneecap with the butt of his rifle, causing the figure to fall backwards onto the ground grasping at its leg.

Jonas sprang to his feet and pounced on top of the figure, pressing his weapon forcefully in-between the armor on its chest and the mask on its face.

The attacker tried to fight back, but having lost its weapon in the jarring hit from Jonas, it could only attempt to block Jonas's furious flurry of blows. The final strike landed with a jarring thud at a sharp angle to the attacker's chin, resulting in a sickening crack of its neck.

Breathless, Jonas rolled off the figure and back to safety behind the rock.

26: NIGHTMARE

Brig, having returned to his own safety behind another boulder several meters off the path, furiously tapped at the sat-com on his shoulder.

"Eagle Prime," he shouted, whipping his head violently from side to side at each of the approaching attackers, "...this is...McGraw! We need assistance NOW! We're pinned down. McGraw!"

Brig left the sat-com open and jumped upright.

One of the figures had run up close to him. Brig fired several shots into the group of three that was there, but to his surprise, the bullets from his weapon passed through them, whizzing harmlessly into the fog behind. As Brig squinted at the incredulity of what he had just seen, one of the figures to his side caught him off-guard, hurtling Brig sideways into the rock and dislodging the weapon from his hand.

Taking advantage of Brig's momentary lapse of focus, the figure quickly jumped on top of him and shoved the butt end of its weapon into his throat. Brig countered with a solid blow to the side of the figure's head with his forearm, but it's mask protected it from the force of the hit.

The two wrestled on the soft brush beneath them, trading forceful blows to each other's abdomens, with Brig recoiling in pain after each attempt to hurt the figure through its heavy body armor.

Suddenly, a massive, orange glow filled the area for a moment, the result of a huge fireball ten meters from where Brig fought off his attacker. The two combatants flew apart from the minor shockwave that ensued.

Standing at the edge of the heavy brush leading to the shore was McGraw, the P-77 Plasma rifle in his hands, the tip of its barrel glowing with a white heat.

Farther down the path, just past where Brig lay staring in shock, one of the figures flailed around wildly, most of its body engulfed in phosphorescent flame until it fell to the ground, where it continued to burn.

Seizing the shift in momentum, Brig sprung to action and slammed a boot hard against his own attacker's head, cracking its neck and forcing its skull into an odd slant. He sneered viciously as he watched its life twitch from its body.

McGraw fired two more shots from the weapon into the grove of trees, each generating a massive bonfire out of the brush in which it landed.

Despite the additional explosions, several of the attackers had shaken off the blasts and had begun their rush at the trio once more.

McGraw, having spent the usefulness of the plasma weapon, laid it down against a rock and rushed at the pair of figures that were poised to pounce on Jonas once again. However, as Brig had found, McGraw sailed through their bodies and landed awkwardly on the ground behind them. As McGraw shook off the failed attack, one of the aggressors dove onto his back, forcing him to the ground.

Witnessing his counterpart in peril, Jonas levered himself and fired several rounds at McGraw's attacker, grazing the figure's arm and knocking it away from McGraw and onto its back.

Jonas leapt from his crouch, sailed over the prone McGraw and landed squarely on top of the attacker. He pummeled the surprised figure with his weapon repeatedly as it futilely attempted to defend itself with its bare hands.

The attacker's mask fell to the side of its face as it dislodged from its mount. Jonas quickly disengaged, recoiling in horror at the sight of the figure's face.

"Oh my God, they're just...*kids!*" Jonas yelped, falling backward onto his hands and then away from the attacker, who frantically grasped for its mask to put it back in place with visibly shaking hands.

Jonas, meanwhile, had turned and knelt on the ground. Instead of fleeing, he involuntarily vomited as he tried to push himself up. Before he could finish choking the bile out of his throat, two additional figures grasped him violently by the arms and yanked him backwards down the path.

Brig, having recovered his weapon after the melee with his attacker, quickly stood upright and started towards Jonas. Additional attackers began popping out of the fog by twos and threes, firing their assault weapons, albeit not proficiently, forcing him to dive back into cover.

McGraw, sensing the urgency of the situation, quickly gained the upper hand with his foe, spinning the figure over and onto its back. He swiftly pressed the weight of his forearm into the enemy's throat, causing it to fling its arms in a panic. The attacker spurted a watery gurgle as it gasped for breath.

Reaching into his belt, McGraw extracted his combat knife and dexterously plunged it into its chest plate. The hideous, sharp crack of the knife penetrating the attacker's armor and entering its ribcage split the dense air around them.

The figure emitted a shrill cry and then fell lifeless.

A sudden surge of bloodlust pulsing through his veins, McGraw yanked the dead enemy's mask and glared at its face. Bloodlust quickly gave way to intense dread for McGraw.

His attacker, like Jonas's just moments before, was merely a teenage boy.

McGraw staggered backward, dropping the mask on the ground, as he gazed at the horrific sight laid before him. The sound of projectiles raining around him shocked him back to the moment. He spun and located cover behind the same rock in which Brig crouched with his weapon.

The firefight continued.

Both men peered around the rock and watched helplessly as Jonas, knocked unconscious, disappeared into the brush in the grasp of his two assailants.

Brig knew that their only recourse, and only hope for survival, since he would run out of ammo soon, was to escape to the shore and call in a rescue.

He grabbed at McGraw's jacket and yelled, "Back to the extraction point, I'll cover you. *GO!*"

Brig's assault weapon hummed loudly, as he stood and laid a heavy pattern of fire into the fog ahead, forcing the large group of figures to scatter. McGraw darted from behind the rock and into the brush that led to the shore. Brig quickly sprinted to safety as well, keeping his rifle pointed backward as it continued to spray its deadly armament in a blaze of orange muzzle fire into the forest behind them.

As the two Epsilons emerged from the forest and clambered onto the rocky beach, massive cannon fire erupted from the sky and tore into the brush behind them. The forest, once lush with green foliage, became ablaze with enormous, deafening explosions of crimson and orange fireballs.

The heli-jet had reappeared above the water, the dark sky around it flickering with bright, white flashes, as its cannons hefted hundreds of screaming projectiles into the forest.

In the after-glow of the fireballs, groups of the attackers hastily retreated to their encampment while others, or fragments of them, flew into the air like cooking popcorn.

Moments later, Brig and McGraw, aboard the heli-jet, slumped back in their seats opposite of each other in silence. Every few moments they exchanged knowing, dreadful glances at one another as the aircraft swiftly carried them home.

Present day (2084)...

The door of Bronson's estate creaked open slowly. Brig peered inside. He stood fully in the doorway, glaring down at the splintered wood along the doorframe nearest the lock.

"Looks like it wasn't someone he knew," he said, pointing at the broken wood, "...forced entry."

Steele peered around his shoulder, ignoring Brig's new discovery and motioning at the living room.

"Over there..." she said meekly, indicating the large patch of blood that had now seeped farther into the carpet.

Brig stepped into the center of the foyer and glanced around, gathering in his surroundings.

The absence of a rug nearest the bottom of the staircase, evident by the different shade of carpet that traced its obvious outline, drew his eye. Where the carpet used to be, a thin trail of blood led from the center of the room and out onto the porch.

He did not say anything to Steele. She was still standing in the doorway trying not to stare at the bloodstain on the carpet. He stepped to the edge of the living room and craned his neck to peer down the hallway that led to the kitchen.

Brig knelt next to the crimson stain and gazed at it silently for a moment, and then stared pensively up at the bloodstained curtains on the front wall with his head cocked sideways.

"Well? What do you think?" Steele begged impatiently, tapping her foot nervously on the hard wood frame of the door.

"Well," Brig answered, as he stood upright, still glaring at the curtains. "I'm not going to say that your father *isn't* in danger, because...well..."

He glanced at the stain.

Steele did not respond. She nodded her head and held her hand over her mouth, choking back a sob.

"You said your father was in a wheelchair?" Brig asked, trying desperately to get off the subject of the sickening puddle of blood staring at them.

"Mmm hmm," Steele said in a muffled response, her hand still over her mouth.

"And there's no chance that he could've been standing at any time?" Brig scratched the back of his head with one eye squinted shut.

Steele looked at him, puzzled. "Not at all...*why?*"

Rubbing his chin with one hand and holding the other on his hip, Brig glared at the curtains again. "I don't think your father was the one who was shot here tonight by the looks of things," he said, shaking his head in doubt.

"What makes you so sure, Brigadier," Steele begged.

"Well, for starters," Brig began to explain, approaching the curtains, "the angle of the spray of blood on these curtains suggests that whoever was shot must've been standing. *Then*," he continued, as he turned to scan the rest of the room, "there's no wheelchair here. You'd think that if someone...broke in here and shot him, that they would've at the very least left the chair behind, if not the body."

He faced Steele, put a hand on her shoulder and lifted her chin with his other hand to meet his gaze.

"I'm not trying to give you false hope, Steele. But this looks like a *kidnapping* gone wrong. The bloodstains, no wheelchair, the lights still on...something doesn't add up. Why take the body *and* the chair? Then there's..." He stopped as he faced the door.

"*What?*" Steele pleaded, grabbing onto Brig's jacket sleeve. "What is it?"

"We have to assume this was a Syndicate job. And knowing what we know so far about them, and knowing that they were after you. Why wouldn't they just wait outside in hiding until *you* showed up?" He squeezed his head between his hands, trying to figure out what he could not see.

Steele looked dazed, as she glanced around the room for an answer that was not presenting itself. "What are you *saying*, Brigadier? How could my father have fought off someone *and* lived?"

"I think there was more than one kidnapper...and I think something went wrong and one of them panicked and took your father with them," he concluded, facing her.

"So you think he's still *alive?*" she asked, as she dried her eyes with the sleeve of her coat.

Brig put his hands on his hips again and glimpsed at the room once more. "Well...stranger things have happened, I suppose. But I think we need to keep hope alive that your father is still out there *somewhere.*"

Before Brig could finish his sentence, Steele swiftly grabbed him around the shoulders and hugged him tightly.

"Thank you so much, Brigadier," she gushed, burying her face in his chest.

Brig reciprocated the hug, squeezing her into him tightly, relishing the scent of her hair against his face.

"So...how do we go about finding him?" she said after a few moments, gazing innocently up into his eyes.

"Well," Brig countered with an intense glare, "we don't do anything..."

"But..." she interjected, but Brig forced his finger over her lips again.

"They're already out looking for you. Going to them is just playing right into their hands. You need to go back to your place and sit tight. They don't know where you live. Otherwise, they would've already made a move on you. Besides," he continued, as they both released each other simultaneously, "the less we get seen out together, the greater the chance of you staying safe."

Steele broke her gaze with Brig and glared down at the floor, nodding subtly in agreement. "So what are you going to do?"

"I know the perfect place to start."

27:
Fuel

Present day (2084)...

Brig stood at the entrance to the alleyway, his shadow cast forward onto the wet concrete in the dim streetlight behind him. The rain, which had started up again, pelted against his shoulders and chilled him to his core, penetrating the thin coat that he had thrown on prior to leaving Bronson's house.

The strong sensation of déjà vu jolted him as he glanced around at the empty lane. He had been in this exact spot only a month prior.

He thought about the paradox that had been his recent life: how that it had been seven years since everything went to Hell for him, but yet it felt like yesterday. The time since the incident in the alley a month ago, however, felt like an eternity. So much had happened in the short period of time since then, that he had not even begun to fathom what it all *meant*, or *where* it all led.

The only thing he knew for sure was that he had to find Bronson... and *fast*. Not only for the old man's sake, but for Steele's. She had such a strong tie to her father, and Brig could tell that it was tearing her apart at the seams to have him come up missing.

The Syndicate bagmen; Brig had a hunch that he could find one here, if he just hung out in these alleys long enough. If he stuck to the shadows and observed, eventually they would come.

For the most part, the area was deserted, but *something* brought them to that alley that night, and he was willing to bet that they would be back again. He would find one, which would be the springboard he would need to find out details about Bronson's whereabouts. And maybe even the Syndicate itself: its makeup, its numbers, its safe houses...*its base of operations*. His mind swirled at the thought of the opportunity that lay before him, and all he needed was just a whiff of their scent.

"Focus, Brig, *focus!*" he cursed, shaking off the thoughts of potential grandeur. "First things first, gotta *find* one of them..."

He flipped the wet hair out of his face. Something caught his eye.

Rising over the top of the wall to his left, a faint light emanated from a window at the top of a building a block away. It was not much light, but in the relative darkness of the surrounding area it shone like a beacon. In this part of town, that could only mean one thing – *someone* was there.

Brig grabbed the hanging edge of a nearby fire escape ladder and hoisted himself up swiftly, scaling it within a matter of seconds and stepping over the top wall of the vacant building to which it was attached. The roof creaked with his weight as he carefully crossed it and peered over the adjacent edge, which offered a perfect vantage point with which to see the warehouse across the street, without detection from anyone on the ground.

Two men stood facing each other in front of the warehouse, beneath a dim light mounted to the siding above a set of double doors. One gestured with his hands as he spoke, while the other stood and smoked a cigarette, every so often puffing out a thick, white cloud to his side. The light above the door reflected sharply off the bald head of the talking man, and the exposed tattoo on the side of his skull. The other thug looked around nervously as the first man spoke to him.

"*Perfect,*" Brig whispered aloud, recognizing Syndicate when he saw them.

The rumble of a truck approaching in the distance from one of the side streets drew his attention. It groaned as it neared, turned the corner and stopped in front of the two men with a shrill squeal of its brakes that echoed through the empty streets. Unfortunately, it blocked most of Brig's view of the front of the warehouse.

A shadow, cast under the truck from the other side, moved quickly towards the passenger door, where it stopped. The truck door opened and the vehicle swayed lightly from the shifting of weight, followed by the appearance of a set of additional shadows on the ground immediately afterwards.

The other guard suddenly appeared behind the back corner of the truck. He walked towards the driver's side door, looked around at the buildings, including the one on which Brig stood, and scanned the rooftops. Brig quickly crouched until he heard the sound of the truck door opening and then closing with a loud thud. He waited a few seconds and then poked his head just barely above the top of the roof wall. The shorter man, having just passed the back of the vehicle, headed to the warehouse door and stopped to take one last toke of his cigarette, before flicking it into the empty street.

Brig stood, and then trotted parallel to the roof wall, all the while focusing intently on the front doors of the warehouse below. However, he only managed to see the doors slamming shut behind them. Once again, the neighborhood fell into silence, the rhythmic tapping of the rain on the metal roof attached to the building next to him echoing solemnly into the streets.

Something big goin' on down there... Brig thought, as he rubbed his chin.

He decided on his course of action.

Carefully stepping back across the rooftop and over to the fire escape, he crawled over the wall and descended the ladder with ease, dropping the final meter into a crouch in the alleyway below.

Brig pressed himself against the brick siding of the guard shack, which sat ten meters from the warehouse. He peered around the corner and through the broken pane of glass that precariously hung from the side window frame of the shack, making sure to keep within the murky shade that it offered from the warehouse's external lighting. Small halos of light shone dimly every five meters around the structure.

Two men guarded the front of the building where the others had entered. However, they were not the same pair that he had seen before. Movement caught his eye from the far right. Another armed man slowly walked the perimeter.

Brig quickly made the calculations, and then leaned his head back against the wall.

That's at least eight. Something... or someone... important is in that building, that's for sure, he assured himself silently. *Damn. No way I can take out all three of the outside guards without someone noticing inside.*

He shook his head and inspected the rest of the warehouse from afar. A set of darkened, broken windowpanes lined the top rear of the building. Below the windows lay a grouping of trash containers, which Brig knew were his *only* shot at getting inside.

He watched intently as the roving guard passed and turned the corner at the front of the building, where the guard nodded casually to the other two men and continued on his way, disappearing finally around the opposite side into the darkness.

After quickly scanning the parking lot, Brig emerged from within the shadow of the guard shack. He stealthily sprinted to the side of the warehouse between two of the spotlights, coming to a stop in a crouching position within the darkness of a mangled, metal fence that protruded from the side of the building.

Pausing only a quick moment to catch his breath, Brig sprung from behind the fence and pulled himself up onto one of the trash receptacles. He quickly found that the one he had chosen had a bad wheel when it crumbled with his additional weight, swayed the container sideways and cast him backward onto the concrete with a thud, briefly knocking the wind out of his lungs.

His window of opportunity for scaling the wall had closed for the moment, so he picked himself up and returned to the darkness behind the fence.

Brig sat in silence for a few seconds, positioning himself for the presumed confrontation with the guard, whom he expected to be coming around for another circle soon. His expectation was soon realized; he could see the growing shadow of the guard coming from beyond the back corner of the building, slowly working his way towards him.

The guard passed by the broken fence, unaware of what lay in wait. Brig pounced from the darkness, looped his elbow around the guard's neck and squeezed tightly. Before the guard could utter a word, he lost consciousness and fell to the ground at Brig's feet.

Brig had already realized his tactical error in assaulting the guard; it would not be long before one, or both, of the men in front of the building would notice his absence. Moreover, he knew that his actions had gone way beyond simply interrogating a Syndicate bagman for Bronson's potential whereabouts, and had exploded into his full-blown interference with one of their operations.

Wasting no time, Brig slung the guard's weapon over his own shoulder and swiftly dragged him into the shadows behind the fence, then opened one of the trash containers and promptly stuffed him inside.

"Gotta make it quick, *now*...," Brig muttered, gently massaging the trigger of the Ripper that he took from the guard. He stared intently at the front corner of the building, fully expecting to see the others investigating the noise of the trash bins. However, they did not come.

Leaning on each to test their stability, Brig boosted himself onto a receptacle. The bin made a slight rattle with his full weight upon it. He stopped and peered over at the front of the building again... still nothing. Making a small leap, he grasped onto the bottom edge of the window frame above and pulled himself up and into the opening, dropping quietly onto the floor inside.

The former Epsilon sat on the floor and stared into the pitch of the room, gathering his bearings. Brig breathed easier, as the pelting of the rain outside against the metal roof of the structure fortuitously masked any minor noises from him that would otherwise have been detected.

His eyes having adjusted to the murkiness, he squinted at his surroundings. The room was on the top-level floor of the two-story building that overlooked the warehouse below. A small ledge separated the upper floor from the open air above the main area, with several jagged holes punched into it, where a small amount of light streamed in from the spotty, overhead lighting.

Brig cautiously felt his way across the room, stopping several times to ensure that the wild creaking of the floor underneath his weight did not attract attention, until he reached the half-wall, crouched next to it and peered through the opening.

Beneath him, standing on the main floor, surrounding a palette with several large and small boxes tied together, stood five people.

One, he instantly recognized by his size.

Pollux, Brig thought, *...healed up pretty quickly though. And shorter, too*, he mused.

Next to the giant stood the smaller, dark-haired man that had been standing in front of the warehouse prior to the arrival of the truck. The other man, with the head tattoo, stood on the opposite side of the behemoth, giving the appearance of an odd pair of small bookends.

A large support beam jutted from the edge of the second floor and frustratingly prevented Brig from seeing the other two people in their entirety. Instead, he could only see the movement of their shadows across from the others.

He pressed his ear against the wall and listened purposefully to the conversation going on below, but the din of the rain against the roof hindered his ability to comprehend much other than a couple of words: '*worthless*' and "*I don't know...*"

Something did strike him immediately – one of the voices was... *female*.

Brig sat back against the wall and closed his eyes. "Steele," he whispered. "What the *Hell* are you doing?"

His mind buzzed at the possibilities of what was going on right in front of him. Was she captured? Or *worse*...was she trying to broker some sort of deal with the Syndicate for her father? A wave of anger came over him as the fact that, for the second time in two days, Steele had gone off plan and had done something to endanger both of their lives. Now her latest stunt might get her *father* killed as well.

Brig held his breath as he pressed his ear once again to the wall, hoping that the absence of the sound of his own breathing would somehow make up for the echoing clatter of raindrops above him, but it was no use.

The female's voice sounded familiar to him, and because of the situation that Steele and her father were in, he had to assume that it was indeed her standing down below.

His fingers felt their way over the magazine attached to the Ripper in his hands.

Seven... he calculated by its size.

He knew that any plan to overpower the Syndicate members present and free Steele would have to be beyond precise, leaving less than zero margin for error.

"*Damn it,*" he cursed silently, realizing the futility of such a plan.

Putting the specter of a potential, botched rescue operation to the back of his mind, he leaned over and peered into the crevice once again. The bald-headed man grasped onto one of the smaller crates in front of him and toppled it sideways, spilling a large heap of electronic components and gear onto the floor. He held his arms to his side while giving his shoulders an exaggerated shrug.

One of the people, who Brig had not seen standing opposite of the other three, stepped forward and leaned in to examine the components lying on the floor in front of him.

The man's long, straight, black hair flowed down to the sides of his face, as he tilted his head back and forth trying to make sense of the pile of components. The man stood upright once again, straightened his collar and then proceeded to stroke the thin goatee at the base of his chin. The others stood silently, trying not to stare directly at him.

Suddenly, one of the front doors of the warehouse swung open and clanged against the wall. The elevated voice of someone approaching the group, who had all quickly turned to face the man that had entered, broke Brig's concentration on the gathering below. As the man stepped within the cone of the dim spotlight, Brig realized the man's identity – the guard that he had knocked out and stuffed into the trash bin outside.

"*Shit*," Brig grunted aloud in disgust, knowing that he was mere moments away from being discovered.

He quickly got to his feet, stumbled to the window and stuck his head out to gauge the situation below.

Standing next to the trash bin onto which he had climbed moments ago were the two guards from the front of the warehouse. Both with their weapons drawn, they attempted to peer upwards at the broken set of windows, but the rain and the darkness made it impossible for them to distinguish anything.

Brig pulled his head back from the window and quietly made his way to the wall. He crouched and peered into the hole. Two of the Syndicate members were now ascending the wooden staircase at the opposite end of the room, both of them with weapons at the ready. Brig flopped flat against the divider.

He was trapped.

Gonna have to take 'em by surprise, he thought, as he jumped up, strode silently across the floor, and vaulted himself through the window.

Before he had cleared the empty frame, a massive blast, emanating from the building next door, violently shook the entire warehouse. The two henchmen below flew abruptly onto the ground several meters away, as the blast shattered what was left of the windows along the side of the building in a hail of glass shards. Brig grabbed at the wooden frame with one hand as he sailed through, stopping his fall as he twisted wildly and came to rest against the warehouse's metal siding.

Despite hanging precariously just meters above where the two henchmen laid on the ground below, they had not noticed him in the chaos. The guards furiously clamored upright and ran to the front of the building, and then disappeared around the corner.

Brig let out a snort at the incredible stroke of luck that had just befallen him. Gracefully dropping onto the trash bin below and hopping onto the concrete in one fluid move, he sprinted across the parking lot into the protective shadow of the guard shack once more.

He stopped and glanced back at the warehouse.

Another explosion, louder than the first, flattened the building across the street from it, sending another concussion wave that tossed him backwards onto the parking lot. The blast instantly shattered the remaining glass in the guard shack, and sent a fireball skyward that lit the entire neighborhood in an orange radiance.

"...the *Hell*?" Brig muttered loudly, as he sat up and glared at the Syndicate group frantically pouring like ants from the warehouse.

His attention, however, fell quickly to the female of the group, as she sprinted out behind the man with the long hair, her hand grasped tensely within his as she followed.

To his surprise, it was not Steele.

This woman was taller, and unlike Steele, who had a slender build and longer hair, was more curvaceous and wore her shorter, brunette hair in a ponytail that whipped from side-to-side as she ran behind her partner.

"*Jess?*" he said incredulously. He rubbed his eyes and propped himself on one knee next to the guard shack. Before he could confirm what he had seen, the group piled into the truck and sped away into the night.

28:
Black Out

Seven years prior (early 2077)...

Brig sat at the edge of the exam table, his t-shirt rolled up over his elbow, exposing a small bandage where the medical technician had taken blood some 30 minutes prior.

The device built into his watch twinkled with a bright LED light and emitted a subtle burst of chirps. Brig sighed impatiently as he looked around the room and then glanced at the device, waving his finger quickly over the display to silence it.

A knock at the door drew his attention. It was not the attending physician, whom he had anticipated.

"The doc not coming back?" Brig asked the man, who wore official dress uniform, rather than the standard white lab coat of the normal staff at the medical center.

"He's turned your results over to me, Major Stroud," the man responded in a thick Colombian accent, not taking his eyes from the data pad in his hands. "My name is Captain Mirado. I am a medical ethologist."

Brig stared at the Captain confusedly. "What's that...some kind of bug doctor?" he said in jest.

Mirado chuckled dismissively as he sat down, still peering studiously at his data pad. "No, Major. I study patterns – more specifically, as they relate to human physiological behavior."

Brig clenched his eyes shut for a second, wrinkled his brow and then looked at the Captain. "You lost me...*patterns*? What's this have to do with *my* results?"

"Well, that's what we are here to figure out. Shall we?" The Captain swiped through a couple of data screens, stopped at one while putting on his reading glasses and then read silently to himself. Giving a subtle nod, he removed his glasses and placed the data pad on the chair next to him.

"Major, it says here that you've been having frequent headaches, but nothing that you can relate them to...eating habits, bright light, weather changes or the like. Is that correct?" Mirado asked flatly.

Brig nodded his confirmation. "Yeah, strangest thing…"

"Have you ever experienced blackouts as a result of these…headaches," Mirado continued over Brig's explanation.

"No…" Brig replied, shaking his head before Mirado picked up once again.

"And what would you say the frequency of these headaches would be?" he asked Brig, while curiously examining his eyes.

Brig stopped and thought for an instant. "I don't know…probably once about every week or so. It's hard to say, I haven't kept a log of them or anything."

"Would about every two weeks sound correct to you, Major?"

"Yeah…yeah, I guess it would," Brig replied after pondering the question. "What is this *about*?"

"Major," Mirado began, standing up from his chair, grabbing his data pad and crossing the room while speaking with his back to Brig. "You listed in your diagnosis session with the doctor on duty that you thought your symptoms might be related to the *Clarity Protocol*."

The Captain paused, and then faced Brig with his arms crossed. "It's my duty to follow up on any issues that might be arising from the application of that project as it relates to our military personnel. What makes you certain, or at least speculative that the two might be related?"

Brig frowned and curled his lip in irritation. "It's the only thing that's changed for me in the past year or so, Captain. What else *could* it be?"

"Have you used the Catalyst to date?" Mirado asked, as he glanced down at the floor.

"Yeah…" Brig replied, nodding his head, "just did on my last mission about a week or so ago…"

Mirado rolled his eyes upward as he followed a progression of logic in his head. "And did you experience any headaches as a result?" he asked matter-of-factly. He typed a few commands into his data pad. A display depicting a chart full of numbers expanded instantly on the wall next to him.

"No…*but*…"

"What we are looking at here, Major, is your blood," Mirado continued, casually pointing at the display without looking at it. "Well, at least as represented in terms of data. The green area over here," he said, pointing to a section of data near the top, "represents your PS…your Physiological State, a conglomeration of different...baselines, if you will, that have been established that show your body in its normal, *healthy* pattern."

He peered at Brig to gauge his comprehension, and then focused on the display.

"This data was established prior to your first application of the Clarity Protocol two years ago," Mirado continued, moving his hand to another section of data lower on the display. "This second set of data in yellow is your PS as of today. This set in its own grouping to the right is your PS while on your mission last week. As you can see," he said, turning to Brig, "There is very little change."

"On my *mission*. How did you get *that* data?"

Mirado tapped the back of his neck with a pair of fingers. "The tracking chip that each of you has also doubles as a bio-feedback processor. It allows us to collect data, when needed such as now, to determine what, if anything, might be happening with your PS."

Brig shook his head in frustration at the Captain's explanation. "So what're you saying, that it's just all in my head – that this *Clarity* stuff has nothing to do with it?"

"On the contrary, Major," Mirado replied immediately, raising both eyebrows. "If we thought that it had nothing to do with your...condition...we would have simply ignored the comment and moved on. I'm merely stating that your level of symptoms is not quite equal to that of others..."

"*Others?*" Brig parroted. "You mean other guys are having the same problems?"

The Captain shook his head subtly. "Not quite. Which is why I have to handle each case individually to ensure that we're looking at the right data and on the same level." He crossed his arms, holding his data pad loosely against his chest.

"So what symptoms *do* they have?"

"While I can't go into specifics...it varies. From the mild, like yours...to the...extreme...of some others," the Captain trailed off, gazing past Brig in thought.

Brig bowed his head and flicked his thumbs together as he stared down at the floor. "Do you *give* them anything for it?" he asked, raising his head to peer at the Captain.

Mirado sighed, glanced at his data pad and tapped at a virtual control. The door to the exam room slid shut silently behind him. "We have developed what is referred to as a dampening agent that...*handles*...the symptoms sufficiently, *but*..."

"But what...side effects for *that*, too?" Brig mocked in response without a smile.

"No. It's just that the agent...incapacitates its host long enough for the Catalyst to be metabolized in its entirety – returning the Clarity cells to their normal, dormant state," the Captain concluded flatly.

"Is it something that *I* should be taking?"

Mirado shook his head hesitantly. "Your bio-data doesn't support us prescribing it for you, Major Stroud," he replied. "But...with your permission, we'd like to monitor your bio-processor over the next several weeks to determine if there is a pattern to the behavior..."

"If it's gonna help stop these headaches...sure..." Brig affirmed, and then glared down at his communicator, as it began to emit several tones once again. "Captain, I've got an emergency briefing to get to. Do you need me to come by your office to follow up with this?" He pushed himself from the exam table.

"Not at all, Major. The chip is already registered and can be accessed at regular intervals remotely," Mirado replied, tapping at his data pad again. The door unlocked and slid back open.

Brig nodded, pulled his shirt from the hangar next to the door and threw it over his shoulders as he exited the room.

Brig poked his head into the doorway of the EW lounge, expecting to see the usual medium-sized group of soldiers sitting around, either watching a movie or in a spirited discussion of the latest sporting events.

However, the lounge was quiet. Aside from one Epsilon sitting alone on the far end, it was empty. That one EW was McGraw. He sat with his elbows perched on his knees and his head his hands.

"McGraw...you get called to this briefing, too?" Brig asked.

McGraw lifted his head and stared forward without making eye contact with Brig. "Yeah, I got it. Heading there now," he said, as he arose from the seat and strode past Brig, bumping his shoulder.

Brig had gotten his fill of McGraw's sour attitude towards him over the years. Given what they had just gone through, he was sick of it.

"What's your *problem*?" Brig grunted, grabbing McGraw's

shoulder to stop him. McGraw took a breath and stood still without turning towards Brig. "Look, man, I know that was some messed up shit back there..."

"What...you my *shrink* now?" McGraw growled, spinning around to meet Brig's gaze just centimeters from his face. "My problem is *you* and your habit of puttin us all in danger...*that's* my problem, Stroud," he barked angrily, poking his finger into Brig's chest.

Brig scowled. "Name *one* thing you think I did wrong that put *anyone* in danger..." he replied in confident anger, pushing McGraw's finger away from him.

"That shit you pulled with Slade. You know damn well you should've forced him to take the *Catalyst*..."

"Slade had the choice, and he didn't *want* it..."

"Aww, bullshit, Stroud!" McGraw screamed. "You outranked him. It's *your* job to make sure the flunkies follow orders..."

Brig shook his head adamantly. "Wouldn't have made a difference...we were outnumbered. Don't try to deny *that* fact, McGraw."

McGraw snorted, and then forcefully pushed past Brig with his shoulder. He stopped and abruptly faced Brig.

"Thing is...*you* saw it comin', *I* saw it comin'...and the one guy that *didn't* take the Clarity *didn't* see it comin..." McGraw barked while angrily pointing his finger into Brig's chest again. "And now he's God-knows-where havin God-knows-what done to him. You think *that's* a coincidence? That's on *you*!" he screamed. "And I saved *your* ass, by the way...don't forget *that*!"

"*Saved* me?" Brig replied with incredulity. "All you did was throw the entire area into chaos. We were on our way back to the beach when you showed up with your little toy – and *that's* when Slade got taken – don't forget *that*!"

McGraw took a step closer and stared with disgust into Brig's face.

"Listen you little punk. You may outrank me, you may have that stupid little cluster on your shoulder that says you can tell me what to do, and you may have your *Daddy* to back up your stupidity," McGraw hissed, showing his bright white, gritted teeth. "But none of that means I have to *respect* you. You gotta long way to go for *that*..."

Then, turning quickly, McGraw stormed out of the lounge.

Brig strode the hallway towards the briefing center, taking a deep breath and exhaling heavily, trying to ease his mind from the encounter with McGraw moments before. As he neared an intersection of two hallways, another Epsilon, Captain Pedro Alvarez, caught sight of him and hurried to match Brig's pace.

"Morning, Major," Pedro said.

"Hey, Pedro," Brig answered, flashing him a quick glance, but still keeping his brisk pace towards the meeting. "You headed to the briefing?"

"*Briefing?*" Pedro asked, surprised. "Didn't get any invites..." He squinted at his wrist communicator. "Must be high-level," he concluded. "Hey...you hear about Rodriguez?" he whispered.

"No...what, he finally got that retro-bike finished?" Brig chuckled, as he continued walking.

"No, man..." Alvarez said concernedly, "his wife found him dead in his car last night..."

Brig slowed his pace abruptly and stared at Alvarez in shock. "What? Oh my God. That's *horrible.*" He shook his head in disbelief.

"Yeah...heard he offed himself..." Alvarez mumbled, loud enough for Brig to hear.

Alvarez continued forward, unaware that Brig had stopped and was staring at his back with a blank, shocked expression.

"No...that *can't* be..." Brig said finally, beginning to walk at a slow gait while in deep thought.

"Sorry to bring that to you, Brig. Thought you knew already, man. Sorry..." Alvarez said apologetically while patting Brig on the shoulder.

"S'alright, man. Just a shocker is all. Hey, I gotta get to this meeting. Thanks, Pedro." Brig shook Pedro's hand and returned the pat on his shoulder with his own. "We'll talk later..." Brig said, a concerned scowl slowly growing on his face.

As he had done so many times in the past, Brig entered the mission briefing room, curious, but yet reserved, about what lay ahead.

"Stroud...take a seat and we'll begin..." Commander Falco greeted him flatly, turning his back and stepping to the front of the room.

Brig scanned the room. He had expected to see it full of Epsilons, as was the norm, but only six others, aside from himself and Falco, were there.

"Are we gonna wait for the *rest* of the squadron before we start, Commander?" Brig asked, as he found a seat near the front.

"This *is* all we need, Stroud," Falco replied without facing the audience, or Brig. He tapped a switch on the front console. The door slid shut and emitted a high-pitched tweet, signifying that the lock was in place, sealing the room from the busy corridor just outside.

Brig thoughtfully peered around the room, as he waited for Falco to begin the briefing. The presence of several other lower-ranking Epsilons, including McGraw, quickly diminished any idea that this was a high-level affair. Brig glared at McGraw for a quick second, and then turned his attention to Falco.

"Gentlemen," Falco began, still with his back to the group. "I've preached in the past about our mission caveats... being disavowed or the like. But all of that is out the window *right now*." Falco faced the small grouping of soldiers, sat back on the edge of the console, and crossed his arms. "I'm sure all of you know or have heard by now, that one of our own was captured by enemy forces last week as a result of a failed operation..."

Although he did not need to see him, Brig could feel the angry glare coming from McGraw two rows over.

"We've got several pieces of news on that front, however," Falco continued. "Firstly," he said, pointing casually in Brig's direction, "Major Stroud here had the incredible foresight to deploy a bio-sensor just prior to his team's engagement with the enemy during that same mission, which resulted in a good bit of intelligence gathering about what *actually* happened there..."

"I can tell you what happened...a cluster..." McGraw began.

"...That's *enough*, McGraw," Falco reprimanded firmly.

Falco tapped at the console, bringing up a 3D, overhead map of the engagement area from the previous week. Multiple blue and red dots quickly filled various portions of the display.

"The blue dots here," Falco said, highlighting each using a touch pad on the console, "represent our forces...Stroud, McGraw, Slade. The red dots indicate enemy forces..."

Brig sat forward and frowned at the map. *The display was wrong!*

"As you can see," Falco went on, "there were six enemy

271

combatants present, *despite* what you and McGraw reported, Major."

"That can't be right, Commander," Brig interjected. "There were at least fifteen to twenty of them there. *You* saw them, McGraw," Brig pled, pointing at his nemesis.

McGraw, also engrossed in what the Commander displayed, grunted in agreement, blinking with incomprehension at the results.

"The data doesn't lie, gentlemen..." Falco said adamantly. "But the next piece of data should clear things up, so to speak." He turned his back and continued talking as he stepped towards the display. "The sensor picked up the deployment of a hallucinogenic agent sometime just prior to engagement..."

"*The fog...*" Brig said under his breath, but loudly enough for McGraw to hear him.

McGraw glanced concernedly at Brig.

"Don't take it so hard, Stroud," Falco said, switching off the display behind him and turning to face the room. "We couldn't have prepared you for that. But that isn't the most important piece of news that I have for you men today."

Falco took up the spot at the edge of the console once again. "Early this morning, Intel up at HQ in Boulder picked up enemy chatter that used known codes indicating that we believe to be the location of a POW."

"*Slade?*" Brig asked curiously.

"We don't know that for sure," Falco concluded, as he sat and stared at his men silently.

After what seemed like an eternity of silence, another of the Epsilons, Swanson, spoke. "What about his tracker?"

Falco continued to scan the group with a stern expression, without eyeing Swanson. "Slade's tracker went silent almost the instant that he was taken to the enemy encampment. And, as you know, there are only two ways that can be possible. Removal and destruction of the chip. Or...*complete incineration of the body.*"

The room remained gravely silent, except for several hesitant inhales.

"Until this recent bit of intel hit us this morning, we were forced to believe the latter. Now we are a bit optimistic that Slade may *still* be out there." Falco glanced over the small audience of EWs, witnessing the chord that his news struck with most, if not all, of them.

"Gentlemen, in the display behind me," he began once again,

the display flickering and changing to a geographical map of Eur-Asia, "is our focal point for this mission. The city of Kaliningrad on the southern edge of the Baltic Sea. We have reason to believe that our POW is being held at an old theater that was converted into a prison about twenty years ago." Falco fell silent and peered at the group.

Unlike Falco's normal briefings, usually filled with barbs and jabs between the Epsilons present, each man fixated on every word that came from their leader's mouth.

"Men..." Falco instructed, turning his head to focus on each EW in turn, "this mission is beyond Black Ops, and as such shall remain top secret. The bigwigs up in Boulder don't want another international incident, so we're having to take care of this in-house. Stroud... *this* is your squad."

Despite having scanned the group upon entering the room, Brig did not really pay much attention to the exact makeup of the team. He looked purposefully at each of them.

Aside from himself, there was McGraw, Swanson – an EOD specialist, Johannsen – a Crypto specialist, Evans – an engineer, and Ballard and Delgado, both snipers, the latter a rookie to the EW squadron. Brig had never been in charge of this large, or this specialized, of a team. He nodded silently as he stared at them, and then turned to face Falco.

"You will most likely encounter *heavy* enemy presence," Falco warned, leaning on the railing separating the display console from the seating area. "You are authorized to take whatever measures necessary to bring him home," he emphasized, glaring sternly at Brig.

"Deployment is at twenty-three-hundred tomorrow night, with insertion shortly before dawn the following morning. Rest up, men...you'll need your strength for *this* one. *Dismissed*," Falco ordered. He turned his back to the grouping as they began to file out. "Stroud, stay after a minute. I've got some *additional* instructions for you..."

Brig arose from his seat and approached the front of the room just behind Falco, who leaned against the console with his head bowed.

As the last Epsilon, McGraw, left the room, he turned and shot a curious look at the two men before disappearing around the corner.

Falco tapped at the console to close and lock the door once

again, leaving them alone together in the mission room. He folded his arms menacingly across his chest.

"Son...I've been in this business for over thirty-five years. And I've had to put up with a *lot* of bullshit from the top brass. And they've put me in a position to make calls that *I* didn't feel were right. But there comes a time when enough is enough," he explained, much to Brig's confusion. "I'm not gonna sit back and watch one of our enemies thumb their noses at us and disrespect this outfit by taking one of our own – that's what this mission is about. You *get* that, son?"

Brig frowned and nodded his head. He knew exactly where Falco was coming from...*now*.

"So I just wanted to pull you aside and let you know how *personally* I'm taking this one, and why I *expect* this to be a success," Falco continued.

He leaned into the rail just in front of Brig's face.

"Now you go over there and you bring back that kid, you understand?" he ordered, the pitch and intensity in his voice rising suddenly. "I don't care what the *fuck* you have to do. I don't care how many *Goddamn* bogeys you have to take down."

Falco's face had become flush with a dark shade of crimson.

"I don't care if you have to slice them open and rip their fucking guts out to get to Slade, Goddamn it! You *bring* him back!" he shouted through gritted teeth into Brig's face, spittle flying from his lower lip.

"Yes sir..." Brig stammered, taking a half step backward in surprise at Falco's sudden emotional outburst. "Anything else...*sir?*" he asked, truly afraid of what else the man might have to say.

"Just one thing..." Falco added, tapping the console behind him to open the door. "Don't screw up, Stroud. Or I'll have you busted back to Captain so fast your head will spin. *We clear?*" he said in an alarmingly calm voice.

"Yes, Commander," Brig responded and then exited the briefing room.

29:
Who Are You?

Present day (2084)...

The wind howled through the pines in the distance, across the street and up the hill from Clive's workshop. The latest bout of rain had tapered to a light, shimmering drizzle.

The weather this winter season had been particularly blustery and wet, and up until a few days ago, Brig would have had to brave the elements in his makeshift campsite in those very woods.

Things had changed dramatically since then – not that *he* was complaining. However, he found himself out in the elements once more. As he approached the front entrance to his friend's abode, he tucked his hands tightly into the pockets of his hooded jacket, and snugged his chin against his chest to keep the misting rain out of his face.

Brig was not entirely sure of what role Clive was playing in everything, but his gut told him that it was *much* more than he was letting on. It was time for Brig to get Clive to show some of his hand, and he knew just how to do it.

He stepped into the dim light that flowed down from the small overhead lamp above the doorway.

Suddenly, the familiar groaning of a large truck echoed in the distance.

What're the odds? he thought, unsure of whether the truck's destination was the workshop. He swiftly darted out of the light and ducked behind the fence that bordered the property, adjacent to one side of the workshop.

After a few moments, the truck pulled up to the front of the building, stopped and idled. Someone exited the passenger side, slamming the door behind them. Brig cautiously peered over the top of the fence. Just as he had expected, Clive walked around the front of the vehicle and towards the front door of the workshop.

"You gonna be long?" the driver yelled out to Clive.

Clive turned his head to the driver without stopping. "Just go back to the safe house. I've got some work to do here," he said, continuing to approach the door.

"You're not gonna guard the old man tonight?" the driver asked in a thick Eur-Asian accent, while sticking his head out the window of the truck.

"Not my job, Alexi. Besides, there's two of you there, I think you can handle it. I'll see you guys in the morning..."

Alexi shrugged, poked his head back in the window and put the truck in gear. The truck rumbled off, quickly turning a corner and accelerating as best it could, as Clive entered the workshop and slid the door closed behind him.

Moments later, as Alexi released the steering wheel to stretch his arms in a deep yawn, he suddenly saw a man in the middle of the road, waving his arms wildly at him to stop. Alexi slowed the truck as the man came around to the side of the vehicle and peered up at him.

The hooded man swiped the long hair away from his face. "Thank you for stopping, man...you're a *lifesaver!*" he said to Alexi, panicked.

"What do you need?" Alexi said skeptically, glancing uneasily around the area.

The man pointed excitedly ahead of the truck. "It's my son, he...got bit by a snake down the road in the field. You *gotta* help me!"

Alexi frowned and scratched his head. "I...can't do anything to help you with that, buddy, sorry."

"Please, mister," the man insisted, stepping closer to the door of the vehicle, "you gotta at least come help me get him outta there - he's gonna *die!* I can't lose him. I just can't...he's all I got *left!*"

Alexi sighed heavily and looked around once more. "Alright... get in, let's go take a look at him..."

As the man climbed into the passenger side of the truck, Alexi glared at him curiously. The man's jacket, with the hood up loosely over his head, coupled with his wild, long hair, hid most of the features of his face.

"What's with the hood, buddy?" Alexi asked, glancing back and forth between the man and the road, as he forced the truck into gear and slowly began to accelerate, the truck's engine laboring as it rolled to a slow pace.

"I've got a...*disfigurement...*" the man said ashamedly, while looking out the side window, "...don't like to show my face much anymore..."

Alexi nodded while still peeking from the corner of his eye. "Where's your boy?" he asked the man gruffly.

"About a kilometer and a half up the road just beyond the entry road to the forest." The man held up his finger above the dashboard to show the way.

"The forest? What the Hell you doing *there*?" Alexi grumbled. He pushed the accelerator pedal harder, forcing the engine to emit an even louder groan, as he prodded it forward.

The man fell silent, continuing his gaze out the window. "We like to live off the land... try not stay in the city too much. Too dangerous there anyway..."

"*Dangerous?*" Alexi chuckled derisively. "Sounds like the *forest* is the dangerous place..."

"Only dangerous if you threaten them," the man defended flatly, and then fell silent again. He eyed Alexi's weapon, a small handgun, lying on the dash up against the windshield in front of the steering wheel.

After a few moments of driving, the man tapped on the dashboard to get Alexi's attention. "It's just up here, just up on the right."

"Boy, it's *dark* out here...and I thought it was dark in town!" Alexi marveled, as he began to slow the truck.

"Angle the truck's headlights towards the side of the road over there." The man forced open the door and hopped out onto the pavement, while the truck was still rolling to a stop.

Alexi put the truck in its parking gear and pushed open the door to the cab. He jumped out onto the gravely side shoulder of the road and strode towards the front of the vehicle.

To his surprise, the stranger had already made his way quickly around the front and met him at the corner of the driver's side – with an outstretched arm holding a Ripper to Alexi's face.

"Are you *crazy?*" Alexi cried, wild-eyed, taking a step backward, his arms outstretched.

"I've been told that several times, *yeah*..." Brig said, his hood having fallen back around his neck. He waved the barrel of the Ripper in Alexi's face. "Keep your hands where I can see 'em." Brig took a step towards Alexi.

"Easy, buddy. I don't think you *know* what you're doin'

here..." Alexi cautioned, nervously eyeing the weapon pointed at him. "Let's not lose our heads..."

"*I'll* do the talking right now. Get up here and get down on your knees. Hands on the back of your head," Brig growled, reaching for Alexi's arm and pulling him forcefully several meters in front of the idled truck. He forced Alexi onto to the ground facing away from him.

"I don't have anything for ya, man..." Alexi grumbled, folding his palms loosely over the top of his scalp, just above the ponytail that trailed down behind his neck. He glanced every few seconds back at Brig through his peripheral.

"You only have one thing I want...the *safe house*. Where's it at?" Brig barked, jabbing the tip of the Ripper at the back of Alexi's neck, which made him flinch forward with each touch.

"*Safe house*? I don't know what you're *talkin'* about, man. You got the *wrong guy*."

"Playin' dumb isn't the best thing to do right now, pal. Where's the safe house?" Brig screamed into Alexi's ear, grabbing the shoulder of Alexi's jacket and balling it into his fist.

"I told ya, I don't *know* about any safe house!" Alexi yelled, a hint of disdain in his voice.

Brig grunted in frustration and then shoved Alexi forward, sprawling him onto the headlight-lit, wet pavement. Still pointing the Ripper at Alexi, Brig quickly stepped over to the cab of the truck, extracted the handgun from the dashboard and stuffed it into the back of his belt.

"You doin' this to get my *truck*?" Alexi shouted while pushing himself up with his hands so that he could see his attacker.

"I said *stay down!*" Brig bellowed at Alexi, taking a step towards the front of the vehicle and gesturing with the Ripper.

Alexi placed his face flat on the surface of the road, watching Brig once again dart into the cab of the truck. The engine of the vehicle moaned as the truck lurched forward, forcing Alexi to flinch in shock. He began to back-pedal onto his knees out of the path of the moving vehicle.

Before Alexi could reach a standing position, however, Brig, who had hopped back out of the truck and stood behind him, forced him back onto the pavement with a forceful thud of his boot.

"Now then," Brig said calmly while jabbing the cold steel of the Ripper into Alexi's back and placing one of his boots firmly against his neck, effectively pinning Alexi to the ground, "Wanna tell me where the safe house is?"

Alexi grunted, futilely attempting to free his neck and head from Brig's downward force. "What the Hell? Are you crazy?" Alexi watched the slowly approaching truck, realizing that he was in its direct path.

"I thought we went over that already. Time's runnin out for you...*pal*. Gonna talk?" Brig pressed his boot harder against the base of Alexi's skull, making the prone man squeal in pain.

"I'm not tellin you *anything*..." Alexi said defiantly through his gritted teeth.

Brig glanced at the truck and rubbed his chin with his free hand. "You're about to have four thousand kilos-worth of incentive to talk parked on your neck in about five seconds. *I beg to differ...*" he said coolly. He prodded the Ripper harder into the back of Alexi's ribs.

"You're messin with the *Syndicate*, man! You're a *dead* man! You're crazy!" Alexi said in a panicked wail, his eyes growing large at the sight of the truck's massive front tire. It was now so close that the pungency of the exhaust leaking from around the engine gaskets stung his nostrils, and he could feel the heat radiating from the underside of the engine compartment.

"*You're* gonna be the dead man, buddy. And I'll just find *another* Syndicate slug to get what I need. So it's your choice," Brig replied, shaking his head at Alexi. Brig quickly moved his boot away from Alexi's neck and stomped it hard into his lower back, holding the man to the pavement, as the front bumper of the truck approached close enough to block out the stream of light coming from the headlights above it.

"*Okay! Okay!* I'll tell you!" Alexi screamed in terror. Brig swiftly released his boot from the man's back, grabbed him by the ponytail and yanked him out of the truck's path.

Alexi fell backward onto the wet gravel and watched breathlessly, as the truck continued to ramble forward, finally coming to rest with a dull crunch against a large tree at the edge of the road.

Brig stood next to Alexi and pointed the Ripper at his temple. "Out of the frying pan. You're Syndicate...so I *know* you're familiar with these," he said, tapping the barrel of the Ripper.

Alexi took a deep breath and avoided looking directly up at Brig. "The safe house is out on highway 89 just past the old airport.

But you'll *never* get anywhere close. We've got five guys watching it..." he said, gasping for breath.

"Now see? Wasn't that hard, was it?" Brig commended. He pulled the Ripper away from Alexi's head and reached with a hand to help him to his feet. Alexi stared incredulously at Brig, as he cautiously took Brig's assistance and pulled himself up.

Before he could gather his wits, however, Brig delivered a crushing body blow to Alexi's gut, doubling him over. As Alexi staggered backward a step, Brig followed up by clubbing him over the back of the neck with the butt of his Ripper. Alexi fell unconscious to the ground in a heap.

Brig hoisted Alexi up and over his shoulder, and then carried him over to the truck, its engine whining pitifully as it continued pushing against the massive tree trunk in front of it. He opened the cab door and pushed Alexi into the driver's seat, his head falling with a thump against the steering wheel.

"You're gonna have an awful headache in the morning...but I doubt you're gonna know what hit ya'," Brig mumbled, slamming the door shut and briskly walking away.

Clive stepped off the final step of the wooden staircase that led from his workshop into the secret room under the floor. He flicked on the small LED lamp that hung above his workstation and then tapped on the edge of the display. It emitted a small tone and instantly lit up to a login prompt.

A rapping at the front door upstairs halted him.

"Damn it," he grunted, spun around and climbed the stairs once again. "I *told* you I wasn't coming back tonight, Alexi."

He pulled at the front door to slide it open.

Brig stood with his back to Clive, his wet hair tied back. "Just *me*, Cryp," Brig said, turning around with a sardonic smile. "Expecting some *other* pony-tailed friend?"

Clive rolled his eyes back in his head as he looked up at the ceiling in frustration. "What do you want, Brig?"

"Was in the neighborhood, thought I'd drop by for a little chat," Brig replied, casually pushing past Clive and stepping into the workshop. He scanned the room, as he stopped and turned to face Clive. "Got a few minutes?"

Clive quickly glanced out the front door, and then faced Brig, sliding the door shut behind him. "What about?" he asked impatiently.

"About Steele...and the *work* you did for her..." Brig said intently, keeping up his nonchalant air.

Clive did not respond, but stood with his arms crossed as he glared at Brig.

Brig nodded at his non-response and continued. "I was just wondering why she would have gone through the trouble to have blank cards decrypted. *Any ideas?*"

"I'm sure I don't know anything about it," Clive answered matter-of-factly. "She asked me to decrypt them... I did. And the transaction ended there." He shrugged his shoulders for effect.

Brig shook his head. "*Something* doesn't add up, man." He rotated and slowly began pacing the room. "She gets these cards...comes to you. Then she gets tailed by one of the Syndicate goons...the *same* one that was here a week ago," he explained. He faced Clive. "*Pollux Webb* ring a bell?"

"I don't know what you're getting at..." Clive began to defend, stepping over to the workstation across the room and beginning to tidy up.

Brig pursed his lips and furrowed his brow. "And then, just when it couldn't get any odder, they go and kidnap her *father.*"

Clive stiffened as he listened to Brig talk about Bronson Fox.

"Now what kind of sick bastard goes and nabs an elderly man in a wheelchair?" Brig quizzed slyly.

Brig unzipped the front of his coat, extracted a half-empty bottle of vodka, and placed it on the end of Clive's workstation with a light clunk.

Clive glanced at it briefly, before turning away.

"Oh yeah, brought this by. Thought we could have a drink together...*like old times,*" he said, staring at Clive for his reaction.

"No thanks." Clive continued to clear the desk in front of him. "I need a clear head tomorrow, and *that* ain't gonna help."

"So what do you make of this whole thing, man?" Brig stood back and crossed his arms over his chest.

"I don't know what to tell you, Brig. But it sounds like your girl is in over her head with the Syndicate," Clive answered, facing Brig with a stern expression. "And as *usual*, you don't see that this is probably bigger than just you and her. But yet here you are sticking your nose into it. When are you going to get it through that thick skull of yours?" He walked past Brig, bumping into his shoulder deliberately as he passed.

"Trying to help out a friend. Like *friends* do, ya' know?" Brig countered.

"And if I were *her*," Clive continued, reaching for the front door to slide it open, "I'd just give them what they're looking for so that this all just *goes away...*" He stood aside and looked at Brig.

Brig snorted, nodded his head as he zipped up his jacket, and began strolling past Clive into the doorway.

"Okay, we'll play it your way...*for now*," Brig said knowingly. "Oh, by the way..." he added, turning to Clive, who had taken several steps away from the door and was faced away from him. "...*Jessica's* alive," he said flatly.

Clive tensed but did not turn to face Brig.

"You hear what I *said*, Cryp?"

"Yeah, I *heard* you, and you're *crazy*," Clive responded.

"That seems to be the consensus lately, yeah. But not about *this*. I saw her tonight."

"You've taken too many hits to your head, or that serum is starting to make you hallucinate," Clive said derisively, facing Brig once again with a sneer.

"Not the reaction I *thought* I'd get from you," Brig responded with feigned concern. "But I thought you should know about it anyway. And the fact that I'm gonna' *find* her." He spun and walked out of the workshop, gently sliding the door shut behind him.

Nine years earlier (2075)...

"I can't *believe* you invited McGraw..." one of the Epsilons, Johannsen, sitting on one of the lawn chairs, said to Brig. Johannsen took a large swig of his beer as he eyed the burly, flat-topped McGraw from across the room.

The rest of Brig's EW squadron, 40 in all, mingled around throughout the estate, either inside or out near the pool. A small trail of white smoke wisped across from the opposite end of the Olympic-sized basin, while the sweet, smoky smell of charcoal-grilled meats filled the air within a half-kilometer radius of the mansion.

The Stroud annual barbeque was a tradition, at least among the elite crowd that either knew or worked for Brig's father, Devlin. The event was much larger this year, not only from the addition of

Brig's cohorts from the EWs, but also because of Devlin's recent announcement that he would run for President of the URA.

Brig stared pensively at McGraw as he, too, took a big gulp of his own brew.

"We're all EWs here man...one big happy family," Brig responded with a half-hearted smile.

McGraw had always had *something* against him, what that was, however, Brig had no clue.

"Besides," Brig added with a grin, "if I didn't, that would only make him act *more* like a tool."

"Happy family? What's *he*, the crazy uncle?" another EW, Swanson, chortled. Several other Epsilons, seated around one of the outside corners of the swimming pool, laughed loudly.

"More like the big brother you love to hate..." Brig interjected, looking around the group and laughing at his own musings.

Brig rarely had many friends over to the estate during his childhood. To have *this* many people here on *his* account made him feel important, at least for the afternoon. He also knew that it could help bring everyone in the squadron just a bit closer – even if one of them *was* McGraw.

"More like the big brother you want to smack with a shovel..." Johannsen corrected with a hearty chuckle, raising his bottle to his lips again.

"Clive comin today?" Swanson asked Brig, quickly changing the subject, noticing the change in Brig's expression as they all joked.

"Yeah, he's supposed to be here," Brig replied.

"Who's Clive?" Johannsen asked under his breath to another Epsilon seated next to him.

"Underwood. Brig's new crypto tech," the other answered.

The subtle clang of the door chimes echoed through the front hallway, into the living room just inside, and across from the patio where Brig and his fellow EWs sat.

"That's probably him, be right back guys," Brig said to the others, as he jumped up and darted across the concrete, and through the open French doors. The shadows of Clive and another person reflected through the glass of the over-sized, oak front entryway. Brig grabbed the massive handle and yanked the door open.

"Hey, Brig!" Clive offered with a smile that lit his face, his hand darting forward to offer his greetings.

Brig beamed his own broad smile to his partner and grabbed his hand, forming the familiar 'W' with their arms, the standard EW handshake, which then devolved into a full hug.

"Glad to see ya', man!" Brig said enthusiastically, as they separated from their embrace. "Didn't think you were gonna make it."

Brig stood and stared at Clive and his guest, a demure woman whom appeared to be in her late 50's. An awkward silence ensued as the three stood facing each other.

"Where are my manners...I'm sorry, come on in," Brig finally said, chuckling lightly, as he stepped aside and allowed Clive and his guest to enter the sprawling estate house. "Who's your guest, Clive?" he asked. The woman walked by him and stood next to Clive, just beyond the entryway.

"Brig, man, this is my Mom," Clive responded happily. "Mom, this is Brig Stroud. This is his place..."

"My *Dad's* place..." Brig corrected, lightly grasping the woman's hand and shaking it. "So you're Clive's mother?" Brig asked. "I have to tell you, that's one great son you raised there, ma'am." He shot Clive a quick glance and a wink.

"Thank you...Brig, is it?" the woman queried, as she took her hand back from Brig and hooked it along with the other onto her purse strap that hung in front of her.

Brig nodded. "Brig...Brigadier, whatever you feel comfortable with," he replied with a courteous tilt of his head, fiddling with the half-empty bottle of beer in his hand.

"*Stroud*...you're not any relation to Governor Stroud, are you?" she asked curiously.

"One and the same." Brig turned sideways and pushed the massive front door closed with an elbow.

"I'll bet you are all just thrilled that he's running for President in the fall, aren't you?" Clive's mother gushed.

"Yeah, we're...*ecstatic*..." Brig said sarcastically, taking a swig of beer and giving Clive a knowing smile, to which Clive subdued his own reactive grin by covering it up with his fist and looking away.

Brig *was* happy for his father, but he also felt conflicted, as he felt things like *this* were why he did not have as close a relationship with the man as he could have had.

Brig cleared his throat and quickly changed the subject. "Did

Clive tell you that he saved my life a few months back while we were up in Alaska?"

"No, I don't believe he did. Of course, he doesn't tell me much. Says it's all *classified*," the woman responded with a haughty, but playful, tone, tapping Clive on the back of the head with one palm.

"Yeah," Clive said, sneering at Brig, "we were doin' survival training up there and hotshot here had a little...*accident*."

"Well, dear," the woman said to Brig in a motherly tone, gently grabbing Brig's upper arm, "I'm so happy that my son was there to help you out. He's always been a good boy, very helpful..."

"Mom..." Clive interjected while rolling his eyes, gripping the back of his neck with one hand and rubbing intently.

"You're *never* too old for me to embarrass you, remember that..."

"Aren't you going to introduce me, Brigadier," a woman, whom they had not noticed standing behind Brig, added to the conversation.

"Oh...*Christine*..." Brig said, somewhat surprised. "Yeah. This is Clive Underwood, one of the EWs in my squadron. And this is his mother, um..."

"...Claudia..." Clive's mother added, holding a hand towards the other woman.

"Right...Claudia Underwood," Brig continued, a bit embarrassed.

"Hello, Claudia. I'm Christine, Brigadier's mother..." Christine reached to shake Claudia's hand.

"You call your mother *Christine*?" Clive said under his breath, leaning towards Brig.

"No, I call my *mother* Mom. I call *my step-mother* Christine," Brig said loudly so that the group could hear, much to the chagrin of his stepmother, who curled her upper lip and frowned at him.

"Well if we're talking about someone needing saving, then *I'm* here to save you, Claudia," she added with feigned laughter. "No need for you to have to sit around and hear all of the boys tell *their* war stories, now is there?"

Claudia raised her eyebrows and lightly shrugged her shoulders. "I don't mind."

"Come now, the other ladies are out on the terrace enjoying some sweet tea. Doesn't that sound more inviting?" Christine smiled with conceit as she grasped Claudia's forearm and led her away from the two men, jabbering away continuously as they walked.

"Talk to you later...*Mom*," Brig said mockingly, but drew no response from Christine. "So hey, man, *you're* late..." he said, facing Clive and walking with him towards the back patio entrance. "Good thing you got here when you did, these guys like their burgers and dogs, that's for sure..."

"Yeah, sorry about that," Clive replied. "Brig, lemmee ask you. You been having any...*health problems* lately?"

Brig stopped and stared at Clive, his brow rumpled heavily, as he tipped his beer bottle to his lips. "*Like?*" Brig said with a mouthful of brew.

"I don't know, man. Like headaches, dizziness or anything?"

"Nothing out of the ordinary, I don't think..." Brig replied after thinking for a split-second. "Why, what's up?"

Clive shook his head and scratched his chin with one hand. "Been having these...I don't know what to call it...*episodes*, I guess," he said and then stood for a moment in silent thought. "You been part of that new program...uh...*Clarity?*" he asked finally in a lowered tone, glancing around at the other Epsilons that he could see.

"Yeah... our whole squadron's been part of it I think," Brig answered, now taking more of an interest in what Clive had to say.

"It's just that...ever since they started that crap, I've been having things like this. Get the sweats, big time. A couple of times I've almost blacked out," Clive explained, looking at Brig with a hint of hesitation.

"Sounds serious. Seen the docs about it yet?" Brig asked, putting a friendly hand on Clive's shoulder.

"You know me, man. I've always prided myself on being physically fit, so...yeah. They even gave me some of this...*serum*... to take if it happens..."

"Is it *helping?*"

"Been too afraid to try it. I don't like meds, man. Just figured I had the flu or somethin'...but it hasn't gone away, only gotten *worse*," Clive replied apprehensively.

"Who's that with Stroud?" one of the Epsilons, sitting next to Mercury McGraw on the other end of the room, asked. The group surrounding McGraw glanced over at the two men.

"That's Underwood, Stroud's crypto..." another one replied.

"Damn, *another* one?" the first responded. "What'd he do to run the *other* one off?"

"He's a loose cannon," McGraw said, swigging his beer

forcefully, staring with disdain in Brig's direction. "No one wants to work with him for very long, and if they do, he runs 'em off when they don't play ball with him and his daddy."

Several of the EWs in the small group laughed uneasily.

"Yeah, it's funny 'til someone gets hurt," McGraw added flatly without taking his eyes off Brig. "The sooner they drum that joke out of this outfit, the safer we'll *all* be..." He forcefully chugged the remainder of his beer and strode out onto the patio.

"So you're gonna introduce your friend to Cruella there, but not *me*?" another female said with dripping sarcasm from behind Brig.

"Yes, because she's just *so* special," Brig said playfully, as he put his arm around the girl, giving her a small peck on the side of her head. "Clive, this is my sister, Jessica. Jess, this is Clive Underwood. He's my partner in our squadron."

"Nice to meet you, Jessica," Clive said, holding his hand out politely to shake hers.

"You can call me Jess," she replied, taking his hand and locking stares deeply with him.

"...*Jess*. Well, I can see where all the attractive genes went in this family," Clive joked, jabbing at Brig's arm, also not taking his eyes from Jess.

"A charmer! He's my *new* favorite of your playmates, Brig," Jess said playfully, placing her hand lovingly on Clive's upper arm.

Brig felt the bubbling of the odd chemistry between the two, as he stared back and forth at them.

"*Dad* gonna make it today?" Brig asked his sister, trying to break the unspoken tension.

"You didn't hear? He's got a summit in Rio this weekend," she replied, rolling her eyes for effect, as she smiled coyly at Clive.

"Wow, tough job," Clive said, still not taking his eyes off Jess.

A man poked his head in from the patio behind them. "Hey Brig, your grille's smokin man."

"Ah, hey, gotta go check on that stuff," Brig said. He stepped to the doorway, shaking his head and wearing a look of consternation.

"You're in this big ass house, got people serving drinks, and *you're* over there flippin' burgers?" Clive mocked incredulously.

"Hey," Brig countered, stopping and facing Clive and Jess, "I can train a monkey to serve drinks, but it takes an *artist* to make burgers like I do, *right* Jess?"

Jess rolled her eyes again and winked at Clive. "Show off," she said.

"Hey man, you can go grab somethin' to eat if you want. There's a whole table of burgers, dogs, chicken... whatever you want..." Brig offered to Clive.

"He's in good hands *here*, Brig. Just go tend to your grille," Jess told Brig, turning her attention back to Clive.

Brig nodded, raised an eyebrow and then disappeared out the patio door.

A few moments later, Brig stood at the grille, moving several pieces of meat from one side to the other, and stabbing at others to test them.

"Hey, man," Clive said suddenly, standing behind Brig, placing one hand on his shoulder, "What's her...*situation?*"

"*Christine?* Oh, she's married to my Dad..." Brig said facetiously, not looking at Clive.

"Ha ha... *jackass*. I mean Jess."

"Married. Well...*separated* technically. Why?" he asked, while curling the corner of his lip upward coyly.

"Your sister's cute, man. Just wanted to know if you were... okay with me getting to know her better," Clive said hesitantly.

"She's a *handful*, man..." Brig said. He pondered for a moment before continuing. "But if she's ok with it, then I guess I am, too." He patted Clive's back.

"I'll take some of *that* when it's ready, Brig," Clive said with a smile, pointing at the grille.

As Clive walked back into the house, Brig continued to prod at several pieces of meat in front of him.

My best friend and my sister... hmm, he thought silently. *Guess that's not too bad.* He let out a heavy sigh, then picked up a plate and dropped a piece of chicken and a hot dog onto it. As he turned to re-enter the house, he caught sight of McGraw standing across the other side of the pool.

Hell, what am I saying... Brig's thought continued, *...Clive would be great. McGraw and my sister - now that would be an epic catastrophe.* To be sure, he could not honestly think of someone better than Clive – after all, the man *had* just saved his life.

Clive leaned next to Jess and held a picture in his hands at an angle to catch the natural light flowing in from the patio area.

"And who are we looking at here?" Brig said from behind the pair, holding the plate of food in one hand out to Clive, who took it with his free hand and set it on the table in front of them.

"That's my folks in the back row, Brig," Clive said, pointing at the picture. "You met my Mom. Next to her is my Pop."

"Handsome...I can see where *you* get it from," Jess said with a coy smile.

Brig pulled Clive's hand closer to him. Next to Clive's mother in the picture stood a tall, solid-built, dark-skinned man, handsome, as Jess had pointed out.

"Good lookin' couple," Brig observed while staring attentively at the photo. "That the *one*...you told me about?" he muttered, only loud enough for Clive to hear.

"Yeah," Clive answered tersely.

"I didn't *know*..." Brig began to observe.

"*Yeah*," Clive countered with disdain immediately, and then snagged the picture back, shoving it into his pocket.

For a moment, Clive caught the fleeting, apprehensive look on Brig's face. It did not last long, but it *was* there.

"*What?*" Jess asked, glancing between her brother and Clive, confused at the looks the two men were silently exchanging.

"Nothing," Brig chuckled. He walked around the front of the couch, held out his wrist communicator and aimed it at the pair. "Say cheese..." he instructed with an exaggerated smile, tapping the side.

"I want a copy of *that*..." Clive said with a coy smile to Jess.

The two began talking between themselves, laughing every so often as they carried on. Brig shook his head lightly as he looked on at them, and then exited out onto the patio.

30:
Divide

Present day (2084)...

The heavier rain had subsided, but a mist of smaller droplets still filled the air and grated against Brig's bare face, as he guided Steele's retro-bike into the neighborhood of her apartment complex.

The night's encounters held him deep in thought; so much, that he had to spike the hand brake on several occasions to keep from missing turns. On one of the more serious corrections, the bike's rear tire slipped out from underneath it on the wet pavement, causing it to career sideways several meters; almost falling to the ground before Brig was able to get it back under control.

"Gotta slow it down and pay attention, *idiot*," he grumbled at himself, squinting out into the dim beam of light emitting from the front of the bike.

He was eager to get back to Steele's to give her possibly the *best* news that he could have hoped for - that her father apparently *was* alive and being held in a location that *he* knew.

Her terror at the realization of her father's abduction, or worse, was very familiar to him. He knew what it felt like to lose the final connection to family suddenly, and he had hoped beyond hope that something good would come from his hunch. However, he realized he had a short window of opportunity. If he knew one thing about the Syndicate, it was that they would show *no mercy*. Moreover, that there was no honor involved where they were concerned. They were after Steele, and it was apparent to him that taking Bronson was just a chess move in their eyes.

It was going to take a careful plan to free Bronson, but Brig was confident that he could pull it off - he *had* to.

He also felt conflicted about Clive's nonchalant attitude towards Steele's situation. To have Clive turn the issue around and reflect it back on her was just insulting to Brig.

Where was the man that Brig had held in such high regard: the man that had saved his own life – on *many* occasions? The cruel winds of reality had slowly eroded the boulder of respect that Brig had once held in his heart for his friend. Lately, that wind had become a typhoon.

The harsh awakening of it all stabbed at him more than any physical wound he had ever endured in his life. It filled him with disappointed anger and frustration that Clive would not accept a torch from a friend, while he stumbled on his dark path to oblivion. Brig was starting to reach the end of his patience with his friend.

It vexed him even more why Clive would have gone to the trouble of double-crossing Steele, a woman he did not even know, for an organization that for all purposes stood for *everything* that Clive would find appalling.

Then there was Clive's dismissive attitude about Jessica. The fact that there was hope of her being alive should have sparked *something* in Clive.

But was it actually hope, or just Brig's desire to have things back the way they were? Brig tried to convince himself that he did not really see her at the warehouse - but he knew it was all too real. He wanted to grab Clive and shake him to his senses, but with the way things were currently, and the fact that their relationship appeared to be devolving day-by-day, Brig knew that he could not take the chance; for his sake, for Steele's, her father's...and Jessica.

Brig turned the bike onto the main thoroughfare that led past the front of Steele's apartment, then reached under the seat and abruptly turned off the ignition, causing the bike's motor to backfire once loudly and then fall silent, as he began to coast the remaining distance.

Before yesterday, it would have been okay to ride the bike up to the front of Steele's place. But since the attack by Pollux, it was increasingly dangerous to be seen, or heard, on Steele's bike. Brig could not risk giving away the safety of her residence. Steele was a marked target, and now Brig was, too. He knew that separation was *essential* to keeping her safe.

He rode the momentum of the final, motorized push into the suburban housing complex. He quickly made several turns onto various side streets and wound his way onto an adjacent, desolate avenue, hoping to dissuade anyone that might be watching or following him. Finally, he hopped off the bike as it slowed to a stop, pushing it the last several meters up to a curb.

He grunted as he forced the bike up and over the curb, rolling it into the safety of the darkness of a gaping hole in the side wall of a vacant store. Brig shoved the kickstand underneath the bike and turned to exit of the building, taking care to poke his head out and survey the area first. Then, swift as a jungle cat, he sprinted across the street and through an alleyway that led to Steele's apartment two blocks away.

The echoing sounds of the rainwater dripping down the facade of the apartment building and into the stairwells provided the only sounds audible to Brig, as he quickly scaled the steps and cautiously walked the final several meters to Steele's front door. He glanced around once again and then, satisfied that no one had followed, quietly rolled the doorknob in his hand, pushed open the door and disappeared inside.

As he adjusted his eyes to the darkness within the apartment, he could see the motionless figure of Steele lying on the couch. The fact that she had not reacted to his entry told him that she was asleep. While he hated to wake her, he had news that just could *not* wait until morning.

He softly sat on the edge of the coffee table that sprawled out parallel to the couch and leaned in towards Steele. Instead of putting his hand on her shoulder to gently wake her, he found himself gazing at her while she slept.

Although it had only been a few hours, it had felt like an eternity since he had left her here in search of answers to her father's disappearance. He watched as she gently drew in each breath, her abdomen and chest rising and falling very subtly after each inhale and exhale.

She was so at peace, so relaxed...so *beautiful.*

Then, her eyes opened abruptly.

"*Bloody Hell*!" she barked. She quickly sat up and fumbled for the small light on the end table next to the couch, flicking it on after a few unsuccessful tries. "You nearly scared the *life* out of me, Brigadier!" she cried, as she held her hand to her chest and gathered her breath.

Brig promptly grabbed her hand in his. "I'm so sorry, Steele," he chuckled. He kissed the back of her hand while staring into her eyes. "I didn't want to wake you...you looked so peaceful."

"*Ever* the sweetheart," Steele replied, reaching with her other hand and stroking Brig's cheek with her palm, a radiant smile spreading across her face. "What did you find out?" she asked eagerly, knowing already from his expression that he had news to share.

"A few things...all of them rather...*interesting*," Brig said pensively, scratching the back of his neck with one hand.

"I don't suppose Clive gave up anything *willingly*, did he?" she asked with a sarcastic air, as she sat up.

"He didn't admit to anything, but I overheard enough from several sources to know that we're on the right track."

"What did he say?"

"He played it close to the vest, as usual. And he claimed ignorance of anything and everything Syndicate-related. But his reactions to what I said..." Brig explained and then went silent for a moment in thought.

"What is it, Brigadier?" Steele begged, taking both of his hands in hers. "Did you find anything out about my father?"

Brig nodded while pursing his lips. "I *think* it's good news. I...*obtained* the location of one of their safe houses, and the indication I got was that they were holding '*an old man*' there," he said tentatively, not trying to get her hopes up *too* high. "I would think given the situation, that it's probably *not* a coincidence."

Steele's eyes widened as she squeezed his hands tightly. "That's *amazing* news!" she cried. She let his hands drop, stood up and then paced the room several times before turning to him once again. "You know, Brigadier. I've been thinking while you were out." She bit at the tips of her fingernails on one hand, "And I think I've an idea to get them to free my father."

Brig frowned and then peered up at her. "Okay," he said hesitantly. "What is it?"

"Well," she started to explain, once again pacing the floor in front of the window, "they don't know what's on the cards. I believe that if we get word to them that we want to make an exchange..."

Steele stopped and glanced over at Brig, who shook his head subtly with a concerned expression.

"After all," she defended before he could respond, "isn't *that* why they took my father in the first place? Why not just give them what they want...in a sense?"

"No, *absolutely* not..." Brig said adamantly, rising from the coffee table to stand face-to-face with Steele.

"*No?*" Steele mocked with her hands placed firmly on her hips. "This is *my* father, Brigadier. And this plan will *work* – as they're clueless as to what this is all about."

"And so are *we*, Steele..." Brig cautioned. "Don't forget that.

We don't know what they're willing to do to get back what *you* took."

Steele angrily crossed her arms onto her chest. "It's a valid plan," she grumbled through gritted teeth.

"It's a *death* wish, for you and your father," Brig shot back immediately. "What exactly do you think is gonna happen when you walk in there – they're just gonna let you two go? And do you think *I'm* going to let you just walk right into the lion's den...on a *bluff?*" He gently took hold of her upper arms and looked into her face.

Steele wrested her arms from his light grip and turned her back on him. "And I suppose you have a *better* plan?" she asked bitingly over her shoulder.

"Yeah," he replied gruffly, "I go to the safe house and get your father!"

"Just like *that*..." Steele replied with a hint of mockery.

"Yeah, just like that..."

"And what am I to do, just wait here like a *good* little girl?" Steele asked snidely.

Brig stood in silence for a moment, glaring at Steele's back. "It's a Hell of a lot better than sacrificing *both* of you, Steele. You realize you'd be playing right into their hands...*right?*" he asked in a softer tone, turning her shoulders around and tipping her chin upward towards him.

Steele sighed heavily and broke eye contact with him, instead choosing to glance out at the night sky. "It's just that your plans..." she began, but then halted and bit the end of her fingernail.

"My plans...*what?*" Brig asked in a surprised tone.

"Nothing," Steele replied, the frustration in her voice changing to a soothing coo. "Let's just talk about it later."

"We don't have time to sit around and wait on this, Steele," Brig said firmly. "They've got your father, and they're gonna make a move...whether you want them to or not. So the sooner we get him out of there..."

"I don't want to do it *your* way, Brigadier," Steele quipped without waiting for him to finish his thought.

"*Why?*" Brig cried, throwing his hands in the air and shaking his head.

"Because..." she answered without hesitation.

"*Because?*"

"Because your plans always end up with someone getting

hurt...or *worse*," she shouted viciously and then fell silent, turning her back once again.

Brig stood behind Steele, speechless. He felt his heart drop as he stared at her with complete amazement of her callous attitude towards him.

"I'm sorry," he muttered finally. "I...I didn't know *that* was how you felt."

"It's not. I...I'm *tired*, Brigadier. Can we just drop it – I think we both need some sleep," she said flatly, as she began to walk to the hallway that led to her bedroom.

Brig continued to stand at the window, glaring out at the darkness in thought.

"You're not going to go all *wounded* now, are you?" Steele asked sarcastically, turning her head back to him while she walked.

Brig snorted audibly and shook his head, as he glanced over at her. "No. You don't have to worry about *that*. Just go get some sleep."

It was the next morning, and Brig had spent a quiet, sleepless night on the couch. He had decided to head out before daybreak, and before Steele woke up; that way he could hit the road without being seen coming from Steele's place, *and* he could avoid another confrontation with her.

The sting of her barb from the night before still jagged at his heart, and the last thing he wanted to do was reopen the wound; or have her profusely apologize for something she obviously *meant*.

He had made sure to leave a note behind letting Steele know the location of her bike, as she had never gone to the precautions of hiding it in the past and would be clueless as to its location. He did not, however, leave any other indication of where he was going – *or* when he might return.

The morning was cool, with a small amount of fog hanging in the air, and small puddles of rainwater from the previous night's storm dotted any flat, unbroken pieces of asphalt that remained on the roads and weedy parking lots around town. Brig had been walking for nearly an hour before the sun winked its sleepy eyes over the horizon at his back, and was absorbed behind a thick bank of dark clouds just as quickly. He had continued walking an additional hour since then.

The pain in his ribs still radiated throughout his abdomen, and the cold bite of the morning air only made him feel more miserable. Clive's place, while not that far by bike, was a considerable hike for anyone, let alone someone with little sleep and a swollen ankle from the fight with Pollux just two days prior.

However, Brig pressed on.

He took the final bite out of an apple that he had pocketed from Steele's kitchen, and tossed the spent core into a grouping of sage bush on the side of the road. It was not much in the way of sustenance, but he had survived on far less for far longer during survival training in the EWs.

His mind wandered to Clive.

Brig knew that Clive was definitely hiding his involvement with not only the Syndicate, but also with Bronson's abduction. He had tried to keep his mind focused on the task at hand; finding as much information as possible about what was going on, and somehow trying to find a way to convince Steele that rescuing her father *was* the best, and only, possible solution.

However, he had a hard time distancing himself from the pain of her comments from the previous night. It felt like déjà vu to him – '*when you do things your way, people get hurt...*' Clive had made that his mantra for the past seven years, but it hurt twice as bad coming from Steele.

He growled audibly as he shook off the emotional cobwebs that had grown overnight, instead forcing himself to pick up the pace as he entered the edge of the neighborhood of Clive's workshop.

Early enough, he should still be there... he thought, convinced that if he could get another run at discussing everything with Clive, that he just might get Clive to be a bit more forthright about his involvement. He knew it was a long shot, but one that might be well worth it if the result was an alternative option to fix Steele's problem, without endangering anyone else.

As he got within view of the small workshop, tucked away from the street in-between two fences, Brig could see a small amount of light poking out around the shutters of the building.

"Good, I'm not too late..." he muttered aloud.

Then, just as he approached the first fence, the front door of the workshop slid open and Clive emerged, turning to slide the door closed behind him and stepping out to the road.

Brig wrestled with the thought of confronting him on the spot, but instinctively dashed behind the fence, choosing instead to watch his friend's actions and determine how best to handle the situation. As he watched Clive walk out onto the edge of the road and begin to head in the opposite direction of him, as always with the slightly noticeable limp, it occurred to Brig that perhaps the best way to get information from Clive was not to confront him, but to follow him and see where it led.

Brig waited until Clive had gotten nearly out of sight a hundred meters or so down the road before emerging from behind the fence, cautiously sprinting a safe distance behind him off the side of the road and near buildings, when possible.

His conversation with him the previous night notwithstanding, the last thing Brig wanted to do was spook Clive into becoming even less talkative.

As Clive wound his way around several corners, ducking into alleyways and crossing streets with no particular pattern, Brig could tell that he was doing what any well-trained Epsilon would have done to prevent anyone from tailing him; anyone that wasn't another Epsilon, of course.

At one point, Brig swiftly scaled the side of a smaller building in order to gain a vantage point from which he could safely watch Clive's progress from afar, without giving himself away by being on the ground.

Brig watched as Clive disappeared behind one building, only to reappear several moments later. However, not in a straight line from where he would be expected, but usually at an odd, and unpredictable, angle, most often from behind an entirely separate building. The cloud cover and lack of anyone else in the area made it very easy for Brig to spot him, especially from his perch atop the building. More importantly, it allowed him to rest his ankle and ribs.

One thing that had surprised Brig was that instead of Clive heading towards the industrial section of the town, where most of the warehouses, and Syndicate thugs, were - he headed away in the opposite direction, towards the edge of town where it was mostly residential.

"Where the Hell is he *going*?" Brig asked himself aloud, scanning the far distance to see if maybe there was anyone waiting for Clive, whether on foot or, as he had expected, in a truck. However, aside from the normal, empty neighborhoods and charred storefronts, nothing stuck out as somewhere that he might be heading.

As he observed Clive heading out from the protection of the surrounding buildings and into a clearing just beyond the start of the residential section of town, Brig decided that it was time to get back down on the ground. He did not want Clive getting too far out of reach, but also his curiosity had now been piqued, and he wanted to get a closer look at Clive's intentions. He zipped up the front of his coat, as the wind howled down between the small buildings around him.

The day had become drearier by the moment, with the dark clouds that had lined the horizon now hovering overhead. In the distance, Brig could hear the light rumble of thunder. The sudden pelting of light raindrops on his shoulder made him pull the hood of his jacket up over his head.

"Super, *more* rain," he cursed while shaking his head, picking up his walking pace to a light jog as he took an alternative route around the buildings; one that he knew would take him on a direct path to the far end of the residential sector where Clive currently was.

Brig rounded the corner of a building near the end of the main thoroughfare. However, he abruptly jumped backwards and out of sight.

Clive, continuing his fidgety, elusive strategy, had turned into Brig's direct path!

Brig pressed himself tightly against the stucco siding of the building, which provided minimal opportunity to hide him from view. He took a deep breath and slowly rotated his head towards the road, fully expecting to see Clive staring at him in disbelief.

To his relief, Clive had once again changed paths, crossed to the other side of the street and had turned the corner adjacent to Brig's current location. Brig cautiously stepped around the corner and onto the sidewalk, then sprinted quietly across the street and continued the silent pursuit of his ex-partner.

Brig's confidence was low, at this point, as to what Clive could be doing. Clive had already gone completely away from the warehouse district, which Brig thought was a sure thing when he had begun following him an hour earlier. Now, having approached the outer edge of town, where only houses dotted the barren landscape ahead, Brig was unsure what the game was.

Clive, now some 100 meters ahead of Brig, had turned and had begun walking down a dirt road that led past a grouping of wildly overgrown trees, and ended in a small cluster of cottage-like homes. The homes, not visible from the main road because of the way they were situated within the wood, appeared to have been built within the past several years; a very odd occurrence by any stretch of the imagination.

The rain had begun to intensify once again, and the trees that lined the dirt road swayed lightly with the wind's caress. Clive had already passed the first several of the houses and was approaching the fourth, when Brig had decided to make a frantic dash for the edge of the dirt road and take up a hiding place behind one of the larger trees. As he panted for breath and wiped the rain from his eyes, he stared down the long, dirt drive at the small enclave of homes.

Clive was now standing at the doorstep of the fourth house with his hand out to knock on the door. Brig ducked his head back behind the tree, as Clive quickly scanned the area behind him, waiting for a response from inside the house.

After a few moments, a small sliver of light appeared from around the edge of the door. It opened and Clive went inside, the door slamming shut behind him.

"Well, this just got *really* weird. So what's my next move?" Brig questioned aloud, peering behind him.

His first instinct was to simply go up to the house and knock on the door. However, he quickly quelled that idea, as it would most likely only blow apart any chance of Brig discovering anything today.

The grouping of houses nestled in this deserted area eased his fears of detection. If not for the rain, Brig was confident that he could have waited out Clive by just staying by the trees without ever being seen. However, the cold wind made his body shiver, and in turn, his ribs ached worse than they had all day. He decided that since there was only one way out of the area, that he would go back to one of the buildings on the edge of town and at least take shelter until Clive would make his way back through.

As he sat on the top floor of a vacant building that overlooked the main thoroughfare, including the corner that led to the dirt road with the mysterious houses, Brig pulled off his coat and wrung the rainwater out of it. Setting it aside to dry as much as possible despite the moist weather, he stood, leaned out of the window, and looked around at the dark tops of the buildings throughout the town.

On the far end, the warehouse district from what he could determine, twin trails of black smoke billowed upwards into the darkened sky; the remnants of the two explosions from the previous night.

Brig had no idea what had caused them, nor what they had to do with the overall big picture where it concerned the Syndicate. But he was thankful, as it provided him the miraculous opportunity to escape from certain capture. Or *worse.*

Thinking about what had transpired the previous night, he began to think about his sister, Jess.

Ever since the sighting, he had fought himself on whether he actually saw her - or whether it was just what he *wanted* to see.

He had not thought about her in years.

It was a time that he had blocked out of his mind, just another in a long line of traumatic events in his recent life. She was the last connection that he had to family. It drove him over the edge, farther than he had ever been before, when he learned that she was a victim of the massacre outside of Vegas that fateful Sunday during a power play from a gang of marauding thugs.

It did not make sense. She was dead, *right?* He did not like thinking about it. The whole idea of it resurrected the memories of the depression and anger that the tragedy brought upon him.

Brig squeezed his head between his forearms and closed his eyes tightly.

"One thing at a time, Brig. *One thing at a time...*" he told himself repeatedly, as he laid his head down on the windowsill and took a deep breath.

A full seven hours later, Brig found himself continuing his watch over the desolate street below, with no sign of Clive. The sun had danced in and out of the clouds all day, and had finally found a small clearing just above the horizon to the west in which to settle. Sunset would be coming soon, and if he had not located Clive by then, it was going to be difficult to track him with any consistency. Besides which, he was beginning to get very hungry.

The apple he had eaten, along with a handful of berries and a couple of hunks of chocolate, were all that he had taken along with him when he left Steele's place early that morning. He had not anticipated having to take such a long time, and assumed he would have been back in just a few hours.

As he yawned and stretched his arms backward over his head, he suddenly caught sight of Clive turning the corner just down from the dirt road.

"About time..." Brig said aloud.

Clive was alone, and did not have any items with him that would have indicated some sort of drop or exchange.

"What the Hell was he *doing* there for eight hours?" Brig marveled, as he stared down at Clive, being careful not to make his silhouette visible in the window.

Over the past few hours, Brig had made a decision on his next course of action. Seeing Clive leaving just as he had arrived affirmed it. He was going to wait until Clive cleared the area, and then *Brig* would investigate the house in the grove. It was a risk, but one that he knew he *had* to take.

Brig stepped into the hallway outside of the room in which he had been camping all day. To the left of the doorway was a crumbling, concrete staircase that led up to the roof.

"Perfect," he pondered, beginning to cautiously scale it, small pieces of the stairs coming loose and falling in crumbles to the floor with a hollow echo below, as he placed his weight on them.

Once he reached the roof, he quickly went to the edge and peered down over the town. It only took him a few moments to locate Clive, whom had already made his way several streets over. Brig waited a full thirty minutes, well past when he could no longer see Clive's shadowy figure twisting in and out of various buildings blocks away, left the roof and then descended the stairs out into the street.

30: DIVIDE

After a quick jaunt across the road, around the corner and down the dirt path while staying hidden along the trees that lined it, Brig found himself in the center of the grouping of cottages.

The windows, tightly boarded with no light emanating from them, were certainly an eerie sight. Although there were tracks that indicated that vehicles had been there at least in the recent past, none were present. For all purposes, this was a deserted mini-village.

The sun had begun to set, maneuvering within the dark, rain clouds. Its dwindling rays flickered amongst the tree trunks along the dirt drive, filling the small grove with an orange cast, as Brig made his way up to the fourth house and stepped up onto the small porch.

The floorboards emanated a dull creak under his weight. Brig stopped and listened but did not hear any movement inside. He reached one arm behind his back and fingered the trigger guard of the handgun that he had pilfered from the Syndicate thug's truck the night before. He hoped that it would not come to it, but he had to be prepared just in case. After all, he had no idea what he was about to stumble upon.

Reaching over to the door with his other hand, he lightly rapped on it and then stood back a step as he waited. It took several minutes, but finally the door creaked open a few centimeters.

About halfway down the opening was the round face of a Mexican woman, staring out at him with wide eyes and lips pursed tightly.

"You've got the wrong house," she said in a low tone with a thick accent.

"Hi, ma'am. My truck overheated down the road in town..." he explained, pointing back towards the road. "Do you think I could borrow a bucket of water to get it going again? I don't want to be stuck here when the sun goes down..."

"Don't have anything for you, gringo...vamos," she ordered with more emphasis.

"Please, ma'am, just some water – that's all I need and I'll be out of your way," Brig pled with his best charm and a friendly smile.

The woman abruptly closed the door, the echo of the wood-on-wood reverberating off the other cottages nearby.

"Okay, weirder yet..." Brig said under his breath. He peered over at the boarded window. As he craned his neck to look around the group of houses, suddenly the door flung wide open.

The woman stepped out onto the porch, wielding a shotgun pointed at Brig's abdomen. Brig's instinct was to pull his own weapon, but something told him that she would be more willing to shoot him if he gave her that big of a reason than she would if she saw he was unarmed.

He slowly removed his hand from the gun in the back of his belt and raised both arms above his head.

"Ma'am, I'm sorry. I just needed a little help, that's all..." he said slowly and deliberately, taking a step backward.

The woman stepped further out onto the porch and poked the end of the barrel into Brig's ribs, making him wince in pain.

"I said go!" she shouted, angrily pointing her finger away from the house.

Suddenly, a face appeared from the shadows behind her. It was a boy.

"Who is that, ninera?" the boy said. He held onto a portion of the wall behind the door with one hand, while staring out curiously at Brig.

"Vas en la casa, hombrecito," the woman ordered, not taking her eyes, or the shotgun, off Brig.

The boy did not listen, however, and continued to stare intently at this new stranger.

"I'm sorry, ma'am, I didn't mean to bother you," Brig said apologetically, turning halfway to step off the porch and onto the sandy grass while still facing the woman

He could not take his eyes off the boy. He looked oddly familiar.

"Sorry, ma'am. Have a nice day," Brig said with a half-smile, turning to walk back down the dirt trail that led to the road.

He craned his neck once more as he heard the woman step back into the house. The boy had come to the door and was getting one last glimpse of Brig, as she closed the door forcefully behind her.

Brig began his long trek back to Steele's, shaking his head at his most recent encounter. If the grand puzzle that he was trying to solve were made up of smooth, rounded, dark pieces that fit well together; this latest piece was bright neon with jagged edges.

31:
Under Cover

Present day (2084)...

Clive clanked the serving spoon around the edges of the saucepan, the warm aroma of the bland soup stock wafting upwards into and around his face.

It had been a long day of walking for him. The temperature had dipped once again, as the sun had begun to set. He was savoring the simple pleasure of a hot bowl of sustenance, prior to descending the stairs to do some work before retiring for the night.

As he reached above the stove to extract the lone bowl from the cabinet, a gentle rapping came from the front door.

He shook his head in frustration. Lately it seemed that he had no *end* of visitors dropping by at all times of the day and night.

Probably Brig, he thought, recalling the confrontation of the previous night with his former EW partner.

In no particular hurry to have another go around with Brig, he casually made his way across the workshop and slid the door open, fully expecting the usual, sarcastic greeting that he had become accustomed to lately.

To his surprise, it was *Steele*, standing just within the dim light mounted above the doorway, with the hood of her dark jacket partially over her head.

"Oh...it's *you*," he said. He briefly made eye contact with her, and then broke it quickly to scan the area behind her.

"Can I come in?" Steele asked hesitantly, staying put just outside the door so as not to seem presumptuous.

Clive sighed heavily and scratched his head. "Brig's not here..."

"I'm not looking for Brig..." she interjected. "I came to talk to *you*, Clive."

He stared at her for a moment and then turned his head sideways to give a quick glance at his workshop. "Ok...come in."

As she floated past him through the doorway, he quickly slid the door shut and ran his hand across the hair on his head.

"So...I guess you and Brig are teaming up to try to get info out of me now. *Your* turn, huh?" He shook his head and crossed his arms over his chest.

Steele ignored Clive's obvious taunt. "I'm here to ask you a favor..."

"*Favor?* I don't know you. Why would I do *you* a favor?" Clive answered dismissively.

"I came to you because I know that you and Brig are buddies, and..."

"...We're *not* buddies," he retorted derisively.

"That's not the way *he* sees it..." she responded in turn, and then continued on. "As I'm certain that you already *know*, my father's been kidnapped...by the Syndicate."

Clive waved his hand at Steele and strode past her towards the kitchen. "I already told Brig – I don't know anything about *that*," he said, disappearing around the corner.

"Clive..." she said in a tone loud enough for him to hear over the racket that he was now making at the stove. "...I didn't come here to ask you about my father. I came to...ask you to please get Brig to back off any plans that he has to rescue him."

Clive reappeared suddenly from the kitchen, holding a bowl of steaming soup in his hand. He chuckled as he set the soup on the table and pulled out a chair, sat onto it and grabbed a spoon.

"You're kidding me, right?" He shook his head once again and slurped a spoonful of the hot liquid, then recoiled when he found the soup to be too hot. "What makes you think I have any sway over what *he* does?"

"Of the two of us, you seem to hold more persuasion with him," she said condescendingly.

"If you really think that, then you don't know Brig that well," he grunted sarcastically, cooling his dinner with several puffs, and then taking a spoonful into his mouth, making no eye contact with her.

After a few more slurps, he could not avoid the fact that Steele was still standing with her arms crossed, glaring at him.

"Look, I don't know what you want out of me here. It's not like he listens to anything *I* say," he explained, still without looking in her direction. "Brig marches to the beat of his own drummer... whether it's right or not." After a few seconds of silence and no response from Steele, Clive glanced up from his bowl.

Steele, biting one of her fingernails pensively, quickly looked away.

He sighed and pushed himself up from the table. "I don't know how well you know him, or what your history is exactly. But I've had enough experience with him to know that he's gonna do what *he* wants to do. And nothing me *or* you...or anyone else for that matter, is gonna change what he has set in his mind."

Steele stood silently and stared at Clive, as he picked up his bowl and spoon, walked back into the kitchen and tossed them into the sink with a loud rattle.

"I realize that Brig is the way he is. But he respects you...more than you know," she explained calmly, glancing around the workshop behind her. "I was just hoping that something you could tell him would trigger a bit of reason within him. I don't want my father hurt..."

"It's getting kinda late. Not sure you should be out here this time of night with...well, you know...*what's going on...*" Clive said awkwardly.

As Steele turned and began walking to the door, Clive followed her. She slid open the door and stepped into the doorway.

"Look," Clive said suddenly, making Steele turn to face him. "...I'll...do what I can with him. But if he doesn't listen...and he probably *won't*...you need to be ready for the fallout from it."

Steele nodded her head in quiet understanding, turned and left.

Seven years prior (Early 2077)...

The crowd chanted wildly, as they stood behind the marked area that the local police had set up for them.

"We're live in thirty seconds..." the cameraman said.

The reporter stood in front of the camera and quickly fluffed the side of her hair with her fingers, as she prepared for her remote broadcast. She glanced around at the crowd that had gathered. The cameraman held his hand up, indicating that their feed was about to begin.

"This is Starr Rizzulo reporting to you live from the URA Capitol in Boulder, where literally *hundreds* of protesters have gathered this weekend to give voice to their growing, heated concerns over the purported rumors of improper and unethical testing of biological and genetic agents on *this* Republic's military personnel," she said stoically into the camera.

The crowd, listening intently to her report, stirred as they began to shout various anti-government slogans and waved their brandished picket signs towards the camera.

"This show of solidarity," she continued, as the crowd noise died down, "comes after months of leaked, but *unconfirmed*, internal reports of a rash of suicides within an elite group of military commandos. Adding fuel to the fire are the tragic events last month at the Guadalajara Air Base, where a Special Ops team member killed his family and then took his own life. Military authorities have *refused* to comment on the possible motives of the multiple murder-suicide, but comments from an anonymous source within the DMST have raised speculation that the..."

The reporter stopped mid-sentence, as she spotted several men in white lab coats emerging from a vehicle that had pulled up near the front steps of the Capitol building.

"*Doctor!*" she said loudly, stepping in front of one of the men, forcing the microphone in front of his face. "Can you comment on the reports that the events at Guadalajara and the high rate of suicides of specific military personnel are tied to the URA's experimental testing policies?"

The man, caught off-guard by the reporter's presence and pointed questioning, scoffed and waved his hand in front of her.

"The two issues aren't related *at all*. The DMST has strict guidelines for human testing and *everything* we've done to date has been strictly in line with..." he defended, but then another man in military dress abruptly pushed him aside.

"No more questions...no more questions," the man said forcefully, pushing the reporter aside and shoving his hand into the camera lens. "If you have anything additional that you need answered, you can contact the URA press secretary. *Now step aside.*"

The man, obviously military legal counsel, along with the doctors next to him, pushed past the reporter, as the cameraman quickly spun to get a shot of them storming away and up the steps towards the Capitol.

The crowd's chanting intensified as several protesters stepped outside of the cordoned area and rushed into the range of the camera.

"You can't cover this up!" one of the protesters shouted with an upraised fist. "We have a right to know what's going on with our boys!" The crowd nearest him roared its approval and began to push inward towards the doctors and the military lawyer.

In an effort to regain control of the situation, several military police, toting assault weapons, stepped down from the Capitol steps and stood in the way of the protesters; who quickly stopped their advance and stepped back into the crowd.

"Well," Starr said, facing the camera once again, "I'm afraid we're left with more questions than answers here. But rest assured this story *hasn't* reached its end. We'll bring you more information as it becomes available. Now, back to Leylah Rodriguez at our news desk in Sao Paulo."

Present day (2084)...

The door of the bar creaked open, and Brig casually stepped in, the moonlight casting his dull shadow forward onto the floor in front of him. His shoes, still wet from the day's earlier rain, when he was following Clive to the mystery house on the edge of town, squeaked on the wooden floor as he entered the room.

He scanned the darkened bar. Of the very few patrons that still remained inside at this time of night, most sat in the shadowed corners away from prying eyes.

To his surprise, and delight, Clive was sitting at the bar, partially hunched over his drink and not paying attention to anything, or anyone, around him.

Brig approached the back of Clive's chair, patted him on the back as he sat down on the empty stool next to him, and waved his hand towards the bartender.

"Just like old times, huh partner?" Brig said to Clive, facetiously.

Clive rotated his head only slightly and peered at Brig out of the side of his eyes, and then turned his gaze back forward without much reaction. "What...you *following* me now?"

"No...just took a chance that you'd be here," Brig replied, continuing to stare pensively at Clive.

Brig was being truthful. He had actually given up his pursuit of his friend when he decided to investigate the mysterious house that Clive visited earlier in the day. The fact that he found Clive in the bar at this time of night was pure luck.

"Thought maybe we could pick up our conversation from last night," Brig offered.

"Think all was said that *needed* to be..." Clive responded flatly, while taking a sip of his drink.

"Nah, I don't think so," Brig disagreed, shaking his head, as the bartender clunked a mug of beer down on the wooden bar in front of him. Brig picked up the beer and took a sip. "Besides, I wanna give you another chance to change your mind and come with me."

Clive snorted derisively and shook his head. "Come with you? *Why* should I help you?"

Brig finished a large gulp of beer and set the glass down in front of him. "Because you know it's the right thing to do. But wait, you've *heard* that one before, haven't you?"

"Even if the person you are trying to help doesn't *want* your help?" Clive asked, glaring at Brig and making eye contact with him for the first time since he had sat down.

"Now how would *you* know *that?*" Brig parried curiously.

"Spoke to your little girlfriend last night. She told me *just* that..." Clive countered, swirling the beer around in his half-empty mug.

The corner of Brig's lip curled upward in anger. He leaned in towards Clive and pointed his finger angrily into Clive's shoulder. "You stay away from her, you got that?" he said in a low grumble.

"*She* came to *me*, man. You don't believe me...ask her. Maybe you don't know *her* as well as *you* think..."

Brig quickly swigged the rest of his drink and plunked the empty mug down on the bar. Pointing casually in Clive's direction, he looked over at the bartender. "*His* tab..." he said as he got up from his stool.

"You know," Brig said to Clive matter-of-factly, "there was a time when I thought you were a stand-up guy. When you wanted to do the right thing. When you wouldn't put yourself on the wrong side of something like this. Whatever happened to *that* person, Cryp?"

"Time passes, people do stupid things. People change, Brig. *You* know that better than *anyone*," Clive answered without looking at him.

"Well...*I don't know you* anymore. But I wanted to let *you* know I'm goin' after him. Not that *you* care." Brig stood and glared down at Clive, awaiting any kind of response.

After a few seconds, Clive set his drink down on the bar. "I won't back you up on this, man. You're stirrin' up a hornet's nest and you just don't see it...*as usual.*"

"Won't? Or...*can't?*"

"What the Hell's *that* supposed to mean?" Clive asked angrily, spinning his head to peer up at Brig.

"We both know *exactly* what *that* means."

"I'm tired of these little games you're playin', Brig," Clive resigned in frustration.

"*You're* the only one around here playin' games, Cryp. It just took me a while to realize it. And your allegiances...they certainly aren't what they were...or *should* be," Brig replied, pointing an angry finger into Clive's face.

Brig turned to stride towards the door.

"I'm goin' out to that safe house tomorrow, and I'm comin' out of there with her father – *count* on that," Brig affirmed, reaching for the door handle.

"I mean it, man," Clive reiterated, as he spun around on his stool to glance at Brig leaving the bar, "you're on your own on this one!"

Brig nodded his head and ground his teeth together, as he walked through the doorway and out into the cool night. *There. Trap's set*, he thought. *Now we'll just see where his loyalties lie.*

32:
I, Warrior

Seven years prior (early 2077)...

The stars shimmered in the cold, dark, Baltic Sea night sky like silvery beads of dew across a dark canvas. Several barges and other assorted sea vessels called out to the lonely darkness, as they slowly and quietly moved past one another in and out of the harbor on the way to their destinations.

Unnoticed by the dock workers, who diligently went about their daily tasks, loading and unloading various crates and pieces of equipment from cargo ships that made port; seven dark dots silently descended from the cloudless sky and drifted inland, staying aloft as they passed over the busy docks.

The small team of Epsilons, led by Brigadier Stroud, sailed forward into the darkness, dropped moments earlier from their undetected transport kilometers above them. Each carried an assault weapon on their backs tucked underneath a black, state-of-the-art jump outfit.

The outfit, playfully referred to as the "bat-suit" by both EWs and the DMST engineers that designed it, allowed the wearer to not only dive and control his descent, but also to decelerate and land on the ground without the need of a parachute. The design eliminated much of the bulk of a normal drop, and provided an incredible amount of stealth for such an insertion.

As the team drifted over a darkened stretch of highway below, Brig signaled to the others that it was time to make the final descent.

Like a well-traveled flock of gulls, the Epsilons performed an incredible, synchronized roll and darted towards the ground. They stretched their arms outward and slowed their descent, then stealthily touched down, one after the other, into a small, lightless field next to the road.

The group quickly came together to plan their first move.

"We need to get a scan of the area ahead to see what we're

dealing with. I could see the grouping of bogeys in the square on our way down," Brig said to Ballard.

"*Already counted them.* Forty-four, Major," Ballard replied immediately.

Not wanting to repeat what was the perception of failure from the last mission, Brig ensured that everyone on the team had taken the Catalyst prior to their insertion.

And it was *already* paying off.

"Forty-seven, *actually*," McGraw shot back, snidely.

"Good, then those extra three are *yours*," Ballard quipped back to McGraw, returning his sneer to his much taller teammate. McGraw answered the stocky Ballard with a one-fingered salute.

"*Shit.* They knew we were comin'...*again*," Brig muttered aloud, staring into the distance where the light from the square emanated upwards into the dark sky like a beacon. "McGraw - I need you and Johannsen to scout ahead and make sure we didn't miss any snipers hanging around the rooftops."

Brig turned to face the other four Epsilons.

"Major...I'm not feelin' so hot," Johannsen said, kneeling down and holding his hands against his stubbly, blonde hair. "Headache...kinda nauseated..."

"You gonna be okay to go on with the mission or do I need to keep you back?" Brig asked, placing one hand on Johannsen's shoulder.

"Nah, I should be okay in a few. Think I just got vertigo on the way down is all..." Johannsen reassured him, waving Brig off with one hand.

McGraw shook his head in disgust at both men.

"Okay then, Evans - go with McGraw. Make sure we're not goin' in blind," Brig ordered. Evans, his tall, lanky frame silhouetted in the moonlight, nodded and then sprinted off into the darkness with McGraw.

"So what's the plan, boss?" Swanson asked Brig in a hushed tone, as the remaining EWs gathered together.

"We wait to hear back from our scouts, *then* we move ahead and station ourselves as close as we can to the square," Brig answered. "They're guarding *somethin'* big with those numbers..."

"Forty-seven to seven's kinda some tough odds, don't you think, Major?" Ballard added to the conversation. "We actually gonna *try* that?"

"I'm not worried about *their* numbers, Mitch," Brig told him. "I've already got *that* part of the equation figured out."

Twenty minutes later, the two scouts, McGraw and Evans, quietly reemerged from a set of bushes lining the side of the highway. Their assault weapons clunked softly against their backs and thick clouds of breath flowed from their panting mouths, as they ran to the group.

"*Well?*" Brig asked McGraw, the next senior member of the group after him.

"Nothing there, Stroud..." McGraw grumbled.

"That's *Major*, Captain..." Brig corrected through slightly gritted teeth.

"*Victory*...Major," McGraw answered sarcastically, bumping by Brig's shoulder and quickly swigging some liquid from his canteen.

"Alright then," Brig said, shaking off the usual, expected insult from McGraw. "We're clear to go. The square's about two kilometers in that direction," he said while pointing into the darkness away from the group. "Silence until we get there. Then we take up stealth positions along the side of the culvert there under the small overpass to the south of the town. *We clear?*"

McGraw approached Brig and stood just centimeters from his face.

"You're leadin us to *slaughter*, Stroud!" McGraw growled through his teeth, just loud enough for Brig to hear him. "*What's your plan?*" He stared fiercely into Brig's eyes.

"I got this covered, McGraw...stand down," Brig barked back, shoving the bigger man backward a step. He looked at the rest of the group. "Anyone *else* have any concerns, let me know *now...*" Brig snarled. He glanced at each one individually, to which all but McGraw looked away from Brig's menacing stare. "Good, then let's head out!"

McGraw shook his head once again as the other Epsilons nodded at Brig's instructions. Some tightened the straps of their rifles, while a couple of others took turns refreshing themselves with drink or a small bar of chocolate from their belt packs.

"And one *other* thing..." Brig said, stopping to face the team and focusing his gaze on McGraw. "Limit the body count – no reason to go ape shit if we don't have to…"

McGraw snorted and began to stride past Brig, as he pulled the assault weapon from his back and cradled it across his arms. "Tell that to my *gun*," he mocked, as he disappeared into the darkness, followed by the rest of the EW team.

Brig closed his eyes, clenched his jaw and took a breath before sprinting after them.

After ten minutes, the group had reached the far end of the dirt channel that ran parallel to the brightly lit town square, which sat four hundred meters to their north.

One-by-one, they dove onto the side of the embankment and shimmied down until reaching the base of the trench. The cold, hard earth crunched beneath their boots as they slid along the side, before reaching the frozen mud of the bottom with a muffled 'clump'.

Brig, in an effort to show his tenacity to the team, had sprinted ahead of them and led the charge into the culvert. He took up the first position on the opposite side and began scoping out the view of the town square, as they each plunked down behind him.

McGraw quickly staked a position beside him, taking in the sight of the large gathering of soldiers that filled the small area.

"Headache's gettin worse, Brig," Johannsen said breathlessly to his leader, as he got to one knee and bowed his head.

Brig did not want to admit it; partially to keep his squad from worrying, but also to keep his own nerves calm. *He*, too, had been suffering from a headache since the jump, but had chalked it up to the cold weather.

"Suck it up, Johannsen," McGraw snarled. He turned to Brig. "Russian Troopers. They're *waitin'* for ya, Stroud…what *now?*"

Without returning McGraw's cocky glare, Brig calmly tapped the sat-com on his shoulder.

"Rufus, this is Wild Stallion. Auth code one two, seven, four three alpha delta, do you copy?" Brig said in a low tone into the device.

After a few seconds, the sat-com chirped softly. "Roger, Wild Stallion – go for Rufus," a mechanized-sounding voice responded.

"We need a clearing on my mark plus point twenty-five, November Echo – copy?" Brig responded quickly.

"Roger, Wild Stallion. Nightlight on your mark plus point twenty-five, November Echo in three – confirm?" the voice repeated back to him.

"Confirmed, Rufus – out," Brig replied, tapping the sat-com once again to deactivate it.

He turned to the group, as he pulled a small pair of goggles from his belt pack and placed them over his head.

"Goggles on, you don't want to *miss* this…" Brig instructed the group with a coy smile, turning to peer at the town once again.

The other six Epsilons knelt in the hard grass on each side of Brig, and looked in at the town square. After a few silent moments, and numerous, curious looks between the men when nothing appeared to be happening, a sudden small whispering sound came from the sky above them.

"*What the…*" Lieutenant Maurice Delgado, the junior member of the squad, remarked in his thick, Peruvian accent, stroking his thin mustache as he peered up into the dark sky.

Just as the rest of the group turned to take in what Delgado had seen, a shadow passed across them in the dim moonlight, and then disappeared on its way towards the town square.

A small, dark sphere darted along noiselessly, yet very determinately, just barely visible and a mere ten meters above the ground, until it reached the edge of the town. It hovered for a moment, and then increased its altitude by a few meters, as it moved into the center of the square.

Several of the Troopers present glanced up and pointed in curiosity at the black orb, as it stopped and rotated very slowly fifteen meters above them.

Before they could react, however, the sphere rapidly split open and expelled six smaller, similar orbs that took up positions perpendicular to it. In one synchronized fraction of a second, all seven of the spheres immediately began to emit rapid bursts of brighter-than-white strobes across the entire square. The area lit with an intensity that not even the hottest sun could produce on the brightest day in a white-sanded desert.

The small band of Epsilons, even with their protective eyewear in place, each raised their forearms to block out the massive amount of luminosity that streamed from the center of the city.

Then, without warning, the light show ceased, with each of the orbs rocketing skyward in a shower of sparks, as they jetted faster than the eye could follow out towards the sea.

The area was once again silent and in dim moonlight.

Before any of the others could speak, Brig, who was already surveying the area ahead through a set of night-vision binoculars, turned his head over his shoulder towards the men.

"Ballard - give me a bio," Brig barked in a hushed tone.

Ballard, like the other men next to him, was standing and staring in confusion at what they had all just witnessed.

"Yes...yessir, Major." Ballard fumbled to pull a small device out of his belt pack and tapped at the screen several times. "*No one standing there, Major*," he reported after a few seconds of studying the data scrolling across the scanner.

"Good, then let's move! And remember - we get in, get the package and get out..." Brig ordered, as he quickly scaled the side of the embankment and began jogging towards the now-quiet town square.

The remaining men traded several apprehensive glances amongst them, before climbing the side of the hill and following Brig into the darkness in their pre-established formation.

Brig pulled the scope from his assault weapon and cautiously put it around the corner of the building, as the others waited silently, pressing themselves up against the stonework of the facade.

"Scope's not reading any movement," the EW leader reported in what almost seemed like a relieved tone, stepping away from the building and turning towards his men. He stared purposefully into the empty park that spanned the center of the small square, and just beyond at the large building that stood above all of the other buildings in the area.

"*That's* our target." Brig pointed at the building without looking back at the others.

While none of the structures in the city seemed recently built, this one stood out. It was a mammoth building in relation to the others, its Greek-inspired architectural style lent to an era sometime in the late nineteenth century, and it stood out visually comparative to the other buildings in the square.

"Don't make 'em like *that* anymore," Evans observed, stepping up next to Brig.

"Ballard, what do you see in that one?" Brig asked over his shoulder, nodding subtly to Evans in agreement.

Ballard, already having begun the scan before Brig had even asked for it, peered up from his scanner. "One..." he reported.

"One...*what?*" Brig asked curiously.

"One *person*...and they're *sitting*..." Ballard clarified, glancing at Brig with a stern, but bewildered, expression.

"Have to assume that's our package..." Brig scratched his chin in deep thought. "They stack everyone outside and leave him in there all alone with no guards? Doesn't seem right, *does it?*"

"Sounds like a *trap* to me," McGraw interjected. He stood on the opposite side of Brig, his hands at his hips.

Brig held up his hand in dismissal of McGraw's comment. "That's our objective – we go in and get it," he said, as McGraw grunted his disapproval.

The men quickly, but cautiously, moved into and across the square. They held their assault weapons at the ready, as they passed by the prone, motionless bodies of the Troopers.

Delgado stopped and approached one of the fallen soldiers, staring curiously at the man's face. A small glop of white foam caked the side of the man's mouth and flowed out onto the pavement beneath him, to which Delgado wrinkled his brow.

"Did it *kill* them?" Delgado asked incredulously. He gently nudged the man's side with his boot. He realized as he looked around, that the rest of the soldiers on the ground had the same appearance as this one.

"Nah," Brig answered, taking a quick glance at the man on the ground. "Probably just a seizure before he passed out. Let's get moving, Delgado..." he ordered, deliberately not focusing on the disturbing scene in front of them.

As they entered the massive, stonework doors of the former museum, the men stopped abruptly.

Brig had encountered the first obstacle.

"Iron portcullis...anyone bring their torch?" he asked, as he examined each edge of the gate, but did not find any sign of a release.

"Gotcha covered, Major," Evans said.

He quickly pulled a small, ion blowtorch from his pack and

began to apply the bright, blue orb of energy to the lower spikes of the gate that stuck into the ground beneath it.

The vestibule around the men flickered in an azure glow, as Evans steadily worked at his task. Seconds later, the blowtorch ceased and Evans stood up to face Brig.

"No more gate," Evans said with a smile, as he stowed the torch back into his pack and stepped behind Brig.

Brig, having already approached the portcullis, pushed it upward and into the ceiling.

"Ballard?" Brig asked without turning back.

"Up the stairs and to the right, Major," the security specialist barked immediately, glancing up from his scanner.

Brig turned to face McGraw.

"*You're* the other sharp-shooter of the group..." Brig said sarcastically. "I need you out at the front doors making sure no one comes in behind us."

Brig knew that he had two primary snipers on the team other than McGraw, but also relished the thought of keeping him occupied elsewhere.

"*Yippee...*" McGraw grumbled, as he stormed past Brig and down the hall towards the front doors.

"Delgado...stick here at the bottom of the stairs. Same deal..." Brig instructed the junior member of the group.

Delgado nodded enthusiastically and took a position just beyond the railing and out of sight.

"The rest of you, up the stairs with me," Brig said, motioning with one hand, as he quickly started scaling the concrete stairs to the second floor.

As the five Epsilons reached the pinnacle of the staircase, Brig slowed and sighed in frustration. The remainder, with Johannsen panting as he brought up the rear, cleared the top step and stood alongside Brig.

"*Another* one..." Brig pointed out an additional door, this one a thicker, steel chamber entry that sealed off the small alcove at the top of the stairs from the rest of the floor.

"Those Ruskies sure like their heavy doors," Swanson observed with a chuckle, as he stood next to Brig. Swanson was significantly shorter than Brig, and he stared up at his leader through his thick eyeglasses.

"It's a *prison*, Jason. No welcome mats here," Brig joked back to him, and then turned to Evans. "Batter up, Evans..." he said, waving his hand as if presenting the door to him.

"Sure thing...just give me a sec..." Evans said. He extracted the torch once again from his pack and made quick work of the large hinges that stuck out from the side.

However, this time, just as Brig was about to yank on the large, metal handle to pull the door from its frame, Swanson grabbed Brig's hand.

"Booby-trapped," Swanson informed Brig, pointing up at a small piece of wire protruding from the top corner of the entryway.

"*Good catch...*" Brig said with a sigh of relief. "*You're* EOD... can you take care of this one?" he asked, as he faced one of his closer friends in the squadron.

"Easy peasy," Swanson answered confidently. He stood closer to the door and examined the wiring. He pulled a small device from his pack and held it cautiously against the top of the door relatively near the wiring, before removing it and placing it back into his pack.

"Standard trip wiring...and a little sloppy at that. *Shouldn't* be too hard," he told Brig, as he removed his pack and began fumbling through it.

"Alright then, take care of it. We'll wait halfway down the stairs," Brig informed Swanson, following proper EW procedure for such a scenario.

Brig, Evans, Ballard and Johannsen crouched patiently on the stairs and exchanged glances with each other. Johannsen propped himself against the stone wall, as glistening sweat drained from his forehead.

"You gonna make it, bro?" Evans piped up.

"I...*think*..." Johannsen began to answer, but then suddenly slumped to one side, and began to tumble end-over-end down the stairs, where he fell in a heap at the base at Delgado's feet.

The other Epsilons clamored in surprise to aide their teammate, standing around him and shouting in an attempt to revive him.

"Calm down, calm down. Get him some air," Brig said, breaking into the middle of the group and kneeling next to Johannsen.

"What's going on *here*?" said McGraw, suddenly standing just behind the group.

"Why are you out of position?" Brig barked, his voice echoing hollowly throughout the stone halls of the museum.

"*Relax*, Stroud," McGraw replied condescendingly. "They're *all* unconscious out there. Not like they're gonna wake up and come get us..."

"Major, I'm through," Swanson's voice called from just beyond the top of the stairs, "and I think you need to *see* this..."

Brig scowled at McGraw, and then leapt several stairs at a time until he reached the top, where he found Swanson standing in the small hall just beyond the doorway that he had opened.

In front of him, sitting on a chair against the far wall, was a man dressed in EW battle attire. He sat motionless with shackles on his feet and arms, and a hood over his head.

"*Slade!*" Evans cried, forcing his way past Brig and into the doorway.

"Wait!" Swanson shouted, grabbing Evans forcefully by the back of his jacket. "He's booby-trapped, *too!*"

Brig rubbed his chin. "Can you get a closer look?" he asked Swanson.

"Sure," Swanson said confidently, as he cautiously approached the chair and knelt beside it, examining the wires that led around to the back.

Swanson bowed his head and shook it dejectedly, and then stepped back over to Brig. "He's pretty wired up. But standard config from what I can see."

"Can we at *least* take his hood off and get him some air?" Brig asked, glancing over at the shackled soldier.

Swanson shook his head and pursed his lips. "It's wired, too. And there's enough K12 powder behind that chair to crater this building if we even move him a *centimeter* without disarming that timer."

"*Shit...*" Brig muttered through gritted teeth.

"I...*think* I can do this..." Swanson offered hesitantly.

"*Think?*" Brig exclaimed, pulling Swanson aside and speaking in a hushed tone. "No room for '*think*' here, Jason..." he said gravely, grasping Swanson's shoulders, "...you either *can* or you *can't!*"

Swanson glanced over at the hooded figure and inhaled deeply.

"Don't be a hero," Brig continued. "Stand down if you have to. I'll call in a team of specialists if that's what it takes..."

Swanson blinked several times in response, turned his eyes to Brig and then nodded. "Yeah...I can do it..." he replied, taking another deep breath and sounding more convincing, as he continued to nod confidently.

Resting on his knees on an anti-static mat laid out beneath him, Swanson began the arduous task of disarming the bomb that protected their squad teammate.

Brig and the remainder of the crew, minus Delgado, who continued to keep watch at the base of the stairs, stood near the top of the staircase just within sight of the EOD specialist.

The other men nervously glanced at each other, as they could hear Swanson having a conversation with himself.

"Wait...*red* was the battery, white-red was the secondary and *green* was the timer," he muttered loudly, enough for the rest of the crew to partially understand him. "Yellow was the interrupt. There's a secondary interrupt. *Shit...*" he cursed, nodding his head, realizing his mistake and then rectifying it. He took a second to wipe his brow with the sleeve of his jacket.

"He doesn't look too sure, Stroud..." McGraw mumbled into Brig's ear. "You *might* want to get him out of there."

Brig pushed McGraw away with one hand. "He's fine," he said dismissively, although concern was starting to seed in his own mind, as he listened to Swanson growing slightly irritated.

Johannsen, lying at the bottom of the stairs under the watchful eye of Delgado, had begun to regain consciousness.

"He's waking up," Delgado said in a loud whisper up to Brig, who nodded his head and refocused his attention on Swanson's efforts.

"...head...spinning..." Johannsen began to spout incoherently, as he grasped the sides of his temples. "...On *fire*..."

"Keep him *quiet!*" Swanson shouted in a hushed tone from the room atop the stairs. "He's messin' up my concentration!"

Swanson tried to conceal his obvious level of unease: the uncontrollable tremor in his hands, the cursing under his breath and the sweat that poured off his forehead and into his eyes. Unfortunately, he found himself at the mercy of his nerves. "I can do this. I can do this. Okay, interrupts are taken care of..." he told himself aloud in a slightly elevated voice.

"...blood is hot!" Johannsen said, raising his voice ever so slightly with each word.

"Brig, he's gettin' *worse!*" Evans called up the stairs to his leader.

"He's lost it, Brig. You need to do something or we're all *dead!*" McGraw growled at Brig.

For the first time since he had met McGraw, Brig realized that he had never called him by his first name...until *now*. Something about that fact curdled his blood, as he glanced between McGraw, Swanson and the men down at the bottom of the staircase.

Suddenly, Johannsen, who had been sitting up, broke free from Evans and Ballard, and stood up.

"My blood is boiling! *Oh my God*, my head is burning!" he cried. The two Epsilons quickly grabbed Johannsen's arms and wrestled him back to the floor.

"Shut him up, Brig! Shut him up!" Swanson shouted frantically from upstairs.

"Get him out of there! *NOW!* He's lost it! He's..." McGraw bellowed.

Swanson suddenly turned to face Brig and McGraw, a black wire dangling from his fingertips.

"I...there's *never* a tertiary timer. I didn't see it. I'm sorr..." he tried to explain.

Before he could finish his sentence, the room ignited in a brilliant, momentary flash of flame. The room crumbled away, as it ripped both Swanson and the prisoner apart, and sent a torrential hail of concrete and ash that spewed outward towards the open stairwell.

The blast lifted both Brig and McGraw, still standing near the top step, and tossed them like kindling down the stairs, where they landed in separate heaps.

Brig had never experienced such a dark shade of black as he did at that moment. The horrifying realization of what had just happened agonizingly dawned on him, as he lay crumpled over on his side.

The bomb had exploded, and he had failed yet *another* mission. Swanson's warning replayed with a dull echo in his head: *'There's enough K12 to crater this building...'* and it *did*.

Worse, Brig had died in the process.

They had *all* died – and *Brig* had killed them.

The silence of the scene was deafening. Brig felt numb, yet his head felt like it was going to cave in from the pressure from within.

Then, he realized it – he was not dead after all! Somehow, he had survived the massive explosion that tore apart the very structure of the centuries-old behemoth of a museum.

A high-pitched, muffled squeal doused his ears and slowly replaced the silence. A strange, red glint filled his eyes, as he blinked away the debris that had been sprayed into them, and looked around the room. A billowing cloud of dust flowed down from the prison cell at the top of the stairway and burned his throat. He raised his head and peered up the stairs.

A gaping hole stood where the cell was just moments before.

As he slowly scanned the rest of the area around him, he spotted McGraw, face down on the floor just a few meters away.

Brig had to blink several times and rub his eyes to be certain, but he thought that he saw McGraw covering his eyes with his hands.

Sobbing.

He was not sure which stunned him more – the explosion, or the fact that McGraw was showing a *human* side.

Before he could call to McGraw, Brig had his head forced off the floor by someone grabbing him by the collar. Brig looked up in surprise.

Ballard stood next to him, gripping Brig's coat and looking into his eyes. Brig stared in confusion, able to see Ballard's mouth moving and hearing the muffled sound coming from the man's lips. The words, however, were garbled.

Brig pawed at the side of his face with one hand, feeling the hot blood oozing from the side of his head, and then stared, senseless, at Ballard. He watched Ballard's mouth move and mouthed the words in unison to himself.

Are...you...ok, Brig thought, still in shock and unable to speak. *He's asking you if you're ok. Yes, yes...say yes!* he screamed in his mind, but he was dumbfounded and could not form the words to reply.

Brig nodded his head slowly, as he tried to blink away what felt like a moist fuzz spreading across his brain.

With Ballard's help, Brig pushed himself to his knees and put both hands on his ears in an attempt to clear the ringing sensation. Ballard held Brig's shoulder tightly to aid his leader's recovery from the blast.

Ballard's face was awash with a look of utter shock and confusion as he stared at his leader.

Brig's eyes were red.

The sound of Brig's surroundings slowly began to grow clearer in his ears as the ringing subsided.

"I'm...ok," Brig said, at last able to speak with a strained effort. He shook his head a few times to regain his focus, and then slowly pushed himself up to his feet. He instinctively tapped at the sat-com on his shoulder, but nothing happened. After several more taps, Brig closed his eyes.

"Shit. Comm's down from the blast concussion..." Brig said to Ballard and McGraw, who had also gotten to his feet and was standing behind him. "Alright...we need to get out of here...get back to the extraction point..." he said, the words laboring their way from his mouth, as he rubbed his head with both hands.

"How're we gettin' outta here without the *radio*?" McGraw growled, cautiously rubbing the back of his head. "Looks to me like we're stranded..."

"Get to the extraction point, we can pulse a beacon from Ballard's scanner," Brig responded, pointing at Ballard. His senses were getting sharper, but his skull continued to throb, as he glared at the rest of the team.

Suddenly, from behind both men, Johannsen emerged from the back of the stairwell pointing his sidearm at Delgado.

"I can't take it anymore!" Johannsen shouted maniacally.

Delgado took a step backward in shock.

Johannsen waved the gun in Evans's direction.

"It's taking over my head! Oh my God, make it stop! My brain's boiling!" he cried, alternating pointing the gun at each Epsilon, in turn.

"Dave...put the gun down, are you *crazy*?" Evans shouted frantically, as he, too, took a step backward.

"It's gonna kill us *all*, man!" Johannsen howled uncontrollably, gripping his head with his free hand, tears flowing down his reddened face. "I can't take it! I can't take it!"

Brig, in the midst of the confusion, had taken several steps away from the group, and had circled around towards Johannsen's side. Hoping to get the gun away from his teammate, he slowly began stepping towards the confused Epsilon.

Just as he had gotten within a meter of ending the crisis, Johannsen turned his gun abruptly in Brig's direction and fired a single shot, striking Brig in the face.

Brig immediately spun and fell face-first onto the hard concrete floor, a puddle of blood quickly forming underneath his head, as he lay motionless.

"Shit! Brig's down! Brig's down!" Ballard screamed in panic to the others, taking a step in Brig's direction.

Johannsen's face contorted into a look of pure terror, as he glanced down in horror at his fallen leader.

The realization of what he had just done took hold in his mind.

Then, looking up at the others with a wide-eyed, pale face, he lifted the gun to his own temple and squeezed the trigger.

The single gunshot echoed like a clap of thunder off the tiled walls of the museum.

Johannsen fell lifeless to the floor.

The remaining Epsilons stood their ground, speechless and in shock. McGraw, never one to let a moment leave him without words, stared in disbelief at Johannsen's body, and then over at Brig's.

"Merc, what do we do?" Evans exclaimed, tears forming at the corners of his watery eyes.

"Just what Stroud said...*we* get out of here..." McGraw ordered, his voice suddenly cracking.

As he turned to face the others, a single, high-powered shot rang out from outside of the building. A slug instantly pierced the back of Delgado's ribcage, and flew out the front of him in a bloody cloud of flesh, as he fell forward and onto the floor at McGraw's feet.

McGraw looked down at Delgado's lifeless body, dumbfounded.

"Sniper on the roof across the square!" Ballard yelled, as the three remaining Epsilons dove for cover.

McGraw scanned around him from behind an old, overturned museum pedestal at the surreal scene unfolding before him. From his vantage point, he could see the bodies of his fallen comrades – Delgado in the hallway; his cold, dead stare piercing his own gaze, Johannsen by the stairwell, his neck and one of his arms bent horrifically underneath him, and Brig, lying face down in a substantial pool of syrupy blood, just three meters from him.

"Captain, what's the plan?" Evans shouted from across the room.

McGraw did not respond. A shell-shocked, void expression tattooed his face, as he blankly stared around the room at the carnage.

"*Captain*! What's your orders?" Evans repeated, again to no response. "McGraw! God damn it, snap out of it!" he screamed.

Turning to glare at Evans with wide eyes, McGraw screamed, "Ballard! What's out there?"

"We've got...*twelve!*" Ballard responded frantically.

"Damn it!" McGraw cursed loudly. "The Troopers woke up..."

"*No...*" Ballard corrected. He pulled his scope from his assault weapon and aimed it around the corner at the front door, "...we got commandos out there, Captain..."

As Ballard pulled his scope back, two commandos entered the hallway from the front door.

McGraw quickly stood from behind the pedestal and poured a volley of rounds into the two men, making them fall back awkwardly and onto the floor, dead. Then, retreating to his hiding spot, he sat and shut his eyes tightly.

He could not believe what was transpiring. Nothing could have prepared them for this, but still he was aggravated that he did not see it coming.

Suddenly, he opened his eyes and looked down at his vest, realizing what his only...*their only*...option was.

"Here's the plan," McGraw shouted across the room to Ballard and Evans, who glanced over at him, as they hid just beyond the corner of an adjacent hallway. "I'm gonna throw two flash-bangs down the hallway and out the door. As soon as you hear them go off – we're gonna rush the hall. You two follow me with suppression over my shoulders!" he exclaimed at the two men.

"That's *suicide!*" Ballard shouted back.

"They're gonna storm this building any time now and we're gonna die! At least we got a shot out there behind those concrete pillars," McGraw reasoned gruffly.

Ballard sat back against the wall and took a deep breath, as he looked concernedly at his partner, Evans. He glared down at his scanner and cursed silently. "Four of the Troopers woke up, Merc... you *sure* you wanna do this?"

"You a gambling man, Ballard?" McGraw asked, peering around the pedestal down into the hallway.

"Never have been," Ballard answered without making eye contact with McGraw.

"Might want to start - these are some messed up odds. But we got no choice. On three I'm tossing the grenades," McGraw insisted.

Counting silently, McGraw stood and tossed the two grenades, one after the other, into the hallway, where they clanked off the portcullis and into the square just beyond the steps.

Frantic shouts accompanied the ensuing few seconds of silence, as the commandos and Troopers nearest the building futilely ran for cover. Two deafening blasts and a blinding flash followed. The hallway outside lit up in an eerie glow, before going dark once again.

"*Go! Go! Go!*" McGraw ordered in a growling shout, as he emerged from behind the pedestal. He grabbed Delgado's rifle from his body and darted towards the hallway, the muzzle of both assault weapons ablaze with fire, and the metallic clank of shells hitting the tile floor ten at a time reverberating off the stone walls as he ran.

Ballard and Evans quickly followed him; each three meters behind, each of them squeezing off sporadic rounds of suppression fire past their new leader, as they sprinted for the front entrance of the building.

As the Epsilons reached the front door, they split and headed for cover.

McGraw quickly dove behind the nearest pillar to the right of the entrance, while Ballard and Evans, barely missing a hail of sniper's armament, took up positions on either side of him.

Ballard looked to McGraw, who held up his fist to signal that he wanted them to sit and wait for the enemy commandos to make their move *first*, rather than waste what little ammo they had left. The two men nodded their understanding of McGraw's order and flattened themselves against the concrete of their respective pillars.

McGraw emerged from his protective cover to fire several shots into the street at the enemy commandos, who took turns spraying the facade of the museum with bullets.

Suddenly a blur of motion caught his eye. Someone, or something, sprinted out of the main doors, vaulted the concrete staircase that led out to the square and landed in the midst of the battle, a loud growl emanating from him as he passed.

In one smooth motion, the man stood and engulfed a rotating radius of the square in a hail of bullets, with an assault weapon in each hand that hummed in unison with the other. Flames spewed from their barrels as they took down their targets two- and three-at-a-time.

It was Brig. Although to McGraw, unlike he had *ever* seen him.

Brig's eyes glowed a crimson red, as he stopped firing briefly and turned towards McGraw.

"What are you waiting for?" Brig howled in an unrecognizable, gravelly, guttural tone.

McGraw, Evans and Ballard raised their weapons and began firing into the square.

One by one, the commandos and Troopers that had regained consciousness either retreated in terror towards the other end of the square, or attempted to take down their assailants to no avail; their torsos ripped into by the storm of metal armament being thrust upon them.

Brig continued firing until both of his weapons spent their munitions or had locked up due to overheating, and then threw them down. He extracted a pair of handguns from the back of his belt and continued firing.

The other Epsilons watched in disbelief, as several enemy soldiers along Brig's path became unfortunate victims of his merciless assault.

As he exhausted the ammo in the handguns, Brig tossed them away and quickly grasped onto the collar of a passing Trooper that was attempting escape. He gripped the man by the neck with his other hand and twisted until a sickening snap ended the brief engagement.

Brig glared around with a ferocity in his eyes that, even though he was unarmed, made the enemy combatants flee at the very sight of him. He stomped maniacally through the square, kicking the bodies of the fallen as he passed to ensure that none lived.

He approached a troop transport that had delivered the fresh set of commandos. One of the commandos had stayed behind and had decided, unwisely, to hide behind it.

Brig swiftly rounded the corner of the vehicle, scooped up the cowering man and held him aloft in an insane display of raw power with one hand, dangling him a half meter off the ground.

The enemy commando futilely flung his arms at Brig in an attempt to knock himself free, but Brig's grip was unnaturally strong, given that he was only using one arm to hold him. Brig snarled at the man in a tone that could easily have been mistaken for an enraged jungle cat, a small amount of white froth expelling from the corner of his mouth.

"You're gonna *die!*" Brig vomited with a roar that echoed off the buildings around him, as he reached with his free hand and yanked off the riot mask that the man wore tightly about his face.

To his shock, *it was Clive.*

"*How...*" Brig stammered with a growl. He glared up at his friend, who somehow came to be a member of a Russian Special Ops team.

"Let me down, Brig!" Clive squawked. He tried once again to get a firm grip, unsuccessfully, on Brig's forearms.

"Cryp...what are you *doing* here?" Brig snarled incredulously, placing his other hand around Clive's neck and squeezing.

"Let me go...you son of a bitch..." Clive demanded with a strained voice.

"No! What are you *doing?* What have you *become?*" Brig said furiously, shaking Clive like a rag doll.

"What have...*I* become?" Clive mocked, as he swung one of his legs forward to kick Brig's chest, but missed. "Look at *you.* What have...*you* become," he choked. "You're some kind...of...*animal.*"

"*No,* Cryp. This is what *we've all* become..." Brig purred with a wicked smile. "...all the Warriors have it in them. Even *you,* Underwood. You just don't know how to use it yet."

"No one has...*this.* They drop over from...super migraines and kill themselves but you..." Clive coughed in reply, but had to stop due to lack of air.

"You're *wrong...*" Brig insisted. "You don't understand...the power. The raw power. And the rage...the *RAGE!*" he growled intensely, pulling Clive in closer to his face. "This is...a *gift...*it makes you...unstoppable!"

Clive closed his eyes tightly and gritted his teeth, as he struggled to free himself from Brig's immense grip.

"Come back with us, I can make this right," Brig pleaded maniacally.

"No...not like *this...*" Clive tried unsuccessfully one last time to free his neck from Brig's clutches.

"Then you're gonna make me *kill* you, Cryp..." Brig warned, flexing his arms and increasing the grip around Clive's neck. "Don't *make* me *kill* you, Cryp!"

"You do...what you...*have to do...*" Clive gurgled, as he closed his eyes again. *This is it...* Clive thought, *he's gonna strangle me to death right now...*

The crimson in Brig's eyes illuminated brighter than ever before, as he flexed his forearms and held his former partner aloft, his hands shaking visibly.

"Cryp...help me, I'm losing control..." Brig screamed, a small stream of drool glazing the side of his mouth. "I don't *want* to kill you..."

Just when Clive was about to take what he knew to be his final breath, he realized that Brig's grip on his neck had loosened a miniscule amount. He opened his eyes and peered down at his former partner.

To his surprise, a single tear flowed down Brig's cheek as he glared up at Clive.

He was giving Clive an out!

Knowing he had only a split second before Brig reapplied the pressure and choked the last breath from his lungs, Clive fumbled with one hand, reached into his side pouch and extracted his field knife.

He swiftly plunged it into Brig's upper arm.

Brig instantly dropped Clive from his grasp and took a step backward, howling like a wounded animal while he looked down at the knife handle protruding from his bicep. He grunted with a sick smile, yanked it from his arm and tossed it aside with a clank on the pavement beneath him. Brig snorted a wicked laugh as he looked down at the blood spurting wildly from his bicep.

Clive regained his footing and began pummeling Brig with blow after blow to his face. The blood from Brig's prior facial wound splattered after each contact, along with fresh blood from gashes that he opened with his barrage.

Brig did not fight back. He stared at Clive in between punches with an emotionless, almost relieved, expression.

He had given up.

Just as Clive was about to deliver the final blow in his mercy killing, he felt the crushing impact of a hit to the side of his face, causing him to fall to the ground in a heap at Brig's feet.

McGraw quickly turned his assault weapon around and aimed the barrel into Clive's back, as he stood above the motionless soldier.

Before he could pull the trigger, however, Brig grabbed McGraw by the collar and tossed him three meters away onto his back.

"What have you done?" Brig snarled at McGraw.

McGraw sneered up at Brig, as he pushed himself up to his elbows.

"Saving your fucking ass...*again!*" McGraw yelled at Brig while pointing an angry finger at him.

"This one's *mine!*" Brig bellowed, his red eyes becoming even more intense with each word. "He's coming back with us..."

"You're out of your mind, man..." McGraw corrected fiercely. He started to get to his feet, reaching behind him for his weapon once again.

Brig pounced with one swift step onto McGraw, slamming him back to the pavement with a hard thud and a brutal grunt. He straddled McGraw with his knee forcefully into his chest.

"If anything's happened to him I'm gonna make *you* pay!" Brig roared into McGraw's face. "Now go help the other men get our teammates back to the transport – I'll take care of this one..." he screamed, as he jumped up from McGraw and stood over him with a vicious gaze and bared teeth. "That's an order!"

McGraw, seldom speechless, nodded shakily, scrambled to his feet and ran off towards the others, who were finishing the mop up effort of the enemy combatants near the museum.

Brig emitted a single, ruthless chuckle, followed by a grunt of self-actualization, as he stared off at McGraw and the other men. Then, he turned to scoop up Clive and personally carry him to the transport.

Clive was *gone.*

The heli-jet lifted agilely from the sea surface, a fine mist of seawater filling the air from the thrust of its quad rotors that assisted its dart upwards and into the pre-dawn sky.

Small pockets of dockworkers, not sure what they had witnessed, stood around and pointed at the vanishing craft in the sky while chatting with each other, a story sure to be told amongst their families for years to come.

In the darkened cargo hold at the rear of the aircraft, tucked neatly side-by-side into vinyl containers, lay the remains of four Epsilon Warriors that saw their final action in the port city of Kaliningrad.

On the end of the row lay Lieutenant Maurice Delgado, the youngest Epsilon to see action on this fateful day, struck down by an overlooked sniper's bullet.

Next to him, Captain's Jason Swanson and Jonas Slade, or at least the remains that the others could find of them, victims of an ill-fated rescue attempt.

Finally, on the opposite end, was Captain David Johannsen, his life taken due to an experiment gone awry and ultimately, by his own hand.

The muffled sound of the twin turbine thrusters on the bottom of the chassis powering up filled the tomb-like cabin with a low rumble.

The solemn ride home began for the fallen teammates, friends and brothers for life.

In the crew compartment just behind the weapons stow, the four surviving Epsilons sat, two abreast and opposite one another in the corners of the craft.

Captain Mitch Ballard sat back against his seat with his eyes closed and arms crossed, no doubt attempting to dismiss the horrific images of the night's events.

Lieutenant Albert Evans sat opposite of Ballard, leaning forward with his elbows on his knees, his short, black hair glistening as he stared blankly out at the water zooming by in a blur.

Next to him on the bench a meter away was Captain Mercury McGraw, his chiseled biceps gleaming with sweat and blood in the low overhead lighting. Of the group, he was the only one to make eye contact with any of the others. He gritted his jaw tightly, as he glared across the cabin.

Across the aisle, and the target of McGraw's gaze, sat Major Brigadier Stroud, his field jacket bundled up tightly with the collar wrapped up around his face.

Brig stared out intently at the passing landscape. His chest heaved up and down in short bursts, as his hot breath fogged the window next to him. He glared out at the horizon, where the sun had just begun to get a jump on the day, lazily creeping up into the sky. It cast an orange haze across the cabin, forcing the others to turn away or close their eyes as the jet banked to head out to sea.

But not Brig. He continued to peer out of the entry door glass, casting his own glare from the red glint in his eyes.

33:
Almost Easy

Present day (2084)...

Brig awoke early the next morning. He had hoped that Steele would at least wait until the sun rose to get a start on her day, and he knew that it was the perfect time to catch anyone at the safe house by surprise.

They had not spoken since the night before last, when he had his ego, and heart, stomped on by her vicious choice of words.

He pushed himself off the couch and quietly made his way down the hallway, stopping just outside of Steele's bedroom door and peering through the cracked opening.

Steel lay peacefully in her bed, her long hair mussed across her face.

Brig could not help but be a bit mesmerized by the peaceful beauty of the moment.

He was sure that he was doing the right thing. After it was all over, she would see that *he* was right.

Satisfied that she was sleeping soundly enough for him to leave without detection, he carefully clicked her bedroom door shut and left the apartment.

After an hour, and having retrieved Steele's retro-bike from its hiding place a few blocks over, Brig slowed as he spotted the turn-off from the highway ahead of him a half kilometer on the right. Preserving the element of surprise, he once again shut the motor of the bike off, coasting to a stop just beyond the shoulder of the highway into a patch of wild grass.

Aside from the early morning moonlight shining across the barren highway and reflecting off the signage that marked the entrance to the safe house's subdivision, the area was unlit and desolate. While he pondered the remote area's significance of being a hot spot for Syndicate activity, he did silently understand that it would be the perfect, out-of-the-way location to hold a hostage.

His ankle and ribs still burned with pain from the confrontation with Pollux days ago, but Brig put it out of his mind and trotted through the high grass that bordered the perimeter of the subdivision ahead.

Brig's mind thought forward to how he was going to distinguish the safe house from any other houses in the area. And suddenly, how he was going to manage bringing back a wheelchair-bound, elderly man.

I'll cross that bridge when I come to it... he thought, as he emerged from the higher brush into an overgrown back yard of one of the edge houses.

Instead of some form of lighting on the properties that stretched out before him, no matter how dim, Brig was surprised to find that the area inside the subdivision was just as dark as the highway that he had left minutes earlier.

He shook off any notion that this was the wrong neighborhood, or that Alexi had given him false information, and pressed forward. He skirted the edge of one of the houses and stopped, as he emerged onto the main street of the grouping of homes. Brig stood within the darkened shadow of one of the houses, scanning both sides of the street.

Of the fifteen or so that dotted each side of the road, only one had any lighting.

"That's *got* to be it," he muttered softly, and then stealthily moved along the row of houses to his right, until he reached one that was exactly opposite of it.

As he crouched and silently watched the house for movement, fully expecting to see a guard or two making rounds, he heard the sound of a footstep on the broken pavement of the driveway behind him.

He turned abruptly to find Clive standing silently, the moonlight creating a dim aura around his head.

"Can't say I'm surprised to see *you* here," Brig said, turning his attention back to the house across the street. "Change your mind about helping me out?"

"I can't let you do this, Brig," Clive replied flatly.

Brig chuckled and shook his head. "You can't let me do this..." he repeated in incredulity. "And why is that?"

"Because...it's a *trap*."

"Unbelievable..." Brig barked at him with upraised arms. "The first time I came to you about this, you acted like you didn't know anything about any of it. Then, I came to you a couple of nights ago about her father...and you acted clueless again. And I tried to give you *one* more chance last night to do the right thing...and you still acted like you didn't know about anything going on."

Brig turned his head and scratched his chin for a moment in thought. "And now...all of a sudden you're here, where you said you didn't know anything about – and you're telling me it's a *trap*? How the Hell does *that* work, Cryp?"

"Look...I'm not here to make a big conversation out of this," Clive said, waving his hands dismissively. "I'm just tellin' ya you're walkin' into a trap."

"Like *you'd* know..." Brig said sarcastically.

"*I* know..." Clive quipped right away.

"Yeah, and you'd know...*how*?" Brig asked, already knowing the answer.

"Let me paint a picture for you, hot shot," Clive shouted, pointing his finger angrily at Brig. "You walk in there...they're gonna catch you, and they're gonna *kill* you..."

Brig shook his head in disgusted disagreement.

"*No*?" Clive said mockingly. "Well, maybe *this* will wake you up. Once they take you out, then they're gonna go after your girl and kill *her*, too. *That* what you want?"

Brig gritted his teeth, turned his head to glare at the house, and then faced Clive again.

"What choice do I have, Cryp? I don't do this...they're gonna kill both of them anyway, *right*? Isn't that the way the Syndicate operates?" Brig asked angrily through his gnashed teeth.

"You don't know that..."

"You seem to know an awful lot about how *they* do things," Brig said accusingly.

Clive, rather than responding to the bait, shot Brig a silent, annoyed glare.

"In case you haven't been picking up on my hints lately," Brig continued, moving in close to Clive and lowering his voice to a heightened whisper, "...I *know* you were at her father's house a few nights ago..."

"You don't know what the Hell you're talkin' about," Clive dismissed with a sneer.

"I *don't*, huh? Well, let's see if I'm in the ballpark. You know what *I* think this is all about?" Brig asked, but Clive held his reply. "I think *you* almost botched kidnapping a helpless old man in a wheelchair. And when I came sniffing around looking for answers and told you I was comin' here today, you got to thinkin' that your bosses aren't gonna like it too much when someone that's known to associate with you shows up and just takes him away from *them*..."

Clive shook his head and turned away from Brig.

"What's the matter, Cryp – hit a little too close to the truth? *Once a traitor, always a traitor, huh?*"

Clive spun angrily and grabbed Brig by the collar, pushing him against the stonework of the house in front of which they stood with a hearty, resounding thud.

Brig instinctively parried, turned Clive against the wall, pulled the Ripper from the back of his belt and held it up to Clive's chin.

"*This* the way you want to play it? *Huh?*" Brig screamed, as he glared angrily into Clive's eyes.

After an awkward moment of silence, Brig released Clive, took a step back and tucked the Ripper back into his belt.

"I'm not gonna force you to be someone that you obviously aren't anymore, man," Brig explained, rubbing the back of his neck with one hand. "But I'm givin you *two* choices here. You can either go in there with me, like *brothers*, and we rescue him *together*. Or *you* can just walk away like a coward."

Clive took a heavy breath, as he glared away from Brig once again, his hands on his hips.

"But either way, *I'm* goin' in there." Brig spun and began to walk across the street, but then stopped abruptly and pointed angrily at Clive. "And you *know* it's right! What's *wrong* with you, man?" he screamed, his voice barely choking back his emotions.

"I don't need this..." Clive said flatly.

He did an about-face and disappeared into the night.

Brig stared after him in disbelief for an instant, wiped his mouth and eyes on his shirtsleeve, and then turned back towards the street.

Brig carefully hid himself at every opportunity as he crossed the street, ducking behind an abandoned car, and then sprinting up to the house alongside a neighboring one. He peered out from around the corner of the house and waited for a few moments, still expecting to see at least one guard outside.

After a few more minutes, no one came.

No sentry...hmm, he thought, as he scanned the rest of the neighborhood, thinking that maybe they were watching the house from afar.

The warning from Clive of this being a trap stuck in the back of his mind.

He's tryin' to get in your head, man. Do what you need to do, Brig reassured himself. He emerged from behind the adjacent house and darted into the shadows of a row of overgrown hedges that separated the two properties.

He extracted the Ripper from his belt once again and fingered the trigger guard, as he hesitantly scanned the area. Not wanting to go in blind, he quietly approached a window on the side of the house. A small amount of light emanated from behind the closed curtains. Brig peered in through the worn spots.

In the dim lighting within, a figure sat in a wheelchair. Next to him stood a man, whom Brig recognized from the truck two nights previous.

Brig decided that it was time to move in.

Knowing that entering through the front door would not be a wise move, Brig made his way around to the darkened rear of the house, stopping at a window just past the corner.

"Looks like you're gonna help me whether you like it or not, Cryp..." he mused to himself with a chuckle, extracting a field knife from his pocket, one that he had stealthily removed from Clive's belt during their fisticuffs moments earlier.

With a careful hand, he made quick work of the screen that lined the outside of the window frame, released the locks along the grooves and tossed the frame aside into the grass.

"An unlocked window will make this a *Hell* of a lot easier," he mumbled, gently pushing upward on the glass with both hands.

To his surprise, the window slid open easily.

Brig pulled himself into the opening, ignoring the sore burn from his ribcage, and dropped silently to the floor inside.

The room was not lit, but the light coming from the hallway gave him enough illumination to see that it was obviously a bedroom; perhaps one that the guards used in shifts while watching their prisoner.

The sound of voices coming from the end of the hallway, presumably from the room that he had seen from the window outside, made Brig jump to his feet. He pressed himself up against the doorframe and listened intently, his finger finding the trigger of the Ripper in anticipation.

"Don't worry, old man," a voice that he recognized as Alexi, said in his thick Eur-Asian accent, "The truck will be here in a few hours to take you to the boss. But I don't think you're gonna enjoy the ride," he laughed derisively.

Brig suddenly felt vindicated in his actions. Had he shown up just a few hours later, he might have missed his opportunity to save Steele's father.

One thought did bother him. What were they thinking leaving this person alone with Bronson? Brig had hoodwinked him into divulging this location already, what made him think he could take Brig on again, this time armed?

Either I'm extremely lucky, Brig thought, *or they're incredibly stupid.*

He stretched his neck around the corner and peered down the hallway. A hooded figure sat in the wheelchair just in front of a standing Alexi.

Brig had not seen Bronson Fox in quite some time, so he was not sure what to expect. Because of that fact, he had to assume that the figure was indeed him. It could not have been a coincidence that they had a man in a wheelchair held prisoner – *could it?*

Moving silently and deliberately, Brig traversed the hallway and entered the small living room, stopping just behind Alexi.

"Fancy meeting *you* here," Brig said sarcastically, pointing the cold steel of the Ripper into Alexi's neck.

Alexi instinctively raised his hands, revealing a small, semi-automatic handgun.

"Drop the gun," Brig ordered. He grabbed Alexi's free arm and twisted it viciously up behind the surprised guard's back.

Alexi grunted and dropped the gun onto the floor. Brig quickly grabbed it and shoved it into the back of his belt, all the while not releasing the pressure on Alexi's arm.

The man in the wheelchair remained motionless, as Brig pulled Alexi away from him and pressed the grunting guard up against the far wall.

"You're just *full* of mistakes, aren't you pal?" Alexi snarled, looking at the wrong end of the Ripper in Brig's hands.

"Who's here with you?" Brig asked, ignoring Alexi's taunt.

"Gonna give you a chance to live. Walk out that door and don't look back, and as far as I'm concerned this never happened…" Alexi said, nodding his head towards the front door.

Brig snorted and pressed his forearm into the back of Alexi's neck. "I'm not leavin' without *him*," Brig growled into Alexi's ear.

"I'm not goin' anywhere with *you*," a voice from behind Brig said suddenly, as the hard steel of a gun barrel jabbed into the back of Brig's ribs. "You shoulda' listened to Alexi there...*pal*."

Brig turned his head to try to see his surprise attacker. The wheelchair was empty. The hood was crumpled on the floor beside it.

Shit... Brig thought.

Before he could react, the other guard clubbed Brig over the back of his neck with the butt of his weapon, making Brig sprawl forward forcefully onto the floor.

As he lost consciousness, Brig felt a small prick of a needle in his upper arm.

Brig opened his eyes to darkness. As he swung his head from side-to-side, he realized that it was not the room, but rather the shade of a smooth, satin hood over his head.

His skull throbbed, and not just from the blunt force of the hidden guard's weapon. His mind felt foggy, and the darkness warped oddly around him.

He groaned as he squinted, trying desperately to see through the cloth sheathed over his eyes. The rope binding his hands and feet cinched tightly around the chair with such little slack, that he could feel the skin on his wrists rip with even the slightest struggle.

His brain became sluggish. He could see his thoughts stalk towards him, as if they were treading through a soggy marsh, barely able to lift their heavy feet. However, despite their slowness, he was unable to avoid them as they approached, bumping shoulders with his conscious as they passed.

Brig thought about Steele. How disappointed she would be that he went through with his plan despite her adamant reservations – and failed. And she was right – *he* had let her down. He loved her, and he longed to be with her right now – to tell her how sorry he was, and to ask for forgiveness.

Screwed... he tried to think, finding that he was only capable of single-word thoughts now.

But they still came in a frenzy.

His mind wandered to Clive.

Trap, he realized, shaking his head in disgust.

He loved Clive, too. Despite everything that had happened, despite their tumultuous, sometimes explosive, relationship – he did not want to believe that Clive was capable of the treachery of which Brig had accused him. He was the closest thing he had to family. He was his brother. Brig wanted to find him and tell him how he felt and to tell him, too, how sorry he was.

Suddenly, from what seemed like a great distance, Brig heard a pair of voices speaking. He could not understand them, but he thought that he had caught a couple of words in Russian. The Eastern Eur-Asian dialects were never his biggest fluencies during language training in the EWs. Not that it would have mattered now, because his mind felt like an over-saturated sponge.

Then, the door to the room opened and closed quickly. The voices were now next to him, although they still sounded as if they were talking into a tin can far across the room.

Two men stood next to Brig, exchanging words so quickly that it made Brig's head swoon, as he cranked his neck back and forth to determine their location. He felt one of them tug the hood from his head.

Brig shut his eyes tightly to block out the blinding light. Slowly, he opened them and peered up at a pair of shadowy figures standing in front of him.

"Hello," the first man said in a thick Eur-Asian accent.

Brig blinked several times – he could not find the words to say, his mind would not let him.

"Do you know where you are?" the man asked, tilting his head side to side as he bowed in towards Brig.

Brig could only shake his head.

The man turned his head and said something to the other, to which the other responded and then left the room, closing the door behind him. The first man turned his attention back to Brig, standing up fully and folding his hands behind his back.

"Do you know how you got here?" the man queried flatly.

Brig clenched his eyes shut, trying desperately to remember the exact sequence of events that led him here. "Clive..." he managed to mutter.

"Your name is Clive?" the man asked curiously, his full face now becoming clearer to Brig, despite the rest of the room remaining very blurred.

Brig shook his head again. Then, it occurred to him.

They're using a truth agent! Brig shouted inside his mind. *Don't tell them anything... fight it!*

"Then what *is* your name?" the interrogator asked, turning his back and pacing the room in front of Brig.

"Br...Br..." Brig began to stammer, using all of his strength to prevent saying his name. "Br...ody..." he blurted finally.

"Brody?" the man repeated. "And Brody...do you have a *last* name?"

"Sss...s..." Brig started to respond. "Sampson..." he said and then closed his eyes, the pain in his head beginning to intensify.

"Brody Sampson. That is your name?" the man said back to Brig.

Brig nodded his head. "Jess..." Brig moaned.

Shut up! Brig's inner voice bellowed.

"Pardon?"

"Where's..." Brig started.

Don't do it, Brig – just shut up! the voice demanded.

"Where's...Jessica..." Brig managed to ask aloud.

The man abruptly stopped pacing and faced Brig with a look of concern and shock.

"Jess!" Brig shouted, as he closed his eyes tightly.

The man quickly grabbed the hood and forced it back over Brig's head.

"*No!*" Brig roared, but by the sound of the door slam, he could tell that the man had already left the room. He growled loudly in frustration, his voice echoing off the walls of the tiny chamber.

After what seemed like an eternity to him, which in reality was only twenty minutes, he heard the sound of the door opening and closing quickly.

Instead of the clomping of hard shoes on the tile floor that he had heard when the other two men had entered, this time the sound was much more reserved, much lighter, much more... *feminine.*

"Mr...Sampson?" a woman's voice called suddenly.

Brig lifted his head in the direction of her voice but did not respond. *A woman? Really?* he thought incredulously. *They couldn't get anything from me and now they're gonna pull this?*

"*Brody...Sampson?*" the voice called again, this time more deliberate.

That voice... Brig puzzled, *it sounds so familiar...* He tried to glare through the fabric of the hood unsuccessfully.

"*Jess?*"

"Brig? Brigadier, oh my God..." she answered quietly, swiftly pulling the hood from Brig's head and standing back to look at him.

Brig shook his head violently from side-to-side, certain that he was dreaming.

"Jess, is that *really* you?" he asked with eyes wide in amazement, ignoring the effects of the truth agent, which had now worn down to a dull buzz in his head.

Jess flung both of her arms around Brig's neck and squeezed tightly.

Brig felt the tears welling up in his eyes. He could not believe what he was seeing, despite that he thought he had seen her just a few days earlier.

"Brig...you *jackass*, what the Hell are you doing here?" Jess cried in a heightened whisper, as she pulled back away from him.

"*Me?* What the Hell are *you* doing here?" Brig parried immediately in a louder tone. "And *how* the Hell are you here? And *how* the Hell did you know *I* was here?"

Jess motioned her finger to her lips, as she pointed at the door with the other hand. "Brody Sampson? You think *I* wouldn't remember the name you used to call yourself as a kid when you'd run off to the county fair when you were mad at Dad? Why are you here?" she asked. "...For *me?*"

"Love to sit here and talk, catch up and all. But if you can just untie me we can get the Hell out of here..." Brig said matter-of-factly, flexing his arms to show his bindings.

Jess crossed her arms across her abdomen. "I...*can't do that*, Brig," she said hesitantly.

"What the Hell? Why not? Let me out of here, damn it!"

"Shhhh! If Yemi hears you getting loud he's gonna come in here!" She placed her hand softly over Brig's mouth.

"Jess, what are you *doing?*" Brig said finally after she pulled her hand away. "I'm your *brother*. Why can't you let me go? And who the Hell is Yemi?"

Jess pointed nonchalantly at the door. "The *guard* that was in here."

Brig shook his head in confusion. "Why did he let *you* in here?"

"He owes me. I caught him stealing from the liquor room a while back," she explained, "He'd do anything to keep from getting in trouble for *that*..."

"I don't understand, Jess. What's going on here? What *is* this place?" Brig pled, closing his eyes tightly, ironically hoping this was all a weird dream.

Looking perplexed, Jess turned away and held both of her hands against her temples.

"Jess! You *need* to untie me. They're gonna *kill* me, you understand that?"

"You need to calm down, Brig...or you'll get us *both* killed. Just wait a second. Let me think," she reprimanded calmly. "Yeah. *That's* it. I think I can get Yemi to help out."

She spun and made for the door.

"A *guard* is gonna help me escape?" Brig said in complete puzzlement.

"No," she replied without looking back. "But he can go get someone that I know *will...*"

As the door softly shut, Brig sat in amazement and confusion. Not only was his sister alive, but she was here at the enemy compound – and refusing to let him go. His world was upside-down at the moment, and he was not sure what to think next.

A few minutes later, the door opened and Jess reappeared once again.

"Okay," she said softly, as she approached Brig and knelt to eye level with him. "The wheels are in motion – but you need to promise me you'll just play ball with these guys. Don't be a hero. And *don't* tell them we talked!"

"You're not making any sense, Jess. What the Hell is going on? How are you *alive?*" Brig demanded.

Jess sighed and locked eyes with Brig. "I don't have a lot of time to talk, but I'll tell you what I can," she replied. *"Bruno's gonna want to see you soon..."*

"*Bruno?*" Brig questioned, his brow wrinkled in confusion.

"Yeah...*my husband*," she said flatly, as she glanced away.

34:
Saints and Sinners

Five years prior (2079)…

"Good evening, everybody," the woman said in a bubbly tone to the crowd of 30 people that had gathered in her home in a suburb of Las Vegas.

"Thanks for showing up. I know that with the circumstances the way that they are it's hard to get word out to everyone," she said, peering around with a sheepish smile. "If you'll just give us a few more minutes, we're waiting on a few more people to show up that want to present something to the entire group. There's drinks out on the patio if you're interested…"

"So Tom, who's showing up that we don't know about already?" one man, Craig, asked another. He took a sip of his drink, while both men stood by the sliding glass doors.

"Rumor has it that the *Mayor* might be here…" Tom replied, shrugging his shoulders.

"*Mayor?*" Craig questioned with a puzzled look.

"Well…*former* Mayor, you know what I meant…" Tom corrected.

"You think he's got a plan to get things running again?" Craig asked.

"Anything's gotta be better that what we've got right now, I'll tell ya that much."

"Thank you everyone for your patience, we'd like to get started," the woman continued once again, moving to the front of the room where everyone present could see and hear her.

"Some of you may know this gentleman already, but if not I'd like to introduce you to former City Councilman Albert Latham. He would like to speak to us all about some very important issues that we've all…well, we've *all* been worried about." She moved aside for another man, a stocky, gray-haired man in his 50's.

"Thanks everyone for coming out tonight. It's good to see so many folks all in one place…" he began.

"Why are we here?" one man in the crowd interjected loudly

over him. "We're all supposed to act like this is some sort of cocktail party and everything's just *fine?*"

"Well, no, sir," the Councilman responded, holding both hands up in front of him in protest. "I think we *all* realize the hardships that everyone has had to endure these past two years..."

"You *really* think he has a plan?" one woman in the crowd whispered to her husband standing next to her, her ponytailed brunette hair bouncing to the side as she spoke. She playfully mussed the hair of her four-year-old son, who clung tightly to her leg.

"I don't know, *Jess*," Davis, her husband, responded while shaking his head, not taking his eyes from the front of the room. "I don't know that any of us have the resources to even get the power back on, let alone set things right."

Davis scanned the room to gauge the crowd's reaction to the Councilman's speech. One man in particular caught his attention.

"Who invited *him?*" Davis asked Jess, while he pointed at him.

The man, dressed in a silk suit, wore his shoulder-length black hair slicked back from his forehead.

"I think his name is James?" she replied pensively. "Well, he *has* been at the last few meetings – so I guess he has *some* right to be here..."

"Mr. Latham," James said politely, raising his hand to be spotted in the crowd. His Irish accent made more than just a few people turn their heads to get a good look at him. "What is your plan to restore power to the greater Las Vegas area?"

The Councilman pursed his lips and darted his eyes around the crowd. "Well...the resources for that type of plan just *don't* exist as we speak right now. As you know, the area has been devastated economically because of the disaster – but that's not a situation that's unique to just *us*..."

"But Mr. Councilman. People are dying – *have died*, and *continue* to die on a daily basis without the simple fundamental necessities of life," James added haughtily. "There have been reports out of the East that possibly millions have died. One can only assume that on a global scale that number is growing to astronomical proportions. *Surely*, you have some sort of plan to address these basic issues? Otherwise...aren't we just wasting our time here?"

"I think we need to have faith in our local and state governments to come up with a plan that..." Latham began to defend.

"Mr. Latham," James interrupted, "no one has heard from anyone at the local or state, or even national level for that matter, in nearly a year. We have no communications whatsoever, we've lost critical functions such as power and water, but yet you say we need to have faith in our officials?"

The crowd began murmuring amongst themselves. The Councilman glanced around the room nervously, beginning to feel the swell of distrust growing.

"And Mr. Councilman," James continued, "what is being done about the general security of the populace? The rumors coming in from other cities across the land are that the government and security forces simply no longer exist. Many major cities have become desolate wastelands where lawlessness and anarchy reign."

"Well, sir, we need to treat them as such...rumors," Latham responded confidently, still scanning the group unevenly, as they watched the conversation intently.

"Where is the Mayor this evening, Mr. Councilman?" James asked purposefully. "It was said that he would be in attendance."

"I...I don't know. But rest assured, I'm certain he is working with the government to come up with a plan..." Latham replied unevenly.

"Another government official missing in action, aye?" James chortled derisively.

Latham cleared his throat into his hand. "I'm a firm believer of unity – and I believe that if we stay together, with or without the Mayor, anything's possible."

"A very *political* answer, Mr. Latham, in a very non-political time," James barbed back at him.

"We don't need *your* input, James..." Davis barked over the crowd, whom had taken to jabbering amongst themselves.

"Ah, Davis. I wondered how long it would be until you graced us with some of your wisdom," James said sneeringly, rolling his eyes. "Unlike you, I have come with a plan that not only restores the basics of everyday life, but also uplifts our community from the *brink of extinction.*"

"We're not *all* foolish enough to believe that. We know about your associations," Davis denounced adamantly. "Don't listen to him, he's part of the Syndicate!" he shouted to the others.

"Mr. McKechnie, please," James said dismissively. "I'd suggest doing your homework before showing up and presenting baseless accusations. I admit that I have connections...*yes.* And my family has resources that others might consider *excessive*. But that in no way links me with the likes of common thugs which you are inferring."

Davis snorted derisively.

"People, people. Let's keep it civil..." Latham interjected.

"*I'd* be open to hearing James's plan. We're living in the dark and scraping the bottom to come up with even the basic supplies!" Tom offered over the crowd's light chatter.

A sly smile flowed across James's face as he scanned the crowd without moving his head.

The Councilman continued his speech, asking members of the crowd to input their ideas as to how they could regenerate their community.

"I can't believe they're willing to listen to that...*Euro-trash*," Davis grumbled fiercely to Jess.

Jess cleared her throat and raised her eyebrows at her husband.

"Davis, Davis. Can't we all just get along?" James said coyly, as he stopped next to him, and then bowed politely to Jess and her son.

"I don't have anything else to say to you, James," Davis said sharply, holding up a hand in front of him.

"Why...I merely came to plead my case to my biggest detractor," James said smoothly.

"Go fool someone *else*. It's not working here..." Davis shot back.

"*Davis...*" Jess censured with a furrowed brow and a prod to her husband's arm.

"Jess, *not now...*" Davis insisted with a growl, pushing her hand away.

"Jess? Short for...Jessica, I presume?" James said suavely, turning his head and locking gazes with her.

Jess nodded and smiled politely.

"Fabulous...and what would your name be, my young friend?" James asked the young boy, bending over to make eye contact with him.

"His name's Elijah. Say 'hi' Eli..." Jess said to her son. Eli grabbed his mother's leg and hid behind it, as he stared up at James with trepidation.

"Well, Jessica and Elijah, it is a pleasure to make your acquaintance. I'm James...*James Muldoon*." James held out a hand and gracefully shook hers.

"That's enough, Muldoon. You can go now," Davis insisted, putting his hand against Muldoon's chest and pushing lightly, breaking his contact with Jess.

"Short-sighted as always, Davis. I'm just making polite conversation," Muldoon replied, calmly removing Davis's hand from his suit jacket. "I think you'll see I'm quite harmless once you get to know me...*and my ideas,*" he said, peering over Davis's shoulder at Jess.

"We don't want your ideas. All *you* wanna do is get us all under your thumb," Davis parried. "...*Just like the other cities.*"

"I'm sure I don't know *what* you're referring to," Muldoon scoffed, as he straightened his tie. "I offer food banks and restoration of basic services. Is that a crime?"

"It is the way *you* do it..." Davis growled sternly.

Muldoon put his finger to his lips as he looked up at the ceiling in thought. "Not the cry, but the flight of a wild duck," he began to recite eloquently, "leads the flock to fly and follow."

"Spout your garbage somewhere else. Haven't we all suffered enough? Some of these people might be polite enough just to let you talk. But believe me, when you turn your back they can't *stand* you," Davis said adamantly. "Just go away, we'll solve this on our own."

"Tsk, tsk," James said cunningly. "Casting aside salvation to placate your *own* prejudice is rather foolish in these dangerous times, Mr. McKechnie. *Don't you think?* I'd hate to see anything happen to that beautiful family of yours just because *you* were too obstinate to see the light..."

Davis pushed himself forcefully up against Muldoon's chest and snarled into his face. "*You* stay away from my family, you son of a bitch. I don't care *who* you're connected to – I'll take you out myself..."

Jess grabbed Davis's arm and pulled him away from Muldoon. "That's enough!" she barked quietly to Davis, as Muldoon leisurely tugged at his collar with a fulfilled smile.

"No, it's *not*..." screamed one man in a semi-drunken slur, emerging from the crowd. "We don't need Syndicate telling us what to do here. Go back to where you came from!" he said, shoving Muldoon backward a few steps.

"I see the drink has hidden the car keys to your brain," Muldoon observed wryly. He turned from the man to re-address Davis.

"I said you're done here, damn it!" the man bellowed, shoving Muldoon again. "This is a *Reformation* party. *You* have no place *here*."

Muldoon reached his hand partially into his jacket, then withdrew it suddenly, as the man extracted his own gun and pointed it into Muldoon's face.

"Whoa, whoa! That's *enough*, Gary!" Davis yelled, reaching for the man's arm.

Gary yanked his elbow away just before Davis could touch it.

"We've been pushed around enough already, McKechnie. And if he's who you *say* he is, this is a good time to show 'em just how much we're sick of it!"

"Not like *this*, Gary..." Davis pled, glancing between the two men.

Another man came from behind Gary, his own handgun held out towards Muldoon.

"I'm with you, Gar," he said with a growl.

The crowd, already starting to form a semi-circle around the three men, began chanting '*Ref-orma-tion! Ref-orma-tion!*' as Gary and the other man swatted their arms upward to egg them on.

Davis, meanwhile, retreated to Jess and Eli, pushing them gently away from the crowd, seemingly out of harm's way.

Before Muldoon could retreat from imminent danger, a third and fourth man jumped from the group behind and grabbed him by the arms, preventing him from retreating from the armed men in front.

Gary turned to the crowd, raised his gun skyward and roared, igniting the energy of the already-overzealous group.

"Take his jacket off..." Gary commanded the two men that were holding him, to which they happily complied. Gary stepped over to the fireplace and yanked a bullwhip from the mantle's decorative display.

"Oh my God...we need to *stop* this..." Jess said under her breath, leaning against Davis.

"I...I don't know if I can..." Davis replied in shock, as he watched the proceedings.

"*I hereby claim this first victory in the name of the Reformation!*" Gary taunted the crowd.

They cheered loudly as he pulled his own jacket off and tossed it to the floor. Then, with a sloppy windup, he let loose a crack of the whip onto Muldoon's back, tearing a swath of fabric from it, exposing his bare skin underneath.

Muldoon grunted in pain as dark, crimson blood began to soak the fabric around his torn skin.

Jess recoiled in horror and grasped Eli tightly against her leg, as she buried her head into Davis's chest.

The loud snap of the whip echoed off the walls of the modest, split-level home. Gary reached back again and again, each time finding a new spot on Muldoon's back, each time resulting in a terrifying scream from the man, as he leaned forward onto the arms of the two men. The back of his shredded, white dress shirt was now completely red with his blood, and his chest heaved from the shock of each impact of the whip as he tried to catch his breath.

"Let *me* have a shot..." the second armed man told Gary. He grabbed the handle of the whip from his cohort's palm.

Just as he reared back to deliver a merciless blow to Muldoon, the front door burst open.

Portions of the group retreated farther back into the living room as two men, each wielding automatic weapons, sprinted in from the front porch.

The first raised his gun and squeezed off a burst of shots, two of which found their target in the back of the whip-wielder's head, dropping him forward onto the ground.

Gary spun around lazily and fired two shots from his own gun, but because of his intoxication, they clumsily found the wall a meter from the intruders. The first intruder made quick work of Gary – firing a single burst into the man's chest, which exploded in a mist of red as he fell backward onto the floor.

The crowd screamed in terror as they stumbled over one another to find cover. None was to be found, as most of the furniture in the room had been removed to accommodate the gathering.

The two men that held Muldoon quickly dropped him to the floor, each of them in a terrified stupor as they backpedaled away from the carnage unfolding in front of them.

Muldoon slowly pushed himself up from the floor, but crouched down, holding his weight with his hands on his knees, as he glared up at the two intruders.

"It's about time..." Muldoon said flatly to them with a sneer.

"Sorry, boss," the first intruder said apologetically. "We couldn't find the house..."

"*Enough...*" Muldoon choked.

Muldoon wiped the heavy drool from his chin with the sleeve of his shirt and stared with a dark intensity at the two men. The second man nodded at the silent command and turned towards the crowd.

Muldoon stood upright and faced the room.

"*Where there is no vision, the people perish,*" Muldoon bellowed to the crowd, who had begun to file back into the center of the room, believing that the danger had passed.

"And I see no vision here. Jesus Christ was misunderstood. Am I to understand that you would crucify your *New Messiah* as well?" he screamed, glaring wild-eyed around the room. "You will kneel before your King!" Muldoon barked maniacally, raising his hands like a victorious monarch.

Before anyone could realize his intentions, his pair of henchmen squeezed the triggers on their weapons, spraying hundreds of bullets into the group.

In an instant, all of the members of the Reformation that had gathered that night lay on the floor at Muldoon's feet; each bleeding heavily from the wounds incurred from the pair of guns that delivered their wrath upon them, each wearing their death stare – one of shock and fear.

Muldoon then held his hand up, to which the henchmen immediately ceased firing.

"Check them all. If you find any alive...*kill them,*" Muldoon ordered coldly, turning his back.

As the men dispersed and began searching the crowd of bodies lying haphazardly around the room, Muldoon picked up his jacket, brushed off dirt from the floor, and then gingerly placed it over his back.

Jess, who had dove out of the way along with Eli when the firing began, both miraculously surviving, lay on the floor near the back of the room, her precious son hidden beneath her. She glanced over to where Davis lay a meter away from her.

"Davis..." she whispered, but as she gazed at him, she could tell it was too late.

He was dead.

A thick trail of blood globules streamed from the side of his head where a bullet had found its target deep in his brain. He stared blankly back at her, the last, tragic seconds of his life written on his face for her to see.

She shut her eyes tightly and leaned into the back of Eli's neck. "Eli...baby. Are you okay?" she asked softly.

"Yes, Mommy," Eli answered with a whimper.

"Shhh..." she instructed her youngling, placing her finger over his lips to silence him. "I need you to do me a favor, sweetheart..." she said, choking back the shock of the night's events. "Remember how we play Cowboys and Aliens?"

Eli nodded silently.

"I want you to pretend that the aliens have invaded and they've hit everyone with their stun guns. Can *you* do that for me, my love?" Jess asked, wiping away tears from his face.

Eli nodded again as he peered up at his mother.

"Mommy, I want to go home..."

Jess hugged him tightly. "Can you pretend for Mommy?" she pled. "Can you pretend to be stunned and knocked out for me?"

"Yes, Mommy," Eli whispered lightly.

"And no matter who tells you it's ok to look up...*don't do it*, not for anyone but Mommy. Do you understand?" she said, as she stared into his eyes, prompting a nod from him once again. "One more thing, my strong little boy..." she said, sobbing without sound. "After you hear the aliens leave and close the door, promise me you'll get up and run out the back door. *Run as fast as you can.* Don't look back. Go to the Wilson's house next to ours. Do you remember where they live?"

Eli gave a nervous nod.

"I love you, Elijah. Mommy will come and get you from the Wilson's soon. We'll have ice cream, okay? You are such a strong, courageous young man," she said, hugging Eli as tight as she ever had.

She slowly raised her head and peered around.

The henchmen were still on the other end of the room, prodding the bodies on the floor with their feet or weapons as they passed. Every few moments, a single, gut wrenching shot would ring out in the room as they found another survivor, making her flinch and lose her breath momentarily. Jess quietly rolled off Eli and lay beside him, wincing as she realized that her arm had been hit in the volley of bullets.

Following his mother's request like a brave soldier, Eli lay face down on the floor, his arms spread awkwardly out beside him, pretending the imaginary aliens had struck him.

Jess quietly dragged herself to Davis's motionless body, and then, after taking a deep breath to calm her nerves, swiped her hand through the thick puddle of blood that had formed under his head, collecting enough to cover her fingers fully. She gulped back a momentary reflex to vomit and turned to Eli. Moving slowly as to not draw attention to herself, she smeared the blood into Eli's hair and onto the side of his cheek.

Knowing that she only had seconds until the henchmen would be near, she pushed herself painfully away from Eli and laid herself flat on the ground.

After a few moments, one of the henchmen approached the back of the room where she lay with her son.

"Found a live one back here, boss," the man said. He raised his gun and aimed it into the upper portion of Jess's back. "A woman..." he said, as he fingered the trigger.

"*Stop*!" Muldoon commanded in a loud bark.

The henchman abruptly raised his weapon over his shoulder. Muldoon stepped past him and looked down at the ground.

"Mrs. McKechnie...*Jessica*..." Muldoon said soothingly.

"Get away from me you *animal*. You killed my family!" she screamed, pushing herself away from him.

Muldoon glared over at the bodies of Davis and Eli.

"Yes...how *unfortunate*," he said derisively. "But you knew the consequences of allying yourselves with *this* group."

"Why?" Jess cried, tears flowing heavily down her face from her watery, brown eyes. "James...*why* did you do this? *Why*?"

Muldoon wrinkled his brow and pursed his lips as he looked around the room.

"James. I've always *hated* that name. So regal, but yet so... *British*," he said with an air of disgust. "*The Brits...such snobby twits*," he cooed. "*You*, Jessica, can call me *Bruno*."

Muldoon knelt next to Jess and gently grasped her arm.

"Bruno was my father's name..." he said casually, looking at her bullet wound. "Why on Earth he allowed my mother to name me James is *beyond* me." He stood and extended a hand towards Jess. "Come, we'll get you some medical attention for that wound."

Jess again pushed herself backward and wrinkled her freckled nose. "I'm not going anywhere with *you*!"

"*I didn't ask*," Muldoon sniped immediately. He motioned to one of the henchmen, who quickly grabbed Jess around her waist and picked her up from the floor.

As the three men and Jess exited the front door and made their way down the driveway towards an idling truck, Muldoon grabbed the arm of the other henchmen.

"*Burn the house...*" Muldoon ordered inhumanly.

The henchman nodded, jogged ahead to the truck, extracted a canister from behind the cabin and then ran back to the house to perform his task.

As the other henchman assisted Jess into the truck's cab, she peered over at the house. For a brief moment, she thought she saw a young boy sprinting along the fence line, disappearing into the neighbor's yard.

Present day (2084)...

The light from the candles flickered, making the shadow that it cast of Bruno Muldoon on the wall behind him rise and fall erratically. Sitting quietly in a kneeling position, Muldoon gazed peacefully towards the front of the room, staring in deep, pensive meditation at the set of darkened, round masses placed upon the table several meters in front of him.

He took a deep breath and closed his eyes, holding his palms together calmly in front of his chest, as he began to put himself into a deep trance.

A knock on the frame of the door, which he had kept open to allow airflow into the windowless room, broke the serenity of the session.

"Boss?" the gruff voice of Pollux called from just beyond the doorway.

"I asked you to *never* bother me in here, Pollux," Muldoon said in a soothed tone.

"Yeah...um...I know boss, but this is *important*," Pollux insisted, standing with his back to the room, avoiding looking inside.

Muldoon sighed heavily and rolled his eyes open. "It's *always* important, isn't it?" he said mockingly. "What is it *this* time?"

"It's Underwood, boss. He uh...wants to have a meeting with you," Pollux stammered, while he folded his hands nervously in front of his hulking mass.

"What do I *pay* you for, Pollux?" Muldoon asked with an air of increasing frustration. "Could you not have just taken a message from him and *relayed* it to me?"

"He said he needs to speak to you in person. *And in private.*"

"Very well," Muldoon resigned. "Go pick up Mr. Underwood and bring him here to me. Anything else?"

"No, boss. Sorry, boss. I'll be back as soon as I can..." Pollux strode out of the adjoining room into the hallway, closing the door quietly behind him.

As he began to return to his meditative state and gazed upon his altar, Muldoon's brow rumpled. A wicked smile formed at the corner of his lips.

"Time to show your hand, Mr. Underwood," he whispered and then closed his eyes.

35:
Heroes and Pawns

Present day (2084)...

Clive rested his chin on his folded hands, as he stared intently across the room. The SAT phone device that he had retrieved from Bronson Fox's mansion a few nights previous sat on the shelf on the other end of his small, secret room. The room's LED lighting shone dully against its black, leather outer case.

He had come downstairs to his private workroom under the floor to finish decrypting data that he had found on Steele's cipher cards before getting some rest. For the good portion of the past hour or so, however, he found his mind wandering to the mystery and possibilities of what the device represented.

"What were you *doing* with Quantum tech, old man?" he said aloud.

Clive shook his head in subtle confusion, as he turned his attention to the cipher cards, which sat halfway out of their box next to the terminal display, resting on the bench in front of him.

He pulled the set of cards from the box and inserted the first into the reader below the terminal, and then sat back in his chair awaiting the display to register their content. As the data scrolled on the screen, he mumbled the words to himself aloud, closing his eyes and committing several pieces of the information to memory.

He paused the data output, as one particular piece of information caught his eye.

"No way. Well...*this* is a game changer." He scratched the back of his head with one hand and clicked a key nonchalantly to restart the data display.

Just as the data had begun to scroll once more, an error flashed in the center of the screen.

"End of data?" he read frustratingly, his eyebrows furrowed. "Right in the middle? Can't be..."

He re-entered the commands into the keyboard, repeating them once more as his fingers gracefully flew across the keys.

"Rescan partition..." he said, and then sat back again to wait a few seconds while the terminal performed its task.

"Invalid end to partition..." he repeated, "...partition partially overwritten with *hidden* sector data?" He sat back and stared at the error on the screen, perplexed.

"Hmm..." he grunted loudly, sitting up and typing in another quick command. "Encryption scan..." he mumbled, typing and then resting his head within his palms while he waited for the results.

After a few more moments, the screen flashed another message accompanied by a subtle tone. Clive leaned forward and read it aloud as well.

"Encryption level consistent with URA SA cipher block – do you wish to decrypt? Well...," he said playfully. "Let's see what a naughty little girl you've been here..." He answered 'Yes' to the prompt.

After several more minutes, the screen began displaying information in a highlighted, crimson text.

"Top Secret Omega..." he started to read to himself. "Project *Red Vision*? What the heck is that..."

He continued to scroll through the data presented in front of him.

"What...you've got to be kidding me. That can't be right...*can it*? What's the date on this data. Gotta' be in research mode..."

He tapped several keys rapidly to display a pop up screen that displayed the date.

"2075. But, that would mean that..,nah, can't be possible."

Clive frowned, as he rapidly scanned through the top of the data, one finger tapping impatiently on his temple. His eyes darted back and forth through the information.

"Implementation...*completed*?" he read aloud, and then sat back in his chair with an astounded, blank expression.

"Oh my God..." he said to himself, folding his hands over the top of his head and closing his eyes, "I can't...*believe* it..."

A heavy knocking at the front door of his workshop abruptly pulled him from his pensive trance. Clive glared up at the stairs and pursed his lips, shook his head and decided to put it out of his mind.

"Sorry, we're closed for the evening..." he said facetiously under his breath, turning his eyes back to the screen.

After a few silent seconds, however, the rapping at the door grew louder and more intense.

"Damn it!" he cursed aloud.

Clive pushed himself up from his stool, reached with one hand and unsuccessfully flicked at the power switch of the terminal. The light of the LED terminal from the room below poked out around the cracks of the door frame, as he pushed the swinging door back in place and threw the area rug over it.

"Damn it, Brig. I thought I told you..." he began to chastise, as he slid the door open forcefully.

For the second time that night, he was surprised that it was not Brig.

"Pollux. I wasn't expecting...*you*," Clive said hesitantly.

"Underwood," Pollux grunted. He stood and glared at Clive with his arms folded across his broad chest.

"By all means, come in. Mi casa es su casa," Clive said derisively with a mock, partial bow, while pointing the way inward with one hand.

"Don't start with your gibberish, genius," Pollux grumbled, passing Clive and entering the workshop. He stopped in the center of the room and faced Clive, the modest lighting illuminating the large man's face.

"Well...you've...looked better, if *that's* possible," Clive observed with a light chuckle, not able to take his eyes from the massive wound on the giant's face.

"Listen - if the boss hadn't sent me here, I'd put my fist through the back of your skull *right now*," Pollux growled with an outstretched, angry finger. "Seein' as how it was *your* buddy that did this to me."

Clive's smile slowly faded away as he held his tongue for a moment, not wanting to anger the brute any more than he already was. He also realized that this almost certainly was Brig's handiwork, based on their most recent conversation.

"Yea-ah," Pollux affirmed with his own derisive chuckle. "You alone, or is that creep hangin' around?" he asked gruffly, rotating his mammoth head back and forth on his tree trunk-like neck, and his knuckles snapping loudly like dry tree branches as he flexed his massive fists.

"No...just you and me, Pollux," Clive answered calmly, still staring at Pollux's face with a half-smirk. "What do you need *this* time?"

"I told the boss you needed to see him, one-on-one," Pollux replied, turning his full attention to Clive.

"You came all the way here just for *that*? Really...you didn't *have* to..." Clive said, holding his hands on his hips.

"Don't be stupid, professor," Pollux grunted. "I came to take *you* to the *boss*. He wants to see you as soon as we get back."

"I...I'm not *ready*..." Clive replied hesitantly, peering past Pollux towards the closed, hidden door near the back of the workshop.

"Now *you* know better than that, egghead. The boss *always* gets what he wants," Pollux grumbled. "Now go get what you need and let's get *outta* here."

Eight years prior (late 2076)...

Bronson Fox quickly strolled the hallway, the graceful click of the heels of his dress shoes striking the patches of marble that interlaced with carpet across the broad corridors of the URA Executive Building in Boulder.

As he walked, various interns and other political assistants passed him, offering polite greetings, to which he offered transparent smiles in return.

He focused his eyes forward away from the busy work going on in the open rooms that he passed by. A small chime emanated from his wristband. Upon tapping the device, a colorful, three-dimensional hologram of the stocky Director of the URA Security Alliance, William Hanley, stretching nearly fifteen centimeters in height, suddenly popped above it.

"Good morning, Bronson," Hanley bellowed, tweaking the spectacles perched precariously upon the bridge of his nose. "I assume you're ready to speak to the President today?"

Bronson, eyes still forward, as he strolled swiftly from one corridor to the next, smiled meekly.

"William...already on my way," Bronson replied tersely. "But I'm still perplexed at why *you* aren't meeting with him yourself."

A hand, holding a data pad, appeared from just out of range of Hanley's hologram as he chuckled in reply. He signed it with a quick swipe of his fingers and then quickly returned it out of sight.

"Fox, you know the President is already on *our* side," Hanley explained, training his eyes on Bronson once again. "But we feel it's essential to have someone with *your* credentials to make the final budget push to the General Assembly."

"Very well, William. I'll be in touch shortly," Bronson replied, tapping the device once more, making the image of Hanley abruptly dissipate into static before it disappeared.

Bronson slowed his gait as he approached the desk of the President's primary assistant, her desk a mammoth, oak holdout of a more opulent period.

"The President is waiting for you, Director Fox," the secretary offered upon seeing Bronson approach, quickly standing up and rounding the corner of the desk to guide him into the office.

Bronson nodded and strolled past the desk behind her and into the oversized doorway.

"President Stroud," Bronson announced. He entered the stately office, slowing to a halt in the center, just at the edge of the URA seal emblazoned on the carpet under his feet.

The President, engrossed in an electronic brief displayed on his data screen, looked up fleetingly at Bronson.

"Director Fox," he said in a monotone voice, as both men eyed the secretary.

She turned, exited the doorway and pulled the door closed quietly behind her.

"*Bronson* - wonderful to see you," the President gushed warmly, springing from his desk and extending a hand to Fox.

"Devlin, it's been a while. How's the family?" Bronson replied tersely, accepting the President's welcome with a single shake of his hand.

"Fine, fine..." He completed the handshake and then sat back down into his chair. "You and the missus have to come up for a weekend soon," he continued bantering, grabbing his reading glasses from the top drawer of his desk. "The ladies can go take in a spa day while we catch up on the golf course."

Bronson nodded quietly, his hands folded neatly in front of him as he stood.

"You wanted to see me about the budget?" Bronson asked impatiently, not veiling the fact that he wanted to get to the heart of the conversation.

"I spoke to Hanley," the President said, glaring with concern at Bronson, while pointing with one finger at his data display, the stem of his reading glasses perched at the tip of his lower lip. "What am I supposed to do with *this*, Bronson? This is an *awful* lot of money you're asking for..."

"I *assume* he shared the latest forecasts with you?"

The President nodded silently while pursing his lips. "Still, requests like these don't go *unnoticed* in front of the GA... *especially* when there's such a large overage from your last budget," he said while shaking his head in doubt.

"Perhaps I need to explain the *need* for the extra funding..." Bronson began to explain, his air of condescension becoming apparent.

"Nonsense, Fox. You know *I* understand your data," Stroud argued. He stood from his chair and paced to the window. "But a sanitized version of the business case won't fly very far in their eyes, Bronson. You *know* that," he chastised, peering around to make eye contact with Bronson.

"I don't know what *else* you want me to tell you, Devlin. We *need* this funding. This project *relies* on it. And given the... *circumstances*...I would think my sincerity in this matter is plainly evident," Bronson replied flatly.

The President stood in silence and pensive thought, as he stared out the window at the mountains in the distance.

"When I took the oath of this office two years ago, the people of this Republic entrusted *me* with ensuring their stability. And that *includes* the economics of running this government..."

"And your numbers have never been higher, Devlin. You should be proud of that fact. But *you* should also realize *that* should be your catalyst to try to make this deal. Strike while the iron is hot, as they say," suggested Bronson patronizingly.

The President snorted, as he continued to take in the majestic scenery outside the window.

"You want *me* to go in front of the GA with an 1800% increase to your budget, citing a Top Secret, *Omega-level project* that neither *they*, nor the *citizens* of the URA, get to know about? *That's political suicide, Fox!*" Stroud cried in a lower, hushed tone, turning fully to face Fox.

"Mr. President," Bronson admonished. "Surely *you* are not going to let *politics* be the deciding factor in a crucial moment like this...*are you?*"

"What is my recourse, Bronson? Turn my back on the GA *and* my party?" Stroud replied, holding up both hands in frustration.

"Or turn your back on the *people* of this great Republic?" Bronson responded in turn.

Stroud looked away and shook his head in disbelief, as he glanced out the window.

"Devlin...*Mr. President*...if I may be so bold as to suggest... *EBP*?" Bronson offered coyly.

The President remained silent for a moment, turning his head slightly sideways at Bronson's suggestion.

"Emergency Budget..." Bronson continued.

"...*Provision*..." Stroud interjected.

"It *would* be the quickest path to resolution," Bronson reaffirmed, staring at the President's back with a telling grin on his face.

"I certainly wouldn't be making myself a hero in the GA's eyes..."

"*Aspire to be a hero than merely appear one*," Bronson parried.

"*Gracian*?" Stroud queried, turning his head in Bronson's direction again.

"Your classical education serves you well, Devlin," Bronson responded sharply with a semi-bow. "Mr. President, you can't afford *not* to be that hero," he observed.

The President turned his head again, and then bowed it in thought. "I'll do what I can, Bronson. But I can't *promise* anything."

"That's *all* I ask, Mr. President," Bronson said with a sly smile.

Present day (2084)...

"Keep it moving, the boss wants you up there *now*..." Josef, a brutish Syndicate thug, ordered in a thick middle-Eur-Asian accent. He shoved at the back of Brig, making him lunge forward and almost face-first onto the concrete steps of the stairwell in which they ascended.

"Hard for me to go fast with my ankles tied together, buddy," Brig quipped in a muffled tone from underneath the dark, cloth hood that covered his head.

"Watch the backtalk, or you'll find yourself flyin' out a window *before* I getcha' there..." Josef replied with a growl, grabbing the back of Brig's shirt to prevent him from falling.

As the two men exited the stairwell and entered the long hallway that led to Bruno Muldoon's residential suite, Castor suddenly squeezed his massive frame out from a nearby room.

Castor pushed his hand forcefully into Josef's chest, stopping the man instantly and making him almost lose his balance.

"Just deliverin' the prisoner to the boss, Cas..." Josef informed Castor.

"Boss can't see him *now*," Castor replied, pointing back towards one of the rooms behind him. "He's got another... *appointment* right now that can't wait."

Brig rotated his head slightly to hear Castor's voice. *That sounds a lot like Pollux...* he thought, *...not good.*

"So what do I *do* with him?" Josef asked, pointing at Brig and grasping his arm tightly.

"Take him back to the holding room, *idiot...*" Castor quipped sarcastically, forcefully turning Josef around by one arm and pushing him back into the top of the stairwell, along with Brig.

"*Your* lucky day," Josef muttered to Brig, as they exited the stairwell on the floor below. "Now where the Hell was that holding room..." he mumbled to himself aloud, stopping and scratching his head, staring at the various closed doors along the hallway.

Not having paid much attention to where he had previously retrieved Brig, and not being particularly bright, Josef shook his head and silently selected one.

He pushed Brig into the darkened room and forced him onto a chair, re-locking the chains around his ankles and wrists to it.

"Now don't you *go* anywhere," he taunted with an evil chuckle, as he spun and left the room, slamming the door shut behind him.

Brig sat in silence for a few moments, sighing heavily. He attempted to move his arms and legs, but realized he was bound too tightly to attempt an escape.

"Damn, man...can't you at *least* take the hood off?" he hollered loudly, his words echoing off the walls of the relatively empty room.

"They like their hoods, that's for certain..." a voice with a deep, British accent said calmly from the other end of the room.

Brig turned his head in the direction of the voice.

"*Mr. Fox?*" Brig asked hopefully.

"Not who you are looking for, I'm afraid," the man replied.

"You Syndicate?" Brig queried curiously.

"No, and judging from the sounds of your entry, I could guess neither are *you.*"

"Can you untie me?"

"Sorry...chained, just as you are," the man said.

"So *you're* not Syndicate then, I assume..."

"My instincts tell me that I shouldn't answer that query. After all, *you* could just be one of them trying to get *me* to talk, now couldn't you?" the man said smartly.

"We're both in the dark, chained to chairs, with bags over our heads..." Brig replied sarcastically, "...somehow I think our *instincts* aren't the sharpest right now."

"Well put," the man said with a chuckle. "I suppose I should be pleased that I'm able to talk to *anyone* other than those buffoons. My name is William...William Bryce."

"Nice to meet you, William. I'm Brigadier Stroud," Brig replied warmly. "I'd shake your hand...but, well...*you know*," he added with his own chuckle.

"Quite," Bryce retorted. "Stroud. Uncommon name. Not perhaps a relation to..."

"...One and the same," Brig interjected with an air of exasperation.

"How does one such as *your* lot end up in a spot like *this?*"

"Sticking my nose where it doesn't belong, I guess," Brig said after a brief pause.

"Looking for this Fox fellow that you mentioned earlier?"

"Something like that. Although I'm not sure any more that I'm not just chasing a *ghost*..." Brig reflected.

"There could be *worse* things I suppose than chasing ghosts," William observed.

"Judging by your accent, I guess you're not from around these parts?"

"From the East Coast, actually. Since the walls came tumbling down, as they say," William mused, "You'd be surprised at how many came across the pond to be here."

"So how did *you* end up out West chained up in a dark room?"

"Blokes here think they've got themselves a high-ranking member of the Reformation in their hands," William replied with an air of jest.

Brig snorted and shook his head in the darkness. "Blind leading the blind around here I take it."

"They're *not* wrong..." William parried quickly.

"Really? You guys *still* exist?" Brig replied with incredulity. "I thought that group died out in the late seventies..."

"Not quite," William corrected. "We've had to take things a bit *underground* after some of the more...*high profile incidents* didn't work in our favor. But make no mistake, the Reformation is *alive* and *well.*"

Brig pondered silently to himself. "Well, maybe if you just play dumb and don't let them know who you are, they'll let you go?"

"No, no," William laughed lightly, "I'm afraid *that's* not going to happen. These chums never let their hostages go. They just keep them around to make an example and then...well..."

"*Oh...*" Brig said quietly.

"But I suppose we've been making enough of a nuisance of ourselves lately that they need to make an example of someone. What is it that *you* do, Brigadier?" William asked, changing the subject to lighten the mood.

"Used to be in the EWs..."

"EWs? Oh...*commandos*, yeah?"

"Yeah," Brig confirmed flatly. "But just sort of been...*existing* since then."

"Ever think of allying yourself with a group like ours? We could certainly use someone with your experience."

"I guess I never really gave it much thought. I'm not sure what good I would be. My heart really wouldn't be in it. No offense," Brig replied honestly.

The two men stopped talking momentarily and sat in silence, as the sound of a pair of muffled voices from outside the door caught their attention.

"Well, I suppose my clock has all but ticked out," William observed.

"William...*you're not afraid to die?*" Brig asked.

"*Everyone's* afraid to die, Brigadier," William imparted stoically. "But it's the name in which you offer your final tally sheet that counts...and makes it all worth the while. The battle *will* rage on after me, after all..."

"You're a brave man, William."

"Brigadier...should you ever need our assistance, we have contacts that frequent local pubs all around the Southwest. Simply tell someone that you are willing to 'Fight the Good Fight' and tell them that I sent you..."

"Thanks for the company, William. Good luck to you..." Brig replied, as the sound of the door unlocking from the outside echoed throughout the room.

"And Godspeed to you, Brigadier Stroud," William replied, and then was forcefully pulled from his chair and out of the room by Josef.

Bruno Muldoon sat at the table quietly, his eyes closed and his hands folded under his chin, as he pensively mulled his upcoming meeting. He was quite aware of the unease that he inflicted on his employees and enemies alike when he feigned disinterest in their topics by partaking in a lavish dinner.

"Bruno, thanks for seeing me on such short notice..." Clive called out, as Castor showed him into the room and closed the door behind them, taking up his usual spot at the wall next to the doorframe.

"*Bruno?*" Muldoon mocked in a surprised tone. He sipped at a glass of wine, and then tucked his dinner napkin into his collar. "My family and closest friends call me Bruno. Do you consider yourself one or the other?" he asked, turning his head towards Clive with a raised eyebrow.

"Neither..." Clive responded tersely.

"Then as my *employee* I would ask that you show some respect."

"I'm *not* your employee, either..." Clive corrected.

"Is that so? Then tell me, Mr. Underwood. Exactly what *is* our relationship?"

"We both know I'm more of a...*freelance consultant.* I provide you services when needed. And in exchange your goons leave me alone. But that doesn't *make* me your employee," Clive explained casually.

Muldoon silently nodded his head and raised his eyebrows in educated surprise, as he picked up his dinner utensils and began to saw into a piece of pork that came from the roasted pig in the center of the table.

"So, Mr. Underwood...what is it that just absolutely could not wait?" Muldoon took a small bite of the meat from his fork.

"Could we talk without Castor here in the room?" Clive asked, pointing his finger over his shoulder at the big man.

"I'm *not* leavin' you in here alone with the boss, egghead," Castor said pointedly from behind him.

Muldoon turned his eyes to Clive, and then looked back at his dinner.

"Castor, leave us for a few minutes. My safety is not in jeopardy with Mr. Underwood," Muldoon ordered nonchalantly.

Castor shot Clive a stern look and then stepped out of the room, closing the door quietly behind him.

"Proceed, Mr. Underwood." Muldoon took another sip of his wine and then began to carve at another piece of pork on his plate.

"I've come across some...*information* that I believe would be mutually beneficial to both of us," Clive began to explain.

"I believe what you *meant* to say, Mr. Underwood," Muldoon corrected, holding a piece of meat aloft with his fork, "is that you came into possession of the material that the *girl stole* from me..."

"*How* I got the information is irrelevant to this conversation, Muldoon," Clive said matter-of-factly.

Clive hobbled to the twin French doors that opened out onto the terrace, and peered out at the view of the mountains in the distance, his limp apparent as he passed Muldoon's table.

"A beautiful view, isn't it?" Muldoon said coyly. "A pity about your leg, Mr. Underwood. However, I hear the Russian surgeons did an outstanding job on it."

Clive did not respond. He tightened his lips as he gritted his teeth, while still staring out the doors.

"But then, you're *not* Russian...*are you*, Mr. Underwood? Truly remarkable how *that* worked out," Muldoon hissed with a wicked smile, and then shoved another bite of food into his mouth.

"We're getting off topic," Clive said flatly.

"Indeed," Muldoon replied. "Mr. Underwood, have you stopped to think of why I wouldn't just shoot you right now. And then just have Castor and Pollux ransack your...*home*...and bring the material to me anyway?" He joyfully popped a roasted potato into his mouth.

"You *could*..." Clive answered knowingly. "And then you could also *try* to figure out what the information was, but it would be useless without me and my...*talents*...to help you get to it."

"And you're confident *you're* the only one with...*talents*...left that could do it?"

"I *know* I am..." Clive retorted immediately, turning to face Muldoon. "Otherwise, why else wouldn't you just keep me under close watch here like one of your lackeys?"

Muldoon chuckled, took a sip of wine and then sat back against his chair, a wild smile on his face.

"*Touché!* Although I would hardly consider you a lackey, Mr. Underwood. But rest assured...we know *everything* you do." he said, the smile fading from his face. He focused on his food once more. "So this...*information*...that you have. You are certain it is something that I would want?"

"It's something you *need*," Clive corrected.

"I'm *rarely* in need..."

"*This* will change your mind."

"I'm still listening. Why, I don't know," Muldoon said dismissively, as he sipped his wine.

"*Weaponry*..." Clive said and then waited for Muldoon's reaction.

"I *have* weaponry, Mr. Underwood," Muldoon replied disinterestedly. "What else do you have for me that is worthy of my time?"

"I'm sure your Rippers and small, automatic handhelds help you keep the general populace in line," Clive replied mockingly. "But I'm talking about *advanced* weaponry. Things that you didn't *know* existed."

Muldoon snorted his lack of interest.

"You said it yourself. What we have now does the job superbly," Muldoon replied, waving a floret of broccoli in the air next to him, and then shoved it in his mouth.

"You're thinking too small," Clive insisted. "What if I told you I could put weaponry in your possession that wouldn't only ensure your stronghold on this continent – but also make your organization one to be feared *globally*?"

Muldoon put his silverware down and folded his hands under his chin. As he stared at Clive and chewed a mouthful of food, he raised an eyebrow and nodded his head as a silent prod to continue.

"I'm talking zero-charge plasma rifles. Negative field ion grenades. Nuke fusion rail guns. Dark energy suppression cannons..." Clive said slowly and deliberately.

"Almost as if from a *comic book*..." Muldoon quipped, still showing only partial interest, as he wiped his mouth.

"But the lethality is *real*..."

"And this technology exists? And more importantly is still *functional* after..." Muldoon asked, peering up momentarily at Clive.

"...the *Event*. I would think so. The DMST tended to keep stuff like this pretty well protected from things like that..."

"Alright, Mr. Underwood. You've presented the stakes – at least for *my* part of the deal," Muldoon said. He held up his hand and sat back in his chair. "Now...what is this all worth to *you*?"

Clive took a deep breath and clenched his jaw tightly, as he glared down at the ground.

"You're *hungry*..." Muldoon said in a low tone, his eyes flattening into small slits as he gazed at Clive.

"No, not particularly..."

"I can see it in your eyes, Mr. Underwood," Muldoon continued, sitting up and beginning to eat once again. "You're willing to trade the *world* for something that means *more* than that to you...aren't you?"

Clive remained silently still, making Muldoon look up from his plate to see that he was staring intently at him.

"Well?" Muldoon prodded.

"I want you to let Jessica go," Clive said boldly.

Muldoon crumpled his eyebrows and frowned.

"Jessica is *not* a prisoner, Mr. Underwood. She is free to leave any time she pleases," he informed Clive matter-of-factly.

"That couldn't be *further* from the truth," Clive replied with a stern expression. "I can see it in her eyes..."

"And how long have you been interested in my...*domestic situation*?" Muldoon asked pointedly, wiping his chin with his napkin.

"I'm not. I'm simply offering you a deal. You are a businessman, after all."

Muldoon nodded his head subtly at the suggestion, as he looked away and took a deep breath. "And you're asking for one of my *prized* possessions..."

"In your valuation, what I'm offering you is worth ten Jessicas," Clive said, tensely gritting his teeth at having to make such a revolting comparison.

"You intrigue me, Mr. Underwood. Most men would have asked for wealth, property, possessions," Muldoon said with curiosity, staring at Clive without blinking.

"I told you...this isn't about *me*," Clive reiterated firmly.

"And yet it *is*..." Muldoon hissed.

"I just want her to have the freedom to make her own choices."

"How noble of you," Muldoon said mockingly. "Look around you, Mr. Underwood. Do you think she suffers from *need*? What do *you* have to offer her that she doesn't already have here?"

"It's not what she needs...but what she *wants*," Clive retorted with a noticeable growl.

Muldoon pushed his chair from under the table and stood

upright. As he strode to the double doors that led out to the terrace with his hands folded behind his back, he shot Clive a menacing, penetrating glare as he passed.

"Do you know the location of this equipment?" Muldoon asked deliberately.

"I'm fairly certain I know where it is."

"And *where* would that be?"

"It doesn't work that way..."

"Mr. Underwood, as a...businessman, as you put it...I need assurance that you would live up to your part of any bargain that we would potentially make."

"I have no reason to lie to you, Muldoon," Clive said flatly.

"Still, you understand my quandary," Muldoon added. "Would you be open to having one of the Webbs accompany you to verify the stakes?"

"Not *them*..." Clive insisted adamantly. "...I want Chekushkin to come with me."

Muldoon turned his head and glared in curious suspicion at Clive, and then rotated his head back to look out at the desert sky.

"Do I need to give you a few minutes to think about it?" Clive asked sarcastically.

"You've presented *your* offer, Mr. Underwood," Muldoon said after a silent moment of thought. "I'll take it under advisement and if I'm interested...we'll talk again. You may go now..."

Clive pursed his lips as he stared at Muldoon's back, and then while shaking his head in frustration, left the room.

"You're playing a *very* dangerous game, Mr. Underwood," Muldoon said softly, as he began to pace the room, his chin tucked into his chest, "...but we'll see who controls the stakes in this negotiation."

36:
Your Time Is Gonna Come

Present day (2084)...

"Next one for ya', boss," Castor droned, as he pushed Brig into Muldoon's suite; the latter still with the hood over his head and hands roped together.

Muldoon, gazing pensively at a piece of art on the wall with his hand in his chin, did not react.

"Castor," Muldoon said nonchalantly. "Has your brother returned from taking...our *guest*...back to his place?"

Ah, brother... Brig thought, the realization that he had mistaken Castor for Pollux for quite some time.

"No, boss. But he should be back in a couple'a hours," Castor replied, forcing Brig down onto a chair.

"Did he finish...*taking out the trash* before he left?" Muldoon asked pointedly.

"Uh, yeah, boss," Castor replied. He spun and took up his usual position just inside the doorway of the suite.

After a few awkward, silent moments, Muldoon turned from admiring the artwork and began to pace towards Brig.

"Mr...*Sampson*," Muldoon cooed furtively, approaching Brig and leaning towards him, placing one hand on the table next to him for balance. "You've been a *very* bad boy."

He yanked the hood from Brig's head. Standing upright, Muldoon folded his hands behind his back and tilted his head at Brig.

"Do you *know* who I am?" Muldoon asked.

"Don't have a clue..." Brig replied immediately, resting his gaze upon Muldoon.

"Bruno Muldoon..." Muldoon hissed. "Ring any bells *now?*"

Brig frowned and then shook his head once again. "No, not that I know of. Should I know you?" he asked with a caustic air.

"How should I put this," Muldoon said, laughing lightly, rolling his eyes upwards at the ceiling in mock thought, and tapping his index finger against his cheek. "You've been...*stepping on my toes* quite a bit lately," he gibed, dropping his hands behind his back again. "Impeding my employees. Breaking into places you have no business being in..." he said and then stared at him intensely. "And for all I know, playing a hand in destroying several of my properties."

"You got the wrong guy, I think," Brig replied dismissively.

"Have I?" Muldoon said, mimicking surprise in his tone. "It seems your mere presence here is *evidence* of what I speak."

Brig stoically held his tongue. He shook his head subtly. "I don't know you, why would I lie?" he asked, turning his head in Muldoon's direction.

Muldoon stopped and pushed aside the collar of Brig's jacket to reveal the EW insignia tattoo that had been partially visible on his neck until now.

"That's an...*interesting* marking," Muldoon said prepensely, as he stood upright again. "I know *another* who has the same."

"There was a whole *squadron* of us at one time that had the same..."

"I believe you know *this* one, however," Muldoon replied cunningly. "You're friends with Mr. Underwood, are you not?"

Brig hesitated and averted his eyes from Muldoon. "I knew *of* him. Doesn't mean we were friends or anything," Brig said after a few seconds.

Muldoon shot Brig a glare of skepticism as he began to pace in front of him.

"And how does it feel to know that your friend is the *reason* why you are here? That you've been...*betrayed*?" he asked Brig pointedly.

Brig glared up at Muldoon, who smiled wickedly without looking his way as he passed.

"And what comes to mind when I say '*Fox*'?" Muldoon asked precipitously.

"...*Fox*?" Brig repeated hesitantly.

"Yes, Fox, Fox, Fox, Fox..." Muldoon said playfully, almost as if in song, while he twirled a hand in the air in rhythm with each syllable. "What does it *mean* to you?"

"Um...a small, furry, red animal?"

"Oh *come* now, Mr. Sampson," Muldoon castigated, "...you're not being very forthright."

"I don't know what you want from me," Brig conceded.

"Are you...*Reformation?*" Muldoon asked, whispering into Brig's ear as he leaned over.

"They still around?" Brig asked with an air of feigned ignorance.

Muldoon chortled deep in his throat as he walked past Brig and stood behind him. "One last question for now, Mr. Sampson. How do you know *Jessica?*"

"...*Who?*" Brig replied hesitantly.

"Jessica...*my wife,*" Muldoon elaborated.

"I...I don't know who you're talking about..." Brig stammered unintentionally.

"Castor..." Muldoon called out.

"Yeah, boss," Castor replied, poking his enormous head inside the door, having left the room moments earlier to take care of another task.

"Take our guest down to one of the holding rooms. And feed him some dinner, we're not *animals* here."

As Castor strode past his boss to pick up Brig from his chair, Muldoon turned to him once again as he stopped in the doorway.

"And let me know when Pollux arrives, I'm certain that he may want to have a word or two with Mr. Sampson - isn't that right?" Muldoon said pointedly at Brig, who ignored the comment and remained silent, as Castor yanked him from the chair.

Farther down the hall, the door to Muldoon's residential suite opened. Josef, standing a few meters away, flinched in surprise.

"Josef," Jessica said quietly, poking her head out of the suite. "Have you seen Yemi?"

"No, ma'am," Josef responded with a subtle headshake.

"Can you go downstairs and find him for me?" she asked politely.

Josef turned his head towards Jess. "I'm sorry, Mrs. M – you know I can't leave my post."

Jess pursed her lips, nodded her head and closed the door, disappearing back into the room.

A few moments later, Muldoon strolled the hall towards his suite, reaching inside his jacket pocket for his keys to unlock the door. Before he finished inserting the key into the lock, however, the lumbering form of Castor, exiting the stairwell half the length of the hallway away, caught his attention.

"Boss, I need to speak to you," Castor called out, as he and Yemi, the guard from outside of Brig's holding room earlier, quickly strode towards Muldoon.

"What is it, Castor. It's been a long day already," Muldoon replied tiredly. Josef looked on at the three from his position against the wall.

"Yemi here has something he needs to *tell* you," Castor informed him.

Jess slowly filled the small cocktail glass with vodka, her hands visibly shaking as she set the bottle down on the bar.

"Where the *Hell* is he?" she muttered under her breath. She took a small sip of the drink and set the glass down.

"He'll come...*right?*" she asked herself. "I mean, he has to. They were *best friends*. Oh my God, what if I'm too late..." she said, wringing her hands together. "Get a hold of yourself, Jess," she cursed. She put both hands on her head and closed her eyes.

Opening them again, she caught her reflection in the mirror and turned fully to look at it, staring deeply at herself.

"What are you *doing?*" she said frustratingly, shaking her head in disgust, as tears began to stream down her cheeks. "How can you do this?" Jess cried aloud at her reflection, while wiping away the tears on the shoulder fabric of her blouse.

She closed her eyes tightly and tried to calm herself.

It's the right thing for him... she reaffirmed. *It's the only thing.*

The tears began to flow heavier as she sobbed lightly into the palm of her hand, and turned her head to peer around the room.

From just outside in the hallway, she could hear the familiar voice of her husband, Bruno. Turning back to the mirror, she closed her eyes once again and took several, deep breaths.

As Josef disappeared into the stairwell, Muldoon turned to Castor.

"So, you'll deliver the message *personally?*" Muldoon quizzed.

"Yeah, boss. No problem," Castor responded firmly.

"Good..." Muldoon rotated away from Castor and placed his hand on the doorknob. "Oh, and Castor...your sidearm, please," he ordered, holding out his hand in anticipation.

"Uh...sure, boss," Castor replied with a confused tone, pulling the gun from the holster under his arm and handing the weapon, butt-first, to Muldoon.

Muldoon grasped the gun, cocked back the action to look into the barrel, clicked it back in place and then shoved it into the back of his belt under his suit jacket. Then, giving Castor a knowing glance, he entered the room.

Castor reassumed his post outside of the room next to the door, his hands folded behind his back.

"My darling," Muldoon gushed, as he strode through the alcove of the room entrance, and into the main living area to find Jessica sitting on the couch, her legs folded off to her side.

Jess, anticipating Muldoon's entry, had already wiped the tears from her face completely and was holding her drink at her side.

"Hitting the drink a little *early* today, hmm?" He strolled slowly past the couch and took up a position standing next to the bar, placing one hand lightly on the edge.

"Yeah...just a little...nervous, I guess," Jess responded, shying from making eye contact with him.

"Nervous? Why...whatever for, my dear?"

"I...I don't know. It's nothing I suppose. Just a little on edge lately," she said, as she took another large sip.

"*Indeed,*" Muldoon hissed, staring wickedly at Jess.

"I just think that I...we...need to get away from this..."

"*This?*" he repeated back to her immediately.

"Yes...*this,*" she affirmed, holding her hands out and pointing around her. "This stress, this *life...*"

"And where would you have...*us*...go, Jessica?"

"Anywhere but here. We haven't been anywhere but the

Southwest in years, and I just think it would suit us both to get away from it all," she offered, peering up at him. "It would help us *both*...I would think."

Muldoon smiled coldly and stepped away from the bar, holding his hands behind his back. "Your loyalty to me has *always* warmed my heart."

"I know what's in *both* our best interests..."

"Do you..." he said flatly. He paced past her and stopped just behind the couch on which she sat. "And how would you explain why *you* were in the holding room talking to Mr. Sampson earlier?" he said purposefully, glaring past her and out at the desert sky.

"I...I don't know...I wasn't..." she stammered, as she tensed up, avoiding making eye contact with her husband.

"From what I'm told," Muldoon continued, "you were plotting an *escape*." He strolled past the couch and approached the window, glancing out briefly before turning back to face her.

"His...or *yours*?" he asked, squinting slightly, as if he was staring through her.

"I..." Jess started to respond, but then sighed and closed her eyes for a second. "I knew him from before...*before I met you.*"

"And how does *Mr. Underwood* play into this plot?"

Jess did not respond, not having thought that far ahead when she had visited Brig. "He...doesn't..." she finally added.

"*LIES!*" Muldoon bellowed, making Jess flinch in terror. "Of all of the betrayals that I've withstood over my years, this – *THIS*, Jessica, cuts the deepest!" he screamed wildly through his teeth.

"But I didn't betray..."

"Enough! I spared your life. I *gave* you a life. I've given you *everything*. And this is how you repay me?" he preached in an incredulous rage.

"I'm sorry...I just heard the name and I wanted...I was curious to find out why he was here..." she sobbed, quickly getting up from the couch and approaching Muldoon, grasping his upper arm lightly to turn him towards her.

Muldoon tugged his arm back sharply, rotated and pushed her away. "How am I going to deal with this, Jessica?"

Jess choked down a sob and wiped the tears from her face. "Please don't do anything to them just because I..."

"I will deal with *them* soon enough, my dear. But *you*," he said, his tone lowering to a vicious snarl, as he stopped and stood with his back to her, "...what am I to do with someone that was my closest ally...someone that has betrayed me in the *worst* way."

Jess covered her mouth while tucking one arm tightly under the other, and cried silently.

Muldoon reached under his jacket and into the back of his belt, extracting the gun that Castor had given to him moments earlier, and held it down to his side.

"Please...*please don't, James,*" Jess whimpered, backing up and onto one of the couch cushions.

"*James...*" He sneered coldly. "You've left me no choice, Jessica."

Castor stood stoically against the wall adjacent to Muldoon's suite in silence, listening intently to the muffled sounds of the argument commencing within.

Two gunshots, emanating from inside the room, sliced the silence in the hall.

Castor rotated his head towards the room and then stomped down the hallway, passing Josef as he opened the door to the stairwell.

"Josef, take my post..." Castor said to the smaller man, as he walked past. "I'll be back in a few hours."

37:
When the Levee Breaks

Present day (2084)...

Small clouds of exhaled breath filled the chilled air, as Clive slid open the door to his workshop. It had been a long day for him, and a tasking one, having played a dangerous hand with Muldoon just hours earlier.

The grueling ride on the back of Pollux's latest retro-bike from New Vegas to his workshop in Flagstaff wore him out physically, and his mind was exhausted from the anticipation of what Muldoon's next move might be.

As he closed the door and locked it, turning to head to his cot for the night, a knock once again suddenly made him stop and shake his head in frustration.

He slid the door back open with a heavy sigh.

The large form of Pollux's brother, Castor filled the doorway.

"*Castor?*" Clive asked with a confused tone and a yawn. "What are you doing here this time of night?"

"Got somethin' to *tell* ya, Underwood," Castor said gruffly, as he stood in the doorway.

Clive, fully expecting the large man to push past him and enter the workshop as he normally did, was somewhat surprised that Castor remained standing outside of his door awaiting an invite to come in.

"Well...you *can* come in," Clive said, stepping aside and motioning inward with one hand.

Nodding politely, Castor entered and passed Clive, who squinted in skepticism and then slid the door closed.

"So...what's up *this* time?" Clive asked hesitantly.

"You know..." Castor began, wringing his hands in front of him, "you and me, we've never been...you know, *close* or nothin'..."

Clive blinked in confusion, not accustomed to seeing a human side of either Webb twin.

"...But," Castor continued, "...somethin' happened after you left that...I thought you oughta' know about."

Clive shook his head and shrugged his shoulders subtly. "I don't..."

"It ain't no secret around there about you and the boss's wife..."

"What? That's *ridiculous*..." Clive defended, waving off Castor's comments.

"No...let me finish," Castor interjected. "Sometimes the boss...he gets too comfortable with anyone he sees as loyal to him and all..." Castor said, obviously fumbling for the right words to explain himself properly. "And sometimes see...he doesn't see the whole picture, ya' know? And things can happen right in front of him without him even knowin' it. *Like you and...*"

"Okay...I *get* it..." Clive interrupted, not wanting to hear Castor continue to describe his relationship with Jessica Muldoon. "Go on."

"Well...after you left. Her and the boss, see..." Castor stammered, "...they got in this argument, and I think...he *knows* about you two..."

"Castor. What *happened?*" Clive asked pointedly in a serious tone. He stared intensely at the big man as he took a step closer.

"He...*killed* her," Castor said hesitantly, continually breaking eye contact with Clive.

Clive snorted and shook his head. "*He* put you up to this, Cas? This some sort of bluff?"

Castor, showing an uncommon remorse and even rarer emotion, slowly shook his head.

"It's no joke, Underwood," Castor said flatly, blinking several times with a painful expression.

Shaking his head fervently and pursing his lips, Clive scratched the back of his neck with one hand. "You expect me to *believe* this bull, Castor? Come'on, man. This is...this is just crazy."

"Yemi and me...we carried the body out for him..." Castor replied, and then broke eye contact as he glared down at the floor. "I'm *real* sorry, Clive," he added somberly.

Clive shifted his weight backward and frowned.

The showing of emotion by Castor was odd, but having him hear Castor call him out by his first name, for the first time *ever*, tied a knot in his gut. Was he telling the truth?

Clive turned his back on Castor and paced towards the back of the workshop, as he continued to rub the back of his neck with his hand. He stopped and pondered the odd reality of it all for a moment, as he stared at the cot along the back wall.

"Take me back there..." Clive said abruptly in a low, harsh tone.

"*Huh?*" Castor asked with a grunt.

"Take me back to Vegas. I want to see him...I want to see Muldoon," Clive demanded, spinning around to face Castor, his face flushing red with anger.

"Now come on, Underwood. You know that ain't *smart*," Castor warned. "And you know I ain't gonna let you hurt the boss, no matter *what* happened tonight..."

"This isn't about *you*, Cas. I just wanna hear it from *his* mouth. I want him to tell *me* what he's done!" Clive barked, pointing angrily at the door. "This has gone far enough..."

He pushed past Castor and grabbed for the handle of the door, sliding it open and walking out into the darkness outside. Castor reluctantly shook his head and followed him.

The door to Muldoon's suite flung open, thumping and reverberating loudly against the wall.

Clive, his face crimson with anger, burst into the room. Castor followed quickly behind him, panting breathlessly while lumbering through the doorway and slamming it shut behind him.

"What the *Hell* have you done, you son of a bitch!" Clive shouted, doing his best to dash across the room towards Muldoon.

Muldoon sat in a cushioned chair facing the door with a smug look, his arms crossed over his chest, as if he were awaiting Clive's grand entrance.

Pollux appeared from a door leading to one of the adjacent suites, and quickly put himself in-between Clive and Muldoon.

"*Easy*, egghead," Pollux said gruffly, stopping Clive in his tracks with a single finger to his chest.

"Why, if it isn't my *favorite* poker player," Muldoon cooed, casually turning his eyes in Clive's direction.

"Pol, let him talk," Castor said to Pollux, pulling the bigger man's upper arm and leading him away from the confrontation.

"What did you do...*what did you do?*" Clive repeated

R. JAMES STEVENS

maniacally, his eyes wide with passion, as he stopped a meter in front of Muldoon.

"Mr. Underwood, I'm certain that I don't know *what* you are referring to," Muldoon replied with a coy smile and one raised eyebrow.

"This wasn't part of the deal, damn it!" Clive cursed, as he pointed angrily at Muldoon.

"*Wasn't* it, now?" Muldoon taunted.

"You were gonna let her go...*that* was the deal!" Clive screamed, the pitch and tone of his voice sharply rising with his emotions.

"I took your proposal to heart, Mr. Underwood," Muldoon explained. He looked nonchalantly down at the tips of his fingers. "And I decided to do *exactly* what you asked – I set her free. I'm a man of my word if I'm *nothing*..."

Clive's nostrils flared, as he gnashed his teeth together in annoyed amazement.

"Not like this! That's *not* what I asked for..." Clive shouted, his voice breaking.

"Tomato...*Tom-ah-to*," Muldoon replied suavely. He pushed himself up from his chair and brushed off his suit jacket. "Besides," he continued, gazing at Clive with a satisfied half-smile, "...you didn't really think I was going to *let* you walk away with my lovely wife of five years, now...*did you*? What kind of husband would that make *me*?"

"I'll kill you...you bastard!" Clive yelled, lunging for Muldoon.

Castor, in a surprisingly agile move, yanked Clive by the back of his collar, turned him around and grabbed him by both shoulders.

"I told you this ain't the way to go, Underwood," Castor growled into Clive's face.

Clive turned and stared blankly at Muldoon, Castor still gripping his shoulders tightly to prevent the former Epsilon from reaching his boss.

"How could you? How could you be so cold – she was *innocent* in all of this..." Clive said tearfully.

"Judgment...*from you*?" Muldoon replied with feigned shock. "Thou shalt not covet thy neighbor's wife, Mr. Underwood," he said wickedly into Clive's ear, as he passed by him. "But before you go all 'Old Testament' on me, I'm going to throw you a bone...so to speak."

386

Muldoon strode past Clive and stopped in front of the bar, grabbing a cocktail glass and a bottle of vodka.

"You see, Mr. Underwood," Muldoon explained, filling his glass with the clear liquid, "yours wasn't the *only* indiscretion that forced my hand. Pollux..."

Muldoon snapped his fingers as he sipped his drink.

Pollux swung open the door to the adjacent suite abruptly, and then pulled a man with a hood over his head and hands tied at his front with rope, into the room. He forcefully shoved the man into a chair at the center of the room and stepped back to stand against the wall with an intent glare towards Clive.

"Who's this?" Clive asked with disinterest, wiping his eyes dry with his sleeve.

Muldoon nodded his head silently at Pollux.

Pollux snagged the hood from the man's head.

Clive took a silent, deep breath and squeezed his lips shut tightly in anger, as Pollux revealed the mystery guest.

Brig sat in the chair, his face brutally swollen and bloody from the beatings that he had obviously endured at the hands of the Syndicate. He wore a dazed expression, barely able to keep his eyes open as he attempted to hold his head up.

As he spotted Clive, Brig painfully closed his eyes shut and coughed a stream of blood out of the corner of his mouth.

"*Sorry...*" Brig said incoherently, opening his eyes partly and staring at his friend.

Clive turned his back and rubbed his neck vigorously with one palm.

Muldoon smiled wickedly and set his drink down on the bar next to him.

"I believe you already *know* Mr. Stroud here..." Muldoon crowed maliciously. "I discovered there was a plot afoot, Mr. Underwood. A *mutinous* one at that..." Muldoon hissed. "If I had a plank, I would have had him walk it."

Muldoon stopped and rotated his head in thought for an instant, a queer half-smile wandering across his face.

"That's not a bad idea, Castor. Let's have a *plank* installed on the other end of the building...very *Caribbean*," Muldoon said delightfully to the lesser giant.

Then, Muldoon turned his focus back to Clive.

"I must say, Mr. Underwood...you don't seem to be the *least* bit surprised that he's here," Muldoon asked pointedly.

Clive did not respond. He shook his head.

"And seeing as how you and he shared similar aspirations of 'liberating' my wife," Muldoon added, tilting his head at Clive, "...it makes me wonder if *you* are somehow involved in the same plot."

"Not in the slightest..." Clive replied flatly without making eye contact with either Muldoon or Brig.

"Aye, I wish I could believe that..."

"So what do you want from me then..."

"To live up to *your* end of the bargain, of course," Muldoon shot back immediately.

"*Bargain?*" Clive retorted incredulously.

"Oh come now, Mr. Underwood...let's not be a sore loser," Muldoon cooed. "But first, you're about to bear witness to the punishment that befalls those who *betray* me."

Muldoon extracted a handgun from underneath his jacket and cocked the hammer back.

"Mr. Stroud, I hereby sentence you to death for attempted theft of my property, breaking and entering. And generally stirring up trouble," he proclaimed, holding the end of the barrel against the back of Brig's head. "And I hope that you have learned that trouble will only find *you*..."

"*Wait!*" Clive shouted from behind Muldoon.

Muldoon turned abruptly without pulling the gun away from Brig. "What is it, Mr. Underwood?" he asked in exasperation.

"Let *me* do it..." Clive droned, holding out his hand to the Syndicate boss.

"*You?*" Muldoon mocked with a grin. "You didn't list this sort of...*work*...on your resume. Why should I believe you?" he asked curiously, retracting the gun and stepping aside.

Clive, his face flowing crimson red with angry blood, gritted his teeth as he stared with intense hatred at Brig.

"Because he's had it comin' for a long time. And God knows I've had a *lot* of opportunities to pay him back for the Hell he's caused in my life," Clive explained.

"I *warned* you!" Clive yelled, stepping closer to Brig with an outstretched finger. "I told you to leave it alone. I told you it was only gonna end in disaster, but did you listen? You NEVER listen. And *now* look at what you've done! Are you happy? Look how many lives have to go down in flames because of *your* stubborn ass! It's never enough...*never* enough with you, is it?"

Clive turned away and rubbed his chin as he glared down at the floor.

"It ends...right here, *right now*," Clive said, as he ground his teeth together, the muscles at the corners of his jaw flexing wildly.

"I'm sorry, Cryp..." Brig managed to mumble, lifting his head feebly to look out of one of his eyes, the other swollen almost shut. "It wasn't...supposed to *be* this way."

"It *never* is!" Clive roared, spinning around to face Brig, grabbing the collar of his jacket and lifting him a few centimeters off the chair. "It never is, you bastard. You do your own thing...and people get hurt. People get *hurt*, Brig," Clive trailed off, his voice cracking from emotion, as he released Brig back to the chair with a thump.

"You don't understand..." Brig mumbled. He shook his head and clenched his eyes shut tightly.

"You son of a bitch!" Clive bellowed, winding and delivering a smashing backhand across Brig's cheek, making Brig's head snap abruptly to the side. "Her death is on *your* head!"

"Bravo, Mr. Underwood," Muldoon observed snidely with a mock clapping of his hands, "...I never knew you had it in you."

"You'd be *surprised* at what I've got in me..." Clive snarled in a guttural tone.

"Aye. But let's just see how *deep* that well runs," Muldoon taunted.

Muldoon crouched next to Brig.

"It looks as though you pissed off your friend something *terrible*, Mr. Stroud," he said playfully, a look of nauseating glee adorning his face. "If I were you, I'd pray to your God for a miracle - it looks as though your story has *run its course.*" He stood upright and faced away from Brig, holding the gun flat across his palm in Clive's direction.

Clive glared at the gun for a second, and then grabbed it from Muldoon's hand. He held it down at his side as he stared pensively at Brig.

Muldoon turned and stepped over to the bar.

"But not in *here*, Mr. Underwood," he said, picking up his cocktail glass and raising it to his mouth. "This sort of activity makes an awful mess, and I don't want to have to change rooms...*again.*"

After gulping the remainder of the vodka in his glass, he turned towards Clive once again.

"Mr. Chekushkin – follow Mr. Underwood outside." Muldoon said to Danil, who had entered the room unbeknownst to Clive, and was standing next to Pollux along the far wall. "And once you've ensured that he has...*completed* his task...you will accompany him to the location that Mr. Underwood has specified, so that he can fulfill *his* end of the deal," he added, waving one finger in the air, as he strode towards the other end of the room and opened the door to the adjacent suite.

Danil stepped away from the wall, opened the main door leading to the hallway, and turned to Clive.

"Whenever you are ready, Underwood," Danil said flatly.

Clive grabbed the back of Brig's hair and pulled him brutally from the chair, making Brig grunt in pain as he was forced to his feet.

Pollux, with a swift motion, whipped the hood back onto Brig's head as he passed. Then, without another word between any of them, all three men walked through the door and out into the hallway.

Clive strong-armed the steering wheel of the truck as it rumbled along over the rough patch of highway. Danil sat quietly beside him in the passenger seat, glancing over at Clive every few moments. Clive stared forward, pretending to be oblivious to his attention.

"What is the plan, Underwood," Danil asked deliberately, staring purposefully at Clive. "I do not recall Muldoon telling you to take him on a trip."

"I've gotta make a stop first, it's along the way for both... *things* that we have to do," Clive answered, keeping his eyes forward, as he was acutely aware that Danil was still eyeing him. "Figured might as well take care of both at once."

Danil nodded hesitantly, and then slowly turned his eyes forward to the road. "Back to Flagstaff?"

"*Yeah...*"

Twenty minutes later, the truck pulled to a stop in front of Clive's workshop. The engine moaned as Clive threw the gearbox into neutral and cranked the emergency brake to keep the truck in place.

Danil watched silently as Clive climbed out of the cab, hobbled across in front of the truck to the front door of the building, slid the door open and promptly disappeared inside.

Sitting back and waiting patiently, he rubbed the stubble on his chin, as he pondered Clive intentions.

Moments later, Clive re-emerged from the workshop, closed the door quickly behind him and swiftly made his way back to the truck, a small rucksack hanging at his side from one hand.

As he opened the door to the cab, Clive tossed the sack into the middle of the bench seat and climbed in after it, slamming the door behind him. He quickly forced the truck to lurch forward as he put it back into gear.

Danil stared curiously at the sack and then over at Clive. "Snack?" he asked sarcastically.

Clive glanced at Danil, then down at the sack, and then back at the road ahead while he shook his head.

"No, just something to help...take care of the *problem*," Clive replied, motioning his head towards the cargo area.

Danil fell silent for a few moments, as he stared in pensive thought at Clive once more.

"Your friend must have done something pretty awful to have you respond in this fashion, no?"

"You could say that..." Clive answered tersely.

"What could be so horrible that you would take his *life?*"

Clive did not answer, as he continued to work the steering wheel, the truck leaning slightly to the side as it rounded a quick corner.

"He ruined my life...*multiple times*," he finally responded.

Danil snorted derisively. "Where I am from, we have a saying: *'You make your own path'*. Roughly translated, of course."

"And sometimes you get pushed down that path *against* your will," Clive replied smartly.

"Maybe it is *you* that is just afraid to go down that path?" Danil stared out at the empty road ahead of them.

Clive turned his head and glared at Danil, and then focused on the road once more.

After another tedious hour of driving with both men sitting in an awkward silence, and having entered a remote area of the Arizona desert, Clive slowed the truck to a stop. The headlights sliced through the dust kicked up by the movement of the truck during its abrupt deceleration.

Clive climbed out of the cab and glared over at Danil.

"Stay here, this won't take long…" he ordered.

Danil peered at him curiously, and then re-closed his door, which he had already held half open.

Danil sat and listened, as he could hear Clive rolling up the rear cargo door, fumbling around inside the truck for a few seconds, closing the door once again, and then reappearing around the front of the truck pushing Brig.

"Stop here," Clive ordered Brig, putting a strong hand on his shoulder and forcing him down to his knees.

"You know *why* you're here?" Clive asked, standing in front of Brig, a handgun held down by his side in one hand.

Brig glared up at Clive through the strands of scraggly hair falling down around his bruised face.

"Because *you're* too much of a coward to stand up and do the *right thing*…" Brig grunted with a sneer.

Clive shook his head and smiled disdainfully. "Because you don't know when the Hell to leave things alone. *That's* why," he said angrily, motioning with the gun as he spoke.

Brig shook his head and laughed with disgust. "This was never about Jess, *you know that*…"

"Don't you say her name…*don't you say it!*" Clive screamed into Brig's ear.

"Muldoon wanted a puppet to do his work, and you let him play you like a fool…" Brig replied, showing gnashed teeth through the corner of his bashed, up-curled lip. "How do you *sleep* at night?"

Clive gritted his teeth and fondled the barrel of the handgun as he paced in front of Brig. "I've saved you *countless* times, man. And you just keep steppin' in it. And now you've crossed the line. I can't save you anymore."

"And what about all the times I've saved *you? That* don't count for anything?" Brig retorted sarcastically.

"No...it doesn't. Because you save people just to throw them back in the fire, and I've had *enough* of it..." He slowly stepped behind Brig while staring down at him intensely, cocked the hammer of the gun and pushed the cold steel into the back of Brig's neck.

"Well...this is the *end*, Brig. You only brought this on yourself," Clive said shakily.

"*You do what you gotta do...*" Brig growled slowly and deliberately, tilting his head partially to the side to see Clive out of the corner of his eye.

Clive did not respond. He lifted the gun away from Brig's neck and blinked several times, as he raised his head and glanced around the desolate, night landscape surrounding them. Then, he lowered his arm and let the gun hang at his side once again.

He turned his head and peered back at the truck, where he could see Danil watching with interest from the passenger seat.

"*Don't move...*" Clive ordered, as he quickly headed for the cab of the truck and opened the door.

Reaching inside, Clive grabbed at the pack that he had retrieved from the workshop and pulled it outside with him. He slammed the door shut behind him and slowly walked back to where Brig was still kneeling. He tossed the sack into the dirt in front of Brig's knees, where it kicked up a small cloud of dust.

Brig glanced down at the pack and then at Clive. "What the Hell's *this?*"

Without saying a word, Clive pulled a small knife out of his pocket, swiftly sliced the ropes binding Brig's hands, and then turned his back on Brig, as he stood silently looking back at Danil.

"There's enough rations in there for about two weeks..." Clive said coldly, "and enough *serum* to get you through a couple of months."

Brig leaned back onto his calves, his hands down at his sides, as he stared at the pack.

"There's a town about twenty kilometers to the south that way..." Clive continued, pointing one hand into the darkness ahead, without making eye contact with Brig. "You should be able to make it there with no problem."

Brig snorted as he looked into the darkness. "And what about *you?*"

"Don't come back, Brig. Just…keep moving and don't look back," Clive replied tensely. "I'm *warning* you…don't come back if you know what's good for you."

Then, without waiting for further response from Brig, Clive quickly strode to the truck, pulled himself into the cab and threw the truck into gear. The truck launched forward and past Brig, who was still kneeling in the sand next to the road in the darkness.

"And how does that fit into *Muldoon's* plan?" Danil asked Clive flatly, gazing casually in the mirror back at the dark shadow of Brig in the desert behind them.

"I got rid of him, that's all that *matters* in his eyes…"

"I would think *he* would disagree…"

"You owe me this much, Danil. Let it go," Clive demanded firmly, shooting Danil a stern look and then refocusing on the dark road ahead.

38:
Nothing Else Matters

Present day (2084)...

The lone man sat on a stool in the dimly lit bar. His hair, matted with dirt and crusted blood, swept behind his shoulders as he hunched over his drink.

As he sipped his drink slowly without raising his head, a voice called to him from one of the corners, where a shadowy stranger had been sitting since he had entered, watching him intently.

"You are *Underwood's* friend...*Stroud* is it?" the voice called across the room in a thick Russian accent.

Brig, having been through several of the most tortuous weeks of his life, did not turn his head, but just raised it slightly, as he looked forward and sighed.

"What...you here to take me back to Muldoon?" Brig said quietly.

"The Syndicate does not *own* me, nor am I on official Syndicate business, my friend." Danil emerged from the shadow of the corner and took up a stool next to Brig.

"Then *I* don't have time for you..." said Brig.

"It seems you have all the time in the world. You are lucky to be alive," Danil took a drink from his glass of vodka.

"Yeah..." Brig snorted, "color me Mr. Lucky..."

"To be through what you have and still be alive to talk about it. Where I am from that makes you *very* lucky..." Danil countered.

"This conversation *going* anywhere?" Brig asked, giving Danil a stern eye.

"I am just making conversation, my friend," Danil responded with a light pat on Brig's back. "I am surprised to see you back in town. As I am sure your *friend* would be...*against his wishes.*"

Brig gulped a mouthful of beer and set his glass down.

"Got some unfinished business here. And *he* doesn't make my rules," Brig said matter-of-factly.

Danil nodded his head silently. "The old man..."

Brig peered at Danil out of the corner of his eye and nodded, then glanced down at his drink. "Yeah...somethin' like that," he said quietly.

Danil sat without speaking for a few moments, as he turned his head towards Brig and stared in thought.

"He *is* still alive...the old man," Danil offered finally.

Brig exhaled audibly and shook his head. "Now why should I believe anything *you* say?"

"I have no reason to lie to you."

"Nah. Syndicate thugs would *never* lie to me, right? Probably just *another* decoy to get me back in their hands..."

"If I wanted you, I would have had a knife in your back before you even knew I was here."

"Then *why* tell me at all?"

"Because in my country, we respect our elders. And I do not agree with what Muldoon has done to the poor man."

Brig remained silent and swung his head in Danil's direction, squinting curiously at him.

"There is a power and communications substation about a kilometer from the decoy house you went to..." Danil continued. "You will find the old man there. *Heavily* guarded, as you might imagine."

"Just like *that*..." Brig chuckled under his breath, skeptically watching Danil rise from his stool.

"Consider that my gift to you, Mr. Stroud," Danil said, patting Brig on the back once more and walking towards the door. "But make no mistake," he added, abruptly facing Brig, "...the girl is *still* fair game. If I find her, she is *mine*..."

As Danil exited the bar, Brig sat and slowly finished his beer, pondering the latest turn of events.

The doorknob to Steele's apartment rotated slowly and the door quietly cracked open inward. As Brig entered the darkened room, suddenly he felt a crushing blow onto the side of his head, accompanied by a loud clang.

"*Ow! Son of a...*" he yelled, as he fell to the floor and grabbed the side of his face, feeling the warmth of the blood rushing to the spot of contact.

The light flicked on immediately and Steele, standing over him with a cooking pan wielded down by her side, gave him a shocked stare.

"Brigadier! Oh my God!" she screamed and then knelt to comfort him.

"Nice to see you, too!" Brig groaned. He sat up partially, still holding the side of his face.

"I didn't *know* it was you," she said apologetically. "Where the *Hell* have you been?" she asked with a frustrated tone, as she assisted him in getting to his feet, and then led him over to the couch.

Before she could say anything, he immediately grabbed both sides of her face and planted a passionate kiss on her lips, into which she melted and reciprocated, whole-heartedly.

"I missed you," said Steele softly, looking into his eyes and stroking the side of his stubbled face.

"Got sorta...*tied up*," Brig explained, returning the loving gaze.

"Well you look like you've been out fighting bobcats," she observed, noticing the cuts and bruises still adorning his face. "What *happened* to you?"

"If by 'bobcats' you mean multi-national thugs that think they own the place...then, yeah," he answered sarcastically, "*something* like that..."

"What did you *do*?" she chastised.

Brig broke eye contact with her and moved towards the edge of the couch.

"Went after your father..." he answered hesitantly, glancing at her through his peripheral.

"Did you find him?" Steele asked anxiously.

"Would have...but, *no.*"

"I *told* you that was a bad plan, Brigadier..." she replied haughtily.

"It *was* a good plan...just that I got some bad intel that led me to the wrong place," defended Brig, interrupting her thought. "Otherwise, he'd be sitting right here with us *right now.*"

"Well, can we try *my* plan now?" she asked after a moment.

"These people don't want *you*, or your father. They just want their property back. And when they get it, *they're gonna kill both of you,* just because they can."

"You don't *know* that..."

"I *do* know that..." Brig countered adamantly. "Where do you think I've *been* for the past several weeks? They had me, Steele. And they were gonna *kill* me just for knowing about this."

"And they let you *go?*" she asked incredulously.

"...No, not so much that..." he said softly.

"Then...*how?*"

"A final favor from a friend..."

"Clive?" she asked curiously after a moment.

Brig nodded his head.

"And that's not *all*..." He got up from the couch and paced to the window to look out at the darkness outside.

"*What?*" she said, as she sat and gazed at him.

"They have...*had* my sister," he replied distantly.

"Your sis...but...*how?* I thought she was...*had?*" Steele stammered, now completely confused.

"I thought so, too. She came and found me after they caught me at the decoy house. But then..." he trailed off.

"Brigadier? What is it?" she asked. She got up from the couch and stood behind him, caressing his arms with both hands as she spoke.

"They...*killed her*," said Brig, his voice cracking.

"*Oh dear God*," Steele said breathlessly, as she reached out to embrace him.

"They're not playing, Steele," Brig said, turning around to embrace her with both arms wrapped around her shoulders, a single tear finding its way down his cheek. "And we've got to get your father away from them...*before it's too late*..." he added.

Steele nodded silently in agreement, as she squeezed Brig tightly.

"I love you, Steele," Brig said emotionally, his voice dropping to a cracked whisper. "And I'm *never* going to let you go *ever again*."

"I love you, too," she answered immediately. Steele sobbed lightly into Brig's chest, her hands digging into his back as she looked up into his eyes. "I...trust you, Brigadier," she confessed finally. "I'm so sorry that I said that to you..."

"It doesn't matter anymore," Brig stroked the hair out of her face with one hand while looking longingly down into her eyes. "We're together, and *nothing's* going to pull us apart *ever again*."

Brig and Steele stood across the highway next to her retro-bike, which he had retrieved on his way back to town, looking on at the substation on the other side of the four lanes.

The building was nestled inside a tall, chain-link perimeter fence that was broken in several spots near the corners with several large, bright lights shining down on the area surrounding it.

"Who told you about this place?" Steele asked curiously.

"One of their guys...a *Russian*," Brig responded disinterestedly without taking his eyes off the target.

"*Russian?*"

"Yeah...and he seemed to be quite fond of *you*," he said mockingly with a half-smile.

"Must be that whole 'stealing from the Syndicate thing'," she cooed matter-of-factly. "Oh...and perhaps he didn't like it when I tried to bash his head in with a shovel." Brig chuckled under his breath. "How can you be sure that this isn't *another* trap?"

"I didn't get the feeling that he cared too much for what they did to your father. Besides, he was with Clive when I was set free. So I'd think if he wanted to turn me back in, he *would* have by now. And," he said, squinting off into the darkness at the building, "...they're guarding that place pretty heavily, which makes me believe he's actually in there."

"So...what's the plan then?"

"See that cargo truck over there?" he replied, pointing at smaller truck parked off to the side of the building, partly in the cone of light, partly in darkness.

Steele nodded as she peered across the street.

"*You're* gonna be the getaway driver," he concluded with a coy smile.

Moments later, with Steele hiding in the driver's seat of the cargo truck twenty meters away, Brig stood in the shadows of one of the electrical towers that bordered the inside of the perimeter fence.

He watched patiently as several guards, armed with small automatic weapons cradled across their arms, alternated circling the outside of the building. The guards passed each other every few minutes as they moved in opposite, concentric circles.

"Well, it's *now* or *never*," Brig whispered to himself, seeing an opportunity to catch one of the guards alone near the rear corner of the small, brick facility.

With the prowess of a cat, he swiftly stalked the guard from behind; grabbing him within his clenched forearm until a sickening snap relaxed all of the muscles in the man's body. The guard fell limp to the ground at Brig's feet.

Wasting no time, Brig snagged the man's weapon, lifted the lifeless body and quickly carried it over to the nearest fence opening, tossing it into the darkness beyond. Then, knowing that he only had seconds until the other guard would make his appearance, he sprinted to the corner and pressed himself up against the wall in wait.

Despite his best efforts at controlling his adrenaline, his pulse raced as he stood silently.

Just as the second guard rounded the corner, and before the guard could react, Brig sent his elbow forcefully into the front of the man's neck, making the man instantly drop his weapon and begin gagging while grasping violently at his throat.

Capitalizing on the element of surprise and shock, Brig quickly grabbed the man's hair, which flowed down from the centerline of his head in a spiked pattern, and forcefully dropped the guard's face down onto his knee. The guard let out a quick, throaty grunt as he whipped violently backward onto the ground.

Realizing his mistake at the warehouse previously, where he had given the guard the opportunity to regain consciousness and have the chance to strike back, Brig gritted his teeth tightly and stomped with his entire weight onto the guard's jaw. The man's neck shattered instantly with a muffled crunch.

The final exterior guard, whom Brig instantly recognized as the one from the truck a week previous, stood apathetically at the front entrance to the substation. He toted his weapon carelessly over his shoulder, as he leaned against the building and whistled a non-descript tune out to the darkness of the desert beyond the substation property.

Suddenly, the cold hardness of a gun barrel pressed against the side of Alexi's neck, forcing him to jolt upright.

"Hand over the gun, nice and slow..." Brig growled lowly.

Straining to see sideways without turning his neck, Alexi's eyes widened as he caught sight of Brig.

"You just don't give up, *do* you?" Alexi said incredulously, holding his gun up in the air, barrel skyward, with one hand.

Brig grabbed the gun from Alexi's hand, yanked the magazine

and stuffed it in his pocket, and then ejected the bullet from the chamber, before tossing the gun into the grass several meters away.

"No, I just learn from *my* mistakes," Brig said gruffly. "Now open the door, *we're* goin' inside."

"You'll never make it outta here alive, pal," Alexi warned, as he fumbled for the keys in his pocket and then clicked one of them into the lock on the door.

"We got the element of surprise on our side. And you better hope they're surprised in there, or it's gonna get messy...*for you*." Brig poked his gun into Alexi's back, prodding him to pull the door open and step inside, with Brig following closely behind.

The emergency lighting fixtures were mounted five meters apart along the tops of the walls, stretching the length of the narrow hallway. They reflected brightly off the linoleum tile of the floor and provided an eerie, false daylight that forced Brig to squint while he adjusted his eyes to its harshness. Four doors exited off the main corridor, along with one hallway entrance that ran off to the left perpendicular to where they stood fifteen meters away.

Brig grasped the back of Alexi's neck and jabbed the gun forcefully into his lower back.

"Where are they?" he growled into Alexi's ear.

"In...in the control room..." Alexi groaned in pain, as he pointed forward. "Down that hallway to the left. But...*you'll* never get in there..."

"*We'll* see about that," Brig said confidently. He shoved Alexi forward to the intersecting hallway.

As they reached the corner that led into the other passage, the distinct sound of clomping footsteps echoed off the tile ahead of them. Brig quickly wrapped his arm around Alexi's neck and stepped into the center of the adjacent corridor.

Standing just two meters in front of Brig and Alexi was another guard, a surprised look on his face as he instinctively drew his weapon and began firing. Alexi's body convulsed violently with the impact of the bullets that ripped into him from his counterpart's gun, much to the horror of the other guard.

Before the other guard could adjust, however, Brig lifted his own gun and fired several rapid bursts at him, hitting him squarely in the chest. Blood jetted outward from his ribcage like water splashing from pebbles forcefully thrown into a pond. The guard fell backwards onto the tile floor, the clanking echo of his weapon hitting the hard surface reverberating throughout the hallway.

Brig, releasing Alexi's body to fall limp to the floor at his feet, swiftly seized the other guard's weapon, strung it over his shoulder as he stepped over both bodies, and made his way up to the closed double doors that led into the control room.

Inside the control room, the large, burly guard stood close watch over Bronson Fox. The elderly Fox sat meekly in front of him in a cushioned office chair, his legs dangling limply over the side and onto the floor, as he looked off dejectedly in the opposite direction.

The guard, although tasked to keep an eye on Bronson, was preoccupied with the deck of cards spread out beside him on the control console that stretched in a horseshoe pattern around the entire front section of the room. He lazily stood up from his leaning position against the console, as several loud raps on the door echoed throughout the chamber. He dropped several cards onto the stack in front of him and took a large bite of the apple in his other hand.

The guard yanked at the door handle, expecting to see the familiar face of one of the other guards wanting to enter for shift change.

No one was there.

Holding the door open with one large paw, he stepped partway into the corridor just outside of the control room and glanced through the glare of the lighting down towards the end of the hallway.

As he turned, an annoyed grimace on his face, Brig suddenly pounced from his position above the door, where he had hung in wait for it to open, knocking the guard to the floor, face-first and unconscious.

Having literally only a second to react before the door closed, locking him out of the control room once again and spoiling any chance at surprise for those inside, Brig leapt through the doorway and into the room as the door slammed shut behind him.

Brig stopped to survey the room around him. A hail of bullets met him, raining down from the maze of catwalks that lined the ceiling of the facility above him.

Perched in several locations were three additional guards, each firing their automatic weapons at him from their superior vantage points. Brig ducked deftly behind a nearby pillar, his attackers briefly ceasing their volley as they had lost sight of their prey. He quickly checked the magazines of his weapons and slammed them one-at-a-time back into the bottoms of the stocks, and then jumped from his crouch and sprinted towards the front of the room.

Bullets once again greeted him, ricocheting loudly off the metal surfaces mounted in various sections of the control center. The projectiles tore into the metal fixtures near Brig, as bright flashes of sparks sprayed wildly across the floor in front of him. He squeezed the triggers of both weapons simultaneously as he aimed them up at the catwalks, the storm of bullets from their muzzles instantly silencing the other attackers as they dove for cover. He slid the final several meters across the polished, tile floor and came to a stop just beside Bronson's chair.

"Mr. Fox, hang on...I'm gonna get you out of here..." Brig said breathlessly to Bronson, who stared at him in surprise.

"Who...Brigadier? Is that *you*, my boy?" Bronson said incredulously.

With a nod and one swift move, Brig hoisted the elder Fox, tossed him over his shoulder and began to sprint back to the entryway.

The attackers, yelling commands in their native tongues, sprayed the floor surrounding the two men as they ran. Divots of fragmented tile jumped up from the floor to greet them as they passed.

In one final, valiant effort, Brig swung open one of the entry doors and darted out into the hallway to safety, hurtling the still-motionless guard lying at the entry of the control room and sprinting the length of the hallway in a blur until he reached the exterior door.

Pushing open the door with one shoulder while gingerly holding onto Bronson with the other arm, Brig emerged cautiously from the building. He tactically glanced back and forth to ensure that no other guards had gone unnoticed. Satisfied that they were in the clear, he stepped out into the open where the overhead lights shined brightest.

"You doin' ok, Mr. Fox?" Brig asked between breaths.

"I seem to be okay, Brigadier," Bronson chortled softly. "Although, I think I got nicked by a ricochet back there..."

A dark, crimson stain permeated the cloth of Bronson's shirt just below his ribcage, leaking onto Brig's arm and making him inhale deeply with widened eyes.

"It's okay, *it's okay...*" Brig reaffirmed. "We can get that looked at. We just need to get out of here."

Suddenly several bullets whizzed past Brig's ear, forcing him to flinch and head back to the front door of the substation. To his dismay, however, the door had auto-locked behind him.

Knowing his only chance at survival was to take refuge behind the building, he spun and began a sprint to the corner. Just as he took his first step, however, the cargo truck screamed to a halt in front of him, spraying loose gravel into the air around it and effectively blocking any clear shots the new attackers might have had.

"Get in!" Steele screamed from the cab of the truck, the deafening sound of bullets pinging off the hood of the vehicle, slicing the air.

Brig yanked at the side cargo door, swinging it open just enough for him to gently place Bronson into the cargo bed of the truck on his back, and then jumped in immediately afterwards.

"*Go! Go! Go!*" Brig ordered, pounding on the side of the truck so that Steele could hear him, pulling the door shut with the other hand.

Steele accelerated the truck out of the parking lot and onto the main highway, away from the gunmen hiding beyond the fence.

Brig propped Bronson against the wall inside the truck.

"How you feelin', sir?" he asked Bronson, who appeared paler than he had seen him moments before.

"I'll...be alright," Bronson replied weakly with a partial smile. "Thank you...for *setting me free*, Brigadier."

He patted Brig on the side of his shoulder and closed his eyes to rest.

"We *need* to get your father some medical attention, Steele..." Brig called up to the front through the small pass-through door that led from the cargo area up to the cab.

"And that's not *all*," Steele said in a heightened tone. "We've got company..."

Brig forced himself through the small portal and leaned on the back of the driver's seat, looking over Steele's shoulder and out at the side-view mirror.

In the distance, he could see three distinct, small headlights approaching the back of the truck.

"Damn it," he cursed under his breath. "Go in the back and look after your father...I'll lose them."

Without argument, Steele swiftly climbed from the driver's seat, quickly replaced by Brig, and began to head into the cargo hold.

Before she disappeared, she stopped and turned her head to Brig.

"Head towards my flat..." she said quickly. "There's a medical center nearby that *should* be able to help him out."

"A Syndicate medical center? Are you *crazy*?"

"We've got no choice. Besides, they won't *know* any better..." Steele ducked into the pass-through and entered the cargo hold.

Brig shook his head and then turned his eyes to focus on their new problem. He glanced out at the mirror once again.

Two retro-bikes roared alongside of the driver's side of the truck, single-file.

Brig cleverly lifted his foot from the accelerator, allowing the first bike to pull up next to the driver's window. The rider on the bike quickly aimed his gun at the side of the truck and squeezed off a volley of rounds.

The side mirror splintered, shattering glass and metal into the cockpit and made Brig duck abruptly; forcing the truck to shift violently to the right.

Brig swiftly countered with his own volley, firing directly into the face of the rider and killing him instantly. The rider's bike wobbled wildly out of control and off the side of the road, where it glanced off a roadside crag of rocks and burst into flames.

As the second rider approached Brig's door, Brig once again lifted from the accelerator pedal.

However, not fooled as the first had been, the second rider raced his bike forward and past the truck, where he turned and began firing at the front end. A trail of bullets dotted the windshield directly in front of Brig as he ducked for safety.

Brig accelerated and clipped the second bike, sending it reeling in front of the truck, where it fell sideways and underneath the front wheel. The truck lurched turbulently back and forth, as the bike hung briefly underneath the chassis, and then spewed out the back end onto the road. Brig promptly righted the truck as he caught his breath.

"You *okay* back there?" he yelled into the pass-through.

Before Steele could answer, a hail of bullets screamed through the side of the cargo hold wall in a lined pattern, forcing her to sprawl across her father to protect him.

Another retro-bike had joined the chase and had already pulled alongside of them. Brig yanked the steering wheel to the right suddenly, sending the side of the truck careening into the bike and, in turn, forcing the bike off the road where it ran into a smaller set of rocks.

The bike's rear end lifted abruptly, turning the bike end-over-end, and launched the rider headfirst onto the rocks in the darkness behind the truck.

Brig glanced at the mirror once again and then, after sticking his head out of the driver's side window to scan the area, sat back in relief with a momentary closing of his eyes, as he urged the lumbering truck on towards their destination.

The windshield shattered as a quick burst of machine gun fire erupted from the front end of the truck.

The second rider, who Brig assumed had been run through underneath the vehicle moments earlier, had somehow managed to clamp onto its grille and now climbed in towards Brig. Before he could react, the rider grasped the heroic Epsilon by the throat and wrenched him away from the steering wheel, where he fell onto his side next to the driver's seat.

The truck, now pilotless, began to slow and veer off the side of the road, forcing the rider to fall sideways off Brig as it lurched off course. Seizing the opportunity, Brig grabbed the rider and held him upright, brutally punching him until the rider fell backwards onto the dash. As he lay halfway onto the hood, the rider desperately clutched at the window post.

Gripping the steering wheel to try to get the truck back under control, Brig felt around blindly on the floor underneath him and managed to locate his weapon. He instinctively lifted it and squeezed off a dozen rounds into the chest of the attacker, sending him flying backwards onto the road. The large truck tires quickly flattened the rider as they rolled over him.

Fifteen minutes later, Brig maneuvered the truck up to the side of the small, makeshift medical center, that at one time housed a movie theater. The engine groaned its disapproval, as the squeal of its brakes emanated off the nearby empty buildings.

Brig opened the door and jumped from the cab, made a quick turn around the front of the vehicle and ripped open the cargo hold door.

"We made it...sorry for the rough ride," he said apologetically, as he began to pull himself into the back of the truck.

He stopped abruptly, however, as he noticed Steele still draped over her father.

"Steele, we're here, sweetheart..." Brig urged. "Let's get him in there so they can help him out, ok?"

Steele slowly raised her head and looked at Brig. Heavy tears cascaded from the corners of her eyes as she sobbed loudly.

"It's too late..." she wailed. "*It's too late...*"

She pushed herself up to a semi-sitting position and cried uncontrollably into her hand.

Brig could see the cold stare in Bronson's eyes, as he lay prone and motionless in the back of the truck. A small stream of blood trailed from the wound in his belly and across the bed of the vehicle.

Bronson was dead.

39:
Wish You Were Here

Present day (2084)...

Steele helped Brig put the final few stones atop the makeshift grave that they had dug for Bronson at the back perimeter of his estate. The large oak trees overhead offered final shade over the shallow grave the morning after Bronson's fateful death at the hands of the Syndicate.

It was an unusually balmy March day, and Brig wiped the sweat from his forehead, as he leaned on the old shovel that he had found in the gardener's shack on the other end of the property. He averted his eyes out of respect, as he watched Steele kneel down and bow her head at the foot of the mound of stones in front of her.

A single petal that had fallen from the primrose she had laid at the base of the stone marking the grave caught his eye, buried partly in the dirt at his feet alongside the pile of rocks. Brig bent down and gently picked up the petal between his fingers, and then laid it in his open palm as he looked at it. The sun sank behind a bank of clouds, blanketing the backyard in a dim gray. The wind rustled through the thick wood that bordered the estate properties to the north, whisking the petal from his hand away into the trees beyond.

Brig looked to the west, his shoulder-length hair flowing out behind him as he eyed the clouds.

"Looks like we're gonna get some rain," he said.

Steele only raised her head momentarily, and then bowed it once again with her eyes closed.

Brig sighed silently as he rested his chin on the hand that held the shovel in front of him. He understood what she was going through. She had just lost the only connection to family that she had left in the world. He, *too*, had experienced that pain. He had just lost his only family – *for the second time.*

After a few more silent moments, Steele slowly pushed herself up to a standing position. The wind buffeted her hair forward around her face as she stood and peered down at the grave.

Brig stepped forward and placed one arm around her shoulders.

She did not reciprocate. She stood in silence, chewing the end of her fingernails on one hand as she stared blankly forward.

"Steele, I'm *sorry*..."

"Brigadier – *stop*..." she said instantly. "There is *nothing* that you can say that is going to make this better right now...so please...*just stop*," she said softly, but firmly.

Brig dropped his arm from around her shoulder and placed it at his side, as he stood silently beside her.

He wanted to tell her that he understood; that things *would* get better. He wanted to reach out and embrace her...to hold her tighter than he had *ever* done before. But he knew that what she needed most now was to clear her head and figure out how to put things into perspective.

Brig bit his lip and lowered his head, as he thought about the previous night.

It was the right thing to do... he reassured himself.

After all, the plan *was* a success. They had rescued Bronson from the Syndicate. Against overwhelming odds *and* being insanely outnumbered, Brig had heroically stormed the safe house and pulled her father from the clutches of certain doom. If not for an unseen, stray piece of shrapnel that *miraculously* found its way into his abdomen, severing a critical artery that *no* amount of medical attention would have repaired – she would have been reunited with her father and the sun would be shining again *right now*.

He knew that *she* would not agree, however. She *could not*, and he did not blame her. But he knew better, and he knew that the alternative was a much grislier outcome for everyone involved had he not acted when he did.

He peered up from the ground and his deep thought to find Steele standing directly in front of him, facing him and staring purposefully with watery eyes.

"Brigadier..." she began with a whisper, "would you mind staying here at my father's estate? Now that he's...*gone*...I don't want *them* coming here and desecrating his memory and going through his things."

"Of course," answered Brig immediately. "We can stay here as long as you..."

"Not *we*..." she interjected in a firmer tone. "I couldn't bear the grief of being here. I'm going back to my flat." She lowered her head and folded her hands in front of her. "After all, *you* even said they don't know where I live. So I think I'll be safe there," she said, glancing back up him with a tilt of her head.

"But...*why*..." Brig started to ask, but knew it was a futile argument.

Steele smiled sheepishly as she stepped past Brig, placing her hand gently on his arm.

Brig closed his eyes tightly, wanting so badly to reach out and grab her that it tore at his soul.

No... he told himself, *...let her go.*

He quietly watched her stroll the length of the backyard, not taking his eyes off her for a second, as she disappeared through the front gate between the overgrown hedges, and out onto the street of the cul-de-sac.

Several weeks passed, and the two did not see or speak to each other. Technically, she did not see *him*, for he had made a daily ritual of watching her apartment from across the street from morning to dusk...out of protection much more than obsession.

Each afternoon, he would catch sight of her leaving the building, hear her retrieving the retro-bike several blocks away and then roaring off to the east, not returning for several hours each time. He knew that she almost certainly must have been going to the satellite array field that she had showed him weeks earlier.

He imagined her sitting alone atop the hill overlooking the serenity below, the wind tossing her hair across her face and back behind her shoulders, as she stared pensively at the heavens.

And though it made him happy to see her each day, he missed her almost more than he could bear. But he knew that she would find herself and come back to him. He would embrace her, stroke her hair, imbibe her beautiful scent and tell her that he loved her.

Everything would be right again.

Steele tore open the door to her bedroom and sprinted out into the hallway, looking back in terror as she emerged into the dimly lit corridor. She was not sure *what* was happening outside the window next to her bed, but the blinding light that penetrated the room inside woke her from a deep sleep and panicked her more than *anything* ever had. She fled from the relative safety of her room without even slippers to cover her feet.

As she stopped and stood in the hallway, however, she realized that she was once again in the grand corridor of the URA Security Alliance building in Boulder. Its familiar crimson red, carpet-lined walls stretched for what seemed hundreds of meters in each direction.

The hall, normally bustling with the activity of numerous handfuls of lab technicians and managers buzzing back and forth, was unusually quiet.

A small gathering of people, the only ones in sight, grasped Steele's attention to the part of the facility that Steele knew to be the main foyer.

Suddenly, the light reappeared, melting through the wall like a projector bulb through film. Thick strands of bright amber flowed out into the hallway and onto the opposite wall.

It halted as soon as it began, however, and it left her head throbbing like a pulsing sponge. Her mind suddenly felt full, as if someone had just wrung a wet towel full of thoughts into it from above.

She shut her eyes tightly and grasped her head between her forearms to try to shut out the light that now shined relentlessly into her mind. The images came fast and furious, but too quickly for her to make sense of them as they, and the garbled soundtrack that accompanied them, blurred through her brain in what seemed like a nanosecond.

A sudden darkness and silence, echoing throughout the hallways around her, followed.

Steele hesitantly opened one eye, peering up and down the passage. The strange flashes of light had stopped, both in her head and out, and an eerie silence had settled. Her head still throbbed and, as she rubbed the back of it, her hand instinctively migrated down to the base of her skull, where she gently massaged a spot that burned *intensely*.

She stepped curiously towards the main foyer. The group that had gathered just moments before had disappeared, replaced by two people standing with their backs to her: a tall, lanky man standing next to a young girl.

39: WISH YOU WERE HERE

On the wall above the pair, Steele could see the URA Security Alliance logo, its grand message scrawled across the entire wall for all to see when they entered the lobby. In place of the usual eagle, that normally graced the central portion of the logo, was a vulture with one of its eyes clawed out...a sign of a struggle perhaps. The other eye glared menacingly down at anyone that walked past it in the lobby, as if taunting them.

Below the vulture on a giant, gold ribbon scrawled with, presumably, the vulture's talons, was the phrase 'Reliqua Permanere ad Dimicandum'. To her surprise, Steele found herself mouthing the translation aloud as she read the banner.

"The left behind will continue to fight..." She wrinkled her eyebrows and tilted her head sideways. "That's not what it's supposed to say..." she remarked aloud.

Steele blinked and shook her head in confusion, and focused her eyes on the two people standing several meters in front of her.

The girl, her long, auburn hair draped across the middle of her back, wore a white nightgown that flowed down to her ankles that, to Steele's surprise, very closely resembled the one she was currently wearing.

Odd, Steele thought, looking down in bewilderment at her wardrobe, knowing that she had not worn such clothing since she was a child herself.

"Nadia!" the child called.

Steele glanced up quickly and noticed the young girl turning, pointing in Steele's direction, a wide smile worn across her small face. Steele craned her neck to look backwards over her shoulder, assuming the girl must have seen someone she recognized farther down the hall.

No one was there.

She spun around. The girl, still standing facing Steele, stared attentively in her direction, hiding her timid smile coyly behind her small hands.

Steele shut her eyes and shook her head rapidly, wanting desperately to wake herself, but she could still feel the coldness of the marble tile under her feet. She opened her eyes again only to find that the girl had vanished. Steele once again scanned the lengths of the hallways that intersected into the grand lobby, but she could not locate the girl.

The man remained, however, and still stood with his back to her.

413

She stood in silence behind him, gazing at the back of his head. She *recognized* him! She knew his *build*, his *stature*, his *salt-and-peppered hair*.

It was her father!

Her heart leapt with joy as she stepped forward and tugged at the cuff of his suit jacket.

He did not respond.

"Dad," she said loudly to get his attention, as she tugged harder at the bottom of his cuff, oddly having to reach above her head to touch it.

Bronson turned and darted his eyes around the lobby, and then, noticing Steele standing next to him, glared down at her.

"Hmm? Oh, it's *you*," he said frigidly. He turned fully and crouched in front of her.

She instantly recoiled at the sight of his face. While she could definitely recognize that it was he, the lines of his face distorted as if it were made of putty, and someone had placed their hand on it and twisted violently.

"What are you doing out of your *room*?" he asked curiously, taking her hand and standing back up. "You should go back now..." he said, as he began to lead her down the hallway to her bedroom.

"*No!*" Steele shouted.

She tried to pull from his grasp, but he easily held onto her wrist as he tugged at her. She turned back to face him, but Bronson was gone.

In his place sat a man in a wheelchair, still grasping onto her arm.

Steele became calm once again, as she gazed into his eyes.

It was not her father at all.

He was a younger man wearing a military uniform, who stared purposefully back at her.

"Who..." she began to say, but then realized...*she knew him!* But *who* was he? She squinted hard at him as she tried to recall his name, but she *could not* remember.

"*Save me...*" he said to her, as he pulled at her arm to come closer.

Steele jerked her arm away from the man, causing her to trip and fall backward onto the hard marble.

"*Save me...save me...*" the man repeated, suddenly seeming as though a chorus of men had joined his plea.

She turned and recoiled in horror, as one after the other, men started appearing out of the darkness of the other corridors to stand behind the man in the wheelchair.

Some had missing limbs, while others had a terrifying amount of blood stained in trails coming from their temples down onto their crimson-red uniforms.

Steele let out a desperate yelp and began to claw her way across the floor until she reached the edge of the hallway once again. She turned to look over her shoulder.

The men, too, had disappeared.

She slowly caught her breath and wiped the tears from her face, as she gently pushed herself back to her feet and strolled back into the foyer, glancing in paranoia every few seconds behind her down the hallway.

As she exited the passage, she caught sight of a reflection in a full-length mirror mounted on the wall to her left.

Instead of her own reflection, however, the little girl's image appeared within it. She was standing on the opposite side of a doorway and despite the incredulity of it, appeared to be walking on air.

"*I'm sorry...*" Steele said involuntarily.

The girl, much to her surprise and confusion, was mouthing the words along *with* Steele.

"*I'm sorry...*" Steele repeatedly cried, tears staining her cheeks, as the girl continued to mimic her words silently. "You don't *know* me...it's a *lie!*"

Steele cupped her hand over her mouth in horror as she glanced down at the floor, not knowing or understanding what she was saying, and wanting it to be over.

She glanced over at the girl, but she, along with the mirror, was gone...*again*.

A twinkling of light caught her eye from the center of the foyer to her right.

Rather than the usual, massive receptionist's desk that adorned the entire entry wall, a stairway led downward into the floor. From the entry point, a bright, flashing light beckoned her forward.

For reasons unknown, she felt compelled to answer the call and stepped towards it. She was not sure what she would find, but she felt, with her entire being, that it was an answer that she *needed* to know.

She stood at the top of the stairs and glared downward. The

small LED light that sat on a desk at the base flickered brightly up into the stairwell, where it reflected off Steele's wide-eyed face. A single computer display next to the light scrolled data insanely fast across its screen.

Without realizing it, she had floated down the stairs and found herself standing in front of the display, her eyes still fixated in a trance at the massive amount of information that continued to flow across the screen in front of her.

"*Stop!*" she commanded without thinking, and as she did so, the screen paused, clearing the data that had already overflowed and stopping on one, blinking title.

"*Diversion?*" she read aloud, her face contorted in confusion. "*That's* not right!" she screamed.

She pounded her fist onto the keyboard that sat just below the display. The terminal emitted several rude chirps, and then flickered a crimson text that dropped the room into a deep, reddish hue, as it scrolled backwards across her forehead.

"*Red Vision!*" Steele exclaimed breathlessly, as she bolted upright into a sitting position. Her hair, matted with sweat, flipped forward and over her face.

Her desperate gasps for breath instantly turned to sobs of terror, as she buried her face in her hands and cried aloud.

She knew it was a *dream*, but she also knew now that it was the *key* to providing a critical piece to the puzzle. And she knew *just* where to find it.

40:
Let It Go

Present day (2084)...

Steele hammered her fists against the front door of Clive's workshop, having hopped from her parked retro-bike just meters away.

"Clive, open the *damned* door! I *know* you're in there!" she yelled frantically, unfazed that her voice was loud enough to be heard several blocks away. "*Bloody Hell!*" she bellowed, pounding the door once more with her hand as she spun around, her voice echoing into the dewy night and off the wooden fences surrounding the building.

She was being reckless. Ever since the encounter with Pollux downtown several weeks ago, Brig had made her fully aware that she had a target on her, and up until now, she had *heeded* his warnings. But showing up at Clive's and noisily pounding on the door in the still of the night was only a small pebble in the landslide. His place was almost surely under surveillance of some sort by the Syndicate, and they would most certainly be on the lookout for her retro-bike.

However, she disregarded any concern for her safety as she quickly strode over to her bike, reached under the seat and extracted the metal flashlight that she had always kept for emergency situations. Without a second thought, she stepped into the small alleyway next to the workshop and punched the flashlight through the pane of the window perched about halfway along the side. The shriek of shattering glass flooded the void of silence around the building.

Steele stretched her hand into the small crevice in the glass, craftily popped the lock above the center sill and pushed the window fully open after pulling her arm back.

With the agility and grace of a cat, she performed a small hop, grasped the outside sill and tumbled headfirst into the opening, narrowly missing landing on the remnants of the broken glass on the floor just inside.

She quickly flicked on the flashlight and shined it purposefully at the floor next to Clive's darkened workbench. She was surprised to find that a small amount of light was *already* coming from underneath the haphazardly strewn carpet that normally hid Clive's secret room.

"Knock, knock...you've got *company*," she said coolly, as she strode carefully over to the carpet, shoved it out of the way with one foot and yanked at the handle that was flush with the floor.

The door hinged upward with a small creak of its springs, exposing the staircase that led down into the small workroom below. Although the light was not on, the display terminal *was*. It shone brightly across the room and up onto the stairs with a crimson hue.

Before she realized it, Steele had floated down the staircase and was standing in front of Clive's desk, staring intently at the screen that flashed in front of her. She glanced down and saw a set of cipher cards laid out, with one of them still engaged in the scanner mounted to the left of the terminal display.

"You *bastard*..." she murmured, taking notice of the URA Security Alliance logo at the top center of the screen.

Steele swiftly pulled the stool from underneath the desk and sat, her fingers already dancing along the keyboard, as she began to read the information on the screen. Her eyes quickly darted back and forth. She scanned the data, absorbing more information in those silent, few moments than she had in all of the years since she was a child.

Suddenly, Steele's chest fell as she exhaled a throaty whimper. A single tear gathered at the corner of her eye.

"*No*..." she whispered aloud, blinking away the tear in incredulity.

She opened her mouth, but no words came.

Then, without warning, an outburst of tears streamed down her cheeks and onto her forearms, as she lowered her head into her hands and sobbed uncontrollably.

"*My God*," she cried loudly in-between choking back her raw emotions, her hand finding its way down her neck to the base of her skull and rubbing gently. "This *can't* be true...*it can't. It can't*..."

The sudden realization hit her like an earthquake in the night. The dreams had *led* her here. She was not sure *why*, or *what* she was supposed to find. But somehow, they led her *here*.

And now the *truth*; the *awful, horrifying truth* that she was never *supposed* to know...was glaring her in the face like a distorted, funhouse mirror.

She sat back, her chest heaving violently with her cries, as she gripped the sides of her head with both hands, and stared blankly at the screen.

For the first time in her life, she felt *lost* and *alone.*

The large cargo truck rumbled along the empty highway, its dim headlights piercing the thin layer of fog that had settled next to road and had begun to creep across its two lanes.

"Are you tired of coming up empty in your search for this...depot...that you *claim* exists?" Danil asked, lazily watching the asphalt glide past them through the passenger side window.

"We'll find it," Clive answered tersely, cupping his hand over his mouth to squelch a large yawn, while he held the wheel with the other.

"Muldoon is not a patient man, but it is interesting how he shows no lack of it with *you*," observed Danil wryly, turning his head in Clive's direction to judge his reaction.

Clive did not answer, but silently shrugged his shoulders.

"And what happens when he calls your *bluff*, Underwood?"

"What makes you think it's a *bluff?*" Clive said with a furrowed brow, while glaring out of the corner of his eye at Danil.

"I have questioned many people in my day, Underwood," Danil explained, "that were just as *smart* as you. Or were *not*, but were much *craftier*. And I have learned when someone is bluffing."

Clive ground his teeth together but did not respond. He knew what Danil was up to, and he was not going to fall for it.

"Besides," added Danil, "you showed your hand to me when you let your *friend* go."

"He has nothing to do with this, so what's your point?" Clive replied in frustration.

"I am a student of human nature, Underwood. How a person acts in a pressure situation is *usually* their nature," Danil squinted at Clive knowingly. "Have you heard from Stroud since he...left town?"

"He's *gone*...we don't have to worry about *him*," Clive answered flatly.

"And you are so *sure* of that fact?"

Clive turned to Danil with a curious look. "You *know* something I don't?"

Danil smiled coyly and continued to stare forward. "He is a soldier, *like you*," he explained deliberately. "And in my experience, soldiers will take orders when they are *captive*...but will defy those same orders once they are set *free. Especially* those that have *something* to prove..."

He turned to face Clive and stared at him purposefully. "*Or someone to protect.* You have placed a very dangerous wager on *this* one, my friend. *You* had better hope that he does not show his face any time soon."

"Well, you see, Danil..." Clive retorted after a few seconds of silent thought. "That's where you *and* I have something in common. *You* have just as much to lose as *I* do, *now don't you?*"

Danil peered at Clive in his peripheral and snorted silently to himself.

Clive sneered and turned his focus to the road once again, making one final turn and then pulling the truck to a stop in front of his workshop.

"So we will continue the hunt again bright and early tomorrow, Underwood?" Danil asked, sliding over to the driver's seat, as he watched Clive open the door and begin to climb out of the cab.

"Not too early, I'd like to sleep in for once in my life," Clive answered, turning his back and walking to the front door.

"Okay, I will be here just after sunrise then," Danil shouted back at him. The low, metallic grinding reverberated off the small row of empty buildings that lined the street on both sides, as he forced the truck into gear.

"Gee...*thanks*," Clive mumbled to himself, signaling his goodbye with one quick hand over his shoulder.

As the sound of the truck groaning off into the distance grew into silence, Clive stopped, leaned up against one of the wooden posts that held up the small roof above the entryway to his workshop, and looked up into the night sky.

"Please tell me you're *not* coming back..." he muttered, scanning the starry canvas above. "At least not until *I* find what I'm *looking* for."

He shook his head in frustration, as he reached into his pocket for his keys and unlocked the front door, slid it open and then stepped inside.

As he closed the front door, he stopped abruptly and stared ahead. His eyes darted immediately to the propped-open doorway that led to the stairs beneath the floor. From within he could see the reflection of his display terminal glaring brightly into the darkness above. His heart raced as he reached over and flicked on the small light next to his workbench. He knew for sure that he had not left the secret door open. He could not have, he was always *so* careful.

The crunch of broken glass under his boots made him halt as he stepped towards the open doorway.

Clive peered down at the floor and saw that he was standing in a small field of broken glass, directly beneath the window adjacent to his workbench. He gently pulled aside the shade and exhaled in exasperation as he looked at the shattered window.

He kicked aside the shards of glass in anger, as he strode over to the hinged doorway, bent down and reached into the corner of the panel to turn the light on downstairs. Without descending the narrow staircase, he could already see all that he needed to.

The cipher cards were gone from their compartment next to the terminal display.

The light coming from the far corner of the small, underground room caught his eye as it reflected onto the lowest step. He tilted his head and squinted.

He had not noticed it at first.

A thin trail of dark, crimson blood on every other step leading downwards and then, finally, several dark smudges all around the keyboard and workbench.

"*That son of a bitch...*" he growled through his teeth, hammering his fist into the doorframe.

Clive entered the pub. His eyes immediately wandered to the bartender, who was leaning forward onto the bar. The barkeep, seeing Clive enter, nodded his greeting towards him and then darted his one good, unpatched eye towards the corner. Clive returned the nod and slowly faced the direction of the bartender's focus of attention.

Brig sat at a small table of the dimly lit pub, his back to the room as he faced the corner, his shoulders hunched over, as if he were hiding from the world.

Clive peered around the rest of the room. Aside from him, Brig and the bartender, there were only a small handful of others, who paid no attention to him, as they all nursed their own drinks in other darkened corners of the establishment.

Clive slowly stepped up behind Brig, his boots clunking lightly on the wooden floor.

Brig raised his head.

"What the Hell *you* doin' here..." Clive asked through his teeth.

"Drinkin'..." Brig responded sarcastically. "This *is* still a bar, ain't it? Or is this just a *Syndicate* hangout now?"

"You know *damn* well what I'm talking about," Clive replied, taking a step forward and to the side of Brig, as he stared down at his former partner. "You're not supposed to *be* here...*in town*," he said gruffly, but quiet enough where the rest of the patrons could not hear him.

"I don't take orders from *you*," Brig replied, taking a large swig of beer. "Besides, I got some unfinished business here, Cryp. But you *knew* that."

"Like breaking into my place and stealing stuff?" Clive leaned in with one hand on Brig's shoulder. "That *your* way of paying me back?"

"I don't know what the Hell *you're* talkin' about," Brig shot back immediately.

"What you *took* isn't going to help you at all. So why don't you just give them back."

Brig sighed and sat silently staring at the wall in front of him, his hand resting on the table just beside his glass.

"*You* don't have anything I want, Cryp," said Brig with an air of exasperation. "Besides, that's the *Syndicate's* MO, not *mine*. So why don't you go ask your *buddies* who broke in, 'cause I'm sure it was one of *them*." He sipped the final bit of his drink and placed the empty mug down on the table.

"I'm gonna' let you *think* about it...and do the *right thing*, since that's *your* MO. You know where to find me..." Clive growled.

Then, as Clive turned towards the door, he stopped abruptly and leaned in towards the back of Brig's head.

"And keep outta' sight, not *everyone's* as tolerant as *I* am..." Clive dropped a few Syndicate credits in front of the bartender with a subtle clink, strode towards the door and disappeared into the night.

40: LET IT GO

Brig sat back in his chair and ran his fingers through his hair, as he stared up at the ceiling in frustration.

"What *next*..." he murmured to himself. He pushed himself up from his chair, nodded to the bartender, and strode out the door.

Brig stood outside of the pub's entry door and buttoned up his jacket, protecting himself from the moist air that had settled in the area. He peered to the east, which led past Clive's workshop, and then to the west, towards the area fifteen kilometers away where Steele lived.

Resolving that it was time to put an end to the separation between them, he swiftly turned to the west and began the trek towards her apartment.

Several moments into his journey, the realization suddenly hit him like a brick in the back of the head.

Clive was upset about the break-in because it was *true* that *he* had double-crossed Steele, and the *cipher cards* must have been stolen.

"*That son of a bitch*..." he grumbled under his breath. He quickly did an about-face and headed back towards Clive's workshop. "This ends *tonight*."

41:
Coming Undone

Seven years prior (early 2077)...

Brig squinted and then shut his eyes just as quickly, the overhead light blinding him and forcing him to place his hand over his face.

"...the *Hell?*" he mumbled to himself aloud, painfully pushing himself up to a semi-upright position.

He rubbed the side of his head lazily, pulling it away abruptly as the pain of the wound on his cheek brought to mind the last memory he had before being knocked unconscious.

"Johannsen..." he muttered, "...*shot* me."

As hard as he tried, he could not remember anything beyond that one moment. His mind felt mossy, and the more he tried to recall, the more a small tinge of pain grew deep inside of him.

"Hello?" he called, his eyes still shut tightly, as he rubbed his hands over his head. "You can turn the lights down any time you want..." he said, his voice echoing off the walls around him.

As his eyes finally adjusted to the brightness of the room, he scanned his surroundings. Except for the medical bed that he found himself lying upon, the room was empty.

On the far wall, mounted two meters up from the floor, was a darkened window that ran the length of the wall itself.

"Observation room...*nice*," he said aloud, pushing himself up from the bed and to his feet.

Something tugged him backwards to the bed, however.

He spun around.

An IV trailed from his arm, its syrupy, blue liquid dripping into his vein from a device mounted underneath the head portion of the bed.

Brig quickly yanked the needle from his arm with a small grunt, and watched as the blue substance pooled up onto the floor, creating a sharp contrast to the white room.

He scanned the room thoroughly. It was door-less, at least from what he could see.

"Am I in quarantine? *Huh?*" he yelled at the window.

No one responded.

"Someone's *gotta* be up there. You keep someone in quarantine you *gotta* at least be at the wheel!" he shouted sarcastically.

Brig shook his head and stepped over to the wall just beneath the window, then peered upwards with his hands in the air at his sides.

"Someone's there...*right?*" he called, but no response came. "You can't just keep me in here and not *say* anything..." he continued.

Again, no response.

"*Damn it!*" he finally screamed, pounding on the glass with his left hand, abruptly pulling it back when a sharp pain stabbed at his upper arm.

He glanced into his robe. A bloodied bandage was taped just above his bicep.

"What the *Hell* is goin' on here?" he asked aloud.

Brig stepped back to the bed and leaned on the edge of it, casting a penetrating glare back at the window.

"Alright..." he said, "you want me to sleep...I'll *sleep.*"

He laid his head on the pillow and within moments, even though he did not feel tired, was once again asleep.

The next day, Brig opened his eyes and quickly sat up. He was still in the same room, and the IV once again hung from his arm. He quickly glanced around the room, but there was still no one there.

"*Damn...*" he muttered, swinging his feet around to dangle from the edge of the bed.

One difference, was a small table sitting next to the bed that held a tray of food: steak, cut into pieces, and a grouping of roasted potatoes sitting on a plate next to a glass of plain water.

The smell wafted over to him and made him salivate. He was not sure how long it had been since he had eaten, but he *knew* that he was ravenous. However, before acting on his instincts, he shot a glance up at the observation window.

"Druggin' my *food*, huh?"

He quickly forced himself back onto the pillow and rested his head in his hands, glaring up at the ceiling in protest.

After a few moments, he peered back at the window. Sitting up once again and sighing, he pulled the table towards him, and began to stuff the shredded meat into his mouth.

"Okay, I'll be a *good* little lab rat and eat..." he mumbled loudly with his mouth partially full, "...and then you can do all your little tests. But then you gotta' start talkin' to me, *right?*" He gulped the water and clunked the glass back down onto the tray. "Utensils would be nice, too. I *can* cut my own food, you know..."

The pattern continued for the next two weeks. Each day Brig would wake to the blinding light of the plain, white room, sit up and eat what they had placed next to his bed, and then lay back down for another nap.

However, after what he estimated to be about the fourteenth day of the monotony, Brig awoke to a different experience.

When he opened his eyes, rather than having to squint for the first five minutes of being awake because of the luminosity of the room, he found that the lighting was much more palatable.

The IV, which he had gotten used to ignoring as it hung from his arm while he was awake, was gone.

Brig had decided that enough was enough, and he wanted *out*...or wanted *answers*.

He hopped off the bed and strode over beneath the window. Then, able to lift his arm without much pain, began pounding heavily on the glass above him.

The rattling of the window echoed loudly off the rounded walls of the room.

"Come on, *damn it!*" he yelled, "I've played your little games for *two weeks* now – time to come out and *talk* to me!"

To his chagrin, however, he once again received no response.

Exhaling forcefully in frustration, Brig spun and began to pace back towards the bed. However, before he had reached it, a voice came from the speaker next to the window.

"Brigadier," it said calmly.

"*Dad?*" Brig said in a surprised tone, rotating to face the window.

A portion of the glass had cleared, and he could see the familiar silhouette of his father standing and looking down at him, his hands resting on the console in front of him.

"How are you *feeling*, son?" asked Devlin.

"I...I'm *fine*, Dad," Brig answered with heightened annoyance in his voice. "I just want *out* of here..."

"It's ok to be scared, son. *Everyone* is scared at some point or another in their lives."

"I'm not scared, I just don't understand why I'm here. I'm fine, *believe* me..." Brig insisted, stepping forward and placing his hands on the wall while he glared up at his father through the glass. "I'm *fine*!"

The elder Stroud lowered his head and shook it subtly, as he tapped nervously on the console.

"You've been through a *lot*, Brigadier," Devlin said finally, "These folks here are just trying to *help* you...*sort things out.*"

"*Damn it,* Dad!" Brig growled in frustration, pounding the wall lightly with one fist. "Tell them to let me out. I've got to get back to my squadron. I haven't been debriefed from what I *remember,* and we've got another deployment soon, I'm *sure.*"

"Son..." Devlin interjected, "you've been removed from active duty so that you can...*get better.* And I think that's in everyone's best interests. *Don't you?*"

"What the Hell are you *talking* about, Dad?" Brig shouted, flinging his hands in the air in frustration at his father.

"There's no reason to take that tone with me, Brigadier," his father answered calmly.

"I'm just asking for your help. Can you *help* me when I actually *need* it, Dad?" Brig shouted through gritted teeth.

"We're only doing what's *best* for you, I'm sure you see that, *right?*"

"No...no, I don't. *Wait...you* had them take me from active duty? Why the *Hell* would you do that?" Brig asked with incredulity.

Devlin quietly nodded his head. "I'm sure you understand the position I was put in, son. I had no *choice.*"

Brig growled under his breath. He spun and began angrily pacing in front of the window.

"There you go, talking like a *politician* again," Brig shouted, rotating his head to look at his father and pacing like a rabid beast. "Why am I *not* surprised?"

Devlin paused and gazed down at his enraged son. "What do you *want* from me, Brigadier?"

"I want you to talk to me like a *God-damned father*, not some politician robot...*that's* what I want from you, Dad!" Brig shot back angrily, the heightened emotion starting to crack his voice.

"I've always been there for you, son...and you *know* that," Devlin corrected firmly, his finger held out towards Brig.

"You've *never* been there for me! And when you were, it was only when it was in *your* best interests!" Brig bellowed, pounding both fists once more on the glass in front of Devlin.

"You're flailing, and I understand that..." Devlin said condescendingly, crossing his arms as he stared at Brig. "But given the *alternative*..."

"*Alternative*? I don't *get* you, Dad..." Brig argued loudly, tears beginning to form in the corners of his eyes. "*What* aren't you telling me? What the Hell is going on and *why* am I in here? What was it...that I embarrass you, *as usual*, and you had to tuck me away in a corner somewhere?"

"You don't honestly think that they were just going to let you *walk* away after..."

"After *what*? *What*, *Dad*?" Brig screamed, as he leaned against the wall and glared up at his father.

"Are you telling me you honestly don't know what brought you *here*, son?" Devlin asked.

Brig blinked his eyes in a blank stare and shook his head silently in confusion.

Devlin lowered his head and bit his lip in pensive thought, as he tapped several commands into the console in front of him.

A paused video instantly appeared on the glass between the two men.

Brig watched in bewilderment as the video, which depicted a woman reporter in front of a shopping complex, began to play.

"...And government officials are being tight-lipped this evening about the incident today at the Galleria here in downtown Las Cruces," she began in mid-sentence, "...where a brutal attack that left two men dead and another *critically* injured, was perpetrated by what witnesses are describing, *oddly*, as an *unarmed man* gone 'berserk'. I spoke with one of the witnesses earlier. We have to warn you, the details you are about to hear are...*disturbing*, to say the *least*..."

The video jumped to a recorded interview of a man scratching his head, while he held out his cap to his side.

"Everything was real quiet. You know, a *normal* day here at the mall," he began to explain. "There were these two guys and this gal over here, arguin' I guess. And the one guy started to get kinda loud with the girl. The other guy just stood there with his arms crossed as he watched them goin' back and forth, you know..."

"How did the argument begin. Did you see *that*?" the reporter asked curiously, putting the microphone back into the man's face.

"No...I didn't see that," the man replied while shaking his head. "But they were goin' at it *really* big. A lot of folks were standin' around watchin' them, but not *doin'* much about it. Then all of a sudden this one guy...*military guy* from what I could tell...comes over to them and tells the one guy to knock it off, or somethin'..."

"That was the suspect?"

"Yeah..." the man said, nodding subtly in thought. "So the other guy, that wasn't doin' the arguin' with the girl, pushes the soldier back out of the way and tells him to mind his own business. In the meantime, the other guy reached back and slapped the girl somethin' hard, made her fall back onto the ground. Then he started goin' after her again. But the soldier didn't want *any* of that, picked up the guy by his throat and threw him over two or three meters onto his back..."

The witness started shaking his head in shock, as he began to describe the final few moments.

"I...I was deployed overseas during the *war* back in sixty-eight. And I seen a *lot* of stuff, but this...I never saw *anything* like this happen, not by someone *without* a weapon," he said, his voice shaking.

"It's hard, I know," the reporter said consolingly. "Do you think you can describe what happened next?"

"Well...the soldier, he went up to the guy that was fightin' with the girl...and..." he said with a gulp. "He grabbed the guy's arm and...pretty much broke it in half from behind. The one guy just fell on the ground and balled up. The other guy though, see...he got up and jumped on the soldier's back...tryin' to help his buddy I guess. The soldier just yanked him off his back and tore his throat open. Never saw *anythin'* like that...ever. *Worst thing I've ever seen*...blood everywhere. I'll *never* forget the look on the poor guy's face when he fell to the ground, gaggin' for air while he was grabbin' at his throat. He died pretty much right after that..."

The witness stopped and held his hand over his face, wiping the tears from his eyes.

"Sorry...just, brings back some bad stuff for me. You just never think you're gonna' see stuff like that here in your own country, ya' know?"

"Was that all that you saw?" the reporter asked, trying to calm the man down.

"No...no. Then the soldier goes after the other guy, you know, the one with the broken arm," the witness continued. "I guess he wanted to finish him off or somethin'. I don't know *why*. He was yellin' somethin', hard to understand, but it sounded like '*You can't make me surrender...*' or somethin'. He went up and...stomped on the guy's neck. We all heard it crack. The other guy just flinched for a second and he was dead, too. A couple'a other fellas jumped up to try to restrain the soldier, but that was pretty stupid I guess. He threw one of 'em off him pretty quick and he landed against a light pole over there, hit his head pretty hard and got knocked out. The other guy just backed off. Then the soldier took off over that way, but I didn't see where he went. We were all tryin' to help out the people he attacked."

"Pretty rough stuff from an obviously very emotional witness to this unspeakable tragedy," the reporter said, as the clip switched back live to her reading her notes. "And I can tell you that a small group of military men, described by some witnesses as '*sharpshooters*', showed up right around the time the attacks ended. Witnesses claimed the soldiers shot somewhere between *ten* to *fifteen* tranquilizer-style darts into the back of the suspect before he finally fell and they were able to subdue him. Local police were on the scene moments afterward, but the government and the military officials that were present claimed jurisdiction and took the man into their own custody, *quickly* whisking him away in a nearby van."

The reporter put her notes down to her side and glared at the camera.

"One last clip that we managed to get just moments ago, *reportedly* from the woman who's attack sparked the scuffle by the unknown assailant. *This* one, to me, is the *most* chilling account..."

"Can you tell us what happened?" another woman reporter asked the female victim, holding the microphone down near her face, as the woman sat on the edge of a curb.

The woman shook her head while holding her hands up to her face.

"I don't know...I don't know..." she cried. "Me and my husband, we got into a little fight over there and...he *hit* me." She pulled her hands from her face, revealing a large welt on her cheekbone. She dabbed at the small trail of dried blood around the corner of her nose. "I guess that guy was *trying* to help..."

"The suspect?" the reporter interjected.

The woman nodded.

"...*Oh my God, oh my God, oh my God*...he didn't have to do *that*...he didn't have to *kill* them..." the woman said, her voice breaking with emotion, as she placed her head down into her hands and began sobbing uncontrollably.

The reporter put her hand gently on the woman's shoulder. "Did you know the suspect, ma'am?"

The woman, after several more seconds of heavy sobbing, peered up at the reporter and shook her head. Her eyes were swollen with the burn of her tears.

"His eyes were *red*...*his eyes were red*..." the woman said almost maniacally, as the video halted.

Devlin slowly brought his head up and gazed down at Brig.

Brig, his face frozen with a blank stare, returned his father's glare.

"Do you understand *now*, son?" his father asked him, a small tinge of pity in his voice.

"I *don't* understand, Dad," Brig said in an emotionless drone. "What happened that you're not *telling* me? *Why* are you showing me this?"

Devlin lowered his head and closed his eyes for a quiet moment, breathing a deep sigh and resting his weight forward onto his hands.

"That was *you*, Brigadier," he said quietly.

Brig wrinkled his brow. He attempted to comprehend the video, and how it related to what his father was trying to say. He shook his head in confusion as he looked up at Devlin.

"*How*...that *can't* be. I don't *remember* any of that. I would've remembered..."

"The stress of war can make people do *strange* things, Brigadier," Devlin interrupted. "But I never thought *you* had *that* in you..." he said in a disappointed tone. "These people are going to *help* you, son. I'd suggest you *let* them."

"Like I have a *choice*, Dad?" Brig said, his voice raised to a higher pitch.

Devlin turned his back and began to step towards the exit of the observation room, but then rotated and stared down at his son one last time.

"I *still* love you, Brigadier."

"Dad, *stop!*" Brig yelled.

Devlin did not respond. He pressed his hand against the bio-pad next to the door, to which the door immediately slid open.

"Dad, don't walk away from me, *God damn it*! *You* can get me *out* of here!" Brig continued to curse, pounding his hands rapidly on the glass. "*Dad! Dad!*" he yelled.

It was too late, Devlin had exited the room and the door had slid shut.

Brig wound his arm behind him and pounded the glass one last time, causing a large snowflake of cracks to emanate from around his fists. He spun and slammed himself up against the wall, and slowly slid down into a crouch as he held his head in his hands.

The lion lay on his side, his eyes half-open, as he gazed forward at the handlers that cautiously stepped towards him, their rifles raised.

A few meters away, in a small puddle of crimson blood, his two unfortunate prey lay motionless. They did not stand a chance against his cunning and brutality. He could still smell them, *and* the handlers that now stood over him as they bound his legs, but found he was unable to defend himself.

He tried to move, to fight against certain death from the pair of men, but he lacked the stamina due to the previous night's battle. His paws tingled and his legs felt like heavy logs, and he could not even raise his head to call out for assistance to any of his kind that might be within range.

Such strange weapons... the lion thought, lazily peering out of the corner of his eyes at them. *They didn't slay me. They only made me tired and lose control of my limbs.*

A group of hyenas perched upon a nearby rock and taunted him, as the handlers picked him off the ground and dragged him to their vehicle, where they secured him in the cargo hold and quickly departed. The lion could still hear their jabs through the walls of the truck as it roared away.

Growing more tired by the moment, the lion yawned and closed his eyes, the red glint fading softly as he fell into a slumber.

Present day (2084)...

Brig entered the small neighborhood where opposing rows of small, commercial buildings lined both sides of the street, and where Clive's workshop sat. He stopped and stared at the lone, lit building where he knew he would find, and confront, *once* and for *all*, his former friend.

The heavy sound of rapping on the sliding front door halted Clive in his footsteps, having just cleaned up the broken glass near the window next to his workbench, and on his way back to toss it out in the rear of the building. He slid open the door with an audible sigh, and closing his eyes in frustration, stood in front of Brig

Brig quickly and forcefully pushed past Clive and entered the main room.

"Back to the scene of the crime, *huh?*" Clive said snidely, angrily sliding the door shut with a thump.

"What was *stolen?*" Brig demanded flatly, scanning the room and not making eye contact with Clive.

"Don't play *dumb* with me, man. You *know* what I'm talking about. I've had enough of your *shit*, Stroud. And *I* didn't invite you in...so you can *leave* now. As soon as you return my stuff, of course."

"It was *you*, wasn't it, Cryp?" growled Brig, turning and grabbing Clive's shirt with both hands and pulling him up close to his face. "You *double-crossed* her, *didn't* you? And for *what?*" he screamed.

"Hurts when someone *fucks* with your life, *doesn't* it?" Clive yelled, forcing Brig's hands off him.

"You *son of a bitch...*" Brig snarled, pointing his finger into Clive's face. "You sold her out for your own selfish needs? Who the Hell do you think you *are?*"

"I did it to save *Jessica*, and *everything* was going according to plan until *you* showed up and screwed it all to Hell!" Clive screamed back, shoving Brig backward with both hands.

Brig gave Clive a look of disgusted amazement. Clive *knew* that Jess was alive!

He quickly returned Clive's shove with one of his own, making Clive almost lose his balance, until he caught himself on his workbench stool.

"And you thought it was *okay* to put Steele's life in danger. Did you even *think* of what would happen?" Brig continued, stomping menacingly towards Clive.

"So now you know what it's like when someone *else* is making the decisions that affect your life. Welcome to *my* world, you bastard!" Clive snarled.

"Oh, get *over* it already, Underwood!" Brig screamed in response, waving one hand in Clive's face. "*Everyone* that goes to war leaves *some* piece of them behind. What do you think makes *you* so God damned special?"

He turned his back on Clive.

"It's *more* than that, and you *know* it!" Clive barked. "I *thought* you were my friend...and then you go and get your sister to back away from me. Let's talk *betrayal*, Stroud!"

"What? You're crazy," Brig replied dismissively.

"You *saw* the email, don't act like you had *nothing* to do with it..." Clive countered. "She even *told* me you said something to her about it. You gonna deny *that*, too?"

Brig quickly spun around to face his former partner. "You *just* got back from a mission with a traumatic injury. You needed time to *heal*...physically AND mentally. You were in *no* state of mind to be in *that* relationship..."

"No...no...*that* wasn't all..." Clive interjected angrily. "You told her I had *'issues'* and to stay away from me. What was it, Stroud. You didn't like it that a man with *black* in his blood was sniffing around your high society family..."

"What the Hell...are you nuts? I told her you had things to sort out after that mission, *yeah*. But if you think this has *anything* to do with the color of your skin, or your father's, or whoever, you're just *insane*. And besides, she was *pregnant* and wanted to try to reconcile with her husband. You had *no* right to interfere with that..." He pointed an angry finger into Clive's chest.

Clive smacked it away quickly.

Brig spun around once again and began to storm towards the door, but then stopped as he glanced at the broken window.

He had focused so much on what Clive had told him back at the pub, that he didn't even realize the importance of *who* might have broken in.

Steele... Brig thought.

"*What* was on the cards, Clive?" Brig said calmly, as he stopped, still with his back to Clive.

Clive did not respond.

Brig turned to face Clive with raised eyebrows.

"*Hmm?*" he asked again.

Clive glared back at Brig with a knowing grin.

"Why would she steal the cards *back*. What was *on* them?" Brig screamed as he got into Clive's face.

"Everything about her past that she doesn't *want* to remember..." Clive answered coolly.

"What the Hell is *that* supposed to mean?" Brig asked, knowing that Clive was continuing to play games with him.

Clive smiled wickedly in defiance of Brig.

Brig yanked at Clive's collar, pulling him centimeters from his face.

"Stop playin' games, Cryp! Tell me what was on the cards...now!" Brig snarled, the spittle flinging from his mouth wildly.

"Look around you, Stroud," Clive countered disdainfully. "All of this...everything that's happened. The flare, the power failure, the chaos. *They* knew about it – *before* it was supposed to happen. Her *and* her precious father. And they didn't do anything about it."

"You don't know what you're talkin' about," Brig replied in disgust.

As he released Clive's collar, a queasy feeling of unease grew in his gut. Brig did not *want* to believe it, but the oddity of Steele's actions lately left him with the smallest seed of doubt, but he quickly stowed it away in the back of his mind.

"Yeah, there it is," Clive hissed. "You know it's true...I can see it on your face. That's one classy girl you got there..."

Brig ground his teeth together as he glared around at the room, and then back at Clive.

"And that's not all..." Clive added knowingly, the smirk on his face growing to a sneer.

"What? What other lies are you gonna tell me about Steele, Cryp?"

"I guess you need to ask *her*, now."

Brig flexed his fists and feigned a punch in Clive's direction, then waved dismissively at his former friend. "I don't believe a word you're sayin'. You throw away your life and sell out *everyone around you* just because you lose a girl...and then you go makin' up shit like this," Brig snorted.

He turned his back and began to walk to the door again.

"*You're a pathetic loser...*" Brig said coldly with a wave of his hand, his voice echoing throughout the small room.

Clive, incensed by Brig's remarks, leapt forward and grabbed Brig around the neck with one arm.

"I should have killed you when I had the *chance*, Stroud!" Clive snarled, struggling to choke Brig from behind.

As Clive wrestled his fellow Epsilon, Brig landed a backward elbow into Clive's stomach three successive times, forcing Clive to release him and double-over long enough for Brig to land a crushing blow of his own to Clive's face.

Clive reeled backwards onto his workbench, sending tools and electronics spilling onto the floor in a loud crash.

"You wanna do this *again?*" Brig growled, panting wildly as he rushed Clive.

Clive agilely countered with two successive punches to Brig's jaw, stopping him in his tracks and making him tumble backwards to the floor.

Brig glared up at Clive with hatred in his eyes, as he started to push himself upright.

"And *I* coulda' let you die on that hill in Portugal. Or I could've taken you back with me from Russia to let *you* stand trial for being the *double-crossing traitor* that you are, *you lousy son of a bitch...*" Brig snarled.

"Come on, *Rage*," Clive taunted. "What are you gonna do, turn into an *animal* and finish the job you were too *scared* to do back then?"

Clive turned from Brig and grabbed something that Brig could not see from his workbench, and then spun back around to face him.

"Or maybe I should just *shut* you up before you cause any *more* trouble..." Clive barked.

He waved a small, blue vial of serum in the air with one hand. Setting the glass tube down behind him onto the edge of the workbench, Clive took a step towards Brig and pointed angrily.

"They should have just put you down when you got back like they *wanted* to...but you had *Daddy* step in..." Clive said, gritting his teeth.

Brig growled and pounced forward before Clive could finish his statement, catching Clive across the midsection and thrusting him backward onto the floor.

The two men exchanged flurries of punches, each emitting loud grunts as the blows fell.

Finally, Clive landed with his knee into Brig's throat.

He pulled himself up with the aid of a nearby chest and

stumbled over to his workbench chair, while Brig rolled over onto his side in an attempt to get up from the floor.

Clive lifted the stool in the air over his head.

Just as he was about to critically wound his former friend and EW partner, Brig dodged and, in one motion, did a sweeper kick against Clive's prosthetic leg, instantly knocking him down before he could react.

As Brig swiftly got to his feet, Clive grasped agonizingly with both hands at the area above his knee where the prosthetic had been surgically attached, and glared in shock up at him.

"Act like a *cripple*, people are gonna *treat* you like a cripple," Brig taunted with an angry finger pointed down at Clive, and then turned to the door.

Clive, speechless against Brig for the first time in his life, could only look on as Brig slid the door open.

Before Brig could exit, Clive grabbed the vial from the workbench above him.

"And make sure to ask her about *this*..." Clive growled, angrily tossing it at Brig, where it missed its target and smashed harmlessly against the wall next to the door. Its syrupy blue contents splattered across the wall, the curtains and, finally, onto the floor at Brig's feet.

Brig stopped to glance at the broken vial as it came to rest a meter away from him, and then stepped out of the door into the foggy night.

42:
So Far Away

Present day (2084)...

Brig strode quickly alongside the road on the way to Steele's apartment. The sound of the stones crunching under his feet echoed eerily off the empty buildings surrounding him, giving him the strange sensation of walking through an empty tomb.

Already winded from the confrontation with Clive, and after having walked briskly for almost two hours, he found his feet and legs growing tired. But he was determined to make it there before Steele did anything rash.

What her next action might be, however, was a mystery to Brig. It bothered him that he did not understand her state of mind right now; and why she would *still* be obsessing so much over the mysterious cipher cards, even after her father's death, that she would break into Clive's workshop to steal them.

Brig shook his head in silent thought, as he continued through the darkness.

Clive's words '*Everything she doesn't want to remember...*' kept repeating like a skipping vinyl record in his head.

Brig had initially played it off as just *another* head game that Clive was working at with him, but the more that he put the pieces together of Steele's confusing break-in and theft, the more he wondered if there was *truth* behind the statement.

The soft rumble of thunder behind him from the east filled the quiet, damp night, and a chilling breeze buffeted his face from the west in front of him. He ducked his chin down into his jacket as he strode forward.

A storm was coming.

Brig picked up his walking pace, ignoring the fatigue in his legs, as he knew he *had* to get to Steele before it was too late.

He once again thought of Clive, and even though it angered him to do so, he pondered *his* ex-friend's role in the mystery of the cipher cards.

Clive had said that his plan was to 'save' Brig's sister, and Brig bristled at the realization that someone he had revered so highly was willing to trade one life for another. *Jessica* would not have wanted it that way.

So what was Clive up to, and what was he *hiding*? One thing Brig knew for sure, however, was that he would *never* forgive Clive if any additional harm were to come to Steele because of his selfish actions.

After another few minutes of pondering, Brig finally found himself rounding the corner of the street on which Steele's apartment stood.

He stopped to look on at the front face of the building that overlooked the street below. The lone streetlight on the opposite side dimly cast a beckoning cone of light downward onto the dark pavement below it.

A light mist had begun in the last few moments and, coupled with the nipping breeze that already cascaded over the area, gave Brig chills that ran up and down his arms. The faint, momentary flicker of lightning behind him, followed by a growing thunderclap, urged Brig forward.

A desperate feeling grew in his gut.

He stopped and peered up at the ghostly, dark building that rose up into the night before him. It was the middle of the night, and as such, no lights were visible from any of the small handful of the still-occupied apartments.

The thunder boomed, shaking the ground ominously, as the storm had sprinted to close the gap behind him, and was now essentially on top of the building.

Brig shielded his eyes from the rain that darted from the sky and pelted his head in large, frigid droplets.

From the corner of his eye, he caught the momentary reflection of the lightning on something shiny off to his right at the edge of the courtyard. He strained his eyes as he glared into the darkness some ten meters or so away, but he could not determine what it was.

As he was about to continue on into the building, a brilliant flash of lightning lit the area in front of him, exposing the object that had gleamed for a nanosecond moments before.

Steele's retro-bike lay on its side at the edge of the courtyard grass.

Brig suddenly felt the air expel from his chest, and his heart began throbbing against his ribcage, leaving him panic-stricken as he looked down at the bike.

He swiftly crossed the front courtyard and strode into the main stairwell, making quick work of the first three flights of stairs as he found the adrenaline to leap three steps at once. He exited after the fourth set into the small corridor that led past Steele's door.

As he approached Steele's apartment, he could see the closed door, which gave him both a feeling of relief and of dread at the same time, allowing him to breathe easier, if for just a moment. Perhaps she was asleep, finding the peace to rest for the night, *safely* in her own bed.

He turned the knob silently and pushed the door open, enough for him to poke his head into the apartment to peer around inside.

The lights were off, which he perceived to be another good sign, so he stepped inside and shut the door quietly behind him.

Brig had almost expected, in a *desperately* hopeful sense, to be clunked over the head again by Steele, thinking that he was another intruder.

The apartment was deathly silent.

He cautiously made his way through the living room and stopped at the entry to the hallway outside of Steele's bedroom, taking a deep breath to calm his nerves.

He stepped forward towards the door.

It seemed odd to him that her bedroom door would be open, especially since she had usually made a *point* of locking it when retiring for the night. Brig confirmed his suspicions, however, when he peered into the room.

The bed, still made up, was *empty*.

Brig spun and stepped back into the living room, flicking the light switch at the end of the hallway as he did so, illuminating the empty space.

The lamp that normally adorned the end table next to the couch immediately caught his eye. Its clear base was toppled onto its side on the floor at the foot of the table.

The hairs on the back of his neck stood at attention.

A small trail of dark blood extended across the carpet and onto the tile beside the small, island countertop that divided the living room from the kitchen adjacent to it. The trail stopped in front of the sink. A bloody shirt sat crumpled haphazardly on the countertop, along with a few droplets that were speckled into the sink.

Brig's eyes immediately gravitated to a small grouping of plastic cards sitting on the island itself.

"The *cipher cards...*" he mumbled aloud.

Although he had never seen them in person, he realized *exactly* what they were. He snatched them up with one hand and stared.

Bloodstained and smeared fingerprints marred the face of the top card. Brig forced the cards into his jacket pocket, turned and yanked open the door.

He shut it with a slam behind him and took a step towards the stairwell that led downstairs and back into the courtyard.

The clunking sound of another door, followed by the howl of the wind escaping into the corridor around him, stopped him.

He turned to face the stairwell on the opposite end of the hallway that led upstairs.

"*Roof...*" he said aloud softly, his whispers echoing off the walls around him, as he leapt from his position by Steele's door and sprinted to the steps.

As he reached the top of the stairwell and forcefully pushed open the roof access door with one hand into the driving rain, his heart sank.

At the edge of the roof, Steele stood, precariously perched on the railing of the metal fire escape that ran up the side of the building, her back to him with her arms calmly down at her side.

"*Steele!*" Brig called, as he stepped out into the heavy downpour, the lightning flashing his shadow against the wall next to the access door.

She did not respond.

"You shouldn't *be* here!" he cried. He took several steps forward, raising his voice to be heard over the storm.

As if awoken from a trance, Steele slowly turned her head over her shoulder to look at Brig. Her long hair was drenched and matted partially onto her face, and the skin around her eyes swollen from tears.

"Go *away*, Brigadier," she sniffled loudly, and then turned her head the other way.

"Steele, *please...*" pled Brig. "Come down off of there, sweetheart. Nothing's *this* bad!"

Steele shook her head slowly as she peered down at the street below her.

"I *love* you, Steele...*please!* Don't *do* this, it was *all* my fault..."

Brig continued. "I didn't *think* about the consequences, and I'm sorry it turned out the way it did...but *please* don't..."

"You *love* me?" Steele droned. "You don't *know* me, Brigadier."

"I know you better than I've ever known anyone in my *life*, Steele," Brig argued calmly, taking another step closer to her.

"*Stop!*" Steele cried maniacally through her tears, turning her head to face Brig. "Don't come any closer..."

Brig stopped and held his hands out to his side. The rain pelted his head, making his hair fall straight down around his face.

"Whatever this *is*, Steele, we can work through it. We can get through this *together*," he begged, his voice cracking.

Steele cupped her hand over her mouth and began to sob heavily, as she turned to look down at the street below.

"It's a *lie*...*it's a lie*..." she said repeatedly.

"I don't *understand*, Steele. What's going on? *What's* a lie?" Brig asked frantically.

Steele turned once again to Brig with a blank expression.

"*I'm sorry...I'm sorry*..." she cried, shaking her head, her eyes slanted almost shut as the tears flowed out of them.

"Sorry? You don't *have* anything to be sorry for, sweetheart. *Please*..." Brig countered.

Before he could finish his plea, Steele leaned forward and plunged off the ledge.

"*NO!*" Brig screamed with a shriek that reverberated off the buildings across the street, his voice booming over the storm that raged around him.

The group of three boys and two girls stood in a circle, as they shouted at a smaller girl with pigtails that sat on the ground in the middle. She looked up at them with tears in her eyes.

The bigger of the two girls had pushed the small girl to the ground, and rather than defend her, the others had joined in, laughing and hurling insults at her.

"Limey!" one of the bully girls shouted down to the girl in the circle, to which the rest of the group laughed and pointed, while the girl covered her eyes and sobbed.

"Stop it, go away!" the girl cried, waving the group off with one hand.

Adding to the insults, one of the boys yanked at a pigtail sticking out from the side of the girl's hair, making her yelp in a high-pitched tone. The group erupted with taunting laughter once more as the boy whipped the pigtail into the girl's face and stood back with a sneer, taking in the jeers and taunts from the rest of the group.

As he reached in to repeat his deed, another boy, outside of the circle and not involved with the bullying session, pulled him backwards.

"That's *enough!*" the boy yelled, grabbing the bully boy's shirt and yanking him forward. He balled his fist up behind his head as he prepared to dole out justice for the little girl.

The bully pushed at the boy, who released him as he stumbled backwards, but instantly swung around and tagged the bully just below one eye, sending the bully reeling backwards holding his face in pain.

The rest of the group of bullies dispersed. The girls ran off down the street towards their homes while the boys gathered around the new boy.

"What's *your* problem, kid?" one of the bullies yelled at the boy.

"Leave her alone!" the boy growled, as he swung again, nailing another of the boys directly in the gut and doubling him over.

The remaining bully quickly punched at the boy as he recoiled, hitting him square in the jaw and making him fall backwards onto his rear.

"Mind your own business, *punk!* What's an eleven-year-old doing sticking up for a little girl *anyway?*" the biggest of the bullies said to the boy, while pointing an angry finger down at him. Then, he turned and, along with the other two bullies, strode past the girl on the ground and flipped at her pigtails once again.

"You're lucky your little *boyfriend* came along..." the larger bully taunted, as the group crossed the street and disappeared around a hedge.

The boy stood up while rubbing his jaw and stepped over to the girl. He held out a hand to help her to her feet.

"Thanks," the girl said with a distinctive, British accent.

"Can't *stand* those guys," the boy replied with a heavy hint of West Texas twang in his own voice.

"You didn't have to *do* that, you know," the girl offered. She brushed the dirt from her knees while looking up at the boy. "I may only be *eight*, but I can take *care* of myself."

"Yeah, it looked like it..." the boy chuckled, flexing his jaw back and forth. "You're not from around here, are you?"

"No...just moved to the Republic about a month ago."

"That's a weird accent," the boy teased with a smile.

"I could say the same about yours," the girl retorted, returning the boy's smile with her own. "I'm Steele, *Steele Fox*."

"*Wow*, cool name..." observed the boy with raised eyebrows. "I'm *Brigadier Stroud*, nice to meet you."

"*Brigadier*," Steele giggled. "*That's* a funny name."

"Thanks," Brig said with a sigh and a flat smile.

"Well, thanks for helping me out, Brigadier. Those boys were just *dreadful*. I hope I don't run into them anytime soon."

"Don't worry," Brig replied. "If they bother you, you just let me know and *I'll* take care of them for you."

The milliseconds passed like minutes as Brig sprinted towards the edge of the rooftop. The rain slapped his face in slow motion like a mini whip, but he steadfastly cut through it in his desperate dash to save Steele.

He reached the edge of the roof and peered over the side wall down at the street.

His heart fell.

Steele lay motionless, face-down and at a horrifying angle on the deserted street below. The lone street light nearby cast a small, dim beam of light down onto her crumpled body as it lay on the wet, glistening asphalt.

Brig's jaw tightened. He threw himself over the edge of the wall and onto the fire escape with a loud clang, and then, without regard to his own safety, raced to descend the slick, rattling staircases with an unparalleled amount of speed. He slipped several times and barely caught himself, preventing a neck-breaking fall.

Finally reaching the bottom rung, he leapt and landed on the concrete sidewalk beside the overgrown hedges that lined the side of the building.

Steele flung the line of her fishing rod forward. It landed with a plunk in the serene lake that stretched almost a half-kilometer in front of her, as it wound through and around the forest that lay just to the east of a small set of waterfalls.

She peered over at Brig, who was staring mindlessly forward at his own line, and not paying much attention to her struggles.

"I never really *liked* fishing much," she said to Brig, as she yanked at the line, pulling an old shoe from the bottom of the lake. "But I *do* appreciate you having your family invite me along on your camping trip. It has been a lot of fun."

"Well, we've been friends for a couple of years now, figured you'd *wanna* have some fun. Looks like you caught dinner there," Brig teased, slowly dragging his line back towards him across the top of the water.

"If we're all relying on me to provide dinner, there are going to be a *lot* of hungry mouths, I'm afraid," she jabbed.

Brig snorted and recast his line, holding one hand above his eye to block the glare of the mid-day sun, as it beaconed across the water from the opposite end of the lake in the distance.

"You need to get your line out farther," he instructed.

"Sorry I'm not as strong as *you*, Brigadier," Steele quipped. "I've an idea, though."

She flung her pole over her shoulder and strode up the bank of the lake past Brig, bumping into him playfully as she passed.

Brig snickered as he gazed forward out at the horizon, not paying particular attention to what Steele had in mind.

Meanwhile, Steele had climbed onto a log that jutted out over the water a short distance from him, balancing with her arms out as she paced to the edge of it.

"Think *this* is far enough?" she called to Brig with a shrill laugh.

"You're crazy!" Brig replied, shaking his head in amazement at the young girl. "Gotta be careful out there, that log might not be..." he added, but then the log crumbled beneath Steele's feet, sending her splashing into the lake.

"Help! I can't *swim*..." Steele shouted.

She paddled maniacally with arms and legs pounding back and

forth in the water. Her head dipped underneath the surface every few seconds, as she attempted to stay afloat, while she slowly rode the subtle undercurrent that flowed out towards the first waterfall.

Without hesitation, Brig dropped his pole and dashed towards the edge of the lake, diving headfirst into the water and swimming at top speed towards his young friend.

As he neared Steele, she fell silent and motionless on top of the water. Brig frantically grabbed her arm, threw it over his shoulder and towed her swiftly back to the shore.

Exhausted from the swim and breathless from the shock of seeing Steele unconscious, he laid her down onto the soft grass.

Brig fell to his knees as he looked down at her. His hands shook uncontrollably as he pushed the hair from Steele's face.

Suddenly, she grabbed Brig by the shoulders and smiled at him, gazing deep into his eyes.

"My hero!" she said mockingly, pulling him into a flat-faced kiss, all the while giggling as she did so.

Brig pulled away, falling back onto his behind on the wet grass.

"What are you *doing*?" he asked incredulously.

Steele held her hand to her mouth and giggled profusely at Brig.

"Weren't *you* the one that said we should be having *fun* here?" she teased with a wink.

Brig shook his head with a coy smile and playfully pushed at her arm.

For the next hour or so, the pair sat opposite one another: Steele with her arms around her knees, staring at Brig every so often, and Brig leaning back on his hands as he looked out at the lake.

"I can't wait to come back next year." She turned her head towards Brig. "That is...if I'm *invited*."

Brig smiled for a second, but then let it fade from his face. "Don't know if I'll be around next year..."

"Why not?"

"Dad enrolled me in some *military school*, so I'll *probably* miss camping season," he said dejectedly.

"Maybe I can get my Mum and Dad to let me come up and see you there?"

"*Maybe...*" he said with a distance in his voice. "Dad says it'll *change my life*...for the *better* is what he said. I'm kinda bummed."

"I don't think it will change you, Brigadier. You'll *always* be the same to me," Steele replied, placing her hand gently on Brig's shin.

Brig gazed at Steele and smiled.

As he got up from his landing crouch, Brig darted forward as fast as his tired feet could carry him.

The adrenaline in him was flowing so heavily now that he had not even paid attention to the fact that he had painfully twisted his ankle during the final drop from the fire escape seconds earlier. Not once did he take his eyes off Steele, lying on the ground just ahead of him, as his feet slammed into the puddles of rainwater that gathered within the cracks of the broken sidewalk.

Although the distance to her was only several meters, Brig felt as if though a giant, invisible hand had grabbed the back of his jacket and tugged him backwards.

The sounds of the heavy thunder clapping overhead rang solidly off the stone facing of the buildings surrounding him, but he did not hear it. The world was silent in his ears, and all he *could* hear were Steele's faint breaths pouring out of her broken body ahead of him.

He leapt the final meter from the sidewalk, over the curb and came to a sliding stop on his knees next to Steele, rolling both of his arms underneath her and turning her over in one gentle, loving motion.

Brig softly brushed the hair from over Steele's face with a shaky hand. He stared down at her, the tears from his eyes pouring heavier than the rain coming from the sky above him.

The buzzer sounded rudely from the train platform behind Brig, as he stood looking down at Steele.

She nervously bit the tip of her finger while tapping her foot, not making eye contact with him.

"So, you're going for the full year, *yeah*?" she asked, peering up at him through her peripheral, her green eyes peeking out in-between her brunette trusses that fell around her face.

Brig nodded and smiled down at her. "You won't even *know* I'm gone..."

"Not likely," she replied immediately, glancing away as she caught sight of the bullet train making its way around the corner in the distance. "You've *always* been there for me, Brigadier," she said sadly.

Brig opened his arms and pulled her into an embrace, closing his eyes as his face nestled into her long hair.

"And I *always* will, Steele...you know that," he said lovingly. "You've been like a little sister to me, and I'll never let anything happen to you...*ever*."

As if beckoning him specifically, the buzzer sounded once again in what seemed a more obnoxious tone than before.

"I'm going to miss you *so* much," she said with a small whimper, squeezing Brig more tightly.

"You need to keep in touch," he said firmly, kissing her forehead before he held her out at arm's length, gazing deeply at her.

"I *promise*," Steele replied with a quick nod, wiping away a small stream of tears that had escaped from her eyes.

Brig patted Steele lightly on the side of her arm with a loving smile, picked up his bag and then strode past her to board the train.

Brig stroked the side of Steele's swollen face with a soft palm as he held her across his lap.

He tried to find the words to say to her that might magically make her open her eyes, but at the moment, he had trouble even finding his own breath.

"It's okay...*it's okay*..." he repeated softly, pulling her into his arms tightly and nuzzling his face into her neck, the strength to hold back his sobs fading with every second.

A gurgling cough made him bolt upright once again.

Steele, trying to open her eyes wide, awkwardly blinked her eyelids as she looked up and through Brig.

"*Mum*..." she said, a small stream of blood trickling from the side of her mouth. "*Mum*..."

"It's okay, sweetheart..." Brig reassured, moving his face closer to hers and gazing directly into her eyes.

"Is *Dad* home yet..." she asked with a vacant stare, not even attempting to blink away the rain that continued to pour from the sky. "He'll be *so* proud, Mum," she continued. "I got Best Girl today. Oh, he'll be *so* proud."

Brig looked at Steele as he stroked her hair continuously.

"It's okay...it's okay. I'm *here*, sweetheart," he repeated to her, his words wet with emotion.

He continued to gaze into her eyes.

A good portion of the whites in them had turned red with fresh blood that had started to overflow out of the corner, and washed into a pale pink from the rain.

Steele closed her eyelids and coughed once, expelling a larger clump of blood from the corner of her mouth.

Brig sobbed as he wiped the blood from her chin with his sleeve.

She opened her eyes once again, however this time she looked directly at Brig. Then, shaking painfully, she placed her hand on Brig's cheek.

"You were...*always* there," she said weakly, trying to force a smile.

"And I *always* will be..." Brig answered, kissing her forehead, as he cried silently.

"*Brigadier*..." she said, pulling his face gently away from hers and gazing into his eyes. "You have to...*save yourself*," she said, nodding her head at him as she, too, began to cry.

Brig pursed his lips and nodded, refusing to stop stroking her hair, as he held her tightly.

"*I love you*," Brig sputtered.

Steele attempted a smile through her tears.

"*Promise* me..." she demanded in a broken voice.

Closing her eyes, she coughed violently once again as she began to shiver from the cold.

She opened her eyelids to gaze up at Brig one final time, her eyes wider than they had ever been.

"*Red Vision*..." she said, nodding her head vigorously, as she pawed lovingly at his face.

The blood now flowed heavier than before from her mouth and eye.

"*Red Vision*..." she repeated.

Brig nodded and held her face close to his, kissing her forehead while he refused to let her go.

The grand oak trees at the edge of Bronson's estate swayed in the morning breeze, presenting their comforting shade as the sun above offered its mourning through the wispy clouds that filled the sky around it.

Brig leaned in and gently placed the final few stones atop the fresh grave that he had dug in the earth for Steele alongside her father's. He leaned back on his haunches and stared down at the broken ground in front of him, the realization of the moment numbing him to his core.

As he held the Primrose in his hand at his side, a light wisp of wind kicked up from behind him, but he refused to let it take it from him *again*.

Brig sat quietly, still and alone for hours that day, his hands on his knees and the flower gently resting between his fingertips, as he stared on at the pile of stones that marked Steele's resting place.

As the morning turned to afternoon and the sun began to descend from its peak, he had made his mind up about where he wanted to be. It was not *here*.

Pushing himself to his feet, he cast a longing gaze once more down at Steele's shallow grave, and then secured the flower up against the flat piece of slate at the head of the plot with a few smaller rocks.

He ran one hand through his hair and looked up at the sky.

Brig turned and walked to the front of the estate property, pushed open the gate and roared off towards the highway on Steele's retro-bike.

The afternoon sun had dipped beneath the clouds once more, casting the blurred landscape around him into a dull gray as he rode. His shoulder-length hair flew wildly out behind him as the wind buffeted his face.

Brig had experienced solitude in his previous years, but *nothing* compared to the bitter emptiness that had accompanied him since the pre-dawn hours of this morning. It stung him and numbed him all at the same time, leaving the outside world in a hazy and meaningless cloud.

As the sun prepared for its daily slumber, forcing its final rays through a cloudbank near the horizon to his back, Brig navigated the bike along the divided, desert highway. Then, as if on autopilot, he guided the bike off the main highway onto the dirt road that led to the familiar path up between two foothills. The dust behind him billowed into clouds that hung in the moist air like a sandy fog.

Brig brought the bike to a halt, climbed off and then, after reaching underneath the seat, slowly walked over to the patch of scrub grass that lined the bluff ahead. He stepped onto the cushiony seating and noticed the heavy matting in one spot where someone had been very recently.

He sat down next to the spot. A warmth cascaded over him and he smiled for the first time today.

He was home.

Looking out over the vast array of satellite dishes in front of him, Brig leaned back on his hands and closed his eyes, letting the cool breeze wash over his face. He opened his eyes and peered skyward. The clouds had started to overtake the blue sheen behind them.

The storm was still out there, *always* threatening, *always* unrelenting.

He reached for the half-empty bottle of vodka that he had pulled from the bike moments before and unscrewed the top, and then released a large mouthful of the potent liquid into his throat.

Brig gazed out across the tops of the defunct, technological mammoths in the valley below, finally understanding why *she* loved this place.

Although the world had changed drastically and there were plenty of serene places to be found, *none* of them offered the strange paradox of civilization and exiled peace that could be found *here*.

He placed his hand down on the matted grass next to him. He could feel *her* warmth and knew that she was *there* with him, *even now*. Brig tipped the bottle in the air once more, draining the remainder of the contents into his mouth and swallowing hard.

With a swift motion, he flung the bottle forward into the valley below, where it shattered harmlessly against the face of one of the dishes with a lonely clang.

42: SO FAR AWAY

The breeze subsided and the air became still. Brig reached into the back of his belt and extracted the handgun that he had retrieved from one of the Syndicate thugs weeks before. He laid it flat onto his lap, where he glared down at it in pensive thought.

'Save yourself...' she had made him promise to her before she left him.

He was not sure that *this* was what she had in mind, but to *him*, this was the *only* way to do just that. He had lost *everything*: his family, his friends and *most* of all, the one person that he cared for the most deeply in the world.

Brig closed his eyes once more and slowly lifted the end of the barrel until it gently massaged the edge of his temple. Then, as the numbness settled deep within him and scoured the pain away, he instinctively pulled the trigger.

Instead of the release that he expected, the hammer emanated a hollow click. Brig sighed heavily, checked the action and the chamber of the gun, and then repositioned his finger over the trigger.

Before he could finish the task, a strong gust of wind pushed against his back and forced him forward, so much so that he dropped the gun onto the grass in front of him while putting out a hand to prevent himself from falling forward.

As he put his fingers onto the butt of the weapon, his eyes wandered to the distant corner of the field several kilometers away. A small, red, steadily blinking light caught his eye.

He scrunched his eyebrows in perplexity. He had never noticed it before, and it seemed rather *oddly* out of place.

"Guess *this* can wait a sec..." he said to himself wryly, repositioning the gun into the back of his belt and pushing himself upright, wobbling slightly as he did so. Brig placed his hand over his eyes and scanned the horizon, but could not see the light anymore. He had ingested a lot of alcohol, but he was *sure* that he saw it.

Intrigued, he remounted the bike and fired up the motor, its raw roar echoing fiercely off the lifeless, metal faces in the valley below.

Brig squeezed the throttle of the bike, forcing the horses beneath him forward along the highway that he projected would have run parallel to the field just beyond the foothill to his left.

After a few minutes of riding and scanning the landscape for signs of what he might have seen, he came to the end of the foothills and realized that they simply flowed out into empty desert beyond.

He pulled the bike up to an idle at the side of the road and looked back along the path he had just traveled. Brig shook his head in confusion. He dismounted the bike and staggered into the desert just beneath one of the larger foothills in sight, scratching his head and scanning the area around him.

After what seemed 30 minutes of trudging through the sand and scrub grass, a strong wind had kicked up and a swirling wall of clouds had formed all around him.

Dust storm, great. Guess I'm gonna go one way or the other... he thought, knowing that there would be no way for him to survive without protection from the elements out here.

He climbed blindly up and down each of the dunes as he reached them, holding his face underneath his jacket for protection. He squinted to see anything beyond the cloud of dust that had formed a seemingly impenetrable wall of blackness, but he could not even see his own hand.

Suddenly, he realized that, through no intention of his own, he had not only climbed the bluff on the opposite end of the array field, but that he had also just stepped off it.

Brig tumbled clumsily head-over-heels down the side of the hill, grunting as he bounced off several rock abutments that found his ribcage. He finally came to rest with a dull clang against a large metal post.

He sat up, winced and rubbed his painful side with one hand. Next to him, he eyed the object that he had run into: a metal fence. Brig instantly noticed it as the type that he and McGraw had placed along the perimeter of the missile range some nine years prior.

He pulled himself up by a few exposed chain links and stood staring down the edge of the fence line. The barrier stretched for kilometers in one direction and came to an abrupt end in the other into the side of the hill, covered with a thick, immovable, tarpaulin material.

The cloud cover had passed mysteriously. Or at least in the area where he stood, as he gathered by looking back up at the hill from which he had just fallen, and saw that the clouds still remained at the top.

Brig spotted a tear in the fence covering twenty meters away, where the fence had apparently been damaged and was lying partially on its side.

He quickly covered the distance, darting into the opening without a sound and stopping on the other side, when he ran face-first into a large, metal wall that stood ten meters high by what he estimated to be twenty meters wide. Brig stumbled along the barricade, keeping his balance with one hand as he stepped, as the alcohol had begun to enhance his impairment to a great degree.

It was like a dream to him; he could not understand what he was looking at, or even how he got there. But something beckoned him forward, and his common sense had already fallen asleep at the bottom of the vodka bottle several kilometers ago.

As he reached the edge of the metal wall, he turned the corner and leaned against it, squinting forward into the open space beyond. Brig had to shake himself into coherence as he took in the sight before him.

A large, circular, vertical ring, centered in the open space and mounted onto a raised platform by several metallic braces, angled upward into the sky. An outer band of pulsating, red lighting glowed as it rotated around the structure, accompanied by a droning hum that vibrated the air. Blackness occupied the area in the center of the ring, but he could *see* through the opposite end. The sky beyond the back of the structure warped like heat lines on a desert road, where it met the metal and stretched upward for what seemed to be a kilometer at the very least.

Brig wrinkled his brow further and leaned his full weight against the wall, then abruptly pulled back as he recoiled in pain.

A large, jagged edge of a wooden splinter protruded from his palm. The wall he thought he was leaning on was actually a row of wooden crates. Brig painfully extracted the wooden shard from his hand, and blotted the flesh against his jacket as a copious amount of fresh, crimson blood flowed from the wound.

As he moved to retake his spot next to the crates, a large insignia imprinted on the side caught his eye.

"*Red Vision...*" he murmured. He took a step back to focus on the words.

It hit him like a delayed bolt of lightning as the words left his mouth, making him step back even further until the gun in his belt clanged loudly against the metal barrier at his back.

He scanned the row of crates. They stretched on for as far as he could see, all with the same crimson insignia emblazoned on their sides. Beneath the lettering were additional descriptions that differed for each crate. Some read, 'Perishable: Citrus Seeds' while others simply said, 'Ore' or 'Polymers'.

His curiosity piqued beyond comprehension, Brig trotted along the row of crates until he found an aisle that led inwards towards the center space, and then darted between the rows.

The sound of voices coming from beyond the crates made him halt. He pressed himself flatly up against them and caught sight of two men carrying a larger version of the very crates behind which he hid.

Not seeing or hearing anyone else present, Brig stepped forward around the corner of the tower of crates and into its shadow, taking up a crouching spot just behind a second, shorter row of containers adjacent to it.

He peeked up towards the hill behind him.

The swirling clouds, formed much like a hurricane eye wall, stretched around the entire area and reached into the sky beyond his sight. Every few moments, subtle claps of thunder erupted from random locations up and down the wall, accompanied by small flashes of light.

Brig turned his attention forward again and watched the men with the container ascend the flat, elongated stairs that led up to the ring. He scratched his head.

The men turned, descended the stairs and disappeared from view. Brig's instincts told him to take a closer look, but before he could act on them, the ring's monotonous hum increased to a low roar and the crates next to him began to vibrate. Brig could feel the air forcefully pressed from his lungs. He peered over his shoulder. The lightning that traveled the wall of clouds above him became violent; long fingers of jagged, white sparks jumped from side to side into the dark clouds beyond.

Suddenly, a blinding, white aura surrounded the container on the platform. Then...it disappeared.

"...the *Hell*?" Brig said aloud.

He watched in amazement and confusion, ignoring the intoxicated buzz in his brain.

Just as he had arisen from his crouch to get a closer look, he felt the heavy sting of a blunt tool, as it crunched down onto the back of his neck.

The force of the blow shot Brig forward, where he sprawled out haphazardly onto the concrete tarmac, unconscious. The shadow of his attacker fell ominously across his body.

ABOUT THE AUTHOR

R. James Stevens, born in a small, sleepy town in Western Pennsylvania, had always taken a deep interest in reading and creative writing as a young boy. While focusing primarily on Sci-Fi and Fantasy as a child, he also found reading historical novels fascinating. Several of his literature teachers throughout his academic career encouraged him to pour his mind out onto paper when doing assignments, which freed his ability to write stories they way he imagined them, rather than sticking to strict conventions of storytelling. During his time in the US Air Force, he met his wife. He happily put writing on the back burner for nearly 15 years while he worked at his career to support his growing family, hoping that some day he would find a reason to put pen to paper once more. That day came when he and his son-in-law put their heads together to try to produce a comic book series. While that effort fizzled due to the pressures of everyday life, it did give birth, eventually, to the story contained within these covers.

Catch up with R. James Stevens:

Facebook: facebook.com/rjamesstevensauthor

Blog: rjamesstevens.com

Twitter: @RJamesStevens

This book is an entire work of fiction, and I would be remiss if I glossed over, or minimized in any way, two subjects that were contained within these covers as purely a vehicle to tell the story.

Two of them in particular:
There is nothing fictional about the reality of suicide. Thousands of people each day struggle with the unfathomable: the decision to take their own lives. While no two situations are ever alike, the one commonality for all is that there are many people willing to stand by you or a loved one; to talk or listen to them, to aide them in their crisis.

PLEASE. If you, or someone you know, are contemplating suicide, contact the resource listed below. The meager few seconds it takes to make a call may seem trivial, but it could mean the difference of a lifetime.

National Suicide Prevention Lifeline:
1-800-273-TALK (8255)
Or
TTY: 1-800-799-4889

Violence is part of our culture, has been for eons, and most likely will be for the foreseeable future. However, one particular form of violence doesn't have to happen.

Domestic violence affects millions of people per year, men and women alike. It is the leading cause of injury for women, and the costs go far beyond monetary for either sex. There is a plethora of help available, and I urge anyone that is a victim of abuse, or has witnessed it, to contact the resource below.

Nat'l Domestic Violence Hotline:
1-800-799-SAFE (7233)
Or
TTY: 1-800-787-3224

22729798R00270

Made in the USA
Charleston, SC
29 September 2013